WHOLE LOTTA LOVE

ERIKA KELLY

WHOLE LOTTA LOVE

Erika Kelly

ISBN-13: 978-0-9992585-5-2

Cover design and formatting by Serendipity Formatting

Editing by Kristy DeBoer

Praise for The Calamity Falls series

KEEP ON LOVING YOU

"I adored this book! It is exactly what I love in a second-chance romance. The characters are so vibrant and real, I was rooting for them with every page." —*USA Today* Bestseller Devney Perry

"*KEEP ON LOVING YOU* is such a fun and sexy second-chance romance that I didn't want it to end. Their connection is a swoony blend of tender first love and sizzling heat, and Erika Kelly delivers a highly entertaining and sigh-worthy romance that shouldn't be missed."
—Mary Dube, USA Today

WE BELONG TOGETHER

"I loved every sweet, heart-wrenching, crazy, mixed-up minute of this book. It was an emotional journey from the first chapter to the last. This is Erika Kelly at her best, and this is a not-to-be-missed book!" —Sharon Slick Reads, Guilty Pleasures Book Reviews

"Erika Kelly damn near pulled my heart from my chest with Delilah and Will's story. It's so well-written that you feel everything. My heart got tugged so hard! I honestly cried at a few moments in the book. I fell all the way in love with "Wooby." It's hard not to, really." —Ree Cee's Books

THE VERY THOUGHT OF YOU

"Wow, THE VERY THOUGHT OF YOU was simply OUTSTANDING! This second chance, friends to lovers romance is enchanting and entertaining." —Spellbound Stories

"I just finished this story, and I want to start all over again. Or maybe at the start of series. To once again feel the events, the emotions, that brought these amazing characters together. To hear the banter and the arguments, the sorrow, the loss and the happiness that brought a family together and closer." —Nerdy, Dirty, and Flirty

JUST THE WAY YOU ARE

"An alpha cowboy and a smart, sassy princess collide in JUST THE WAY YOU ARE in Erika Kelly's latest, and it was fabulous! I was cheering for Brodie and Rosalina with every page. If you love stories with heart, steam, and plenty of swoon, don't miss this one!" —USA Today Bestselling Author J.H. Croix

believing five-year-old who will steal your heart! I cannot gush enough about how spectacular I thought this book was." – Bookcase and Coffee

WHOLE LOTTA LOVE

"BRILLIANT! This book was incredible, I could not put this book down, that is how good Lu and Xander's story was. I fell in love with these two characters instantly." – Harlequin Junkie

"Whole Lotta Love was absolutely perfect! You will instantly love this couple and their journey to find happiness!" – Just Love Books

YOU'RE STILL THE ONE

"Griffin and Stella really are soulmates. They bring out the best of each other, and when they're together, everything is better. Their world is better with the love they feel for each other. And I think they made my world better a bit, too." – Jersey Girl's Bookshelf

"WOW! WOW! WOW! Welcome to all the feels! I ADORED Stella and Griffin's story. I was completely lost in this book and didn't want to put it down. I FELT everything, and I can't tell you how much I loved it." – Books According to Abby

Sign up for my newsletter to read the EXCLUSIVE novella for my readers only! You'll get two chapters a month of this super sexy, fun romance! #rockstarromance #teenidolturnedboyfriend Also, get PLANES, TRAINS, AND HEAD OVER HEELS for FREE! I hope you'll come hang out with me on Facebook, Twitter, Instagram, Goodreads, and Pinterest or in my private reader group.

This book is dedicated to Melissa Panio-Petersen. Your patience, your generosity…I mean, just everything you do.

Acknowledgments

- To Superman, my heart: there's no one else I'd rather share this wild ride with.
- To Olivia: thank you for reading this one and helping me work through plotting issues! You'll always be my little punkin pie, Livi bean!
- To Sharon: I love our friendship. You're the very best friend in the world.
- To Kristy DeBoer: damn, woman, you're so insightful and smart, and you always make my stories better. I can't thank you enough for that.
- To Melissa: I don't know what I'd do without you; thank you for all you do to make my life easier.
- To Erica: as always, thank you for your patience and generosity. I love working with you!
- To the romance writing community: I couldn't do this without the bloggers and reviewers like Obsessed with Romance, Guilty Pleasures Book Reviews, Reading in Pajamas, Zoe Forward, Shirin's Book Blog and Reviews, Reads and Reviews, and Isha Coleman—to name just a few; and my friends in writer

groups like the Dreamweavers, the DND Authors, Romance on Main Street, and my monthly plotstormer girls.

Prologue

May, Sophomore Year College

HER FIANCÉ BURST INTO LAUGHTER, AND LULU Cavanaugh turned to watch him across the crowded restaurant. Surrounded by her dad and his football cronies, Trace was totally in his element.

Happiness spread through her in a dizzying rush. That tall, gorgeous, life-of-the-party man had chosen *her* to spend his life with. And she didn't know how she'd gotten so lucky.

I'll never be alone again.

The thought came out of nowhere, delivering a stark relief that nearly buckled her knees. She thought about all those New Year's Eves when her sisters—gorgeous and glittering—would race out the door with their boyfriends, leaving her home alone. The Valentine's Days when her roommates would get dressed up for romantic evenings, leaving her in a cloud of perfume.

From now on, she'd never feel that painful loneliness again. Because tomorrow she'd marry Trace Heller.

Look at him.

How in the world did I get a guy like that? Starting linebacker for Penn State, big man on campus, he was genuinely nice, smart, and funny. Everybody liked him—professors, students…the cafeteria staff had a smoothie ready for him every morning at six a.m.—and it wasn't even on the menu. He was the golden boy.

And he's mine.

An arm settled around her shoulders and snugged her in close. "I don't think I've ever seen you so happy."

Lulu tucked her face into the crook of her older sister's neck. "Thank you for being here."

"What kind of thing is that to say? Of course I'm here." The lead singer of an all-girl pop band, her oldest sister was in the middle of an international tour. She had virtually no control over her life—down to how she dressed and the color of her hair—so it really was a big deal. "You excited for tomorrow? Actually, knowing you, you're probably more excited about the honeymoon."

Joy bubbled through her at the thought of Tokyo, where she'd get to spend time in the kitchens of Michelin-starred restaurants. Yet another reason to love her future husband—he didn't mind her cooking on three of their vacation nights.

"I just want to get this whole production over with." Lulu preferred a small, intimate wedding, but Trace and his family had fought her hard on that. They had hundreds of people they absolutely could not "snub."

Her fiancé came by his outgoing nature honestly—his parents and siblings were all big-time extroverts. They lived on a cul-de-sac in Iowa that threw weekly summer block parties, and their house was party central during football season.

She'd conceded, of course. Lots of people found her quiet intensity a turn-off, so if he accepted her, she could absolutely respect his big personality—even when it meant she didn't have his full attention in public.

When it meant she had to walk down the aisle with four hundred people watching her.

Trace lifted his arms, executing a sexy swivel of his hips, as if dancing to a Snoop Dog song. *He's the brightest light in any room.* His welcoming grin served as an invitation. *Come party with me. We'll have a blast.*

A red dress in her peripheral vision grabbed her attention, and she found her younger sister in a heated conversation.

As Stella drained a champagne flute, her boyfriend's big hand closed around her wrist and tried to pull the glass away from her mouth. Nobody tamed the gorgeous, wild seventeen-year old, though, so she twirled out of his reach. Stella wobbled on ridiculously high heels, but Griffin grabbed her, wrapped an arm around her waist and hauled her up hard against him. He lowered his mouth to her ear, and her expression turned sultry, wicked, before she elbowed him in the stomach and freed herself. Just as he turned away, Stella fisted his dress shirt and jerked him back, cupping his neck and kissing him like they were alone in her bedroom.

God, they were a fiery, passionate couple.

"She's drunk," Gigi said.

"I know, and it's so weird." Normally, Stella would be here for her. Her best friend and fiercest protector, her younger sister stuck by her side to make social situations easier. "Why would she do this at my rehearsal dinner?"

"Oh, come on. She's afraid of losing you." Gigi made it sound so obvious.

But that's ridiculous. Stella made friends everywhere she went—everyone loved her. She didn't need Lulu. "She knows better than that." Lulu had a smaller social circle—Trace, her family, and a few close friends—but she was fiercely loyal and kept them for life. "She's going to feel like crap tomorrow." *When I'll need her.*

She's my maid of honor.

"Let me go talk to her." But before Gigi could go, Stella caught them staring and broke away from her boyfriend.

Her hair a sexy tousle of chestnut waves, her make-up as glamorous as a movie star, she rushed up to them. "The tank is full, and my car's right out front. Say the word..." Stella had a devilish glint in her eyes—anyone would take her comment as light and jovial.

But not Lulu. She knew Stella, and her sister wasn't joking. She'd been against Trace from the very first time Lulu had brought him home. "Nope. Not going anywhere." And then she looked her sister right in the eyes, so she'd finally hear her. "I love him, Stella. I *want* to marry him."

Any pretense of joking flatlined, and Stella turned serious. Grabbing Lulu's arm, she forced her to face her fiancé. "Look at him. Why's he hanging around Dad's friends and not you? It's your rehearsal dinner. Shouldn't he be by your side?"

"We don't have that kind of relationship." *Which is why it works.*

"What does that even mean? You're going to spend your life with this man."

"That's right. And we work *because* we're so different.

4

What guy would put up with spending three nights of our honeymoon apart from me? Trace likes that we're not joined at the hip. It means he can go out and party and do his thing without having to take care of his girlfriend. Do you know how freeing it is to do what I love without worrying that I'm leaving him alone too much? Stella, he sees me. And he likes what he sees." It felt good to say it out loud. It empowered her.

Trace is the right man for me.

Stella leaned forward, reeking of booze. "If he likes you so much, then why does he flirt with *me*?"

God.

No one can hurt you more than the people who know you best.

Lulu fought back a rising swell of humiliation and fear. She pressed her trembling hands to her stomach. *Don't let her ruin this for you.* "He flirts with everyone. That's just who he is."

"You're drunk, Stella," Gigi said. "Not a good look for the maid of honor."

"Why are you defending him when you know I'm right?" Stella grew desperate. "You're all out of your mind to let her go through with this wedding." She looked at Lulu imploringly. "I want you to be happy—you know I do—I *love* you—but this guy is not who you think he is."

"Stop it." Gigi's voice was low, threatening.

"No, I'm not going to stop." Clutching Lulu's hands, Stella went wild-eyed. "This is *me*. You have to know I'd never hurt you. I'm trying to *save* you. He's not who you want him to be. He's just not."

Lulu was shaking, but it wasn't from fear. "I know exactly who he is. He *flirts,* but he doesn't act on it. And you, of all people, should know that because he's just like you. He's the life of the party, but he's also loyal and just as protective of me as you are."

"God, Lulu." Stella was almost shouting. "You're only seeing what you want—"

"No." Wrenching her hands free, Lulu took a step back. "Your job as my maid of honor—as my *sister*—isn't to tell me what's right or wrong. Your job is to stand beside me, and if things go sideways, you can hand me a pint of chocolate fudge ice cream, a spoon, and a box of Kleenex. But I'm telling you right now, if you can't support me, then you won't be standing with me at the altar tomorrow."

Lulu turned away from them, making a beeline for the kitchen.

"What is your *problem*?" she heard Gigi say.

"How can you stand here and let her make the biggest mistake of her life?" Stella said. "Why is everyone acting like this wedding is okay?"

The back of Lulu's neck prickled, as though the eyes of everyone in the restaurant were on her, pitying her. As if they all knew something she didn't about Trace.

But it wasn't true. She did know him.

He was a football player who'd dreamed of playing professionally since he was a little boy. Obviously, he was enamored with her dad, loved hanging around him and getting career advice. What was wrong with that? She *wanted* him to be close to her family. And he flirted with everybody—the bus driver for away games, the security guard at the mall.

That's just who he is.

Unused to high heels and tight dresses, she grew self-conscious and wished like hell she'd been born with a tenth of Stella's confidence and style.

But she hadn't been, so she sought the comfort of the one place on earth she felt like her best self. As she pushed through the doors, the heat hit her first, followed by the scents of grilled meat and chopped herbs. Nothing soothed her like being in the beating heart of a restaurant, with the steam rising, oil sizzling, and everyone busy at their workstations.

Here, she felt competent and in control. She felt beautiful in the only way that mattered to her—she created dishes that made people sigh with pleasure.

Jonny Lee James, the owner and executive chef, spotted her. A big grin cracked his rugged features. Wiping his hands on a dish towel, he opened his arms and came towards her. "My sweet girl."

She fell against him, breathing in the scents of caramelized onions and sautéed garlic embedded in his chef's jacket.

"Have you come to boss me around?" Tipping his head, he grinned. "Make my béchamel sublime?"

But she didn't feel like joking, so she nestled in, comforted by his embrace. He got the message and held her instead of talking.

She should be happy. She should be on top of the world.

But she didn't think she could do that without Stella's support. In fifth grade, when Lulu had a crush on Danny Keene, Stella had invited him over for a playdate. Stella had been *eight years old*.

When Lulu didn't have a date for the junior prom, Stella surprised her with a weekend in Seattle. They'd had an absolute blast, posting pictures on social media, so everyone would think she couldn't make the dance because of a trip with her mom and sister—not because no one had asked her.

So, for Stella to not like Trace—to not *trust* him—it meant something. She didn't want to choose between her husband and her sister. She shouldn't have to. But if Stella couldn't accept this marriage, this relationship…how would that work? Every time her sister and Trace were in the same room, would Stella accuse him of hitting on her? Would she start avoiding them?

Lulu needed her sister. Couldn't bear the idea of them growing apart.

"There she is." Her mom's voice rose above the kitchen noises. "I knew I'd find you here."

Chef Jonny pulled away to greet the tall, slender, and beautiful Joss Montalbano, a former supermodel who'd passed her poise and confidence on to all her daughters, except one.

Me.

"One day, she's going to get this place a Michelin star." Her mom beamed at her with so much pride, Lulu almost felt guilty for choosing Penn State over Le Cordon Bleu, as everyone had expected.

She probably should've gone to Paris, but she'd wanted so badly to be normal. To have fun and party and go wild. Unfortunately, it hadn't taken even one semester to accept that she just wasn't that person.

But she'd found Trace, and that made attending a big university worthwhile.

"Trust me, she'll do much bigger and better things than The Homesteader Inn." Chef Jonny squeezed her shoulder.

Lulu shook her head. "If Michelin covered Wyoming, you'd have a star. No question." People came from all around the world to stay at the romantic inn nestled in the woods of the Teton Mountain Range. A twelve-course meal prepared by Chef Jonny was on bucket lists—people booked reservations a year in advance.

"Well, come on, sweetie, we're about to do toasts," her mom said.

"Excellent." Chef Jonny untied his apron. "Let me find my lovely bride, so she can open the champagne."

Her mom hooked an arm through hers, and together they made their way back to the head table, where her dad still talked with his friends. Only, Trace was no longer with them. She scanned the dimly lit room.

This restaurant…it was so beautiful. Low, beamed ceilings made the large space feel cozy and warm, and the stucco walls with antique sconces gave it a European feel.

Her love of cooking had flourished right here. When she was thirteen, Chef Jonny had walked into her pop-up restaurant in the center of town, tasted her food, and said, "I didn't take you seriously. I thought your parents were letting you play restaurant, that you'd be selling hot dogs or grilled cheese sandwiches." He'd looked her right in the eye. "I was wrong."

She smiled, remembering the way his eyelids had fluttered closed, the way he'd moaned when he'd tasted her garlic aioli sauce. He'd told her right then and there that one day, when she was old enough, she was going to cook for him.

She'd started the very next summer and had worked in his kitchen every holiday and vacation since. Chef Jonny loved to parade her around the restaurant, warning people to "look out for this one. You're going to be reading about Lulu Cavanaugh one day."

Her mom leaned over. "Go get Trace so we can start."

She didn't see him anywhere, so she reached out to her dad. "Do you know where Trace went?"

He spun around with a big smile. Everyone loved Tyler Cavanaugh, not because he was one of the best quarterbacks who'd ever played, but because he listened to their stories. He cared.

He was such a good guy.

"No idea." He glanced at his wife, who held up a champagne flute. He gave her a nod, then reached for Lulu, enfolding her in his arms. "Okay, but before we do toasts, let me just say one thing. Tomorrow, I'm symbolically giving you away, but you'll always be my little girl. You know that, right?"

She nodded against his chest. When he was about to pull away, she looked up at him. "Do you think I'm making a mistake marrying Trace?"

He grew alert, as though hearing a burglar in the house. "We've talked about this before." He searched her eyes. "You know my concerns, but you said you loved him and wanted to be with him. Why are you bringing it up now, the night before the wedding?" His concern drew a sting of tears to the backs of her eyes. "If you're having second thoughts, tell me now. I don't care how far along it's gotten, we'll call it off, no problem."

"No, no. I'm not calling anything off. I just want to know…never mind." He was right. Multiple times over the past eighteen months, he'd suggested Trace was spending way too much time with him, and Lulu had told him she liked that he fit in so well. It gave her the freedom to cook and the comfort to know they'd always live close to her family—and not his.

"You sure?" Her dad looked concerned.

"Positive."

He gave her a nod, trusting her, and then reached for a knife. Tapping it against his water goblet, he turned to face the room. "Can everyone take a seat, please? Champagne's coming around, so grab a glass."

Chairs scraped, and the conversation grew even louder as people decided where to sit.

"We need Trace," her mom said.

One of her dad's football buddies cupped his mouth and called, "Anyone seen the groom?"

Lulu grabbed a glass from a passing server. Excitement started to roll in, as she pushed aside her doubts and focused on the moment.

"Oh, good," she heard her mom say. "You're here."

She turned, eager to have Trace close, needing his reassurance. He always knew how to make her feel special.

But it wasn't him. It was Gigi. "You're giving the first toast," her mom said.

Nodding, Gigi took a sip, eyeing Lulu over the top of the flute with a saucy lift of her platinum eyebrows.

I should've chosen Gigi as my maid of honor.

"Should I text him?" Lulu asked.

Gigi shook her head. "He's not paying attention to his phone right now. Not with all his friends here."

Together, they scanned the room, but between the shadows created by the low lighting, the potted plants, and the wait staff setting bread baskets on the tables, it was hard to make out individual faces.

Any minute now, he'd pop his head out from a big group of people—probably at the bar—and he'd jog across the restaurant, bumping fists and slapping palms on his way to the head table.

"Thank you all for coming tonight." Her dad's commanding presence had people quieting down. "It's great to see faces we haven't seen in a while." He shoved a hand into the pocket of his dress slacks. "Lulu came out of the womb with a spatula in one hand and a sprig of parsley in the other." He paused for the titter of laughter. "And her first word was 'kitchen,' breaking her mother's heart."

Laughter erupted, and her dad continued talking. But noise filled her brain. There were only a few people still standing, and Trace wasn't with them.

"Right, sweetheart?" Her dad wrapped an arm around her shoulder and drew her up against him. She'd missed that last sentence, but the guests were laughing, so she didn't have to answer. She just stood there and smiled.

And that's when her gaze snagged on a red dress.

She had to do a double-take.

Because at the back of the restaurant, behind the fronds of a potted plant, right where the fairy lights dripped down the stucco walls, Stella was making out with someone that wasn't Griffin.

Lulu went rigid. She had to take a moment to make sense of what she was seeing because her mind was tricking her into seeing Trace.

Lots of men wore crisp blue suits. Lots of them had neatly trimmed dark hair.

But no one else wore a neon yellow silicone wristband signifying the Penn State football team's annual fundraiser for The Children's House.

"Now," her dad said. "I'm going to hand the mic over to Gigi, who's got a little story to tell."

But time had stopped. A clammy chill coated her skin.

"Lu?" Her dad squeezed her shoulder. "What's going on?"

Fear fisted her lungs and squeezed with all its might.

Clothing swished, chairs scraped on the hardwood floor, as everyone followed Lulu's gaze to the back of the room, where Trace's hands clutched Stella's ass. He kissed her with the franticness of a man on a sinking ship.

"That fucker." Gigi charged across the room. "I'm going to cut his dick off."

"Is that Trace?" her mom asked. "Who is he...is that *Stella*?"

"Oh, my God," someone called.

In the flurry of activity—Gigi storming across the room, people jumping out of their seats—Lulu set her flute down on a table. A commotion broke out when one of Trace's brothers pulled him off Stella.

Lulu's heart pounded, her mind insisting she get out of there, but her feet...God, her feet were rooted in place, her legs nothing but dead weight.

Deep pain, the kind that would never go away, slowly sank into her bones.

Only when she found pitying eyes on her did she find the strength to turn and walk out of the room.

Her sister had stolen her future.

And that once exciting canvas had just gone blank.

Chapter One

Seven Years Later

I'M A LIAR.

Lulu Cavanaugh chopped the cilantro, reminding herself that soon, her family would know the truth.

Another week, max.

Scraping the herb into the marinade, she focused on the steady crash and drag of waves, the squeals of children playing in the sand, and the happy chatter between customers and servers. Anything to get out of her own head.

Because this whole thing was killing her. The shame, the waiting, the *lying*.

"What'cha makin' today?" Big Eddie came up and filched a strip of grilled skirt steak.

She pointed to a tray. "This one's a Sapporo-beer braised short rib taco with wasabi crema."

"That sounds out of this world. What's that one?"

"That's Pulpo Frito. It's got citrus slaw, shrimp, and roasted pineapple. It's not quite right, though. Still tinkering with it."

He lifted a crunchy shell, juices dripping down his meaty hand and shoved one end in his mouth. "Stop tinkering. It's perfect." He chewed like the police were busting in, and he was hiding evidence. "Damn, girl. Everything you make is out of this world. They don't call you a prodigy for nothin'."

"You can't be a prodigy at twenty-six." *Obviously.* "And I thought you weren't going to look me up online anymore. I'm an open book." *Sorta. Kinda.*

Well, she used to be.

Back when she'd had nothing to be ashamed of.

When he noticed the third tray, his eyes went wide. "What's this one?"

"It's a tres leches and coconut taco with chocolate fudge ice cream and banana peanut sauce."

"Are you kidding me? Why are you not in charge of cooking for the entire universe? Gimme."

Laughing, she batted his hand away. "Wait. I have to fill it with ice cream."

"Just a bite." He hip-chucked her aside to snag one.

She got all warm inside. Nothing made her happier than someone enjoying her food. Slicing open a lime, she squeezed the juice into the marinade.

"Unreal." Eddie's eyes rolled back in his head. "This is…it's like the perfect marriage of flavors. I can't believe you're slumming it with me."

"Slumming, sure, if your definition is cooking on the beach in Maui for a boss who lets me make whatever I want."

"Boss." He chuckled. "Sure, if your definition is a guy

whose business has quadrupled since you started cooking in his truck and who doesn't pay you a dime for it."

"You buy the ingredients. *And* you let me live in your house."

"Yeah, because you keep my belly full of all this goodness. I'd give my last dollar for a tres leche taco." A grin split his plump face.

Happiness bubbled up. "You make everything okay, Eddie."

He gave her a warm, affectionate smile.

"Big Eddie, my man," a surfer called from the pass-through. "What's on special?"

Anxiety ripped through her. *Was* that a surfer? Because it sounded an awful lot like her future brother-in-law.

Then, she heard laughter. And *that* voice was unmistakable. "I'm *starving*. Get me one of everything."

Gigi.

Every muscle in her body tightened.

This is not happening.

What was her sister doing here? *She's got an album to finish. She's supposed to be in the studio.*

Big Eddie nudged her. "These ready to go?"

Stunned, all she could do was give the barest of nods.

"Dude, this is your lucky day." Eddie headed to the customer. "My girl Lu's here."

"Lu?"

Oh, yeah. That was him all right. Cassian Ellis. Her sister's fiancé.

Oh, God.

"Lulu?" her sister called.

She hated lying to her family—hated it—but she'd wanted to come clean at the right time. On her own terms.

She didn't want to be caught in a taco truck.

Not when they thought she was the chef de cuisine of The Orchid, Maui's fanciest restaurant.

Setting the knife down, she wiped her hands on her apron. Slowly, she turned. "Hey."

Cassian cocked his head, confused. "What're you doing in Eddie's truck?"

The big man watched her, stepping aside so she could greet her family. "Making tacos?"

Of course, they weren't alone. No, coming up behind them, her parents trudged through the sand, laughing, holding hands, happy as could be.

Adrenaline burst in her core.

Her sister, she could handle. But her parents?

"Don't eat too much," her mom called. "We're going to have a huge dinner. Lulu's tasting menu has ten courses." Her gaze flicked up to the pass-through window. "*Lulu?*"

Her mom's horrified expression hit like a punch to the gut.

Her parents reached the truck. "What're you doing here?"

"Hang on. Let me…" Lulu backed away from the window and made her way outside. Stepping onto the sandy asphalt, she found herself surrounded by her family, and she felt overwhelmed with their curiosity, confusion…their accusation. She did a slow exhale. "I work here."

"Do you mean part-time?" Her mom's tone said, *I don't get it*. "Don't they pay you enough?"

"No, Mom. I *work* here. This is my job now."

"You left The Orchid?" her mom asked. "It hasn't even been two months."

"Come here, sweetheart." Her dad pulled her into his arms, one big hand cupping the back of her head.

She buried her face in his T-shirt, inhaling the most familiar scent in the world—clean cotton, fresh mountain air, and something she could only describe as *comfort*—and it made her feel eleven years old all over again. "I'm sorry."

"Lulu, what's going on?" Her mom grew impatient. "Why would you quit your job?"

She pulled away. "I didn't quit." She felt sick to her stomach, about to say words she'd never imagined uttering in her life. Words she still couldn't believe were true. "I got fired."

Her dad led their little group away from the truck and under the shade of a tree.

"Who the hell would fire *you?*" Her mom pressed a palm to her forehead. "This doesn't make sense."

"No, it does." She wanted a sinkhole to open up and take her deep into the belly of the earth. But since that wasn't going to happen, it was time to come clean. "I couldn't handle the job."

"Couldn't handle it? You've worked in some of the finest kitchens in the world. Chef Jonny, Chef Paul... they adore you. Everyone loves your food." Her mom turned to her husband for answers. *How does this make sense?*

He watched Lulu with concern. "What happened?"

"The food wasn't the problem. It was everything else. The budgeting, the hiring, the vendors..." She shrugged. "They were right to fire me. I couldn't do it."

"They didn't have to *fire* you," her mom said. "They could've just hired someone to handle the business side of things."

"That's the job, Mom. That's what a chef de cuisine does. And I failed."

"I don't believe that. Not for a second. You're a gifted—"

"Mom." She said it too harshly and immediately felt bad. But she couldn't hear it. Not one more time. About her gift, her talent.

"I'm sorry. I know this has to be hard for you." Chastised, her mom's tone softened. "When did this happen?"

And now we get to the worst part. "A month ago."

"A *month* ago?" Her mom glanced to the taco truck. "You've been working here all this time?"

"Yes." She straightened. Now, that she'd told the truth, she felt better, stronger.

"Why didn't you tell us?" her mom asked. "I don't understand."

"I've been working on something. I was going to tell you as soon as I got the green light."

"Oh, honey." Gigi pushed past their mom and pulled Lulu into her arms. "That sucks so bad. I'm really sorry." Into her ear, she said, "But you know you could've told me, right? I'm here for you. Always."

"I know." It was easy enough to say the words, but the fact was…Gigi had reached the pinnacle of success. Lulu had come close—and then immediately crashed and burned.

"So, what've you been working on?" Her mom sounded hopeful.

Lulu stepped out of her sister's embrace. "I'm not ready to talk about it yet. Give me a few more days to see if it goes through."

"Are you opening your own restaurant?" Her mom's eyes gleamed. "*Yes.* This is what you were born to do." She sucked in a breath. "Tell me you've got Chef Paul backing you. Tell me it's in Paris."

"And you're wondering why she didn't tell us." Gigi shook her head.

"What's that supposed to mean?" her mom asked.

"Because, in your eyes, if it's anything less than a Michelin-starred restaurant, she's a failure." Gigi's frustration sounded like it bordered on anger.

"Lulu could never be a failure. She's too talented." Her mom grew defiant. "Besides, it's not *my* dream. It's Lulu's. Ever since she was a little girl."

"Little girls don't dream about Michelin stars, Mom," Gigi said. "*You* put that idea in her head. You pushed her too hard. All of us. You made our entire lives about accomplishments."

"That's not—" her mom began.

"But I did fail." Lulu's tone caught their attention, and they stopped arguing. "And if I can't manage to run the kitchen at The Orchid, I'm certainly not going to start my own. I'm not ready for that yet, so I'm…swerving. But it's okay, because it's still going to get me where I want to go."

"Are you happy with this new direction?" her dad asked.

She loved him so much. Though he had four daughters, he made each of them feel like his special little girl. She could've told him the truth, and he'd have been cool.

She just hated disappointing him.

No, it's Mom. She's the one I don't want to disappoint.

"I think so. We'll see. It's something I've never done, so I can't say if I'll like it or not. But the good news is, if this project works out, it'll be happening in Calamity. In fact, I'm meeting with someone there next week."

20

"Calamity?" Gigi looked hopeful. "You're coming home?"

"Yep."

"Oh, my God." Her sister flew into her arms. "I'm so happy about this."

"Wait a second," her mom said. "Whatever you do next, shouldn't it be based in a major city like New York or Paris?"

"Joss," her dad said.

"What? Of course I want her home." Her mom grew defensive. "I'm thinking about her career."

"So am I," Lulu said. "And the only way to get a project like this off the ground is to have a unique angle, and there's nothing cooler than our wild west town in the Tetons. We've got Owl Hoot, the bison preserve, world class extreme sports...I mean, our county is ninety-seven percent national park, and yet we have some of the best luxury hotels and restaurants in the world."

"We've got quirky events, too," Gigi said. "The Pole, Pedal, and Paddle race is next week."

"It is? That'd be really good timing." She'd have to check the dates, see if the producer would be in town for it. But she wasn't too worried. She'd already sold her on the setting and content for the show. Now, they just needed to make sure her live personality matched her recording. "But what're you guys doing here?" In a million years, she would never have thought they'd come to their vacation home on Maui. Not when Coco was two weeks away from her due date.

Her mom gestured to where Cassian stood eating tacos with some of his friends. "Oh, you know. It's the annual trip he throws for the guys who help him at summer camp."

"He rented a place for them," Gigi said. "It's a few houses over from ours."

"We figured we'd come with him, take a quick trip to surprise you," her mom said. "We had it all planned… even made the reservation under a fake name. We were going to ask if we could meet the chef, and then you'd come out and find us all there."

"That would've been fun." She'd have loved that.

"Once Coco has the baby, it'll be months before we can get out here." Her mom looked hurt. "We just wanted to celebrate your new job."

The humiliation had burned out, leaving Lulu nothing but exposed and vulnerable. "I'm sorry for not telling you. I wanted to wait until I had some good news."

"You didn't have to wait," her mom said. "We love you no matter what's happening with your career."

"I know, but this is the first time I've failed, and I only wanted to tell you about it once I'd recovered."

"I just hate that you've gone through this all alone." Her mom's expression turned fierce. "We believe in you. Whatever you set your mind to do, we know you're going to succeed."

"No pressure, though, right, Mom?" In spite of her teasing tone, Lulu could feel herself doubling down on her determination to win over the producer.

Now that her family knew the truth, she had to get this show.

If she didn't…nope. Not going there.

Failure is not an option.

Well, a second time anyway.

. . .

Lulu sat with her sister on a blanket, her toes tucked into cool sand. A warm ocean-scented breeze fluttered the hem of her sundress and teased the bare skin of her arms.

A few yards away, the football players gathered around a bonfire on the private stretch of beach in front of Cassian's rental house. "I thought he wasn't planning these kinds of trips anymore?"

As the new kid on the team, Cassian had thrown lavish parties to win over his teammates. The press had labeled him a hard-partying playboy, and that had made it hard for him to win back Gigi, the love of his life.

"Well, it's not *that* kind of trip. Nothing decadent or crazy. But you know Cassian. He likes to do nice things for the guys, so we came up with a compromise." Gigi watched her fiancé tussle with a huge behemoth of a man, bringing him down to the sand with a playful bump to the back of his knees. "He's rented a house and stocked it for the week, but we're only here for the weekend. Besides, it's a whole different crew than the ones who trash hotels and yachts." She reached for Lulu's hand. "I'm so glad you'll be home this summer."

"Me, too." Even if her show fell through, she'd still be in Calamity. Until she found a new job, she had nowhere to go.

From the time she was thirteen, she'd built one success off another. That's why this fall felt catastrophic.

"I'll be in the studio a lot, but I'm still around. It'll be the first time we're all home since—" Gigi cut off abruptly, looking guilty.

Why was everyone so careful with her? "It's okay to talk about her." *I didn't cause the rift*. Stella had done this.

Sometimes Lulu wondered…if she'd reacted differently, if she hadn't dropped out of Penn State and flown across the ocean to enroll in culinary school…would her youngest sister have run off?

But, come on, Stella had *kissed* her fiancé.

At my rehearsal dinner.

In front of everyone they'd known their entire lives.

Stella had left town right after high school graduation, because she'd made a fool of herself.

"What would you do if you saw her?" Gigi asked. "Like, if she just strutted back to Calamity one day?"

"I honestly don't know. Believe me, I've thought about it. Every time I'm on an airplane, I imagine her coming down the aisle." *Sitting in First Class with her Louis Vuitton luggage and her Italian lover.* "When I'm in the grocery store, I glance at the magazines, expecting to see her on a cover."

"But are you still angry? Do you forgive her?"

"It's hard to answer that. I've moved on, obviously. And to be honest, I don't think about her all that often." *I'm too damn busy.* "But I also haven't had a serious relationship since Trace, so…do I forgive her?" She gave it some thought, sorting through the tangle of emotions in the box she rarely opened. "Not really, no. But it's not like I blame her entirely. I blame myself for having such bad judgement in men. I trusted Trace."

"And you trusted Stella."

"Right." After the rehearsal dinner, Stella had begged her to understand that she'd been drunk, desperate to save Lulu from a bad marriage, but it hadn't mattered. Stella had flirted, and Trace had jumped right in. That kiss…he hadn't held anything back.

She sifted sand through her fingers. "The thing is…I don't trust myself." She'd never admitted this to anyone before. "You all saw Trace for what he was, and I didn't.

The whole town saw. God, every time I come home, I dread the way people are going to look at me."

"Well, let's see. Mrs. McCoony's husband ran off with the nanny. Tongues were wagging for *weeks*. Remember Jason Everett? That guy who installed speakers at Mom and Dad's house? Well, he stole from his clients—just a little thing here and there—to support his kid's soccer dreams. Oh, and Candi Evans farted during a town hall meeting. They still talk about that one."

"Did she really?"

"Oh, yeah. It was the fart heard all around the valley. Apparently, she stood up to argue about the new development off Featherlegs Lane, and she got about five sentences into her speech, when she let one rip so loud it woke up Cammie Barrett's baby."

Laughing, Lulu tipped her head back to take in a sky brilliant with glittering stars. "Oh, my God, I would have *died*."

Both their phones buzzed. Lulu and Gigi looked at each, and at the same time said, "Mom."

Chapter Two

Mom: Since there's no reason to stay any longer, we're leaving first thing in the morning. We want to be home if Coco goes into labor.

A second later, her mom sent another text to Lulu only.

Mom: do you want to come back with us on the jet since you have a meeting next week anyway? We can close out your house later.

Lulu glanced out at the dark ocean, lacy white crests surging toward the shore.

And here I thought I'd fallen as low as I could go.

Lulu: already got out of my lease and sold my furniture.

With her decent chef de cuisine salary, she'd rented a lovely cottage right near the beach. She'd plastered images of it all over Splashagram, so her family and friends had all seen it.

Mom: where have you been living????

Jesus, take the wheel. Her mom was going to love this one.

Lulu: the owner of the taco truck's been letting me live in his guest bedroom.

Mom: you're breaking my heart. I don't understand any of this. I wish you'd told me. You could've stayed in our house. It's been empty this whole time.

Lulu: I know. Sure, I'll come home with you tomorrow. See you in the morning.

Cassian approached them, his bare feet kicking out sand. "Got your mom's text." He leaned in and kissed Gigi on the mouth. "You ready to head back to the house?"

It awed her how unabashedly in love this powerful, gorgeous man was with her sister.

"Sure." Gigi got up and wiped her shorts. When Lulu didn't join her, she said, "Aren't you coming?" She glanced over to the loud and wild football players and the entourage they'd gathered.

"Well, let's see." Lulu lifted one palm as if weighing something. "Party with strangers…" She lifted the other. "Or go with you and get into it with mom?"

Gigi laughed. "Yeah, that's a tough one."

She definitely didn't want to hang out with a bunch of strangers, and she'd deal with her mom on the jet tomorrow, so that left one choice. "I have to pack, so I'll just go home." She got up, shook out the blanket, and folded it loosely.

"I'll walk you," Cassian said.

"Oh, no." *Ha.* Big Eddie didn't live anywhere near this ritzy neighborhood. "I've got a car. I'm fine. Don't worry." She got up.

"Okay," Cassian said. "See you in the morning."

Gigi leaned over and hugged her sister. "I love you so much, and I'm glad you're coming home."

"Love you, too."

"Hey, hey, hey." A big, beefy guy jogged over. "You're not takin' the taco lady with you, are you?"

"We've got an early flight." Cassian gestured to Lulu. "And the 'taco lady' has a name. Lulu, meet Ryker, the best wide receiver in the NFL."

"Nice to meet you, Ryker."

His giant hand swallowed hers up. "Those were the best damn tacos I've had in my life."

"Well, I'm glad you—"

"Tacos?" Another guy joined them. "You makin' tacos?"

A teammate jogged over, carrying a bikini-clad woman on his back. "I'm down for tacos."

When half the group joined them, Gigi waved her hands. "The taco truck's closed. If you're hungry, Cassian and I stocked the kitchen. You should be set for the week, and if you run out, we left a bunch of menus on the counter. Go for it."

"But I want tacos." Ryker pointed a finger at Lulu. "*Her* tacos."

"I never even got one," one of the guys said.

"Well, whose fault is that?" Ryker gave the giant man a pointed look.

"He was eatin' another kind of taco," someone said.

"The juicy kind." The giant laughed.

"Hey." One of the guys pushed forward and smacked both men on the backs of their heads. "Knock it off." He was different than the others. Not as thick, he had lean, hard muscle.

"Yeah," Ryker said. "Not cool, man."

While Lulu had heard plenty worse and didn't need anyone protecting her delicate ears, she still appreciated the lack of tolerance for that kind of talk. She turned to Cassian and her sister. "Did you guys buy tortillas?"

He nodded. "But you don't have to cook for them."

Lulu could go back to Big Eddie's and pack, replaying her mom's expression when she found out Lulu had been fired, or she could cook. "I don't mind. Won't take long."

Gigi gave her a look that said, *You sure?*

"Positive. Go."

As her sister and Cassian turned to walk down the beach, Lulu led the way to the rental house.

"You need help?" Ryker asked.

"What does she want help from your ass for?" someone said.

"I cook," Ryker said. "I could be her sous chef."

"You make *one* dish. And it's your momma's recipe."

Reaching for the handle of the French door, she said, "I'll let you know when they're ready."

Through the glass-fronted doors, she could see flames ignite in the fire pit and the whole crew gather around. The moment someone set down a huge cooler and popped it open, greedy hands fished out cans and bottles.

Okay, let's see what they've got. After a quick scan of the refrigerator and pantry, she got a sense of what she wanted to cook and grabbed the butcher-wrapped paper of fresh fish, a couple packages of corn tortillas, and some limes from the fruit bowl. Setting her ingredients on the granite island, she set off to find a cutting board and the right knives.

The French doors opened, and a man burst into the kitchen, heading for the stairs. A moment later, music blasted from an upstairs bedroom. When the guy came back down, he left the doors wide open.

Which gave her a view of a couple kissing against a

table. The man gripped her bottom and lifted her onto it. Her ankles crossed at the small of his back.

Things are heating up. Maybe she'd set out all the ingredients and let them make their own. *Get out of their way.*

Yeah, that's a good idea.

A bark of laughter drew her attention outside again. Ryker stood with a few others in a small circle, having a private conversation. Nearby, the lean guy—the one who'd called out his friend for referring to women's "tacos"—was sprawled out in an Adirondack chair. Long legs stretched out, head tipped back, he gazed up at the sky.

He kind of intrigued her, though she didn't know why. Just before she turned back to the cutting board, a woman in a red swimsuit sat on the arm of his chair. When her fingers glided up his chest, he lurched forward. Another woman plopped down on his lap and wrapped her arms around his neck.

Where his teammates laughed, drank, and flirted, this guy seemed tense and…well, pissed off at the world.

Lord, though, he was handsome. She was such a sucker for the clean-cut look and athletic build.

Right then, his gaze found hers, sending a bolt of energy through her.

Caught staring, she could feel her neck and cheeks burn, and yet she couldn't look away.

She just couldn't.

The man was intense, everything about him reeking of power and unshakable confidence, and she felt ensnared by his attention.

Giving herself a mental shake, she turned back to her work. *What was I doing?* Right, a marinade for her fish tacos. Using the flat of a blade to crush a garlic clove, she blocked out everything going on around her.

A familiar sadness settled over her. The thing about being an introvert was that she loved her life, loved cooking, loved great talks with close friends. She didn't mind working twelve to fourteen hours a day as a chef, because she got to make delicious food for a living and, when she got home, she could just zone out. She didn't need a social life to be happy.

But the other side was an acute sense of being *alone*. Because most people didn't want to have meaningful conversations all the damn time. They wanted to have fun. They wanted to go to bars and clubs, have big dinner parties.

Cutting a look to the handsome man in the Adirondack chair, she wondered if he felt the same way. Even though he was flanked by two gorgeous women and his teammates, he didn't smile, didn't flirt. He seemed like a loner, too.

Oh, no you don't. Don't go there. Classic Lulu. Seeing what she wanted in people, inventing some kind of magical connection.

But it was too late. Longing clenched from deep within.

All she'd ever wanted was to find the one person in the world whose soul mirrored hers.

My match.

For years, she'd thought it was Griffin. She'd crushed on him for most of middle school and all the way through high school. She'd convinced herself that, if he'd only look her way, take the time to talk to her, he'd find his kindred spirit. He'd have the connection he didn't even know he craved.

And look how wrong she'd been.

The whole time he'd been in love with Stella.

Okay. She wasn't going back to the horrible, soul-crushing night in high school when she'd finally worked up the nerve to confess her love for him—only to find him making out with her younger sister.

But she was a slow learner, because she'd done it again with Trace. Bought the whole soulmate thing once again. He'd pretended he wanted to be alone with her at frat parties, that he didn't mind the deep conversations that fueled her. *Ha*.

She'd thought she'd found The One in him, when all he'd wanted was to be part of her celebrity-rich family.

"X-Man," someone shouted. "Wait up."

Ah, so the guy in the Adirondack chair was X-Man? Alexander Wilder was Cassian's backup quarterback, which explained the lean physique. He headed around the fire pit, ignoring his friend.

The big guy caught up with him right before he stepped into the kitchen. "Which one you takin' upstairs?" Drunk, he spoke loud enough for Lulu to hear him over the music. "Or you want both tonight?"

"Marcus." X-Man sounded gruff, almost annoyed.

"'Cause I got my eye on the one in the red bikini." He grinned big and wide. "And I know you like blondes."

Irritated, X-Man pushed past him and strode to the refrigerator. Grabbing a water bottle, he twisted off the top and then turned to watch her.

Oh, Lord. She was acutely aware of him standing at the other end of the island, that gorgeous man with bulging biceps, ripped abs, and dark blue board shorts. He didn't say a word, which only frazzled her nerves.

Well, she might be an introvert, but she wasn't shy. "Hey. We haven't actually met. I'm Lulu. Gigi's sister."

"Xander." He tipped his head back and drank,

eyeing her over the bottle. "You need help?" He had a guarded look about him, like a man who lived in the shadows, keyed into everything going on around him.

"No, thanks. Actually, can you see if there's any chorizo?"

He went back to the refrigerator, opening and closing drawers. "Nope. But there's Italian sausage. If they've got smoked paprika and apple cider vinegar, I could add it, get that chorizo flavor."

Now, how would he know that?

When she didn't answer right away, he said. "Or I could run to the store."

His unrelenting stare unnerved her in the worst way, because it was equaling thrilling and scary. He seemed to look beneath the surface...and what if he didn't like what he saw?

She tore her gaze away. "That's okay. I can work with whatever we've got." *Focus on food.* As she diced the jalapeno pepper, she thought ahead to the sauce. She'd keep it simple. Sour cream, hot sauce. Cilantro, if they had it. *Unlikely.*

"Were you going to do breakfast tacos?" His voice pulled her out of the fog she always fell into when cooking. "With the chorizo?"

Right. "Yeah, thought I'd make two kinds since there's not enough fish for everyone." She smiled. "I don't think Cassian and Gigi were counting on the number of friends you guys would make."

He stiffened. Oops, she definitely hadn't meant to sound judgmental. She truly didn't care what these guys did. Anyone could see they were having a blast.

Then again, maybe she cared a little bit what *he* did—

considering she was invested in whether he'd be having a threesome tonight.

But instead of going back outside to the waiting women, he went to the refrigerator. "I can make some breakfast tacos with scrambled eggs, bacon, and avocado. Does that sound good?"

"Ooh, it does. Maybe some black beans and jalapenos? Give them a little kick?"

With a nod, he got to work, pulling out Monterey Jack cheese and grabbing a couple of limes.

"Now I know why Cassian bought fresh mahi mahi for you guys." She stirred the marinade. "One of you can cook."

He shrugged. "We take turns cooking at camp every Friday night. So, I think a bunch do."

"That sounds fun." She thought about the snacks in the pantry. "Training camp's not for a few months, right? I saw all those bags of chips and pretzels. I guess you don't have to worry about your diet for a while."

"It doesn't really work like that. Everyone has cheat days, but it's too hard to get back in shape." He set the ingredients down on the counter and busied himself with finding a skillet and pulling the right knives out of the block.

As she breathed in the ocean smell of the fish and the earthy peppers, they worked in companionable silence, but she couldn't help noticing the flex and pop of his biceps when he opened jars and pulled a cutting board down from a cabinet. All that smooth, tan skin, the round bubble butt…and his sexy lips. God, she'd never seen such a sensuous mouth.

Since Trace, she'd mostly dated people from the culinary world. Who else did she meet?

"I heard what happened this afternoon."

Snapped out of her thoughts, she felt her stomach pitch. He couldn't mean the conversation outside the taco truck?

"I just wanted to get that out there. We were all sitting at a picnic table eating tacos, so we heard your conversation."

Perspiration popped out along her hairline, and she felt uncomfortably warm. She wanted to defend herself, explain. But she didn't know what to say.

He cracked the eggs into a ceramic bowl. In a separate pan, bacon sizzled. "I thought you should know. Doesn't seem right for you to be hanging out with us, not knowing what we overheard."

She couldn't think clearly enough to know if that was nice of him or totally unnecessary. "I appreciate that." *Maybe?*

Actually, these guys would be in Calamity all summer for Cassian's football camp. *That's why he's telling me.* Plus, she was their captain's future sister-in-law. It *was* nice of him. Respectful.

And that loosened her tongue. "I feel like an idiot." She swiped the dampness off her forehead with her forearm. "I've never lied to my family before."

"Why did you?"

Okay, wow. She hadn't expected him to ask such a direct question. *Not exactly something I'm dying to talk about.* She poured the marinade over the fish and rubbed it all over.

"You don't have to answer. It's none of my business."

"No, I'm just thinking. I mean, the short answer is that I was embarrassed. I got the dream job—and lost it the first month. But there's a lot of history behind that."

"Your mom."

He said it so matter-of-factly, it surprised her. "Yes, she thinks big."

"It's the expectations."

It wasn't so much that he was perceptive. It was more that he'd paid attention to her. *I like that.* "Not just hers, though. When you're good at something, and you start getting feedback...well, it's a long story, but I'm sure you get it."

"I do. When did you start cooking?"

"Oh, really young."

"Yeah?"

He seemed to want more, so... okay. "When we were kids, my parents used to take us to the farmers market every Saturday during the summer. Each of us got to buy one thing. My sisters always got a treat—like a muffin or a scone, a cupcake. But I was the weirdo that chose some kind of vegetable or fruit."

"I probably would've done the same thing."

"Really?" After rinsing her hands in the sink, she looked around for a dish towel.

He pulled one out of a drawer and handed it to her.

"Thank you." She shouldn't be touched by such a simple gesture...and yet she was. "I mean, I could have a muffin any old time, but a jicama? I used to drive the vendors crazy with my questions—what's it taste like? How do you use it? They'd humor me or laugh it off, but this one guy—Sam—he'd give me challenges. He'd hand me the jicama or dragon fruit—whatever—and tell me to take it home and figure out how to eat it. He'd go, 'Come back next week and tell me what you did with it.'"

"That's cool."

"I loved it. Eventually, he gave me the idea to start my

own garden." Ugh, she'd better get to the point. *This story's going on too long.* "In any event, I lied because—"

"So, you did it? Started a garden?"

She thought about the question his friend had asked him, if he wanted the woman in the red bikini or the blonde…or both.

Wouldn't he rather be with them than talking about jicama?

If he did, he'd be out on the patio with them. *Trust a man's actions.* That's the advice her dad had given her after Trace. "Oh, yeah. I got really into it, growing all kinds of things and figuring out how to cook them. And, of course, I made my family taste everything, and that's where it really all starts, you know? That positive feedback. It made me want more of it. When I was thirteen, I opened a pop-up restaurant in town, and people raved about my food so much I was featured in local magazine and newspaper articles. One day, the chef of a fancy restaurant came in and told me I'd be a star one day. So, the feedback kept getting better and bigger, and it just fueled me, you know?"

"Yes. I do."

She wondered what that meant, but with his attention so focused on adding cheese to the scrambled eggs, she knew he didn't want to explain. "I wound up working in his kitchen for years, every holiday, vacation, all summer long…and he'd parade me around the restaurant, telling people to remember my name…" She loved Chef Jonny. Loved the way he'd taken in a girl who didn't fit in anywhere and gave her the space to be creative in his kitchen. "All that to say…I lied because I've always excelled, always surpassed everyone's expectations…" She hated saying it out loud. "Until I got fired from the dream job, the one it takes most chefs twenty years of experience to get."

"I got the impression you didn't lie to them so much as not tell them about it."

He was intimidatingly handsome—thick lashes that framed cognac-colored eyes, surfer-blonde hair, and those defined muscles...*gah*. He was so hot.

And he's real, too.

"Technically, that's true. I never pretended I was still working at The Orchid, but it doesn't matter. The bottom line is that I lied to the people I love most in the world. And now, instead of just being embarrassed about it, I've got the double whammy of being fired plus being ashamed of myself."

He cocked his head. "Ashamed? You're pretty hard on yourself."

"Well, it's easy to be a good person when things are going well. The true test of your character is how you behave in the tough times. And I bombed that one." *It's a party, there's music, food, drinks...let the man have fun.* "But lesson learned, right? Anyhow, I'm just going to grill the fish, whip up a quick sauce, and then I'll leave it all out for you guys. A do-it-yourself taco bar. Sound good?"

He flipped the bacon. "The fact that you let yourself down and feel like shit about it pretty much means you don't have bad character."

"What *does* it mean, then?"

He stopped working to come closer and look her right in the eyes.

For one long moment, she became nothing but a painfully beating heart and a rush of blood thumping in her ears. *What does he want? What's he going to say?*

"That you're human." He said it softly, gently. Sincerely.

She didn't realize how much she'd needed to hear those words until he'd said them.

He got back to work, breaking the spell he'd cast. "And, since it was more of an omission than a lie, I think you should probably give yourself a pass." He opened the can of black beans. "Given how disappointed in yourself you are, I'll bet you don't do it again."

"I won't, but can I just tell you how glad I am to hear you say that?"

He set the perfectly cooked bacon on sheets of paper towels. "It's not easy when you don't live up to expectations."

"Spoken from experience?"

"I was labeled a phenom, and I—"

The door opened, bringing in laughter and conversation. Just like that, he shut down.

One hand holding a beer bottle, the other pumping in the air to the beat, the woman in the red bikini headed right for him. "There you are. I wondered where you went." She sidled up to him. "What're you making?" She picked up a strip of bacon and bit into it. "You need some help?"

"No."

Lulu suppressed a grin at his terse tone, but the woman didn't seem to care.

More people came in, crowding into the kitchen, pulling bags of chips and pretzels from the pantry. Lulu forced herself not to watch the women flirt with Xander, choosing instead to focus on whisking her sauce. It wouldn't be as good without cilantro, but she'd make-do.

A sexy song came on, and the woman in the red bikini

starting swaying right in front of Xander. Slowly, she shimmied to the floor and back up again.

When jealousy got a good grip on her, Lulu knew she needed to get going. *You know what? I'm not heating tortillas.* She'd just use the boxes of taco shells she'd seen in the pantry.

They could figure out the rest on their own. After flipping the fish, she washed her hands, tidied up her work area, and then turned off the burner. Using a fork, she broke the mahi mahi into bite-size chunks.

The scents of herbs, lime, and ocean wafted up to her nostrils, and her mouth watered. *Always a good sign.*

She grabbed her tote bag and started out of the kitchen.

Don't look at him.

She just…she'd really liked talking to him.

But that pull she felt? She recognized it. It was nothing more than a misguided longing.

Xander Wilder isn't my match.

By the time she'd made it halfway across the living room, she couldn't stand it. She risked one final glance at Xander and found him pulling a baking sheet of warm tortillas out of the oven, while the woman in the bikini kept up a steady stream of conversation.

The music got louder, and more people came into the kitchen, attacking the food. She took a moment to watch their expressions when they bit into her tacos. Ryker shouted, "Aw, man, so good." Another of the guys chewed, shaking his head, "Fuck, yeah."

They loved it.

Awesome. She lived for that.

Red Bikini scraped a hand through Xander's short hair, and really, enough was enough. *Go. Get out of here.*

Forcing herself to walk right through the strange pull of resistance, the urge to stay and be with him, she headed out the door, pulling it closed behind her.

But it didn't shut.

Out of breath, Xander stepped onto the porch. "You forgot your blanket." He held it out to her looking…well, eager.

And it made her smile. "Forgot all about it. Thank you."

He'd noticed her leaving and raced to get it to her. That was incredibly sweet.

He stood too close, not releasing the blanket. A million thoughts swirled in his eyes, but his expression remained frustratingly blank.

"It was nice meeting you." She hitched a thumb toward the street. "I should get going."

"Don't you want to try one of your tacos?" The rush of color to his cheeks endeared her.

She didn't want to leave him. "I've got an early flight, so I'd better pack." She brought the blanket to her chest, as if it could somehow alleviate the ache. But when the silence grew uncomfortable, she broke away. "Goodnight."

At her car, she glanced over to find him still standing there, watching her.

And then the woman in the red bikini jumped onto his back, her blonde hair spilling all over his chest. With a hand gripping her wrist, he stepped back inside and closed the door.

She wished she'd never had that glimmer of connection with him.

Because now she just felt lonely.

Chapter Three

Owl Hoot was the craziest damn place Alexander Wilder had ever seen. Once the original settlement of Calamity, the Bowie family had turned the wild west ghost town into a high-end resort. To bring the history to life, they'd refurbished the original buildings, paid costumed actors to walk the streets, and staged regular shoot-outs.

It had boardwalks, a gondola to take visitors up the mountain, and a concierge who could hook you up with any kind of outdoor activity imaginable.

Tonight, Gigi Cavanaugh had launched the summer tourist season with a concert in the amphitheater. Xander remembered her from her days fronting the Lollipops, an all-girl pop band, and he much preferred her current Alt-indie rock sound.

Her parents had rented out the resort's restaurant for the after-party, and it had quickly filled with people. He stood at the bar with Gigi's dad—a Hall of Fame quarterback—and Cassian, the captain of his team, but instead of joining the conversation, Xander found himself scanning the room for the woman he couldn't seem to forget.

He didn't think Lulu would miss her sister's show...*so, where is she?*

If he asked, they'd want to know why he cared, and what could he say to that? *I don't know. I just liked being around her.*

And when she'd left, he'd wanted more.

She didn't seem to like parties much, so he could imagine her standing in a corner somewhere, wishing she were anywhere but here. But she wouldn't do that, would she? No, she'd be in the kitchen. He'd seen what cooking did for her. She'd get this flare of anxiety, and then she'd turn back to the food, and her whole body would relax, her features softening, and she'd lose herself in the scents and textures.

At the memory, interest sparked in his chest, spreading warmth through him.

When her thumb had idly stroked the lime, goose-bumps had sprouted all over his body.

I like the way she makes me feel.

The men laughed, tuning him back into their conversation, but they were still talking about football.

Jesus, mother of God. That's all anyone in his life talked about. His dad, his brothers, his teammates...one track minds, all of them.

"Hey, Dad."

He jerked so hard at the sound of the female voice, the seltzer in his glass sloshed over the side.

Tyler Cavanaugh's face lit up as he embraced his daughter. "Hey, sweetheart. Shouldn't you be home?"

Given the swollen belly, she had to be Coco, the pregnant daughter. Xander reached for a cocktail napkin to wipe his hand.

"Yeah, we're leaving." She handed him a black box tied up in silver ribbon. "I did the chocolates for the party, but I made these specially for you."

"Have I ever told you you're my favorite daughter?" Tyler tugged the bow and pried off the lid, revealing four artisan chocolates. Examining them as if he only had one shot to find the one with the golden ticket, he finally made a choice and popped it into his mouth. "Damn." He closed his eyes and slowly shook his head. "This is unbelievable. What is it?"

"Remember the Venezuelan beans I bought? So, this one's forty-one percent cacao with a mix of caramel and nuts." She turned to the other men. "Hey, Cassian. What'd you think of Gigi's show?"

The quarterback stood there with a goofy expression of adoration. "I think she's a superstar, and I'm proud of her."

His heart...fuck, that pinch. He felt it every time he was around his brothers or friends, anyone in a happy marriage. He'd never seen himself as a guy who'd get divorced. He'd wanted to be married, be done with the whole dating scene, but he hadn't managed to figure out the balance between work and home life.

But that hadn't been the problem, had it? He doubted he'd ever lit up when talking about his ex. He'd never loved her the way Cassian loved Gigi.

He just wasn't built that way. Didn't feel big emotions. Never had.

Tyler's beautiful, elegant daughter smiled at him. "Hi, I'm Coco." She patted Cassian's back. "His future sister-in-law."

He held out his hand. "Alexander Wilder, his future replacement."

Her smile faltered, but Cassian laughed. "In his dreams. He's my backup."

"Well, it's nice to meet you." She rubbed her belly. "Are you coaching at his camp this summer?"

"I'm not on the roster, but I'll help out when I can. I'm starting training at the Antigravity Center, so I'll be in town till July."

"That's a good, long stay. I'm sure I'll see you around. Okay, I'm going." Coco kissed her dad on the cheek and hugged Cassian. "It was nice to meet you, Alexander. Come by the shop, and I'll put together a box just for you."

"I'll do that. Thank you." As she wandered through the crowd, he kept his eye on her, thinking she might say goodbye to her younger sister. Instead, she fell into the arms of a big, fit guy who—given the tender look he gave her—had to be her husband.

"Want one?" Tyler held the box of chocolates close to his chest.

"Sure, thanks." Xander reached out, but Cassian chuckled and said, "He's being polite. Don't mess with the chocolates made *specially* for him."

"Yeah?" Xander flicked his fingers over the box. "They sure look good."

"They are." Tyler cracked a grin. "They're real good."

"Don't worry about it." Xander patted his stomach. "I start training in a few days. Gotta stay one step ahead of my captain." He tracked Coco and her husband, as they made their way out of the restaurant, stopping to say goodbye to people they knew. But he didn't see Lulu.

"Who're you looking for?" Tyler asked.

The jolt of being caught made him feel ridiculous. "No one." He'd spent all of twenty minutes with a woman three nights ago—and suddenly he was obsessed with her?

He was known for his cool composure—on and off the field—and his ability to shut everything out and focus with pinpoint precision. So, he'd just marshal that shit right now. But gazing into his bubbly drink, it was still there, that urgent need to turn around and look for her. Every second that ticked meant he might lose his chance to see her.

"Okay, Tyler, I brought you all kinds of wonderful goodies." A chef, arms loaded with plates, appeared behind the bar.

They all reached out to relieve her of the dishes.

She smiled at them. "Since you're friends, I'm sure you already know Tyler's a total foodie."

"Never seen anything like it," Cassian said. "He's lost to all conversation the minute it's feeding time."

"Man's gotta eat." Tyler examined everything. "This looks great." He pointed to a colorful tower of diced yellow beets with layers of herbed goat cheese and smoked salmon and topped with a dollop of crème fraiche and roe.

A server approached with a stack of small white plates and silverware. "Here you go."

"Thank you." Just as Tyler reached in to scoop up the appetizer, he stopped, aware of everyone watching him. He grinned like a kid caught sneaking a cookie. "Sorry. Delilah, you know Cassian, of course, but this is Alexander Wilder. He's a Maverick, too."

"Wonderful to meet you, X-Man." The gorgeous blonde flashed a teasing smile.

She knows my nickname? As a backup, he was pretty much only recognizable in the football world.

"Cassian grew up here. Everyone watches his games." She shook Xander's hand. "He also brings the guys in a lot over the summer. How come I've never met you?"

He didn't think *because we couldn't stand each other until recently* would go over well, so he just said, "I didn't go out much."

Cassian ran a football camp to offer talented, athletic kids the chance to learn a sport that otherwise might not be available to them. For the sake of the kids and the NFL players that volunteered, he kept it on the downlow.

Xander gestured to the dishes. "Are we sharing the amuse-bouches, or are they just for the big man over here?" He clapped Tyler on the back.

Delilah's gaze sharpened on him but quickly shifted to watch the Hall of Famer shove his spoon under the beet tower and transfer it to a plate.

Tyler took a bite. "Outstanding."

"Thanks." She smiled at Xander.

"Delilah's the executive chef here." Tyler passed one of the appetizers to Xander. "Try it."

Grabbing a fork, Xander cut into it. "Nice." He closed his eyes to experience the flavors. "Is that sage?"

"It sure is." Delilah grinned. "Sounds like someone knows his food."

"My mom owns a restaurant." And, while his brothers were either playing football or watching it, Xander could almost always be found in the kitchen.

"Really?" Delilah asked. "Which one?"

"Café Akasha." He took another bite.

The person sitting next to them swiveled around in her seat to get a look at him.

Delilah pounded the bar with a fist. "No way. You're lying to me." Her eyes glittered.

Tyler and Cassian looked confused.

"You've got to be kidding me." The chef reeled back.

"I'm not. It's true."

"That's one of my favorite restaurants in the *world*. I'm serious. Ask anybody. I'm in love with that place. It's absolutely magical."

"Well, thanks. My mom works hard at it."

"So, is your whole family woo-woo or just your mom?" Delilah asked.

His dad and brothers had plenty of superstitions on game day, but they left the candles and karma to his mom. "Just my mom."

"His dad's Tim Wilder, one of the greatest quarterbacks of all time," Cassian said. "And his brothers are Scottie and Matt Wilder."

"So, we've got football royalty in the house," Delilah said. "Nice. Should've used the fancy plates."

"Considering we used to flick food at each other across the dinner table, these are just fine." Xander sampled the next dish, a risotto speckled with bits of mushroom and red, green, yellow, and orange peppers. "This is fantastic. You put Branchini in it?"

"Okay, you've definitely spent time in your mom's kitchen. Yes, I did. I like the bite it gives to a creamy dish." The beautiful, animated chef leaned across the bar, like she was going to tell him a secret. "I'll tell you my all-time favorite dish at your mom's restaurant. Treasures of the sea."

Pride rushed through him, and Xander grinned. "Yeah?"

"Swear to God, it's out of this world."

"Glad to hear it. When I was a kid, my parents rented a house in Maine. We spent the summer checking out all the fishing villages. Great trip. When I came home, I told my mom I wanted to remember that vacation forever, so I created a dish that reminded me of it."

"Wait, *you* created it?"

"I did."

The woman sitting next to them blatantly turned away from her companion to listen in on the conversation.

"You mean you came up with the idea and the chef created it?" Delilah asked.

"No. It's all mine." Funny how people thought professional players were one dimensional. "I earned my spending money working in her kitchen."

"You sound just like Lulu," Cassian said.

Sunlight poured into his veins, heating him up at the mention of her name.

Tyler smiled. "That girl…everything she makes is like manna from the gods."

"I can't believe this. Treasures of the Sea…it's not just a dish," Delilah said. "It's something you could serve in the best restaurants in the world. It's that good."

"And why am I just hearing about these hidden talents now?" Cassian asked.

"I'm not the only one who can cook," Xander said. "Ryker made a *carne guisada* the night before I left Maui…never had better."

"Sorry I missed out," Cassian said. "But you can bet I'll have him cook for us at camp."

"So, we've got a bunch of football-playing cooks in town this summer, huh?" Delilah said. "I'm thinking we should do something with that."

"I do, too." The woman who'd been listening slid off the bar stool and thrust out her hand "I'm Abigail

Willock. I'm an executive producer at East/West Productions."

When no one recognized the name, she continued. "We make cooking shows. Have you heard of *The Farm Woman* and *Just Bake*?"

"Of course." Delilah seemed impressed, so he assumed they were popular.

"Well, sorry-not-sorry for eavesdropping, but...pro football player, famous family restaurant...my gears are turning, and they've just cranked out the most fabulous idea." She pointed to Xander. "What would you say to starring in your own cooking show?"

"What?" Delilah sounded delighted.

Startled, all he could do was shake his head. "I might've played around in my mom's kitchen, but I'm no professional."

"Oh, believe me, we're up to our eyeballs in famous chefs hosting recipe-based shows. In fact, that's why I'm in town right now, to talk to one. But I'm listening to you and thinking how fun it would be to have a pro athlete chatting with his teammates. It'd be more talk-show format, except each of your guests would create his signature dish in the segment." Her eyes flared with excitement. "Oh, and we could have your guest compete against a chef. With all the talent right here in Calamity, we could get a panel of judges to decide the winning dish. Kind of like *Beat Bobby Flay*, only with football players."

"That sounds amazing," Delilah said.

"I'd watch that," Tyler said.

"Right?" Abigail said to Tyler. "I can't even think of the last time I was this excited about an idea."

"I appreciate the offer, but training camp starts in July." *If I get a new contract.* Fear touched his heart like a hot poker, and he smacked it away. He had enough experience to know fear was insidious. If he let it in, it'd spread through him like a brushfire.

There was only one thing he could absolutely control, and that was his reactions. So, he wouldn't think about contracts until he needed to. "But thank you."

She waved a hand. "It's nowhere near as complicated as making a movie. We could knock out all thirteen episodes in no-time. Seriously, if we film two a day, you'd be done in a month at the most." She gestured to Cassian. "And with your teammates already in town, it's like it was meant to be. We'll film right here."

Cassian grew serious. "I don't want any press on my camp. It'll ruin it for my kids and coaches."

"Understood." Abigail turned serious. "We'll write that into the contract. There will be no mention of it whatsoever. I'm just saying, since the guys are already in town, it's a slam dunk."

"Thank you, Abigail, but I'm only interested in one thing this summer, and that's getting ready for next season." Nothing else mattered.

He *would* get a contract. If the Mavericks didn't come through, another team would.

He just needed to hear from *someone*. It was April, and training camps started in two months.

"Okay, I'll let it go for now." She pressed a card into his hand. "But if you change your mind, I'll be here the rest of the week. I'm vacationing with my family before I meet with the chef."

The woman turned back to her companion, and Tyler clapped him on the shoulder. "I'll tell you what I think." He mentored players. In fact, he'd plucked Cassian out of detention in high school and guided him all the way to the pros.

So, yeah, Xander would listen to anything this man said.

"When's your contract up?"

Xander's gut twisted. "June." And the Mavericks had gone quiet.

"You're too good to be a backup." He cut a look to Cassian, who nodded his agreement. "But you've had two injuries."

Cassian reached for a plate. "That's why he's here. To rehab his shoulder."

"I already did that," Xander said to Tyler. "But Cassian seems to think Fin Bowie's training center can work some magic."

"It can," Tyler said. "They don't just train, they research. They know what they're doing."

Xander perked up. "Fin said they've got some groundbreaking exercises focused on the specific muscles that support my damaged ligaments. He swears they can make my shoulder better than new."

"Your shoulder never separated, right?" Tyler asked. "Neither time?"

"No. Level two."

Tyler nodded confidently. "It'll be all right."

It shouldn't matter. Tyler was a retired quarterback, not a doctor. But it did. Somehow his confidence mattered.

"Right, so, here's what I'm thinking." Tyler set his fork down. "The last time anyone saw you, you were being carried off the field."

Xander didn't need the reminder. He'd finally had his

shot during the playoffs in January, and he'd performed like the phenom he'd once been.

Until three hundred pounds had slammed into him and hurled him to the ground. He would never forget the sickening reality that had crashed over him as his cheek lay pressed to the turf…that everything he'd worked for had just gone up in smoke.

"If you do the show, you'll replace that image with a new one. They'll see you strong, confident, on top of the world. Let them see you having a great time."

"I want them to see me playing football, not doing a cooking show."

"You got another plan?"

Shit. Fuck. "No."

"I'm asking you seriously. Has your agent had any luck getting you try-outs? Has anyone shown interest in you?"

Fear slipped into his bloodstream, burning like acid.

If no one offered him a contract by June, he'd become a free agent.

And, with a second injury to the same shoulder, he might never play again.

If I don't, I'll have flamed out before I ever had the chance to prove myself.

"Hey." Tyler clapped a hand on his shoulder. "None of this is your fault."

I know that. That's what makes it so maddening.

"You won that game, and everyone who matters saw your performance. But that doesn't change the fact that there will always be a whole class of young, healthy kids coming up behind you." Tyler shoved the plate away. "If you do this show, if you interview football players, you're going to have coaches, owners, players…everyone's going to watch. Let them see you've recovered. Be carefree, fun. Show them you don't have a care in the world."

Cassian barked out a laugh. "You want Mr. Intensity to be carefree? He doesn't even hang around his teammates. The only reason he came to Maui was because his agent told him to be seen with the team."

Was Tyler seriously suggesting he do a TV show?

"Look, if it resets your image in the minds of NFL coaches, I think you can fake it for the cameras. Besides, just pretend you're talking to the guys. Block out the lights, the crew." Tyler pushed away from the bar. "You've got an opportunity here—unusual, sure, but it could keep you on the radar."

"It's nothing but a concept right now. Who knows when it'll air?"

"What's the cost? If you get a contract, you'll have wasted a month of your life." Tyler shrugged. "But if you're still unsigned in June, the show will give you visibility."

"You can make it a stipulation in the contract that you want ads going out right away." As the franchise quarterback of the top team in the league, Cassian did a lot of endorsements. He knew his contracts. "You've got the power—there's no show without you—so ask for what you need. In fact, don't most of those shows start with a montage? Let's get the guys together and play some ball. Get footage of one of your sweet spirals."

Xander smiled. "You guys are good."

"At what?" Cassian asked.

"At giving a guy hope."

Chapter Four

Xander's tires crunched over gravel, as he eased his rental car into a parking spot. Thanks to volatile spring weather, April and May were off-peak seasons in the Tetons, which was the only reason he'd been able to get a cottage at The Homesteader Inn. Normally, the high-end suites were reserved a year in advance.

He'd booked a few nights, since he didn't have to check into the training center until the day after tomorrow. Headlights flashed on his cabin tucked deep in the woods. The freshly painted red door stood out against the dark logs. He killed the engine.

His mom would love this place. The reviews he'd read were right—its romantic setting and world-famous cuisine rivaled Café Akasha.

Growing up in Tiburon—a ferry ride from San Francisco—he was used to a small town with an outdoorsy lifestyle. But Calamity—sitting in the valley between the Teton and Gros Ventre mountain ranges—was a whole other world.

Getting out of the car, he pocketed his keys and

breathed in the crisp air, scented with pine and sage. *Damn*. It was cold as balls, and he hadn't brought any winter clothes.

The soft yellow glow from solar lamps lit the walkway to his cabin, and the soles of his boots thudded on the cobblestones.

"You sure I shouldn't stick around?" A male voice carried from the looming main lodge.

"Positive."

His body recognized the voice before his mind did, triggering a jolt of awareness.

"I don't want Chef to be pissed," the man said.

"He won't, I promise. I've cooked in his kitchen since I was fourteen."

"Oh, I know. He talks about you all the time. Lulu this, and Lulu that. He thinks you're the greatest thing since sliced cheese."

"Maybe I am."

Xander grinned. He headed toward the voices, crossing a patch of dew-covered grass and a small employee parking lot to find the hourglass silhouette of a woman framed in the light of the kitchen doorway.

Attraction flickered to life at the base of his spine.

"I don't know," the man said. "It's just...he expects me to lock up."

"Totally get that, and you're welcome to hang around. I shouldn't be much longer."

The man hesitated, glancing over his shoulder. Moonlight glinted off the rearview mirror of a truck. "No, it's okay. I gotta get home. Just don't forget to double lock the door, okay? He gets pissed if you only lock the bottom one."

"You think I'd let down a guy who thinks I'm as awesome as individually wrapped cheese slices?"

The guy let out a huff of laughter. "Yeah, okay. 'Night."

"'Night." She was about to shut the door when her gaze jerked over to where he stood.

He realized how intimidating he must look, so he stepped into the light of a solar lamp. "Hey, it's me. Xander."

"*Xander*?" She straightened. "What're you doing here? Shouldn't you be in Maui?"

"Nah." He came closer. "I start physical therapy at the training center the day after tomorrow."

"Oh."

It was fun watching her try to keep herself from asking the obvious question. He could read her like a book. Finally, he broke out in a smile.

"What's so funny?" she asked.

He climbed the steps onto the porch. "You're dying to ask me why I bothered flying all the way out to Maui, if I knew I had to be in Calamity."

"You can't read my mind." She had the most beautiful smile.

He swore he could draw a full breath for the first time in months.

"But since you mention it, why would you go all the way to Maui just for a couple of days?"

He loved that teasing tone. "Reasons that can only be shared over whatever it is you're cooking."

"Oh, no. That's impossible. This recipe's top secret."

"What if I offer my seasoned palette? I can let you know if what you're making tastes any good."

"Why would I need someone to tell me what I already know?" She turned and headed back inside.

She'd left the door open, which he took as an invitation, and followed her in.

What a crazy night. First, the offer to have his own cooking show and now—out of nowhere—the woman he'd been searching for since the plane's wheels hit the tarmac.

Okay, cool, I found her…now what do I want? His gait faltered. He wasn't all that into hookups, and after a failed marriage, he was absolutely not getting into another relationship any time soon—especially with Tyler Cavanaugh's daughter.

Worse, I'm still a Maverick. Still Cassian's backup.

I'm not banging his future sister-in-law.

And yet…there he was, closing and locking the door behind him, following her down a hallway. He passed an employee bathroom, an office, and a storage room, before entering a cluttered, well-used kitchen.

With her bounty of shiny, dark hair hanging loose past her shoulders, Lulu stood at a gleaming stainless steel counter chopping shallots. She scraped the onion into a skillet with melted butter. When it sizzled and steamed, she lowered the flame. "Welcome to the inner sanctum. Now, what's up with Maui? You spent as much time in the air as you did on the sand."

"You're not familiar with small talk, are you?"

"Says the man whose opening line was about me lying to my family."

He'd wrestled with whether to bring that up for a while, finally falling on the side of respect. He'd want to know if a roomful of people knew something personal about him. He stuttered out a laugh. "Yeah, about that.

When I was in high school, I fought with my girlfriend under the bleachers before a game. For days after, everyone kept looking at me funny. I couldn't figure out why, until I found out that some of her friends had heard the whole thing. It was like walking around with a stain on your jeans, and no one bothering to tell you about it."

"What was the fight about?"

He gave her a look that said, *Really?*

"Oh, come on. You witnessed my most embarrassing moment. You can give me *something*."

"She accused me of hitting on some other girl, and when I didn't deny it, she got all worked up."

"Did you hit on some other girl?"

"No."

"Then why didn't you just say that?"

"Because I needed to be in the locker room with my team." Was that why? It was so long ago. "I was the quarterback."

"Weak. What's the real reason?"

"How's that weak?"

"If the person you love feels threatened, you reassure them."

He couldn't argue with that. "Fair. Okay, well, I was also sick of her jealousy, but I didn't need to discuss it at that moment. In any event, that's why I decided to tell you. I knew you'd be around the guys all summer, and I thought you should know."

"Thank you. I appreciate that." She stirred the onions. "So, how's the weather?"

He chuckled. "Forget it. I think we can agree we both suck at polite conversation."

"Small talk is an unsharpened blade. It's cat hair on a black fleece jacket. It's bits of sand in a bouillabaisse." She measured port wine and poured it into the skillet, and then did the same with red wine. "So, Maui?"

She had a way of moving—he couldn't explain it—but it was deliberate, sexy...mesmerizing. "That was just optics."

"I don't know what that means." She lowered the flame even more, then turned to rest her back against the counter. "But I'm pretty sure you didn't have an ophthalmology appointment in Maui...so?"

He chuckled. "No. It was a team thing."

She cut him a look. "You don't have to tell me if you don't want. I mean, if it's some super-secret football thing a chef could never understand, we could just go back to the weather."

"No, it's just...career shit."

"Okay." Her tone held no judgment whatsoever, but she reached for something that looked like demi-glace and poured a cup into her sauce. She dipped a finger into the mixture and brought it to her mouth. Her tongue licked the tip, and he felt a punch of lust in his cock.

Fuck, he wanted her attention back. And he knew the only way to get it was to be on her level.

He wasn't used to that. His ex cared about superficial things, like how she looked, décor, manners. She was intelligent, fun, lively, charming...but she didn't get deep. He'd been fine with that for a long time—he'd been too focused on the draft, on rehabbing his injury, on training—

Actually, come to think of it, he'd never wanted more until he met Lulu.

He moved closer. "Can this be just between the two of us?" Given that both her parents and older sister were celebrities, he knew she'd understand discretion.

"Absolutely." Tucking the long bangs that kept falling

across her cheek behind her ear, she watched him with concern.

"My contract's up in June. I don't…" He let out a rough exhalation. "I don't know if I'll get a new one."

"Because of what happened during the playoffs?"

"Yes." Of course she'd seen it. *She comes from a football family.* "And my agent thinks hanging around my teammates sends a subliminal message."

"I'm pretty sure coaches don't make decisions based on that."

He appreciated her honesty more than he could say. "No, I don't think so either."

"Is it awful to be around them when you don't know if you're going to be on the team?"

Wow. No one would ever be so blunt—not even his family.

It surprised him just how much he needed to expose those dark, shadowy fears. "Yes. I'm a backup, so I've always been an outsider, but now? The decision might already be made, and they just haven't told my agent yet." His heart pounded, and he scrubbed his jaw with a hand. "I might not be a Maverick."

"That's awful. No wonder you wanted to be anywhere but there."

I wanted to be with you. "Yeah." Those eyes—they were so damn expressive. He could feel her concern, her empathy. "The problem is…it's out of my control." Jesus, now that he'd started, he couldn't stop the words from tumbling out. "I can train, and I can eat right and get enough sleep and perform my best on the field…but I can't make anyone offer me a contract."

"And it's not like you even want to be a backup. You'd rather lead your own team."

"Exactly." Frustration bore down on him. Nothing was in his control.

The way she sniffed the bay leaf, ran her fingernails along the woody stem of fresh thyme to tear off the leaves, made his skin tingle. He wanted to tip her chin, look into her eyes, and taste her mouth.

Which was bad. "So, what's got you cooking this late at night?"

"I just spent the evening with my mother."

"That bad, huh?"

"My mom's awesome. I couldn't have asked for a better mother."

"But?"

"No buts. She wants the best for her daughters. That's her thing in life—making sure we develop our passions into wildly successful careers. But it doesn't allow a lot of leeway to mess up or change course." She lowered her head. "Dammit. That was a but. Okay, fine. My mom's great, *but* she's too damn pushy."

"Yeah, I got that."

She gently stirred, steam rising in lazy curls from the skillet. "Especially when you show a talent for something. Like Gigi. You were at her concert tonight?"

"I was. She's good."

"She's amazing. Not just at singing, but at writing songs." She pressed her lips together in a wistful expression. "I just don't know how happy she is."

"She seems pretty damn happy to me."

Lulu gave a soft, sweet smile. "She's found the love of her life, so there's not much that can get her down. But I don't know that this *career* makes her happy. It just...gets to be too much."

"What, the travel?"

"No." She sounded vague, like she was wrangling her thoughts. "It's like I said before about expectations. About becoming addicted to positive feedback. You start out in little dive clubs, and you get some applause. The following week, more people come to see you. A year later, a manager hands you his card." She made the telephone gesture with her thumb and pinkie. "'Call me.' Pretty soon, you're signing with a label, and it's like your life becomes this quest to climb to the next level. Wherever you are at any point in time isn't good enough. You've got to keep hitting it harder. And then…you make it. You're *there*."

"On stage at Madison Square Garden."

She pointed the spoon at him. "Exactly. And then what? You fight to keep your position. One record goes platinum, and then every single one after that has to make it, too, or else you're a failure and you're left wondering, *Did that record suck? What did I do wrong?* So, you work harder, tour more. And I'm telling you, she's going to hit a wall."

"Are we talking about Gigi right now?"

She flashed him a sexy grin. *Caught me.* "Yes. But also…isn't it true for all of us?"

"Hell, yes."

She held his gaze, those warm hazel eyes assessing and somehow finding him delightful.

No one—not even his own mother—found his broody ass delightful.

Damn, he liked this woman.

"It took getting fired for me to realize all this. It was my first time not working in a dozen years, and it struck me…I don't even *notice* my life. I lived in Paris and worked twelve-hour days. I'm so busy cooking, I forgot about the farmers markets, the food, which was the whole point of starting on this path to begin with. And then I'm just like, am I even enjoying this slice of goddamn cheesecake I just made? Or am I looking at your expression to see if *you* like it?"

"I like cheesecake. I'll bet you make a good one."

Her cheeks flushed a pretty pink. "I make a great one. But do I sit down with a nice cup of tea and enjoy it? No, I don't. And, really, what's the point of owning a Michelin-rated restaurant if you're not enjoying the food you make?"

"So, that's the dream? A Michelin star?"

"That's the dream."

"Look at us." He rapped his knuckles on the counter. "The prodigy and the phenom."

But that wasn't what really connected them. It was that they hadn't realized their potential. That was the link that crackled between them. They got each other.

"And I guess the lesson I've gotten out of this whole experience is that it's good to have goals and work hard for them, but I don't want to miss out on the journey."

"I hear you. But, if we took your mom out of the equation, would you still be gunning for a Michelin star?"

"Well, isn't that just the million-dollar question?" Holding a strainer over a silver bowl, she poured the port wine sauce through it. "Okay, Phenom. I'm throwing it back to you. What's your million-dollar question?" After returning it to the skillet, she added heavy cream.

Easy. "If we took my dad and brothers out of the equation, would I still be gunning for a starting quarterback position?"

"Are you telling me your entire family plays football?"

"Yep." He paused. "And both of my brothers have Super Bowl rings."

"Oh, boy. If I was the only one of my sisters without a Michelin star…" She cringed.

"Exactly."

"We need wine." She left the kitchen for a moment, returning with two glasses. Pouring the red, she handed him one. "Look at us, two free agents."

"I'm not a free agent yet."

"No, you're not." She swirled the ruby red liquid in the glass. "And someone's going to sign you, right? It's just a matter of contract negotiations?"

"Not necessarily. This is my second injury. Same shoulder."

She shut off the flame. "When was the first?"

"In college."

"Ah, so that's how the phenom became a backup quarterback." She said it softly, her eyes full of concern. "What happened?"

"I got sacked by a linebacker from Cal. We'd killed them in the playoffs the year before, and their defense was determined to bring me down."

"Xander." She looked as upset as if it had just happened. "That's terrible."

The memory of that pain still flashed through his body. He'd known—the second he'd hit the ground—his NFL dreams had just died. "So, I went from the number one draft pick to taking a year off to rehab my shoulder. We stayed in touch with coaches, let them know my progress." *Exactly what I'm doing now.* "And then I walked onto the Mavericks, and I've been a backup ever since."

"I'm sorry." When she reached for his hand, he realized he'd curled it into a fist. "That's got to eat away at you."

Her heat, her compassion, eased the tension in his body. "I don't let it. I just keep my focus on the goal."

She didn't say a word.

Because she doesn't believe me.

And she's waiting for me to get real.

He understood. What's the point in having a conversation if people just bullshitted each other? "I've been chasing my brothers my entire life, working to reach their level and never getting there. When I signed with Stanford, I thought I'd made it. When I won the Heisman… that was…" Emotion rose so fast it jammed in his throat. He didn't want her to see him like this, so he marshaled his discipline and shook it off. "Anyhow, it's just never worked out." Given how well he'd performed during the play-offs in January, he'd thought he'd finally done it—and then he'd eaten turf. "If I sucked, it would be one thing. But to be called a phenom…" He sawed a finger across his chin.

"Believe me…" She squeezed his hand. "I know."

Her warmth seeped in, loosening him even more. "I spend every minute of my life going after a goal I may never reach."

She couldn't know the weight of those words he'd never once said out loud. The admission that his career might be over—before it ever really began—was huge. He'd been trained to never give into doubts or negativity.

Stay focused, stay positive. Eyes on the goal.

But he'd said it. And it wasn't nearly as scary as he'd imagined it might be.

In fact, it was pretty damn freeing.

"And it doesn't help that my brothers are always lording it over me."

"Lording what?" Her eyes went wide. "Their success?"

"It's not like that. They're just joking around."

"Xander."

"My brothers are six and eight years older, so they've always teased me."

"But not about *that*. That's just cruel."

The muscles at the back of his neck tightened. "Ah, come on. You're from a big family. Everything's on the table."

"Can you imagine my sisters making jokes about me getting fired?"

No. "It's not a big deal. I'm used to it." He tried to say the words lightly, but they came out raw.

"Give me an example."

"Of the way they tease me?" He didn't have to think about it. "For context, my dad played for the 49ers, I've got one brother playing for Kansas City, and the other for Baltimore."

Lifting her glass, she said, "To overachieving families."

They tapped their glasses and, standing right beside her, he was close enough to find her eyes were a complicated mix of brown, hazel, gold, and green.

And he just knew, if he ever had the time to get to know her, she'd be layers upon layers of interesting, thoughtful, caring, passionate woman.

She sipped her wine, and her tongue peeked out to lick her bottom lip.

His body went hot and hard.

He'd obviously felt attraction before—but nothing like this. When it was a mix of desire, curiosity, hunger…it was so much richer.

He blew out a breath. *Focus.* "Pretty much every time I'm around them, they make a big show out of losing their Super Bowl rings. They think it's hilarious."

She looked disgusted. "How is that even funny?"

"Well, from their perspective, they do it because they

believe I'm a better player than they are, and that as soon as I get my shot, I'll break records. They wouldn't make fun of me if I actually sucked."

"But you're not breaking records, you're not a franchise player…I'm sorry, I know they're your brothers, and I know they love you, but it just seems incredibly insensitive."

"You're angrier about it than I am."

"You sure about that?"

He drank some wine, aware of a rumble deep inside his body. "My brothers are good guys."

"I'm sure they are. I just…that'd be hard for me to take." She poured the sauce into a storage container and then brought the skillet and bowl to the sink.

While she washed dishes, he thought about his parent's thirty-fifth wedding anniversary. During the party he and his brothers had thrown, they'd brought their parents into the garage to give them their gift.

They'd found and refurbished the very first truck their dad had ever owned, and when he'd pulled off the tarp, Xander had heard a plink—gold hitting concrete.

"Oh, no, my ring," Scottie said. "Has anyone seen my ring?"

"Which ring is that, Scottie?" Matt said.

"My Super Bowl ring. You know the really shiny one with a dozen diamonds on it? The ring I won for winning the Super Bowl?"

"Oh, that one," Matt said. "You better not lose it. It's irreplaceable."

Scottie picked up the massive ring. "Not hard to find when it's this shiny, though, right, Matt?" He smirked at his older brother. "'Course you wouldn't know since yours is probably tarnished with age."

His brothers had riffed off each other, and Xander had…well, he'd laughed. He'd played the role expected of him. But inside, he'd been annoyed.

Well, if you're going there, you might as well go all the way.

He'd been hurt.

"You know what?" His voice rang out in the kitchen.

Lulu hit the faucet with the palm of her hand and turned to him.

"I hate it. It pisses me off when they drop their rings in my egg nog and wait for me to get to the bottom of my glass to find it." Damn, it felt good to admit it. "And, worse, my mom always says something like, 'Oh, stop, you two,' which just makes them laugh harder. Like it's some harmless comedy routine."

She dried her hands on a towel. "Have you ever told them to knock it off?"

"No. I'm not making excuses for them, but my brothers and my dad are my greatest supporters. They'd do anything to help me, and when they tease me, they're trying to get me out of my head. I can be…intense. They don't mean to hurt me."

"Okay, but they *do* hurt you. And humor's good, but the elephant in the room is that you might never play again, which means it's not something to joke about." She shook her head. "Ugh. Listen to me. As if you need me pointing out the obvious. I'm only making it worse."

"Actually, you're not. I appreciate your honesty, because everyone just gives me platitudes." *Like Steph.* His ex had never gotten real with him, just gave him empty phrases she'd read in self-help books. Which wasn't what he'd needed. "There's nothing worse than everyone telling you how great you are, how much potential you have, how you're going to get your shot…when it's just not true. I might never get it." Lifting his wine glass, he tipped it back and let the liquid slide down his throat. "I might never play again." Relief swept through him. "It feels good to say that out loud. It isn't easy to stay positive and determined."

"No, it's not."

That sizzling connection hit his skin like static electricity. Her hair looked so pretty falling over her shoulders, and her mouth…fuck, it was expressive and sexy, her lips plump and dark pink.

His heart pounded and desire burned in his blood.

Impulsively, he reached for her hand. "Most people don't understand."

"Most people aren't phenoms and prodigies. And they don't understand that you can't be either when you're twenty-six. It's an adjustment to realize you're just making your way like everybody else."

"Exactly."

It struck him that she wasn't being overtly sexual. She didn't wear provocative clothing, she wasn't giving him seductive looks, and she wasn't playfully touching him.

And yet he'd never been more attracted to a woman in his life.

Because she was passionate. The way she touched food, the way she *savored* it in her mouth. Her heated response to his brothers' teasing. She was a sensual woman, and he wanted to fuck her.

Wanted a dark room and their naked bodies pressed together. Wanted her hands on him because he just knew the kind of pleasure they'd bring. He wanted to know the taste and smell of her skin, and he wanted to watch her expression when she came apart on his tongue.

Her phone buzzed on the counter, snapping him out of his filthy thoughts. Glancing at the screen, she immediately wiped her hands on her apron and picked it up. "Mom?" Her eyes went wide. "What should I do?" She quickly put the cream back in the refrigerator. "Of course. Let me clean up here super quick, and I'll be right over. Wait, do I have time, or should I come right now?" With one hand, she untied the apron and pulled it over her head. "Right. That was stupid. Okay, on my way." She set down the phone and gave him a comical expression of surprise. "Coco's in labor. They're on their way to the hospital. Look at me." She held out a hand to him. "I'm shaking." She looked at the mess she'd made.

"I got it."

She looked surprised. "You sure?"

"Absolutely. Give me the key, and I'll lock up." He remembered what that guy on the porch had said. "I'll *double* lock the door."

Lulu threw herself into his arms, and her sweet feminine scent enveloped him. "Thank you so much. I loved talking to you tonight."

And then she was out the door, leaving him wondering if he'd ever get the chance to see her again.

Chapter Five

NOT WANTING TO WAKE UP HER SIX-YEAR-OLD NIECE by ringing the bell, Lulu peered through the window of her sister's adorable Craftsman house. A single lamp beside the leather couch cast a pool of yellow light on the hardwood floor.

Gigi and Cassian sat cuddled up together. He played with her hair, listening intently as she told him a story.

Lulu's heart twisted with yearning.

She'd longed for that kind of relationship her entire life. She wanted so badly to find her special someone.

Someone like Xander.

Not him, of course. *Obviously. He's only passing through.* But someone she could have good conversations with…whose touch sent a shock through her body.

Gigi laughed, getting up on her knees and wrapping both arms around her fiancé's neck to kiss him. He grabbed her bottom and hauled her onto his lap.

They were so happy.

Back in high school, when her dad was mentoring Cassian, her sister would always find excuses to hang around them. They'd pretended to just be good friends, but anyone could see how much they'd wanted each other. Her dad, though, had worried Gigi would give up her own dreams to follow Cassian's career in the NFL, so he'd kept them apart.

Lulu was glad they'd found their way back to each other, but she couldn't help the squeeze of envy. She loved her family, loved her career, she had a couple of good, close friends, but nothing filled that awful sense of being alone in the world. Because in the end, her parents had each other, her sisters and friends had boyfriends and husbands, and Lulu was on her own.

Quietly, she let herself into the house. Her sister sat up, her expression brightening.

Barefoot, in leggings and a sweatshirt, Gigi hurried to greet her. "Hey." She gave her a hug. "You got here fast."

"Mom said to come right away. Any news?"

Gigi shook her head. "Coco's probably not even checked into her room yet."

"Posie's asleep?" She'd spent so much time overseas she hadn't gotten to know her niece very well. She was a little intimidated about babysitting.

"Out like a light, so she doesn't know yet."

Meaning, if the six-year-old knew, she'd be pitching a fit to be at the hospital with her parents. Posie was dying to meet her new sister.

"Big night in the Cavanaugh family. Your concert and now a second niece."

"Uh, my show at the Owl Hoot Amphitheater's not in the same ballpark as Coco having a *baby*."

"But it was a great concert." Cassian slung an arm around Gigi's shoulders and kissed her cheek.

"Thanks, love." She touched Lulu's arm. "Mom said

you weren't home when she got the call from Coco, but I know you left the party early. Where'd you go?"

"You know that project I was telling you about? I'm fine-tuning it." She didn't have a TV personality, so she figured if she memorized her scripts, she'd perform better during her live audition. The less she had to think about measuring ingredients, the more animated she could be while walking the audience through a recipe.

"In other words, you were in Chef Jonny's kitchen." Gigi said it with a teasing grin.

"Yep. And guess who stopped by for a visit?"

"Oh, God, don't tell me it was Griffin."

Weirdly, Lulu hadn't even considered running into Chef Jonny's son—and Cassian's cousin. "No. Though, this guy's just as broody and quiet."

"Xander?" Cassian asked. "He talked to you?"

Gigi elbowed him. "Why do you sound so surprised?"

"I don't know. He just keeps to himself. Even on the road, he's always done his own thing."

"They thought he was screwing around on his wife," Gigi said. "Cassian and Xander *hated* each other."

"Wife?" *What?* Why would he be hanging out with her if he were married?

She really shouldn't be this disappointed in someone she'd just met.

"He's divorced," Gigi said.

"I didn't hate him," Cassian said. "The Wilders are all about family values, and he projects this righteous, moral face to the world, so it seemed a little hypocritical."

Wait, she needed to know. "But he wasn't? Cheating?"

"Turns out he wasn't. But my point is that he never bothered correcting us." Cassian hunched a shoulder.

"That's how little he talks—not even to defend himself. So, if he talked to you…"

"Lulu does that to people. Mom would be like, 'Hey, can you guys run to the store real quick?' I'd come home with milk and eggs, and Lulu would bring the lowdown on Trudy Jenkin's divorce." Her grin held affection. "People just confide in her. That's her second best quality."

"Second, huh? What's my first?"

"Your passion. You inspire me."

"Me?" Coming from her superstar sister that was a true compliment.

"Yep. Whenever I start to doubt myself, all I have to do is spend time around you, and I get all revved up and want to run back to my studio and immerse myself in words and melodies."

"Wow…that's…I had no idea."

"That's because we don't spend nearly enough time together." Her sister reached for her hand. "Promise me we're going to hang out this summer?"

"Of course. I want that, too."

"We never got to do that growing up, and it always made me sad."

Cassian brushed a lock of hair off Gigi's shoulder. "We should go."

"Right. I have to get back in the studio. Everyone's waiting for me."

"Go." Lulu stepped away from the door.

Gigi grabbed her purse and a bag off a side table. "Here's your costume for the Pole, Pedal, and Paddle race tomorrow."

"Should I even look?" She, Gigi, and their mom had agreed to be teammates—wearing some of the outlandish costumes from her sister's pop star days.

Gigi handed over the bag. "You're going to look hot."

"Is Mom still coming? Now that Coco's in labor? Maybe we should cancel."

"She said she is." Gigi shrugged. *We'll see.* "No matter what, though, I think we should do it. It's a really fun day, and the money goes to a great cause. We can always get someone to take her place. Oh, whatever happened with that person you're meeting? Is she coming to the event?"

"I told her about it, and she sounded interested, but I get the feeling she's keeping her distance. She only wants to see me at the au"—she'd almost said audition—"at the actual meeting." That would've piqued her sister's interest, for sure.

Gigi cocked her head, clearly wondering why Lulu insisted on keeping secrets.

And, as she locked the door behind them, Lulu had to wonder the same thing.

So what if she didn't get the show?

For so long, she'd blamed her mom for calling her gifted, but maybe the only person invested in the idea of her being a prodigy was Lulu herself.

And the only way to get over it was to allow herself to fail.

Hot sun burning the top of her head, Lulu forced herself to paddle through aching muscles. Up ahead, other contestants reached shore, celebrating with waiting friends, while crowds clustered around the food booths and the bouncy house.

After nearly an hour, the rhythmic splash of each oar dipping into the water had turned from soothing to unbearable.

Why had she thought the boating portion would be the easiest?

Fortunately, the race had fallen on a perfect day. A lovely breeze rippled the water and cooled her heated skin.

I have got to start working out. As a chef working impossible hours, she'd had very little time for basic errands, let alone exercise.

With her sights on the inflatable arch that signaled the finish line, she laughed when she saw her two teammates waving, encouraging her on. Just like the other participants, they looked ridiculous in their costumes. Too bad the sexy leather leggings Lulu wore made her feel like she'd been rolled up in a heavy canvas tent.

Right as the tip of her boat nudged the shore, her dad walked into the freezing river and dragged the kayak onto the rocky sand. "You okay, sweetheart?"

"I'm dying, but I made it."

"You sure did." Her mom reached out a hand to help her out of the boat. "Oh, my goodness, look at you. You're red as a beet." She swiped the damp bangs off Lulu's forehead. "Gigi, grab her a water bottle, will you?"

In a white sparkly jumpsuit, her sister dashed off to the event table and pulled a couple bottles out of a large cooler. Her mom looked fresh and lovely, and if she hadn't been wearing a hot pink tutu over black lace leggings, you'd think she'd just had lunch with friends.

"How do you manage to look glamorous after biking twenty miles?" Lulu asked.

"Oh, stop. I've had a while to recover."

Gigi handed her a drink. "We did it."

"We're a bunch of badasses." Lulu pressed the icy bottle to her cheek.

Gigi waved another one. "Let me get this to Cassian."

She headed over to where a group of guys chatted not far away.

"Thanks for doing this with me," Lulu said.

"Honey, you haven't been in town in seven years. I wouldn't have missed it for anything."

"Yeah, but I know you're dying to get to the hospital."

"We saw them this morning, and we'll be there when they get home this afternoon. I *wanted* to do this event with my girls." Her mom shifted, blocking the sun so she could look into Lulu's eyes. "You're important to me, Lulu. You've given me a lot to think about the past few days, and I want to be a better mom for you."

"You're a great mom—don't misunderstand what I said. You've encouraged me and rooted for me and helped me become a damn good chef. What I did with that… that's on me. And, honestly, getting fired sucked, but I think it kind of woke me up."

Her mom let out an exasperated breath. "I still can't believe I actually encouraged you to move to another city when you said you were basing your project here. So, yes, it is partly my fault." With a troubled expression, her mom glanced to the river. A pontoon floated to shore, its captain dressed as a pirate. "You're not the only one who's talked to me about how much I pushed all of you." She glanced to Gigi who stood in the shelter of Cassian's arm. "Gigi says I focused so much on helping you all find your passions that I never let you just hang out and bond as sisters. I feel terrible about that."

"Joss?" her dad called. "Lu?"

Her mom held up a finger before pulling Lulu into her arms. "I love you, sweetheart, and I'm sorry for pushing you too hard."

"Mom, I promise. It's okay."

After they joined her dad's group, Lulu twisted the cap off her bottle and lifted her arm to drink. "Ow. Oh, God."

"Nine miles of kayaking for someone not used to it isn't easy," her dad said.

"Look at them, reveling in their victory." Gigi grinned at the large Bowie clan.

The four extreme athletes seemed to take up the entire beach with their powerful physiques and charismatic personalities. Three of the women in the group wore costumes, so she assumed they made up a team. One wore a toque, the other a frothy gown, and the third a tiara.

"Who are they?" Lulu asked.

Gigi pointed to each one in turn. "Delilah's a chef, Knox is a wedding gown designer, and the one in the tiara? That's Princess Rosalina."

"What's a princess doing in Calamity? With the *Bowies*?"

"Well, they're a little more civilized than when you knew them in high school, but she's engaged to Brodie." Her mom watched a food truck roll in. "Oh, look. Maureen's here. Let's grab a breakfast sandwich."

As her parents headed over to the food booths, Gigi said, "You ready for your meeting?"

"I think so." Her audition was on Monday, and she got a thrill just thinking about it. Right then she knew it was time to stop keeping secrets. "Can I tell you what it is?"

"You know you can. I won't say a word. Not even to Cassian, if you don't want me to."

It shouldn't feel so monumental. But it was, and she was dying to tell someone. "I pitched a cooking show."

Her eyes widened. "You mean like *Chopped*?"

"No, more like *The Farm Woman*. I don't have a big personality like Stella, so I couldn't pull off a show like *Rachel Ray*. And I thought, well, what makes me unique?" She gestured around her. "*This*. I grew up in a wild west town settled by outlaws. Our tourism site calls Calamity the western capital of whoop ass, where the people are wild at heart. We've got everyone from billionaires and celebrities to seasonal workers and recluses like Lachlan Bowie living here." She looked at the people around them, wearing rainbow leggings, cow costumes, and hot pink wigs. "I think I said something like, Calamity's made up of eccentric people who want to live free."

"Well, you sold me. I love it. It's such a cool idea."

"Do you really think so?"

"I mean, I don't watch a lot of cooking shows, but I've seen *The Farm Woman*, and she's always out there in her galoshes gathering eggs from the hen house and feeding apples to her horses...she's adorable and sweet, and her food is so *normal*. I can just see you heli skiing with the Bowies and then cooking a huge feast for them at some big, old farm table."

Gigi got it. She totally got it. Her sister's enthusiasm set her pulse pounding. "I wish I'd talked to you before I submitted." Bouncing ideas off other people would've helped. "I made a video of what I envisioned for the opening credits, panning the Tetons, a still shot of a moose in Ballard's Pond, a family taking the gondola up the mountain."

"Tell me you included the antler archways at the town green?" Gigi asked.

"Yep. And I included enough ideas in my pitch deck to fill an entire season. Like, me visiting the farmers market and talking to the local vendors. Touring a winery, a brewery—"

"A chocolate shop."

"Exactly. And I hear we've got a hydroponic farm. It'd be cool to get a tour, talk about how we can get year-round fresh produce in a mountain town."

"I'd watch it." Gigi touched her arm. "But can we talk about what you said about your personality?"

"I don't mean it in a bad way. I'm not putting myself down. I'm just not bubbly and…and charismatic, you know?"

"No, I don't know. In a big group, you tend to be quiet. But when you're one-on-one or with your family, you're funny and full of energy. But mostly I just want to say, you don't need to be like Stella to draw attention. I'm not sure how she became the standard you measure yourself against."

Simple words, but they packed a punch.

I'm not sure how she became the standard you measure yourself against.

"I told you last night you inspire me, and isn't that what you want for a cooking show? Don't you want people to watch your show and then get so excited they run to the store, buy the ingredients, and start cooking?"

"Yes."

Laughing, Gigi gently smacked her arm. "Well, then, I guess your personality's just fine. I actually think this show's perfect for you."

"Girls, come here." Their mom stood amongst a large group that included the Bowie family.

As they headed over, Gigi said, "Why, so we can congratulate Fin and his brothers for coming in first place for the hundredth year in a row?"

Her dad smiled. "Not this year, they didn't."

"Uh, what?"

"Nope. Your fiancé did." Their dad gestured to the trio of big, bad football players. Cassian, Ryker, and...

Xander.

Chapter Six

HE'S HERE. LULU REACHED TO SMOOTH HER HAIR BUT after an hour paddling in the hot sun, it was pretty much a lost cause.

With his bronze skin, hard body, and dark scowl, Xander stood out among the others and their easy postures and smiling faces. Unfortunately, he was surrounded by excited fans. Ryker, the Viking, flirted shamelessly, Cassian told a story, while X-Man stood stonily, arms crossed over his chest.

"They crushed us." The oldest Bowie brother, Will, had an adorable little girl perched on his shoulders. She was talking to herself and playing with his hair and didn't seem to care about anything other than being connected to her dad.

Things had sure changed in her seven years away. She never could have imagined the Bowie brothers settling down.

"That's what happens when you get all domesticated," someone in the group said.

"Saddest thing I've ever seen," another guy said. "The Bowies gone to seed."

The youngest Bowie brother whipped around. Fin was gorgeous, fit, and fiery. "Hey, we're in the best shape of our lives. We had Ruby with us."

"Oh, sure, blame it on a little kid," a woman teased.

But Lulu only had eyes for Xander. In training shorts and a dark gray T-shirt, his body seemed hard as granite. She'd go over there and say hello, but the woman standing next to him put her hand on his chest, got up on her toes, and whispered in his ear.

His expression tightened, as he listened.

I'm going to do unspeakable things to you, she'd probably said.

One eyebrow hitched, Xander leaned closer. The woman shifted in front of him, gripping his forearm.

"Okay, we're going home to shower and head over to Coco's," her mom said. "Will we see you girls there?"

Lulu had no interest in competing for Xander's attention. "Definitely. I'll leave now, too." Knowing it would take her parents a while to say goodbye to everyone they knew, Lulu headed off to the parking lot alone. She made sure not to look back at Xander. She didn't need to see him with that woman hanging all over him.

As she grabbed the keys off the front tire of her truck, she heard the heavy fall of feet running on the path behind her.

"Lulu." *Xander.*

That deep, sexy voice sent a bolt of excitement through her. Slowly, she turned and gave him a smile she hoped didn't scream, *I'm so happy to see you. Did you choose me over that gorgeous, sexy woman? I hope so. Do you want to go get a coffee or something?* "Hey." She punched the keypad and unlocked her doors. "Congratulations on your big win. No one's beat the Bowies in…well, ever."

"Losing wasn't an option." The corner of his mouth hitched.

"Well, sure, the Bowies *have* gone soft, what with wives and kids." She pressed her fingertips over her mouth. "Oh, sorry, did you think you won because you're big, bad turf warriors?"

He gave her a look that said, *Really?* "You heading back to town?"

She got so lost in that hint of a grin that his words took a moment register. "I'm going home to shower." *Ugh.*

Because he cares about your grooming habits???

"You mind giving me a lift?"

"Sure." She looked behind him to see what the guys were doing.

"They're going to grab some food. I've got a call with my agent."

Oh. For a moment there, she'd thought he wanted to spend time with her.

Silly girl.

"Sure. Hop in." She slid into her seat and started the engine. As soon as he got in beside her, she said, "Back to the Homesteader Inn?"

"Yeah, that'd be great. Thanks."

"No problem." She drove slowly out of the parking lot, crowded with families and people still in party mode. "I hope you realize what you're missing." She glanced at him. "There's a big celebration for the winners. You get up on stage and everyone claps for you."

"Do I get a crown or something?"

"You get a jackalope."

"A what now?"

85

"It's a jackrabbit with antlers."

"And I want that, why?"

"Because it's a jackalope." She gave him a big grin.

"Right. Of course."

The road straightened, and she could see the highway up ahead. "Hey, I never had a chance to thank you for cleaning the kitchen last night."

"No big deal. Everything okay with your sister?"

"Yes, she and Violet are doing great." She thought of that squished little face all bundled up in a soft cotton blanket. "Coco and Beckett make adorable babies."

"When do they come home?"

"Weirdly, today, this afternoon. Doesn't that seem crazy? She gives birth to a human being and then walks out the door the next day?"

"Yeah, I guess it does. I didn't pay much attention when my nieces and nephews were born."

"Big family?"

"My brothers both have two kids."

"Is there, like, a template to be a Wilder man?"

He seemed confused.

"They're all happily married with kids, they play football…"

He chuckled. "Sure, until I went and fucked it all up."

"What does that mean?"

"I'm the only one who's gotten divorced."

When the dirt road met highway 191, she turned towards town. "I'm sorry. That had to be tough."

He let out a rough breath. "I guess. We never should've married."

"Marriage is hard but being married to a football player is impossible. That's what my dad says anyhow. He said he couldn't be a good father and husband *and* break records. And, if he had to choose, he'd rather be the best dad than the quarterback with the most passing touchdowns."

"That wasn't the issue for me and Steph."

She wouldn't press. It was none of her business, and she didn't know him well enough to pry. "Well, I've never been married, but I hear divorce is brutal no matter how amicable."

"It was more embarrassing for us than brutal." His big hand clamped down on his muscular thigh.

"Is she a celebrity?"

"No, it wasn't about the press. We both come from families that stay married. They threw us a big wedding… and then I signed with the Mavericks and…" He rubbed his thigh. "She didn't last three months in Boston."

Hadn't Cassian said they'd thought he was cheating all this time? "How long were you married?"

"Three years, but we were separated most of that time. We only divorced a year ago because she got engaged."

"Ouch. Did that suck for you?"

"Nah. It was a relief."

"So, then, why'd you get married?"

"We dated in college, and when I got injured senior year, she was there for me. I was focused on physical therapy, trying to get back in shape so I could play again. So, when I signed with the Mavericks, we figured we either had to break up or put a ring on it. She wasn't moving across the country as my girlfriend." He lifted a hand, as if to say, *And there you have it.* "She hated Boston. Hated being away from her family and friends. Basically, Steph likes to be a big fish in a small pond, and she didn't like being a nobody in Boston."

"After she left, did you guys go back and forth visiting

each other, spending holidays together? I mean, you were still married."

"That first year, we tried. We did Thanksgiving with my family, Christmas with hers. But we just…lost interest after that."

"Then why stay married?"

"My marriage certificate was the last thing on my mind. My ass was sitting on a bench, and I needed to train, find an opportunity to prove myself. So, between football season and the private coaching I had, getting a divorce was pretty low on my list of priorities. It's hard to explain."

"Is it, though?"

He chuckled. "Right. Forgot who I was talking to for a second."

She flexed her fingers on the steering wheel. It felt so precarious—like, he seemed to want to talk to her, yet if she pushed it too hard, he might wind up resenting her.

And she really, really liked him.

He went back to rubbing his thigh, only more vigorously. "I don't talk about any of this stuff."

"Maybe it's easier with a stranger."

His hand flexed. "You don't feel like a stranger."

A dangerous thrill ran through her. And with a strange sense of urgency to keep him talking, she blurted, "I was engaged."

Luckily, after dropping that bomb, the lodge appeared. Set in the woods with gorgeous landscaping and a sloped roof, it looked like a Swiss chalet had landed in a fairytale. "Here we are."

"Yep. But you're not dropping news like that and then taking off."

"It's a long story. One for another time."

He reached into his backpack and pulled out two water bottles. Twisting the cap off one, he handed it over. "I've got time."

"What about that call with your agent?"

"It's not till later." He glanced down at his hand. "I just saw you leaving and…wanted a ride home with you."

Sparklers went off in her chest. Shyness in this big, broody man just knocked the breath out of her lungs.

Giddy, she tried to keep her voice normal. "Well, it's not long so much as embarrassing."

"And staying married for three years so I wouldn't have to tell my family I was divorced isn't?" He pointed to the lane that led behind the lodge. "I'm just over there."

"Oh, no, it is. Yours is way more embarrassing." She said it straight-faced, but he gave her a look that said he knew she was teasing. Then, he made a rolling motion with his hand. *Go on.* "Fine. So, I'm sure you can tell I'm not the most social person."

"I got that sense when you hightailed it out of the party in Maui." Zipping up his backpack, he tipped his chin. "The one with the red door."

"Right." She eased into a spot in front of the cottage. "So, something happened in high school that made me kind of switch lanes. Instead of going to culinary school, I decided to go to Penn State."

"That was cute, how you did that."

"Did what?"

"Skipped over the 'thing that happened in high school.' That's not how we roll." He wagged a finger between them, before opening the door and planting a foot on the ground. "Come in while I pack."

"You're leaving?"

"I've got my first meeting with the physical therapist

tonight, so I figured I'd just move into the training center now."

"You have to live there?"

"I don't have to. I just didn't see the point of renting my own place." He got out of the truck.

She killed the engine and followed him up a travertine walkway lined in moss-covered stones. "It's so pretty here."

Strings of white lights hung off tree limbs and bushes, windchimes tinkled and swayed in a light breeze, and water rushed from a nearby river.

He let them into his place, which was cozy and charming and smelled of lavender. He went right for the fruit basket on the kitchen table, offering her an orange. She shook her head.

He started peeling off the skin. "All right, so what's this thing that happened in high school that changed the course of your life?"

The sharp citrus smell filled her senses, and she sat on the edge of his unmade bed. "I had my heart broken. Actually, by the son of the people who own this Inn. Griffin James. I can't remember when I didn't have a crush on him. Not that he knew, of course. I barely even talked to him. But finally, after years of watching him from afar and doodling his name in notebooks, I got up the nerve to tell him how I felt."

He watched her intently. "It didn't go well?"

"It went spectacularly bad. It was the summer before senior year, and I knew this was my last shot with him. I either took it, or I'd regret it the rest of my life. He was my 'soul mate.' Tell me you can relate? You've had ridiculous crushes before?"

"I mean, I could make something up…?" He popped an orange section into his mouth.

"Okay, Homecoming King. Anyhow, my sister had always been there for me for everything…*except* this crush on Griffin. When I talked about him, she'd go silent. I thought it meant she didn't want to hurt my feelings because she knew I didn't stand a chance with him."

He kicked out a chair and dropped into it. "I think I need to sit down for this."

"In the summer, Griffin worked at a motorcycle repair shop and, after hours, they let him work on this bike he was refurbishing. Well, I decided I'd bring him dinner."

"Why do I feel like punching someone?"

She smiled, but only so he wouldn't see that the wound still smarted. "Well, I get there, and I'm totally psyching myself up—I'm a strong, creative, interesting woman. I've traveled all over the world, I'm smart, I'm talented. Why *wouldn't* he be interested in me?"

Xander leaned forward, elbows on his knees. "I know I said I wanted the long story, but I think I'm going to need the short version. He was with another woman?"

She nodded. "At first, I just saw him arguing with someone. His body pretty much blocked the other person from view. But then…" God, she would never forget the way Griffin had lunged for her. The way they'd clung to each other, fisting each other's clothes. Griffin had bent his knees, lifted her, and slammed her against the wall.

It was the shoes, the sparkly embellishments on the leather sandals, that made it all click.

"It was Stella."

Xander lowered his head into a hand.

Her sister was kissing Griffin like she was out of her mind with lust.

Lulu wished she could scrub the memory from her mind. "They were making out like…like it was a battle to the death to see who could eat each other's face off the fastest. I mean, I'd never seen anything like it. It was *passion*."

"So, she knew you were into Griffin but was seeing him anyway?"

"She said it wasn't like that, that they'd fought their feelings for years because of me."

His head popped up. "They talked about your crush?"

A flash fire of mortification made her burn. "I don't know. I'll never really know, will I? In any event, that night changed everything for me. Instead of going to culinary school like everyone expected, I went to Penn State. I joined a sorority and partied and did all the things I thought were holding me back from living my best life."

"But you wanted to cook?"

"I wanted to have fun. I wanted my life to feel the way Stella's looked from the outside."

"Did it work?"

"It worked out great because my parents moved me into my dorm, and so right away I was the most popular girl on campus. 'Your mom's Joss Montalbano? Is that Tyler Cavanaugh? He's your *dad*?'" She smiled, but he just looked annoyed on her behalf. "No, it was fine. Think about it. If not for that instant celebrity, I'd have been alone in my room or sitting in a library carrel with a sleeve of Oreos. Instead, I was at frat parties, where I met…" She took a breath. "Trace. He was a total hottie. Football player, king of frat row. And he was great. Seriously, he didn't push me to be something I wasn't. He stuck with me at parties and let me do my thing working in Penn's executive dining room. He—"

"Replaced Stella?"

"Yep. Exactly. He was funny and charming, and we

had all these great adventures. I loved it." The closer she got to the rehearsal dinner, the sicker she felt. "Hey, don't you need to pack?"

"Sure." He got up, dumped the peels into the garbage, and washed his hands. Then, on his way to the closet, he stopped in front of her. Gazing into her eyes, he cupped her chin. She thought he was going to say something. Instead, his thumb gently stroked her jaw. "I'm sorry." A few more sweeps. "What happened with Griffin sucked, and I'm thinking I might have to hunt down Trace for whatever it is he did to you."

Her heart was an ice cube dropped into a hot skillet. It melted on contact.

But then the moment was over. He grabbed his duffle bag and tossed it on the bed. "Go on."

"Well, the best part was that Trace loved my family. *So* much." She said it with sarcasm.

Pulling a shirt off a hanger in the closet, he cut her a look. "If Stella—"

She held up a finger. "She warned me. She kept asking why he always came to our house for the holidays, why he never invited me to his. She kept telling me he was a big flirt, and I said 'Yeah, he's just like you. The life of the party. And I trust him the same way I trust you.'"

"You said he played football." He scooped up a pile of clothes from a chair and tossed them on the bed, folding each piece before setting it into the suitcase. "Was he using your dad to get to the NFL?"

"No, he wasn't good enough. He knew that. He just liked the idea that his father-in-law would be a Hall of Famer who hung out with the greats. He was starstruck." She rubbed one of the blisters on her palm she'd gotten from paddling. "It's embarrassing, I know."

He reached for her knee, gave it a squeeze. "Trace is an asshole. There's no shame in trusting someone."

"Except for the fact that I fell for it." She watched him to see if he agreed.

"I don't know that there's any value in beating yourself up over something that happened when you were nineteen. And I doubt you'll ever fall into another relationship like it again, so you might as well let it go."

"You're right. And, no, it'll never happen again. So, anyway, he proposed, I said yes, we planned a huge wedding—which his family insisted on and I dreaded—but to be honest...I was just relieved."

"That you'd have a wingman for the rest of your life?"

How did this man see her so clearly? "Yes, and that I didn't think anyone would ever get me the way he did. Who else wouldn't mind how much time I spent cooking?"

"So, what brought it all to a head?"

"He kissed my sister at the rehearsal dinner."

"What the fuck? Stella did that to you?"

She loved how he understood the true crime. "She was drunk, and she said she needed to keep me from making the biggest mistake of my life."

"Jesus, Lu."

The only people in the world who called her that were her family and closest friends. She loved hearing it from him. "Yeah, it was awful."

"I'm sorry."

Two simple words that held tremendous power. "Thanks." She started to get up. "What can I do to help you pack?"

But he reached for her hand. "Hey, it's not your fault. What happened with those guys...that's not on you."

"Well, I mean, it was. I didn't even know Griffin, and I only saw what I wanted with Trace."

"Yeah, but do you want to be the kind of person who starts every relationship not trusting? If we don't go in with an open heart, why bother trying? I don't think you did anything wrong...I just hate what your sister did to you."

"Griffin didn't even know me. He was in love with Stella. Who wouldn't be? You'd fall in love with her, too. She's gorgeous and fun and wild and—"

"And you're gorgeous and funny and intelligent, and you've got this passion that's..." He went quiet, thoughtful. "It's sexy, and it makes a man want to know what it would feel like to have all that passion focused on him."

Something wicked coursed hot and fiery right under her skin. He looked at her with raw hunger, and she loved it. She felt seen. Wanted, in a way she never had before.

His gaze drifted down to her mouth, and his eyes went half-lidded.

She wanted to touch all that hard muscle, wanted the weight and heat of him pressing her down on the mattress. But he was holding back, and so she kept her hands to herself. "Which man, exactly, are we talking about?"

With a finger, he tilted her chin. "This one." Desire tightened his features. "You have the sexiest mouth I've ever seen." He leaned in until he was a breath away. "I guarantee there isn't a guy who sees you that doesn't want to know what you taste like."

With his neatly cropped blonde hair and square jaw, this hard, muscular man appealed to every single one of her sensibilities, but it was his soulful eyes, his depth and honesty, that made her half-mad with want. "I'm not a flirt, Xander. I don't need that kind of attention. I just want to feel *this*." She reached for his hand and pressed it over her heart, hoping he felt its wild beat against his palm. "I only want to kiss the man who does this to me."

"Fuck." The syllable came out on a gust of air. He cupped the back of her head and pulled her right up to his mouth. He hesitated—and the moment held so much weight, she stopped breathing.

It was like he tottered on a precipice. Like, kissing her meant something—did he want to go there?

And when he pressed his lips to hers, when the tip of his tongue licked the seam of her mouth, every hope and desire she'd ever clutched deep in her core released in jubilation.

Because Xander Wilder wanted to go there with her.

Electricity pulsed through her, hot and so exciting she didn't think her heart could stand it. She smelled the mountain air in his clothes, the hint of soap and sage on his skin, and it sent her pulse racing.

Kissing her, he groaned deep in his throat, and his fingers fisted in her hair. She thought she might die from the indescribable softness, the slick heat of his mouth. His hunger made her greedy for more. She slid her hand up his strong thigh, underneath his T-shirt, and flattened it on his hard stomach. His muscles contracted, and she caressed up toward his ribcage, tracing every ridge and dip.

She had the strangest sensation of falling, and it was disorienting because her eyes were closed and she was lost in the tangle of his tongue, the scent of him filling her senses, and when her back hit the mattress, her eyelids popped open.

His hand slid under her, gripping her ass, lifting her, his erection trapped between their bodies.

That snapped her out of it. "Wait."

Wild-eyed, he pulled back, confused, concerned.

God, she'd let her hands roam his thigh, his stomach. *Of course* he'd thought she was up for more. "I'm so sorry. I didn't…"

Looking shaken, he swallowed thickly but didn't say anything.

"I shouldn't have done that. I got carried away." She set her hands on his shoulders and gently pushed. "I'm not really a hookup kind of person, you know?"

"This doesn't feel like a hook up. Not to me."

He did it again. Surprised the hell out of her. She kept seeing the battle-hardened warrior, and then he'd go and expose his warm, gooey middle.

The throbbing between her legs ached for him to fill her, but she just couldn't do it. "Neither of us is in any place for a relationship."

"No." He rolled off her, scrubbing his face with a big hand. "That's not something I want right now."

Feeling vulnerable, she sat up. "What do you want?"

He closed his eyes. It seemed to take him a moment to pull himself together. "I want to get a contract and lead my next team to the Super Bowl. That's it. That's all I want."

"Right. And I have to get my career back on track. So…" She swung her legs off the bed and smoothed her hands down the leather leggings. "Is that your rental car out front?"

That impassive mask back in place, he tracked her as she grabbed the keys she'd set on the table by the door. "Yeah."

"Great, so then you don't need a ride." She knew she sounded off.

Two adults attracted to each other, a little fun in the afternoon. *Why not?*

It would be so good. Better than any sex she'd ever had.

And yet she knew herself, knew how invested she'd get. How she'd spend the next few weeks checking her phone to see if he'd called, looking for him around town.

No, she just wasn't the type to have casual sex.

At the door, she turned back to him, though she avoided meeting his eyes. "I'm sure I'll see you around. What with Cassian and..." *Oh, my God, would you shut up and just leave?* "Bye."

She shut the door and hightailed it to her truck.

Once locked inside, she fired up the ignition and backed out. A squirrel darted across the road. Flustered, she nearly pressed the accelerator instead of the brake.

Catching herself just in time, she stopped and idled.

Breathe.

It's all right. I made the right choice.

I probably won't even run into him again.

And if I do, ten bucks says he'll be surrounded by fans, women touching him, whispering naughty things in his ear...

Right.

Let's go home and shower. She'd make some mac and cheese, roast a chicken...maybe some brownies...and bring it over to Coco's. *Keep her family fed the next few days.*

And yet, with every rotation of her wheels away from his cottage, longing tugged and pulled at her.

Because her body still craved all it had missed out on.

Chapter Seven

A<small>FTER A MONTH OF PLANNING, SEVERAL WEEKS OF</small> memorizing and finessing her script, the moment had finally come.

And Lulu was kicking ass.

"See the color?" Her tone was light, pleasant, her smile genuine—because what could be more fun than showing people how to do the very thing she loved? "You want to cook it long enough to get that lovely toasted brown color—"

"Okay, thank you." The producer stepped forward, making a slicing motion with her hand. The red camera light went dark.

Lulu shot a look to the clock on the stove. The audition couldn't be over so soon, could it?

The two crew members Abigail had brought with her were talking and laughing, as they headed toward the refreshment table.

It is. It's over.

She scrambled to think back on what'd she done—had she messed up somehow? Maybe she hadn't looked into the camera enough. Sometimes, she got too caught up in what she was doing.

And then it hit her. *Stories.* Dammit, she was supposed to tell stories about her childhood, her family, chefs she'd worked with over the years. She'd forgotten those parts of the script. "You don't want me to finish?" If they gave her a little more time, she'd definitely add them.

The producer looked up from her phone. "Nope. We're good. Remember, we've already seen your audition tape. Today, we just wanted to get a look at you live."

They'd come all the way across the country—with equipment and staff—to watch her for twenty minutes? Setting the whisk down and turning off the burner, she wiped her hands on her apron and approached the woman. "You can be honest with me. If I didn't meet your expectations, I'd like to know."

"Oh, no, you delivered exactly what you promised." With her short, dark red hair and easy smile, Abigail seemed unperturbed.

Lulu had to believe she hadn't blown it. "So, what's next?"

"We've got some ideas we'll be testing out." The fortyish woman had a gleam in her eyes. "We'll be in touch."

"Okay." The production company had rented a condo for the audition. With the lighting and the huge kitchen space, it made the perfect studio. But had they really gone to all this effort for twenty minutes? "Can I show you around town? I'd like you to see the farmers market and the brewery. My sister's chocolate shop is right up the street."

"We've been here all week. Trust me, we're sold on the location."

"Did you ever make it to the Pole, Pedal, and Paddle race?"

"We did. It was brilliant, and we got some amazing shots."

Excitement flared. They wouldn't have bothered filming unless they were going ahead with her show. Then what did Abigail mean by *other ideas*? "Okay. Well, let me just clean up real quick."

"No, no. You can leave everything just as it is." Abigail maintained her pleasant demeanor but nothing could disguise the undercurrent of impatience.

What is going on? Nothing made sense but standing around wouldn't give her any answers, and it might antagonize the producer. "Well, thank you for the opportunity." Untying her apron, she grabbed her knife set, rolled it, and slid it into her canvas tote.

She scanned the counter. Did she just leave all the ingredients she'd brought? *No way.* Those truffles were expensive. Pulling out one of her storage containers, she filled it with the mushroom. She wished Abigail would just be honest, tell her what she was thinking. Lulu had been unemployed for six weeks now. If she didn't have a cooking show, she needed to come up with a new plan.

She got the crème fraiche out of the refrigerator and the bottle of cognac off the counter. *I think that's everything worth taking.* She headed for the door, watching the three of them talking, and it couldn't have been clearer that they were done with her.

Regret twisted her up. She hated that she'd forgotten to share the stories. That might've made all the difference.

As Lulu hurried down the street to her truck, a gust of chilly wind plastered her dress to her body. Once inside, she tossed her tote in the back seat and turned on the heat.

April weather in Calamity was crazy—hot one day, cold the next.

As she pulled away from the curb, dread sank deeper and deeper. She didn't want to go home, where her mom would be waiting with an expectant expression.

How'd it go? Did it work out?

And what would she even say? *I have no idea.*

So, instead of feeling sorry for yourself, think about your audition.

Did I look into the camera? Not enough. She'd been focused mostly on making sure the butter-soaked flour had browned but didn't burn.

Because how lame would that be—to ruin the béchamel sauce in an audition?

Was I charming? Engaging?

I mean, yeah. She thought she'd done a good job.

At the stop sign, she braked. *We've got some ideas we'll be testing out* didn't sit right with her.

Lulu flicked her turn signal. Determination rolled in. She hadn't come this close to getting her own cooking show, only to run off with her tail between her legs. If they were going to work together, she needed to be part of the conversation. And if they weren't, if she'd done something wrong, she deserved some feedback.

She'd happily tweak her concept.

Whatever it takes to get my show.

Driving around the block, she took the same spot in front of the condo and then marched up the walkway, the heels of her boots clicking on the concrete.

I'll be nice, pleasant…but I've got one shot here to nail down my show.

Through the window, she could see the bright Tungston lights had been turned back on.

Unease skittered across her skin. *What are they filming?*

She opened the door to laughter.

And then she heard deep voices.

"Ah, that's disgusting, man." She recognized that voice. One of the football players?

But that didn't make any sense.

"What's wrong with you?" the man said.

"I didn't know what the hell I was doing." *Xander.*

What the hell's going on?

"How was I supposed to know you had to clean them?" Xander's voice was playful, fun.

Her world had flipped upside down, right along with Xander's personality.

"Because they're fuckin' clams. Oh, shit, sorry. My bad."

Okay, that was definitely Ryker.

"It's okay," Abigail said. "Just keep going. This is great. I love it."

"So, I throw the whole thing together," Xander said. "And set the bowls on the table. My mom's on top of the world, so happy that at least one other person in her family's doing something other than watching game tape, and she takes a bite, and her whole face…"

After a pause, laughter exploded in the room. Lulu had never been more confused in her life. What the hell was Xander Wilder doing in this kitchen, telling stories like he was some stand-up comedian?

Crossing the living room, she stood behind a column to remain unseen while getting a better look.

He and Ryker sat on bar stools, their legs spread in easy postures. The lights highlighted their powerful bodies and strikingly handsome faces.

They were auditioning.

For what?

"I would've spit it out right there at the table." Ryker made a face, like he'd just gotten a mouthful of dirt.

"Yeah, but remember, my mom was trying to *encourage* me. She played it cool, kept on chewing, but my brothers...they took one out of your playlist. They spit out the clams and started hacking up their lungs." He pretended to gag.

Hilarity ensued.

"They both jumped up from the table and raced to the sink, so they could wash the sand out of their mouths." He shrugged adorably.

Where did this personality come from?

She'd only ever seen him pissed off at the world, all stoic and hard. Or quiet, kind, and sweet with her. Who was this charming guy?

Ryker chuckled. "I'd have kicked your ass out of the kitchen."

"Good thing you're not my mom, because I'm a determined little fucker. And you can bet I never made that mistake again. But I made some tweaks, and now this dish has become a restaurant favorite. I'll make it for you, you'll see."

"I'm never eating anything you make."

The two men laughed like they were just two friends hanging out at the bar.

"Cut." Abigail jumped off her bar stool. "I love it. I absolutely love it." Her phone buzzed, and she lifted a finger. "Hang on. It's them."

As soon as she headed out the back door, Lulu charged forward. "What's going on?"

Xander slid off the stool. "Lu? What're you doing here?" Clarity struck, and his eyes went wide. "*You're* the chef she's in town to see?" He reeled back. "Holy shit. This is the project you've been talking about."

"Hey, it's the Taco Lady." Ryker started to greet her, but both Xander and Lulu gave him looks that wiped the smile off his face. He turned on his heel and redirected to the refreshment table.

She lowered her voice. "You told me you're in town to train. What're you doing *here*?"

"Abigail offered me a show."

"Why?"

"Hell if I know."

"Oh, come on. She didn't offer it out of the blue."

"The night of Gigi's concert, I was at the bar with your dad and Cassian. Abigail was there, she overheard me talking about my mom's restaurant and asked if I wanted to do this show."

"What restaurant?"

"Café Akasha."

She took a step back, the world tilting, spinning. "Your *mom* owns Café Akasha?"

"Yeah. I guess you've heard of it?"

"Of course I've heard of it. God, I don't understand any of this. Is Abigail giving you my show?"

"This is supposed to be a talk show format, so I don't think so. I'm not a chef."

"You just talked about a dish you made that's served at Akasha."

"Right. But I have no training. I can't teach anyone how to cook." He glanced at Ryker, who was messing around with the crew. "She knows the guys are in town for the summer and liked the idea of me interviewing them. Some of them cook…" He grew frustrated. "I don't know. I turned her down at first, but then…"

"But then what?"

He shrugged, wrapping a hand around the back of his neck. "Your dad thought it'd be a good idea, so I said I'd do it."

"My *dad*? Oh, this is perfect." Of course her dad would be mentoring the broken down quarterback. "If you really didn't know about my show, why didn't you bring it up? Last night, you said the only thing you cared about is getting a contract."

He glanced toward the back door, where they could see Abigail talking animatedly on her phone. Xander led her to the other side of the living room. "I don't give a shit about this audition. It's the last thing on my mind."

"Yeah, well, guess what? It's the only thing I've been doing since I got fired. This show matters to me."

"You act like I set out to steal your show. I didn't even know you were the chef she was talking about. You didn't tell me."

"I didn't tell anyone." In case it didn't happen. *And now here we are.*

"I just can't believe this is happening," she said. "You have to understand, I spent a month working on a pitch deck. So, for you to just meet her in a bar one night and walk away with my show…" *God.*

"Yeah, I know. I get it." He looked confused. "None of this makes sense."

"I mean, obviously I can see why she likes you so much." She gave him a playful swat. "And where did that personality come from anyway?"

"I don't know. I was talking to Ryker, not even paying attention to the cameras. Besides, I can be anything they want if it'll get me in front of coaches."

She got that. "I'm not seeing how a cooking show will get you in front of coaches."

"Your dad said if I wanted to get signed, it wasn't enough for my agent—the man I *pay* to represent me—to tell everyone I'm healed. He said I should show them." He cut a look towards the kitchen, and his cheeks turned bright red.

When had Abigail come back inside? And why was she recording them on her phone? Everyone stood watching them with big grins.

Lulu'd had enough. She strode back over to them. "What's going on?"

Abigail ended the video. "Looks like you two have already met."

"I thought East/West only produces cooking shows?"

"That's right."

"Then, why are you auditioning an athlete?"

"He's an accomplished chef, his mother owns Café Akasha, *and* he's an NFL quarterback."

Lulu couldn't help checking to see how that comment had landed. And, even as she felt her show slipping out of her grasp, her heart twisted for him, knowing how close he was to becoming a free agent.

She knew, of course, that he hadn't set out to sabotage her.

She'd seen the audition—he was charming, gorgeous, and apparently he knew how to cook.

Abigail checked her phone, lifting her arm in a victory punch. "I knew it. *Yes.*" She grinned at Xander. "You got the very rare, direct-to-series order. We're doing this."

Lulu thought her head might explode. "He's getting a cooking show? I thought training camp starts in July?" *And this is my life.* She'd worked her ass off on that pitch deck. She'd finessed and memorized thirteen recipes, practiced hundreds of times, recording herself to improve her delivery.

None of that matters right now. She had to salvage her show.

"How does this impact me? Does this mean you're not moving forward with *The Wild West Woman?*"

Abigail lowered her phone and turned serious. "We've got a couple options. I know what I'd like to do, but we'll need you both to sign off on the idea. I'm sold on this town, and I like the way you want to showcase it, but we do have quite a few teaching-based shows queued up for the next pitch meeting. What we don't have is anything with a professional quarterback, who just happens to come from football royalty."

"If you're giving his show my setting, where does that leave mine? We can't have two of them in Calamity."

"That's right, but we can merge them. I've already pitched the idea of you co-hosting, and that footage I got just now of you two arguing sealed the deal."

"What deal? What're you talking about?"

"I livestreamed both of your auditions to the executive producers. They love the charming, handsome jock juxtaposed with the passionate foodie. It's a go."

Lulu needed clarity. "So, I'm not making gourmet food accessible to the home cook?"

"No." Abigail drew in a slow breath. "What I'm envisioning here is a morning show format. Xander will interview other football players, and in the second half of the show, his guest will go against you in a competition. The jock versus the trained chef." She paused. "It'll be *The Gridiron Grillers.*"

Lulu's world crashed and burned. It was like she'd been

running on hope, convinced hard work would turn her idea into reality, only to discover her tank held nothing but air.

Gazing down at her cork-soled platforms, she cleared her mind of fear and anxiety. She had to pull something together. She couldn't freak out.

Yeah, and also? I'm a motherfucking phoenix, and I will rise.

"I'm not hijacking her show," Xander said. "This is her livelihood, not mine."

Did he mean that? Would he actually walk away from this opportunity? Lulu watched him carefully, and he seemed sincere. She couldn't believe he'd do that for her. "Can we continue the process for the show I pitched?"

"Sure, but here's the deal. I've been in this business over twenty years. You know how many projects I've seen greenlighted out of the box? Three. And all of those featured celebrities."

Which is awesome for Xander but not all that interesting for me. "Okay, but if I still want to pursue it, what's the process?"

"I'll pitch it in one of our future meetings. If it moves forward, it goes into development, along with all the other projects we're working on."

"How long will it take to make a decision?"

"I can't give you a definitive answer. Sometimes we run out of time before I can pitch it, sometimes there are so many similar projects, I decide to hold off until the next meeting. But the real issue is whether any of the networks will be interested. If they have enough shows hosted by chefs, they'll pass. If they're interested, if it does get picked up, it doesn't get a green light until the upfront presentations in May. If the advertisers aren't interested, then the process stops right there."

"So, I could be waiting a year, only to have the whole thing die."

"That's right. But what we don't have—what no one has—is a pro football player and a chef." She waved her phone. "The entire team loved not only your auditions but your chemistry." She looked between them. "We've got a hit on our hands. I can feel it. So, what do you say? Do we have a show?"

Lulu felt Xander watching her, making sure she was okay. But she wasn't. She couldn't wait a year to find out if she had a show. And if she agreed to *The Gridiron Grillers*, she'd be nothing but a side character wearing a toque.

If she said no, she'd have to go back to being a sous chef.

That's not going to happen.

Nope. Forward-motion only, and that meant she had to get another chef de cuisine job. Which, frankly, she'd get with this show regardless of her role. All she needed was the visibility.

She forced a smile. "We do."

Xander looked to Abigail. "You understand that football's my priority, right? Soon as I sign a contract, the team becomes my employer. They might not allow me to do the show, or they might need me to come work out with the team—"

"We understand." Abigail gave him a calm, reassuring smile. "Like I said, we can film two episodes a day. I promise you, we will knock this show out fast."

He looked to Lulu, as though seeking her permission. What could she say? He was in limbo, too. He'd never realized his potential, either. He needed this show as much as she did. She shrugged a shoulder and gave him a look that said, *Might as well.*

"Let me give my agent a call." He headed across the kitchen and out the back door.

Abigail smiled. "I'm glad you agreed to this new format. Your voice is so soothing…it feels like satin on my skin. And the way you talk about food, it's *inspiring*. And Xander…he's confident and charming…just perfect."

He pretty much was.

"I love that with professional athletes, we'll be able to take advantage of Calamity's outdoor lifestyle. We'll do segments of them white water rafting, rappelling, skiing… The viewers will love it."

You've got to be kidding me. She had to work with this woman, so she kept her tone businesslike. "I'm pretty sure Xander's contract prohibits him from putting himself in the way of bodily harm. But, since I grew up here, and I've dropped out of helicopters to snowboard on glaciers, we're still good to go."

"Point taken. I'm sorry about that." Abigail's phone vibrated, and she read a text message. Smiling, she looked up. "They're chomping at the bit. The sooner you both sign contracts, the sooner we can start filming."

Filming right away? "Is this normal? How can you get a show on the air so fast?"

"No, it's not normal." Abigail's gaze slid away. "But that just speaks to the massive support behind it. I know it's not exactly what you wanted." She squeezed Lulu's arm, as if sending a message. "But trust me, you made the right decision." Her phone pinged, and she read the message. "See that? They've already secured the set."

"But we only just auditioned."

"Right, but I've been working on this all week. I talked

with a local family about using one of the outbuildings on their ranch, and they've just now agreed to our terms."

"We're filming in a barn?"

"It's actually the original bunkhouse on a cattle ranch that's been turned into a man cave, so it's fitted out with a great kitchen and plenty of room for the crew." Abigail brightened. "And it's set right at the base of the mountain."

"You're not talking about the Bowies, are you?"

"You know the place?"

"Of course." How could any production company move this quickly? What was Abigail not telling them?

"Then you know how perfect it is. The outside's got so much character, covered in bear crossing and street signs, paddles and surfboards, but inside? It's gorgeous and kitted out with modern conveniences. Plus, there's nothing but wilderness surrounding it, which means we can park the crew's RVs there. Once you and Xander sign your contracts, we'll fly our best editor out, so he can work right here on location. Talk about fast-tracking a show."

"But the kitchen isn't equipped for two chefs."

"The owners will get an upgrade. We've already lined up a kitchen designer, and we can have it turned over in forty-eight hours, which means we'll be able to bang out all thirteen episodes in under a month. Hell, I bet we can have a reel ready to go out to the networks in ten days."

Why on earth were they already this far along in their planning? Before contracts were signed, they'd already committed to the bunkhouse? Talked to a kitchen designer? Lulu didn't have answers, but she would use it as leverage. "I'll do this show, if I'm an actual co-host. I want to interview my own guests—Chef Jonny from The

Homesteader Inn, Chef Paul from Sublime. And then, Xander—"

Awareness broke across Abigail's features. "Will compete against the celebrity chef."

Lulu held her breath. *Please say yes. Please.*

Abigail burst into a smile. "Done." She reached out a hand. "You've got yourself a deal."

Chapter Eight

Keys in his hand, Xander watched through the window as another RV rolled in, its tires kicking up dust and spitting out gravel.

For the last couple of hours, crew members had crawled all over the bunkhouse, taking measurements, dropping off hard-shell black cases, and taping electrical cords to the hardwood floor. Everyone chattered, excited about the production.

And Xander stood in the middle of all the chaos and activity wondering what the hell had happened. *How'd I wind up on a cooking show?*

Anxiety overpowered the discipline he'd always relied on. He felt like he'd just awakened to find himself on a ship that was slowly leaving the shore. He was desperate to dive into the water and swim back to land. His life—football—was growing more and more distant with every day that passed.

He had the horrible sense he'd signed the wrong contract, and now he'd swung his life in a completely new direction. The only ray of light came from Lulu's smile. At least he was doing this with her.

Last night, he'd met with his trainer. They'd made a plan...*so that's good.* The research on this new kind of physical therapy looked promising and gave him the first hit of hope he'd had in years.

A truck pulled up, and Xander stood straighter, grew more alert. But the doors opened, and strangers spilled out.

Just another delivery.

Where is she? He hadn't seen Lulu since signing the contract two days ago. To bang out filming, the East/West wanted them both to live here in the bunkhouse, but Lulu was from Calamity. Maybe she'd live with her parents or sister. She could commute. He tightened his grip around his keys until the sharp edges dug into his palm.

I want her here.

He'd talked to the Bowie brothers when he'd checked into the training center—all good guys. His kind of people. Knew he'd become friends with them this summer. The crew had invited him out tonight—some bar in town with a mechanical bull.

But for some strange reason, the only person he wanted to be with was Lulu.

And just as if his thoughts had conjured her, an engine rumbled, and her beater Ford 150 appeared in a cloud of dust. One side panel was blue, the other white. It had dings and dents and the fender was mangled. Loud music blasted out of tinny speakers.

Lulu listened to Marshall Tucker Band?

Dammit, it bugged him how little he knew about her. Did she sing in the shower? What books did she read on planes? Was wine her drink of choice, or had she chosen it because she'd already opened a bottle for the sauce?

As the truck came to a stop, he heard her sing along with the music. "*I'm gonna find me a hole in the wall.*"

Deep-throated and rugged, she mimicked the singer well. Xander couldn't keep the grin off his face. He threw open the door and rushed out to greet her. In a dress and cowboy boots, she stood on the running board and hauled a fancy suitcase out of the back.

"I got it." He jogged over.

The big case tumbled onto the dirt. "What're you doing here?"

The question caught him up short. "I'm living here for the next month."

"I thought you had to live at the training center?"

Right. That's what I told her. "I gave up my room. They want us here."

"I just figured, since training and physical therapy are your priorities, you'd live there." She swept back to the driver's side and reached for something. The dress hitched up, exposing the backs of her creamy thighs, and the silky fabric clung to her ass, accentuating the round firmness of her cheeks.

His fingers remembered clutching one of them, as he'd lifted her, rocking his erection between their bodies. He curled them into fists.

Stop thinking about her like that.

But he couldn't shake the sensation, the memory of the way she'd clung to him, pressed against him like she was desperate to get closer.

That kiss. Jesus.

He'd had a lot of them in his life, and he couldn't remember a single one.

Other than Lulu's.

The one that had singed his scalp and made him lose his mind.

"So, it's just you and me in the bunkhouse?" Dragging out a stuffed tote bag, she slammed the door, smoothed her dress on her thighs, and eyed him warily.

"Well, the crew's here." He gestured to the RVs. "They'll be in and out."

He felt jittery and off-balance, and he knew it was because he'd never felt this kind of attraction to anyone.

And I've been married.

But it didn't matter. She didn't do hookups, and the last thing he wanted was another serious relationship. Especially now that they were working together. If things went sideways, and there was hostility between them? The show might tank.

He had an opportunity here, and he wouldn't screw it up because he was hot for a pretty woman.

Hiking the overstuffed tote on her shoulder, she started wheeling her suitcase.

"Here." He grabbed the handle and led the way to the bunkhouse.

"Thanks."

He'd never heard her voice so flat. Either she still blamed him for hijacking her show, or she was just disappointed about the way things had gone down. He couldn't change anything, but he still didn't like to see her unhappy. "I'd rather live here. Look at this place." He stopped for a moment to breathe in the pine-scented air and take in the mountain range, the snow-capped peaks glittering. "I can train anywhere, and I'd rather go for a hike or a run than work out in a gym. And when I have physical therapy, I can use the weight-lifting equipment at the facility."

"I get that." She walked through the open door and did a brief scan of the large, rectangular room.

To their left, the living space had leather couches and sturdy coffee tables, a big screen TV, and every kind of game table imaginable. Straight ahead was a massive kitchen, and to their right, a long hallway led to several bedroom suites.

He led her in that direction. "This one's mine." He tapped his closed door. "Those down there…" He tipped his chin. "One's a green room, one's for make-up…things like that."

She took the one across the hall, and he followed her in. Hoisting the suitcase onto the bed, she started unzipping it like he wasn't even there.

"Anything else in the truck?"

"No, this is it." She examined the contents. "For a woman who's lived overseas for seven years, you'd think I'd have more." She fingered the slinky fabric of a dress. "I worked so many hours, I didn't have much time for shopping. And home was a place to crash and shower, so I never even thought about décor."

He hated seeing her this down, knowing he was the cause. "I'm sorry it worked out like this."

Finally, she looked at him, and it was like his comment pulled her out of her own head. "It's not your fault." She grabbed a handful of lacy underwear and set them in the top drawer of the dresser. "I'm disappointed, but…" She shrugged. "It is what it is. I guess I'm just skeptical about the whole thing."

"What do you mean? You don't think East/West Productions is legit?"

"No, they are. They're the best. That's why I pitched to them. But it doesn't make sense, how fast they're moving. I mean, look at all these people they've hired, and filming starts *tomorrow*. Nothing moves this fast in Hollywood."

"It's not Hollywood, though. East/West is based in New York. In any event, it works in our favor that they're fast-tracking it."

"Oh, I know. And it means something that they're putting big money behind it. It should get both of us tons of visibility."

"That's why I'm here." He ran his fingertip over the edge of his house key. "I just want you to know I never would've followed up with her if I'd known you were the chef she'd come to town to meet."

"I believe you." Like a cool breeze, Lulu swept past him, enveloping him in her scent—clean, sweet, and summery, like fresh-cut peaches. She tossed some flip flops into the walk-in closet.

Weirdly, he got a flash of him following her in there, wrapping his arms around her waist, nuzzling her neck… just holding her in the quiet, dark space. Comforting them both in this new situation. Claiming that intimacy they seemed to share.

But then he imagined her head tipping back on his chest and her ass grinding on him and Jesus Christ, his body went hard with need.

All he'd done was kiss her one time, and he already craved more. Because he knew how those hands would touch him, how that hot, hungry mouth would feel on him.

Desire ripped through him.

She came out of the closet and looked from her suitcase to him and said, "Let's get out of here."

"Where do you want to go?"

"I don't know. Let's get a coffee at Calamity Joe's."

"Okay. I was actually going to pick up some groceries for us. We should probably do that together."

"Perfect. Let's do it on the way back." She pulled a bunch of things out of her tote and tossed them on the bed, before hitching it on her shoulder and heading out of the room.

When he was a kid, he'd wanted to go to Disneyland more than anything, but his brothers were six and eight years older—*been there done that, too old to go again.* He'd begged until his parents had booked a trip.

This moment...following Lulu out of the bunkhouse just to have a coffee with her...rivaled that level of excitement.

Grinning like a fool as he opened the door for her, he didn't even recognize himself. He'd never lost his head over a woman.

The moment they stepped outside, the chill tightened his skin. "When does it warm up?"

"Not till June, really." She climbed into her truck. After he got into the passenger seat, she said, "You're from San Francisco. Shouldn't you be used to it?"

"Are you calling me a wimp?"

"I would never." She flashed him a grin and started the engine.

There. She's back. Playful, sharp, sweet.

Mine.

What the fuck? Where the hell had that come from?

"Here, look, I'll even turn the heat on for you." She made a big show of flicking all the vents in his direction.

"Jesus, stop. That's cold air." He turned them back toward her. "Here, mountain girl. I'm a sharer."

"This mountain girl prefers the windows down and the music blaring when she drives."

"That's fine." He pushed the button to lower his, and cold air rushed in. "I'm down for the full Calamity experience."

"Ha. You couldn't handle it."

"No? Calamity's too wild for me?"

"Oh, yeah." She turned the radio on, and Marshall Tucker Band's "I'll Be Loving You" blasted on the speakers. Grimacing, she pushed a button on her phone, and a Billie Eilish song immediately replaced it.

"I thought you liked Marshall Tucker Band. You were giving a sold-out, live performance fifteen minutes ago."

Smiling, she turned the truck around and headed down the road. "I know, right? But that song was from a different album. I can't listen to anything from *Together Forever.*"

"You're serious? Why?"

"Because it's associated with one of my life's most embarrassing moments.'"

He lifted one eyebrow and shifted his back against the door to face her, settling in for a story.

She sighed. *Fine.* "I was in this week-long cooking class in Idaho Falls over spring break a million years ago, and they were playing in town. A bunch of us went to see the show, and after, on our way back to the car, we saw a limo coming out of a gated parking lot. It was obviously the band. I was having fun, so I ran up to them, waving." She cringed. "Do I have to go on?"

"Absolutely." He stretched every syllable out like taffy.

She gave a long-suffering sigh. "So, they stop and roll down the window to greet me. I hadn't expected that *at all.* I was just being silly with my friends. I figured the car would just keep on going. But, no, there they were, the whole band smiling at me. Well, the wires got crossed in my brain, and I didn't know what to say, but there they were staring, like…waiting for this sixteen-year-old to say, 'Can I have your autograph' or something normal." She paused, and it was adorable because she'd gotten all red-faced. "Instead, I blurted out, 'Are you going to be together forever?' You know, the name of their album. I wanted a meteor to hurtle down to earth and smite me."

"It wasn't that bad." He chuckled. "They thought you were cute."

"Is that why the driver floored it and left skid marks on the road? Trust me, I was ridiculous. It's all I heard the rest of my cooking class. 'Chef Eugene, after this class, are we going to be together forever?'"

He laughed. "You're too hard on yourself."

"I think it's best to keep me in a kitchen. I don't embarrass myself there."

"Oh, come on. Being social's hard for everyone, and we all have ways to deal with it. My ex always knows what to say…that's her coping technique, to storm in and take charge. My mom copes with it by entertaining. She's always serving food or drinks, acting like she's the hostess. It's a personality thing."

"What's yours? To look mean and grumpy?"

He liked when she teased him like this, but mostly he liked getting her all to himself. "Hey, if I come off like that it's because of how familiar people get. They think because I'm a ball player they can touch me, talk to me like we're old friends."

"So, there you go. Mean and grumpy's your coping skill."

"It doesn't work. They still sit on my lap or grab my arm."

"Well, it's better than having your brain get all scrambled. I have this little fantasy of the Marshall Tucker Band coming into my restaurant one day, so I can get a do-over. I'd be so normal. I'd be downright *delightful*."

He grinned. "Yeah, that's what you'd be."

She nudged his thigh. "I would."

"You wouldn't even notice them. You'd be all up in your head." He tipped his head back, sniffing the air. "Steak's ready to be flipped." He petted his forearm. "Ooh, the texture of this lime's *divine*."

She burst out laughing. "Shut up. I don't do that. At least, I don't do it *out loud*." She gave his shoulder a playful shove. "Get out of my head."

"Is this your dad's truck?" He couldn't help noticing the smell of leather and a hint of cologne.

She fought a smile. "What you're smelling is Ian Chesterfield."

"Why's that funny?"

The truck bumped over ruts in the dirt road, and though he'd never been to Calamity before and had only recently met this woman, he had an absolute sense of rightness. He couldn't explain it. If he'd ever believed in his mom's woo woo, every moment of his life had led to this one, where he'd landed in the exact right place and just *fit*.

"Stella dated him. He was one of the seasonal staff members in the village, and the guy literally reeked of cologne—so bad, it was like he showered in it. He went back to England, but he's stayed forever with us because his scent still clings to every fiber inside this truck."

"How many years ago was that?"

"It was before she started dating Griffin, so she was maybe sixteen? And, of course, she was always getting grounded for one thing or another, but my parents knew when she'd sneak out to see Ian because of the smell. And she'd be all outraged. 'I didn't even go out last night. I was in my room watching a movie.' She'd actually have tears in her eyes and be all, 'Why don't you believe me?' And my dad would go ballistic because it was so obvious that the car reeked of that god-awful cologne."

"You guys shared the same truck?"

"Yep. This was the kid truck. My parents had all these hoops we had to jump through if we wanted our own phones or cars or whatever, and we were not having that, so we went in on one together. We bought this baby off Lachlan Bowie." She shot him a look. "That's Fin's uncle. Total mountain-man recluse." She smoothed a hand on the dashboard. "We thought it was the coolest thing."

She turned onto 191 and drove the long stretch of highway back toward town. "Hey, so, you know how I switched things up a little bit? That I'll be interviewing people, too?"

"Yep." He'd heard she'd demanded to be an equal co-host and not just the token chef. Impressed the hell out of him.

"Well, I have an idea."

That smile. *Jesus.* He felt it like carbonation in his chest.

"For my segments, I want to do something more than sit in chairs and chat. That's not to say there's anything wrong with that. It's more that I want to incorporate the setting way more than in just the opening credits."

"You have anything specific in mind?"

"I'm so glad you asked." She grinned. "Calamity's

small, but because of our 'live free' spirit, we get a lot of trail blazers and down-to-earth nature lovers. Which means we're really progressive and cutting edge. I know people don't associate fresh produce with mountain towns, but we've got greenhouses and hydroponic farms, wineries and breweries. And I want to visit those places and use their ingredients on the show."

"I like that."

"Okay, good. Then, for my first interview, I really love the idea of us going to the farmers market and 'running into' Delilah. She's the chef at the Owl Hoot Resort and Spa."

"I met her."

"Like, how fun would it be if we walk around and talk to some of the vendors, and then we bump into her and she hands us two identical baskets of ingredients and tells us to make something with it?"

"And then she judges what we make and decides which one of us wins?"

"And the winner gets to donate something like, I don't know, ten thousand dollars to the charity of her choice."

"Or his choice. I do have some skills."

She hunched a shoulder. "So far, you're all talk. I'm going to need some proof."

"I'll cook you dinner tonight."

"You're on." She slowed as they caught up with a line of cars that'd stopped for a bison in the middle of the road. "This is going to be fun. We get to interview the top people in the fields where we no longer work." She cracked a grin. "Kidding. Kind of." She gave an exaggerated sigh. "Okay, none of that negative talk. We'll be back in our saddles in no time." She raised a fist. "To phoenixes."

This wave of affection crashed over him, and he

grabbed her hand. Impulsively, he brought it to his mouth and kissed her knuckles. "I'm glad we're in this together."

And, really, what the fuck was that? Was he a duke or some shit, kissing her hand?

But when her expression went all sweet and dreamy, when her mouth went soft and kissable, lust boiled in his core. "I don't know how the hell I'm supposed to not kiss you."

Her eyes flared.

"Shit, sorry. I shouldn't have said that. I won't. Kiss you. I know that's not what you want." He checked her response, but she stared blank-faced at the road ahead. Which, he guessed, was answer enough. She wasn't into him. "And now that we're working together, it can't happen."

"Right."

Good job making everything awkward. They drove in silence for a bit, and it gave him a moment to consider. After they'd kissed, she'd said she didn't do hookups. But now they had a whole summer together. At least for the month of May, they'd be roommates, and then he'd be in town for June and the first couple of weeks in July.

That's not hooking up.

Or is it? Maybe by hooking up, she means fucking around for a summer. *But that's all I have.* The moment training camp started, he'd be out of here.

Why am I even thinking about this? He'd had two serious relationships in his life. The last thing he needed was to jump into a third. *Get the conversation back on track.* "So, instead of sitting in chairs interviewing people, we'll take our guests on field trips."

"That's what I'd like." She'd gone serious on him.

He'd do just about anything to keep that light shining inside of her. "Then, we'll make it happen."

"*Yes.*" She pumped a fist when she found a spot right in front of Calamity Joe's. "You think it's silly, but during tourist season, there's no parking anywhere in town." Cutting the engine, she hauled her purse off the back seat and got out of the truck.

Taking in the town green and its white gazebo set against the dramatic backdrop of the Tetons, he met her on the sidewalk. "This place is cool." It was a Wild West town, for sure, with the antler archways leading into the square, Bazoo's Mercantile that sold taxidermy grizzly bears and foxes, and boutiques that sold cowboy boots and belt buckles.

Holding the door open, he followed her into the coffee shop. It smelled like cinnamon and sugar and the rich, dark aroma of roasted beans. With country music playing in the background, the place had glossy wood floors and bookcases filled with merchandise like stuffed moose and bears and stacks of Calamity Joe's T-shirts and sweatshirts.

"Lulu?" The barista came racing around the counter. "Oh, my God, it's so good to see you."

"I haven't seen you in forever." The two hugged, rocking back and forth.

The woman pulled back and greeted him. "Hi, I'm Harley."

"Xander. Nice to meet you."

"She's Maureen's daughter, the owner of Calamity Joe's." Lulu smiled affectionately. "We were best friends growing up."

"How long are you in town?" Harley asked, clearly excited.

"That's kind of up in the air, but I'm for sure here for the summer. Are you just helping out your mom?"

Some of the woman's enthusiasm dimmed. "Uh, no. I'm…probably going to stay for a while."

Lulu's gaze skimmed down the tall, fit woman's body. "Is something wrong?"

Pain flashed across Harley's features before she reset back to happy. "I retired." She glanced to the growing line. "Listen, I've got to get back there before my customers revolt, but let's get together soon. We've got a lot to catch up on."

"I'd love that."

Harley headed back, and Lulu and Xander took their places in line.

"Sounds like there's a story there."

"I guarantee she wouldn't be back in Calamity if something hadn't gone wrong. It's May, so she should be on tour. Last I heard, she was the fourteenth ranked women's surfer in the world."

"Really?" He glanced back at the woman with bright blonde hair. "You guys didn't keep in touch?"

"Barely. With my work hours and her travel…" She gazed up at him. "We're past all the bullshit, aren't we?"

"Yeah, we are."

"Well, the last time I saw my friends, my sister was kissing my fiancé. I've hardly spent any time here since. So, no, I didn't keep in touch with many people." She watched Harley. "But I'm over that now, and no one's going to keep me from Calamity ever again."

Chapter Nine

LULU TURNED DOWN THE UNMARKED LANE THAT LED to the bunkhouse. After a wonderful day out with the photographer getting location shots, she'd taken time for herself to wander the shops and sit outside with a gelato.

She'd been arguing with herself the entire time.

Because when Xander said things like, *I don't know how the hell I'm supposed to not kiss you* she started making shit up. Like, *he really likes me.* And, *We get along so well, we set off sparks like the Fourth of July*...and that made her cross the line from *I like this guy so much* to full-on *I'm crazy about him.*

And she knew she'd entered dangerous territory because denying herself a second kiss had physically hurt.

She'd wanted to pull the car over right then and pounce on him. She'd wanted to straddle his lap, lift his shirt over his head, and find out what it was like to be touched by a man who looked at her the way Xander did.

Because, literally, no one ever had before.

Rounding the bend in the road, she had to lower the

visor to block the glint of sunlight from an RV's metal siding.

But as much as she wanted to get naked with him, explore his hard, sexy body, and hear the sounds he made when she went down on him, she couldn't do it.

Because we live together. That meant, after one or two glorious nights, she'd have to watch him going out with his teammates to bars and restaurants. He was a gorgeous man. Women flocked to him.

And he was single for the first time in his adult life. He didn't want a girlfriend.

Worse, he'd probably bring women home. He had every right to do it. He didn't have to be a monk just because he had a roommate.

The bunkhouse came into view. With the kitchen renovation underway, trucks were parked haphazardly around the RVs, so she eased under the shade of the Aspens and cut the engine. Armed with grocery bags, she entered to find Abigail chatting in the entryway with a crew member.

The producer smiled at her. "Oh, hey, you're back. Good day?"

"It was amazing. We got some great shots." Even as she answered, she sought out Xander. Which was mortifying since she knew she couldn't hide her reaction when she found him in the kitchen surrounded by the stylist, the make-up artist, and two of the locals they'd hired as interns for the show.

She forced her attention back on the producer. "So, you know how we talked about me interviewing chefs? When we were in Owl Hoot this morning, I stopped in to visit Delilah Lua, the executive chef at the resort restaurant. I invited her to be a guest on the show. She's excited about it."

"That sounds great. You just let me know when you want to do it." She gave a slow shake of her head. "I can't believe how quickly everything's coming together. Between you and Xander, we've already got a fantastic line-up of guests."

"How'd filming go?" While she was out, Xander had interviewed Ryker.

"Oh, he was phenomenal. The audience is going to adore him. There's just something so appealing about him —his confidence mixed with that air of mystery. It couldn't have gone better."

"Sorry I missed it."

"Well, I'm just thrilled you guys got so much done today. Okay, let me jump into the editor's trailer. We're going to put a little teaser together to send out to some network friends." She started off.

Was Lulu going to have to fight for herself every step of the way? "Abigail, hang on a second. I know we're moving fast, but can we hold off one day? Doesn't it make more sense to give them something with *both* of us?" Ultimately, she had no creative power over this show. She was just along for the ride.

Abigail moved in closer. "I'm going to be straight with you. And this is just between the two of us, okay?"

"Absolutely."

"We got the inside scoop that The Food Channel's about to pull one of our shows. They haven't announced anything yet, and we're sure they won't until they've filled the slot."

"I knew there had to be a reason why everything's moving so fast."

"Exactly. We haven't gotten the official word, but we want to be ready with a replacement. And to be honest with you, there's no other show like this one—with an athlete and a chef—and that's why I want to send them this reel, before they consider something else. Now you know why I livestreamed the auditions, and why we got the green light. We've got other shows we could push, but we all agree that this is the one that's going to stand out."

"Is it *The Farm Woman*?" The once beloved older woman recently voiced some unacceptable views on social media.

"Unfortunately, yes."

For the first time, Lulu felt excited about the opportunity. "Well, if it'll help to send something out right now, then I don't mind."

"I appreciate that. Let me go ahead and get this clip ready." She smiled. "This is it, Lulu. I can feel it. All right, you get a good night's rest. You're going up against Ryker first thing in the morning." She headed out the door.

Hoping to put away the groceries and make some tea, Lulu started for the kitchen, but Xander, Ryker, and their adoring fans were hanging out there. Since she was all peopled out from the day's adventure, she'd just go to her bedroom until they left.

As she headed for the hallway, two crew members dashed off to the air hockey game. "I'll whup your ass."

"Try me, betch."

"Come on, Xander," the stylist called. "You, me, ping pong. Let me show you my moves."

But Xander was watching Lulu when he said, "Later. I'm going to shower."

As he came right for her, her heart pounded, the rush of blood washing away her words. She wanted to lift her bags and show him what she'd bought today. Entice him to have a night in with her—maybe they'd cook together, share a bottle of wine on the patio.

But just before he reached her, Ryker grabbed his arm. "Shower later. Me and Julie against you and Laurie. Winner buys drinks tonight."

Xander never took his gaze off her. "Come and play."

She didn't want to say no when six people were watching, but two at the air hockey table, four playing ping pong…she'd be the seventh wheel. "Maybe later. I've been out all day."

She could've sworn she'd seen a crack in his impassive expression, but it quickly sealed up as he gave her a curt nod and joined the others.

Leaving her bags on the dining room table, Lulu shut her bedroom door, kicked off her shoes, and changed out of her clothes, all while listening to mallets crack into pucks, the rapid click-clack of balls, loud conversation, and bursts of laughter.

She reminded herself that she could be out there with them. They'd invited her.

But she didn't want to be with them.

She wanted to be with *him*.

And that was a problem.

When the bunkhouse had gone quiet, Lulu came out of her room and put the groceries away. Setting her phone in the docking station, she chose a playlist and turned up the volume. As she washed her hands, Oh Honey's *Be Okay* came on, and the happy tune pulled her right out of her funk.

After uncorking a bottle of crisp, cold white wine and

pouring some into a glass, she contemplated dinner. Like her mom, Lulu preferred a bunch of little things to eat instead of one big meal. So, she got busy cutting a few slices of cheese, found some crunchy wafers, and shook some roasted almonds out into a bowl.

What else do I want?

Oh, she'd make humus. She loved it with sliced peppers, cucumbers, and baby carrots. After finding what she needed in the pantry, she hauled out the blender and dumped in chickpeas, tahini, and some jarred roasted red peppers. She hit the switch and reached for a cracker, topping it with a piece of cheese. Right as she bit into it, her hips shaking to the beat, she got a prick at the back of her neck, like someone was watching her.

Her gaze flicked up to find Xander, hair wet from a shower, standing at the door in jeans and a black T-shirt. The soft cotton clung to his muscled chest and bulging biceps.

Where are you going? she wanted to ask, but all her thoughts got shaken up in her mind like a snow globe. He was a powerful, intimidating figure.

And then, as if the moment had never happened, he walked out the door, shutting it firmly behind him.

Disappointment nearly crushed her good mood, but she wouldn't let it. She'd enjoy her evening alone, recharge. *Tomorrow's another busy day.*

Moments later, the door flew open, and Lulu's heart about flipped over. This time, she'd be bold, ask him if wanted to have dinner with her. She had plenty of food and would be happy to make more.

Maybe they could cook together?

But it was Coco. And she didn't look happy.

Her sister—always elegant, even after having her

second baby two weeks ago—strode into the kitchen, killed the music, and lifted herself onto the counter. "I'm mad at you."

"At me?"

"Yes, at you. Angry enough that I'd leave my newborn." She reached for a slice of yellow pepper and dipped it in the humus.

Lulu tried to grab the bowl. "I'm not done making it."

"Don't care." Coco took a bite and chewed. "Magic, Lu. Magic." She eyed the wine.

"You want some?"

"Violet's nursing every two hours. No wine. I actually only have an hour and twenty minutes before I have to get back home."

"Well, then, you better talk fast. What'd I do?"

She dropped the slice of cucumber she'd just picked up. "You lost your job, you were unemployed for a *month*, and you kept it all to yourself. Think about it. You weren't going to tell us anything until you got a new job. We're talking about a *job*."

"Yeah, I know. I get it."

"Do you, though?"

Lulu nodded. It did seem ridiculous now.

She sighed. "Okay, give me some wine. Literally one drop."

"It's really good." Lulu poured a tiny bit into a glass. "I got it from Hole-in-the-Wall winery. We were out taking location shots today, and I can't even believe how this town has changed."

Coco plopped a square of cheese on top of a cracker. "I already ate dinner, but suddenly I'm ravenous." She tipped the wine glass back. "Mm, delicious." Then, she grew ornery again. "Of course, it's changed. A lot happens in seven years."

With Gigi, she'd take the comment lightly—a poke about keeping in touch. But with Coco, it was different. Seven years ago, she'd gotten pregnant from a one-night stand. One year ago, in an insane twist of fate, she'd run into the man here in Calamity. They'd gotten married and had their second child.

Lulu had missed a lot more than a few new stores popping up.

"When we were kids, I was so jealous of you guys." Coco sipped the wine. "You had Stella, Gigi had Cassian, and I was just…on my own."

"I thought you didn't *want* to be with us. I thought I only had Stella." She sprinkled cayenne on the humus and stirred. "It's funny, isn't it? The way we all grew up in the same family but have totally different perspectives. I thought you were so cool. You didn't let Mom get to you at all. Just looked her right in the eyes and said, 'Nope. Not interested in going to London.' Or Seattle or Boston or wherever the hell she wanted to send you. You just knew yourself."

"I did. But you guys were gone all the time, and I spent a lot of time alone in that house." She gestured to the humus.

"It's ready." Lulu pushed the bowl over. "I thought you didn't like me. That I wasn't fun enough."

"And I thought I was too average for you."

"What? What does that even mean?"

Coco hunched a shoulder. "You were the special kid, covered in glitter."

"I think you're confusing me with Gigi. *She* was the special one. She was so freaking talented."

"For sure, but there's something about you. You're very self-contained, kind of like…while the rest of us are clueless, flapping around like chickens with their heads cut off, you've got this very calm center. Like, Gigi's always been the entertainer, she's all flashy and creative, Stella's the popular girl, who just knows what to wear and what to say, but you…you were grounded. You knew what you wanted, you didn't suffer fools, and you…I don't know how to explain it. But, like, you glow from within. It's like you've got this flame burning inside you. This *passion*. And that's pretty elusive for those of us who don't have it." She swiped a carrot stick through the humus.

"I had no clue you felt that way about me."

"Yeah, well, that's because we don't talk. How long are you in town?"

"Until I get a job offer. I'm only doing the *The Gridiron Grillers*"—God, she had to get that name changed—"to showcase my skills. If it's a hit, I'm pretty sure I'll have my pick of top chef jobs. The brass ring would be investors who want to back me in my own restaurant. If it's not, I can always stay in town and be a fry cook at the lakeshore food truck."

"And this right here is the problem in our family. You're only a success if you're running a Michelin-starred restaurant. Anything else is failure. How sad is that?" She gobbled up a cucumber slice.

"Slow down. It's like you haven't eaten in months."

Coco laughed. "I run a business, I have a six-year-old, a newborn, and a husband. I eat on the go, and right now all of this is going right in my belly. God, I can't remember the last time I actually tasted food." She finished the last little bit of wine. "Anyhow, you know why this whole thing makes me sad? Because I did the same damn thing. I was alone in Europe for seven months, pregnant by a guy I never thought I'd see again, and I didn't tell my family. I mean, I have *three* sisters. We should be there for each other. And starting right this minute, that's what we're doing. We're all going to be best friends. Well, the three of us living in the 83003 zip code anyway. Deal?" She held out a pinky.

"Deal." They linked fingers, but Lulu needed more. She'd been so disconnected from her sisters for so long, the idea that she could actually be close to them hit deep. She leaned in and wrapped her arms around Coco, too aware of all the years she'd had to navigate career choices and friend problems and heartache all by herself. "I wish I'd talked to you guys the day I got fired. I was freaking out. Nothing like that has ever happened to me before. And it was a big job."

"You never have to go through anything alone because I'm here. We're all here for you. I love you, Lu. Come to dinner tomorrow night and get to know my family. Will you?"

She nodded in the crook of her sister's neck.

She'd wanted this her entire life—this closeness with her sisters.

And this summer…she just might get it.

Xander had been in a lot of bars in his life, but he'd never seen anything like this one. Separated into different sections for line dancing, mechanical bull riding, dining, and drinking, the place was huge. Plus, it had antler chandeliers and animal heads mounted on the walls. Not just deer, but big fucking bison with beady black eyes.

"Who's gonna teach me how to ride a bull?" Ryker said to the group surrounding him.

After dinner, Ryker had wanted to see the nightlife in Calamity, so Cassian had taken them to Wild Billy's. It was pretty much impossible to go unnoticed with two of the most celebrated players in the NFL, so the evening had turned into a wild party.

And, of course, Cassian had gone home about twenty minutes after they'd gotten here.

Leaning against the bar, back turned away from the crowds, Xander nursed a beer. He wished he'd left with his captain.

"Here you go." Laura, the stylist on the show, perched on the bar stool next to him and handed him a small plate with hors d'oeuvres. Wings, mozzarella sticks, a couple celery stalks and carrots and a puddle of blue cheese dressing.

"Thanks." He'd already eaten dinner, so he set the plate aside.

She searched his expression, as she'd done all night, trying to figure him out. "Okay, this isn't your scene. Want to go outside? Get some fresh air. We could sit in the gazebo."

It didn't matter what his scene was, when his thoughts were stuck on the bunkhouse. On Lulu. On the look in her eyes when he'd walked out the door.

He'd seen hope, interest. It had only lasted an instant, but he'd known she wanted him to stay home with her.

And, man, had he wanted to.

Dammit, there was just something about that woman that called to him. Something fresh and warm and fucking sexy.

"Nah, I'm going to head back soon. Got an early call."

"Yeah, I know. So do I, you goof." She reached for his arm. "You're not going to bed until you've learned how to two-step. Come on, I'll teach you."

He glanced to the dance floor, found everyone laughing, having a blast. Still…he couldn't muster an ounce of interest. "Think I'll pass."

He'd had to go out since Ryker had stayed in town specifically to do the show. Well, and also because he'd known what would happen if he'd gone back to the bunkhouse. He'd have cooked with her. Which meant he'd have to watch her expression get all dreamy as she fondled a firm tomato and sniffed a lemon. They'd probably take their food out on the patio, and he'd have to talk to her, hear her laugh, follow the trail of her fingertips on her forearm as she made lazy figure eights.

Did she even know how sensual she was? He was positive she didn't know she teased up gooseflesh on his skin, got him hard, and made him pay too much attention to her mouth.

If he'd stayed in, he probably would've gotten so worked up, he'd have swatted the fork out of her hand, grabbed her wrist, and pulled her up onto his lap.

He'd have kissed her, filled his hands with her tits, and slid his fingers under the waistband of her leggings. Fuck, she'd have been slick and hot—

Someone nudged him right out of his fantasy. "What?"

Laura grinned. "You're not nearly as much fun as I thought you'd be."

"No, I'm really not."

And that's why I can't go to the bunkhouse. Because Lulu didn't want to be with him like that. *And I can't be around her and not want to fuck her.*

Liar. He wanted a whole lot more from her than sex.

But she didn't want a summer fling, and they couldn't offer each other more, so…

"There's a cigar bar in Owl Hoot you might like," Laura said.

"I don't smoke."

"Hm, okay. Let me think. Well, it's too early in the season for bonfires at the lake. We could go back to my place, have some wine."

She was beautiful. Long blonde hair, tight jeans showcasing a rocking body…and yet he felt nothing.

Jesus, I'm twenty-six years old.

I've been in two long-term, monogamous relationships…

Why the hell would he want to roll into a third one anyway?

Maybe, while he was in town, he should have some fun. Fuck around.

Yes. Right.

Let's do that.

He looked at Laura. Really looked at her. But his blood was pumping fast, and he was having a hard time drawing a full breath. Because, while his body was here, with this woman, his mind was in the bunkhouse.

Lulu would've finished dinner by now. She might be washing dishes.

An image dropped into his mind. Lulu's soapy hands on his cock, jerking him, as warm water rained down on their naked bodies, steaming up the shower door. Lust roared through him.

Fuck.

He shook it off. "Nah. I'm hanging out with Ryker tonight." Not going back to the bunkhouse. Not until he knew she was asleep.

But that called up another image of Lulu in bed, dark hair fanned out on the white pillowcase, moonlight spilling in through the window. Did she sleep naked? He pictured coming in late, pulling back the covers, and climbing in beside her, her soft smile, fingers scraping across his scalp, welcoming him. Their bodies pressed tightly together, her sweet scent filling all the chilly, empty spaces inside him.

A sense of peace, of home, washed over him.

He'd never felt anything like it in his life.

"Hey, you okay?" Laura's voice jolted him.

And he landed back on the hard stool, awash in people shouting to be heard over the music and bursts of raucous laughter, and the smell of too many bodies pressed together, a clash of perfume, cologne, and shaving cream.

She reached for his hand, ready to go. "Let's go. You and me, away from the crowds."

A woman of action.

And that's when it clicked. Blonde, beautiful, intelligent, full of energy. "Were you a cheerleader?"

"Sure was." She beamed a smile at him. "At Montana State."

She was Steph. She was Kayla.

It struck him hard. *This is what I do.*

He'd met both of his exes at a party, Kayla in high school, Steph in college. Loud music, booze, everyone drunk and grinding on each other on makeshift dance floors. Both times, he'd felt bored and out of place.

And then a beautiful woman claims him. She swoops in and takes charge. And then, somehow, without him even thinking about it, they're dating. She takes control of the social life that doesn't interest him. He goes along, so that he can focus on the things that matter to him—football, working in Akasha, studying.

Kayla and Steph were his wingwomen. Just like Lulu's sister was for her.

The reason he was grumpy and broody, as Lulu liked to say, was because he didn't like social situations. He preferred being one-on-one with someone he knew and liked, but parties, *bars* weren't for him.

Laura's not my people.

Lulu is. And there's nowhere else I'd rather be than with her.

"Thanks, Laura. I appreciate your efforts to make this a fun night for me, but I'm just going to head back to the bunkhouse."

"No problem." And just as Steph would've done, she defaulted to cheerful. "I'll figure out something fun for Friday night."

"See you tomorrow." He made his way through the packed bar, eager to get the hell home.

To Lulu.

Chapter Ten

As pumped as if it were game night, Xander parked in front of the bunkhouse. Two of the RVs were dark, but the third was lit up, music playing.

He got out of his rental car, imagining Lulu reading in bed. He'd knock on her door…and what?

No, if she'd gone to bed, he couldn't bother her. But maybe she'd be out on the patio with a glass of wine. He breathed in the night air, scented with sage and a sweetness that could only come from the profusion of brightly colored wildflowers in the surrounding meadow.

Inspired, he grabbed a handful and brought them inside.

That yellow light he'd seen through the window turned out to be a lamp she'd left on for him. His hopes crashed when he saw no sign of her. Boxes, cameras, extension cords…the place was ready for filming tomorrow. But no Lulu.

Dammit. He'd wasted too much time at the bar.

He listened outside her door, but it was quiet.

He'd blown it. And it wasn't just about tonight.

He'd spent his life chasing after things that didn't matter...all because he'd wanted so badly to be like his brothers.

And, as he stood in the dark hallway with a handful of flowers, he realized he was done with that.

Because, for the first time, he had something that mattered more.

Lulu loved mornings best. Her sisters had always slept in, thanks to boyfriends and parties and all the normal stuff teenagers did.

But she'd used that time alone to make croissants, galettes, or cinnamon rolls...something fun that would elicit squeals of delight when they all came running downstairs, lured by the fabulous scents.

Xander had probably gotten in late, so it was unlikely he'd be up this early. Sliding her feet into slippers, she got out of bed. She'd make a pot of coffee and have some fun looking at the foodie Splashagram pages she loved so much. Anything to keep her mind from jumping back into the endless reel of wondering what he'd done last night—and who he'd done it with.

Had he gone home with someone?

Worse, had he brought someone here? If he did that at some point, would she hear them giggling behind his closed door and watch them making out between sips of coffee?

Why does it matter? I don't want to be his hookup.

Throwing a sweatshirt on over her pajama bottoms, she headed out of the room. She stopped short when she saw a handful of wildflowers right outside her door.

Picking them up, she brought them to her nose and inhaled the earthy sweetness.

Had someone dropped them? That didn't seem likely. *They're literally right outside my door.*

Who were they from? Not Xander, right?

Why would he give her flowers?

He'd left his door ajar, and she fought the impulse to peer in.

Because what could be creepier than watching your roommate sleep?

Heading into the kitchen, she flicked on the light and checked the cupboards for a vase. The designer hadn't spared a single expense. Good for the Bowies, because the woman had bought everything a cook could possibly need —times two.

The space was already enormous, but she'd installed a massive island finished with matching sinks, ovens, and cooktops at either end. Perfect for competitions—but also good for the big events the family threw here.

"Morning."

The shock of Xander's voice in the early morning stillness jarred her. She stuttered out a laugh. "You scared me."

"Sorry." He stood there in red sweatpants and a Stanford T-shirt, his short hair mussed from sleep.

"I didn't think anybody would be up this early."

"I didn't stay out late. Besides, my trainer's got me on a schedule. I've got to get in a run before we start filming." She noticed his gaze fixed on her hand, which reminded her about the flowers.

She lifted them. "I found these outside my bedroom."

"Yeah, that was pretty dumb. I should've put them in water." He reached out to touch the petals. "They're wilted."

"You got them for me?"

He dipped his chin, and her heart swooned at his shyness.

"They're perfect. I love them." *But what do they mean?* She wouldn't ask, so she went back to looking for a vase. "I saw your door was open, so I tried to be quiet. I hope I didn't wake you."

"That's why I left it open. I wanted to get up when you did."

What? She found a crystal vase on the very top shelf. A wall of heat came up behind her, and he pulled it down. She caught a whiff of something uniquely him—like clean sheets and fresh mountain air—a scent that made her want to crawl under the covers with him and spend the day in bed. He stood there for a moment, his chest grazing her back, and she chanced a look at him.

She might not have known him long, but she'd learned that, while his features were often unreadable, his eyes told stories. And Lord, did she want to hear them.

He stepped back, filling the vase with water, as she snipped the stems and put the flowers in.

"They make me so happy." It was an unspeakably sweet gesture—especially since he didn't seem like a romantic guy. "Did you…" Her voice came out funny, so she cleared her throat. "Do you have a nice time last night?" She held the kettle under the faucet and filled it.

"No."

His sharp tone made her glance at him over her shoulder.

He shrugged. "Dinner was okay, but I should've come home after."

Home. "Why, what did you do?"

"Cassian left early, and I didn't want to bail on Ryker, so I went with him to Wild Billy's."

"And drew a huge crowd."

"Yeah."

"You're sounding grumpy again. Too early in the morning for you?"

"No. I just…" He rubbed the scruff on his chin. "I realized some things. I'm not very social."

She set the kettle on a burner and lit the flame.

"I only figured it out last night, but between my family and teammates, I'm rarely alone, and I guess I rely on everyone else do the socializing."

"Cassian said you didn't go on any of the trips he sponsored. He figured it was because you were married."

"There's truth in that. Even though we were separated, I'd never embarrass Steph by partying on a yacht with other women. But now I'm wondering if the reason I didn't push for a divorce was so I could have the excuse *not* to do things like that." He didn't say anything for a moment, and he looked like he was pulling his thoughts together. "I'm not a one-night-stand kind of guy."

He'd said it in such a deliberate way, she knew he was sending her a message.

"Never have been. I guess I need to know someone first. Feel some kind of connection. Otherwise, it's just a bodily function I can take care of on my own."

She went very, very still. Almost like, if she moved, he'd be able to see excitement rise like solar flares on her skin. Because she'd told him she didn't do hookups. And the only message she could put together from flowers, his open bedroom door, and this conversation, was that he wanted to be with her.

In the only way that would work for her.

"Sorry. Was that TMI?"

"Not at all." *So, what do I say? Do I jump into his arms and kiss him and tell him I want to be with him like that, too?*

What if I'm reading him wrong?

Like I did with Griffin ten thousand times.

And then all over again with Trace.

She had a bad habit of reading into things, so she'd hold off. She got her bag of coffee beans out of the pantry. When he didn't offer more, she filled the grinder and turned it on. Then, she poured the grounds into the French press.

"I had a hard time falling asleep last night," he said.

"You still haven't heard from the Mavericks?"

"Nothing. Not a word. But I was up thinking you'd probably heard from Cassian that I screwed around on my wife."

She nodded, keeping up with her task.

"On the road, it's pretty common. You know the stories, girls wait in the lobby, outside your door, inside your room." He shrugged. "It's easy. When I didn't go to bars and clubs with the guys, they thought I was getting laid. I heard them talking about me, how I was a big hypocrite for talking about family values and then screwing around on my wife. But it wasn't true."

She turned, resting her back against the counter. "Why didn't you correct them?"

"They never talked to me about it, just made their assumptions. I've never cheated. Never would. And I'm not the one who talked about family values. When would I do that? How many interviews do you think backup quarterbacks get?"

"So, where'd the idea come from?"

"My parents have been together thirty-five-years, my brothers are happily married. We don't have any scandals, so the press likes to talk about our squeaky-clean family."

"Okay, but don't you guys share rooms? Couldn't your roommates see you weren't out hooking up?"

"I did go out. I just wasn't doing what they thought."

"Well, don't you just get more intriguing by the minute?" She opened a cabinet and pulled down two mugs. "Are you going to tell me what you were doing?"

"What do I get if I tell you?" In spite of the light tone, those intelligent eyes held a challenge.

No, a dare.

She wanted to accept. She wanted to, so badly. But something held her back, so she met him halfway. "What do you want?" Leaving the ball in his court.

The kitchen grew smaller, warmer, as he studied her, his thumb rasping over the scruff at his jaw.

And she had a moment to weigh her own feelings. Did she really want to start something with him? What if it only lasted a night or two…then what?

She'd want more. She'd want so much more than he could give, so she broke the tension by lifting a mug. "I mean, I make a mean cup of coffee. Is that enough to get it out of you?"

For a moment, he looked disappointed. But he quickly shook it off. "It's not that big a deal. Road trips take us to a lot of the same cities every season, so over the years I became friendly with some chefs."

"Wait, are you serious? They thought you were screwing around, but really you were a guest chef?"

He nodded.

She laughed. "You constantly surprise me. Here you are, the big bad athlete, looking all hard and intimidating, and instead of hanging out in bars, you're chopping onions."

She had a feeling she'd regret not being bolder about his dare, and yet she liked this time with him, just talking. "Why do I get the feeling your brothers teased you for working in your mom's kitchen?" That's why he hadn't corrected him teammates' impression of him. He didn't want their ridicule.

"Yeah."

"Want to hear something funny?" The kettle started to whistle, so she switched off the burner. "I had my Sweet Sixteen at Café Akasha."

"Seriously?"

"Totally."

"How did you even know about it?"

"Long story."

He came up against her again, this time reaching around her. One hand cupped her shoulder, and the other poured the hot water over the grounds. "I want to hear it." His morning voice was rough and gravelly. *So sexy*.

Oh, my God. He smelled so good. She wanted to turn around in his arms, stick her face in his neck, and just breathe him in.

She wanted his big hands sliding down her back, rounding the curve of her ass. She wanted to thread her fingers through his hair and kiss that hungry mouth.

That's it.

I want his hunger.

No one's ever kissed me the way he did, and I want it.

When he moved away, leaning against the counter, arms folded across his powerful chest, she found herself at a loss.

Which is my fault. Since she didn't know what she wanted, she had to be giving mixed signals.

Then again, she didn't want to have to read into his words and actions.

I want him to want me so much he can't keep his hands off me.

"Don't you need to get going?" She gestured to his bare feet.

"Not until I hear the story about your Sweet Sixteen."

"You pretty much already know it. It started with Sam and my vegetable garden, and then cooking for people led to me fantasizing about having my own restaurant, and of course if you look up farm-to-table, Café Akasha pops up everywhere. Because it's the most gorgeously romantic place on the planet with all the candles and fairy lights and gazebos. It was my dream restaurant. So, I begged my parents to let me have my Sweet Sixteen there."

He gave her a strange and intense look. "We might've met."

"Well, I don't know. Where were you April twentieth ten years ago?" She said it jokingly, but she could tell he was giving it serious thought.

"That would've been the week after spring break...I was around. I could've been there. I'll have to ask my mom about that."

"She wouldn't remember one party out of thousands over the years."

"One hosted by Joss Montalbano and Tyler Cavanaugh?"

"Good point. Isn't it funny I don't think of them like that?" She pushed the plunger down. "You wouldn't have paid the slightest bit of attention to me anyway."

"Why do you say that?"

"Weren't you with your girlfriend?" She poured the coffee.

"Yeah, I was. Actually, I was thinking about it last night." He grabbed the milk from the fridge and offered it to her.

"No, thanks." She got the cream out instead and dropped a little into her mug.

Setting the milk aside, he did the same. After adding sugar, he stirred. "How I tend to wind up in relationships."

"You go for the hot blonde?"

He reached for a lock of her hair and rubbed it between two fingers. "To be honest, my mom's blonde. My sisters-in-law are blonde. I didn't know how pretty dark hair could be."

Sensation shimmered through her, and her heart pounded.

Kiss me.

Want me.

Instead, he settled back and sipped his coffee. "I was standing at the bar, not really interacting much, and this woman kept trying to find something fun for me to do. And I realized that's exactly how I got together with Kayla and Steph. I met them both at parties, where I wasn't having a good time, and they took charge and just... claimed me."

"But you loved them, right?"

"I..." He let out a frustrated breath. "I can't say I've ever lost my head over anyone."

"Like I did with Griffin."

"Right. Never anything like that." He sipped the steaming brew. "This is really good."

"Thank you." She'd bought the beans in Kona. "Have you ever felt passion?"

"I don't think so."

"Not with your wife?"

"Now that I have a sense of it, I can say no. I absolutely didn't feel that for her. I was attracted to her but passion?" He shook his head.

Now that he had a sense of it?

Is he talking about me?

God, this is unbearable.

I have to stop trying to read between the lines.

"Something you said in the kitchen the other night, about expectations, and reaching goals...I think I've been so preoccupied with reaching mine, that I haven't paid attention to anything else, and Steph filled out the parts of my life I neglected. I don't know if that makes sense, but I'm not sure I'd have had a social life if it weren't for her."

"I get it. I'm the same way. I don't need a lot of people, but I do need my person."

Been looking for him all my life.

"I also think..." He gazed into his mug. "Being the youngest played a part."

"How so?"

Holding his mug, steam rising, he stared unseeing ahead. And then he said, "I think I had to be very careful growing up. Being so much younger meant I wasn't really part of what my brothers were doing, and I felt like if I did anything wrong, they'd kick me out." He turned wistful. "My whole life was about reading their expressions, figuring out the right thing to say that would make them like me. Most of the time, they ignored me. But every once in a while...I'd nail it. And if I could get them to laugh, that was the biggest high. It was like…in that moment, I was in. I was part of the team."

"I can relate so much to that."

"Except your biggest high was when people liked your food."

"Exactly." She marveled at the way he paid attention to her. *Saw* her.

He chuckled. "No one's ever made me think about this shit before."

"Is that a good thing or a bad?"

"Considering I left a bar I didn't want to be in last night and came home, where I wanted to be, I'd say that's a win."

He wanted to be home…*with me?*

There's no use agonizing over this. Unless she wanted to go for it, jump into bed with him and see where things went, she needed to stop analyzing every single thing he said.

It's not like he's making any moves.

Time to change the channel. "Hey, I told Abigail about my idea to meet Delilah at the farmers market, and she's into it. She seems to be giving us a lot of leeway, so I was thinking about your situation and what we could do to promote your agenda in all this."

"Were you now?"

"Why don't we get the chef from The Antigravity Training Center to talk about the care and feeding of extreme athletes?"

With his free hand, he made a rolling motion. *Go on.*

"While I'm getting a tour of her kitchen and the grounds, we can just happen to pass a big field where you're throwing the ball to Cassian and Ryker and whoever else is in town by then."

A slow smile transformed his features into the kind of handsome that made her wobbly.

"While we're getting some shots of you working with the physical therapist, we can do a quick interview with him, and he can talk about the research he's done, the advancements that'll make your shoulder ligaments better than before. Fin could be there, and he could talk you up like, 'Damn, he's better than new.' What do you think?"

He stood straighter, and she could swear she saw his pulse fluttering in his neck. He set his mug down and scrubbed his face with both hands.

"I mean, it's just an idea. I don't even know if Abigail will go for it." When he didn't answer, she put a hand on his back. "You okay?"

"Yeah." He seemed to be working through something, so she waited. "You think everyone falls for Stella, and I've never met her, but it sounds like she's pretty and has a big personality. But that's superficial shit. That's just attraction. I know because that's what I had with both of my exes. The thing about you that's different—better—is that you fucking care. Women like Stella are so busy drawing attention to themselves, they're not really listening. They're reading the room, looking for cues, looking for the pay-off of being pretty and bubbly. But you…you're so in the damn moment, so…invested." He blew out a breath. "I like your idea." He reached for her, drawing her against his chest. "Thank you."

It was just a hug, but it was more thrilling than any touch she'd ever felt in her life. His body shook with the power of emotion—and she'd done that to him. With just a simple, obvious idea. It was like he was starved for someone to see him, to really pay attention.

He shifted one thigh between her legs, his hands

sliding lower on her back. She waited for it—the glide over her ass—but it didn't happen. "Lu?"

Hearing her nickname in that deep, growly voice made her go all fizzy inside. "Yeah?"

"I've felt pretty damn powerless the last five years. I can train and eat right and play my best, but I can't make a coach want to give me a shot. I have to sit on my ass and trust my agent to do his job."

"You have your brothers and dad…"

"Nepotism doesn't work in football. Not when I'm twenty-six with two major injuries. I fight every day to stay positive and not give into doubt and fear. And what you suggested for the show, for my career…it means a lot." He tipped her chin, gazing into her eyes. "Thank you." He lowered his mouth to hers, and desire burst in her chest.

She needed his kiss so badly she shook with it. *Take me.*

This kiss was different from the first one. This was heart-stoppingly slow and sensuous, this one said, *I like you, I appreciate you…I've got to have you.*

And she melted into it. Just felt her whole body give itself over to him, to the sweet stroke of his tongue, the flex of his fingers at the rise of her bottom.

The front door flew open, and Abigail said, "Anyone up?"

They jerked apart, as though they'd been caught.

The producer strode in, followed by a couple of crew members. "I smell coffee." She came up short when she saw them standing so closely.

Lulu stepped around Xander. "You guys are here early."

Quietly, the crew went to work taping down cords and setting up lights. Abigail looked between them. "I told you we'd knock this out in a month." She wagged a finger between them. "We're all on the same page here, right? We all want the same thing."

"Yes," Lulu said. "Of course."

"Great. We're going to shoot the competition between you and Ryker today, so we need to lay out the ingredients and set up, make sure both sides have the same tools and supplies."

Certain she'd just gotten scolded for kissing Xander, Lulu threw on bravado she didn't feel. "I'm always ready to kick someone's ass."

"Perfect." Abigail gave them one more look. "Well, let's do this."

Chapter Eleven

Two hours later, Lulu hardly recognized herself. Laura, the stylist, had her wearing black slacks and a blood-red blouse—not her style at all. The make-up artist had gone heavy on foundation and eyeliner, and her hair had been sprayed so thoroughly a windstorm at the summit of Grant Teton wouldn't move a single strand.

Now, she headed down the hallway to tape the competition with Ryker. And, strangely, she wasn't nervous.

Funny, how wondering whether Xander wants to kiss me gets me more rattled than filming a television show.

"Hang on." The makeup artist came out of the bedroom they'd transformed into a dressing room and raced down the hall. "Let me just…" She gently brushed powder over Lulu's cheeks, forehead, and the space between her nose and mouth. She pulled back for a better look. "There. Now you look fresh and smoldering."

"Not sure it'll last. I'm going to sweat like mad under all those lights."

"You will, but don't worry. At the break, I've got blotting papers to keep you glowing. I got you, girl."

"Awesome, thank you."

At the end of the hallway, Lulu waited for her cue to come out. It gave her a chance to take in Xander, his form-fitting golf shirt highlighting broad shoulders and round biceps. He and Ryker chatted and traded barbs, like two guys hanging out in the locker room. He was charming and handsome, and her pulse quickened with how much she liked him.

If only they'd met at another time, instead of this summer when they were both waiting for their big breaks. Their time together was a blip on his radar. As soon as he signed with a team, he'd go back to football, to a gorgeous blonde beauty who took care of his social life so he could focus on what mattered most to him.

Abigail came up beside her. "You ready to take on the Ragin' Cajun?"

"Oh, God, that's not his nickname, is it?"

"No, just giving you a teaser of the region. Not that there's anything you don't know how to cook."

"Believe it or not, I've never been to New Orleans. Seems crazy, right?"

"You've never had Cajun food?"

"Worse, I've never cooked it."

Abigail grinned. "This should be good."

Lulu wasn't too worried. The kitchen had been stocked with everything she'd need, plus she had her own list of must-have ingredients, so she knew she could wing it.

"Think you can handle going up against Lulu Cavanaugh?" she heard Xander say.

Ryker clapped his hands together. "You bet."

"Should we bring her out here," Xander asked. "Or are you going to use your one call for help?"

"Didn't you say she trained at the Cordon Bleu?"

"Not only that, but she won the student chef of the year award."

She got a kick of joy that he'd bring that up. *He's looking out for me, making me look good.*

"Huh. Now I am a little scared. Yeah, okay, I'll use my call."

The prop master rushed over to her. "Your apron and knife set are on the butcherblock cutting board."

"Perfect, thank you."

"All right," Xander said. "Let's bring her out."

The cameraman rolled back as she walked into the kitchen. Smiling at the guys, she went right to her station and shook out her apron, as scripted.

"You ready, Lu?" Xander asked.

"You bet I am." She nodded to Ryker. "So, what've you got for me?"

He grinned proudly but shrugged like it was no big deal. "Just your basic Creole jambalaya."

"That sounds fantastic." Xander looked to her. "Have you made it before?"

"Nope. Never." She threw the blond-haired behemoth a pointed look. "Have you?"

Ryker laughed. "Yeah, I know how I look. What can I say? My dad's Danish, and my mom's Puerto Rican, but they met in college at Tulane, and I grew up in New Orleans. It's the only thing I know how to make, but I'm telling you, it's the only thing I ever want to make. It's that good."

"It'll be my first."

"You've never eaten jambalaya?" Ryker sounded surprised.

"Never."

"Hm." He faked looking thoughtful. "Maybe I don't

need that call for help after all."

"Probably not," Lulu said. "What's the prize, again, if you win?"

"Ten grand to the New Orleans Mission."

Xander clapped him on the shoulder. "You and your family have volunteered there since you were a little kid, right?"

Ryker nodded.

"Good people. So, what's it going to be?" Xander tipped his chin toward Lulu. "She's never even eaten it before, so there shouldn't be a problem. But if you need to check in with your mom or sisters, just to be sure you don't forget a critical ingredient…" He held up a cell phone.

Ryker deliberated. "You worked for a fancy restaurant in Paris, right?"

"I was the sous chef at Sublime." She looked into the camera and blew a kiss. "Thank you, Chef Paul."

"Yeah, I'm making the call."

Xander handed over the phone. "You've got sixty seconds. Make the most of it."

"No worries. I only need two." Instead of dialing, Ryker set the phone down, tipped his head back, and shouted, "Mom!"

The French doors opened and in walked a beautiful older woman with a Cheshire cat grin. "You called me, baby?"

Everyone on set cracked up, and Ryker enfolded his petite mom in his arms. When he pulled away, he turned to the co-hosts. "Hey, man, you never said what kind of call."

People were howling.

"Great. I'm going against your mom." Lulu gave

Xander a look that said, *Did you know about this*?"

He hunched a shoulder, playing innocent. "All right, ladies. Get to your workstations."

Lulu pulled the pretty gingham cloth off the gathered ingredients.

"Ready?" Xander called. "You've got one hour to create Creole jambalaya."

Lulu did a quick scan of what they'd laid out—onion, celery, bell pepper, chicken, shrimp, sausage. "Yep. Let's do this."

"You've never made the dish, and you've never tasted it," Xander said. "Still think you can win?"

She was itching to get to work, but this was television, and she needed to be as charming as Xander to keep her gig. "I'll leave that up to the judges to decide." She glanced at her competitor. "Either way, that ten grand's going to a worthy cause."

"Amen," Ryker's mom said.

"All right then, ladies, on your mark, get set…" Xander stood next to her with a charming and mischievous grin, and it made her belly flip over. He was so handsome. And then he did a little dip of his knees and his arm shot out. "Go!"

While the other woman took off like a shot, racing to the refrigerator and filling her arms with ingredients, Lulu took a moment to prepare. First, she made a mental list of the basics. Beyond the provided ingredients, she'd need crushed tomatoes, cayenne, paprika, thyme, oregano, basil. She'd need fat, so she'd go with chicken thighs and skip the breasts. Garlic. She always used lots of that.

As she set out her mise en place, she thought ahead to the rice. *Better get that going now.* She filled a pot with water and put it on the burner.

Now, to build flavor, she needed to brown in batches. She got the sausage and chicken cooking in a big skillet, then took off for the pantry and grabbed the spices. Then, in the refrigerator, she exchanged the green pepper for a red one, preferring its slightly sweeter taste.

In the background of her thoughts, she was vaguely aware of conversation, but it wasn't until she heard her name that she looked up.

And found everyone staring at her.

"You're giving that pepper bedroom eyes," Xander said.

"Am I? Or do you need to get out more?" She tipped her chin to Ryker. "Maybe tonight you should take him back to Wild Billy's. Get him two-stepping and riding the mechanical bull."

Ryker pointed at his teammate. "We're totally doing that."

"You do know the clock's ticking, right?" Xander teased.

Lulu waved a hand. "Great things take time. Right, Mrs. Olsen?"

"Mm hm." She raised her eyebrows as she took in Lulu's skillet. "Not that much time."

Lulu laughed. "You guys think you can scare me, but you didn't have Chef Thibaud for a teacher. After his class, there's literally nothing you can do to ruffle my feathers. Grueling hours, frantic pace, and the expectation of perfection? Forget it. Put your feet up, Xander, chat football stats with your buddy, and leave me to my jambalaya."

Once she had a lovely fond, she tossed in the diced onion. As soon as it started to caramelize, she added the garlic. Then, salt, pepper, and chopped herbs.

Again, she heard her name. When she looked up, she

found Xander tasting something Mrs. Olsen had cooked. "Oh, man, that's good. Those spices."

He sauntered over to her end of the island. "You doing okay, Chef?"

She sprinkled in the cayenne. "Just fine."

"Good to hear."

"Why do you ask?" She pushed her bangs out of her eyes with the back of a hand.

"You seem distracted."

"Did you mean engrossed?"

"I *meant* this place could burn down, and you wouldn't know it."

"Oh, I'd smell it, for sure. How do you think I know when something's ready?"

"Now, you're just showing off." He nodded toward her skillet. "Smells good. You think you're going to have it done in time?"

"You trying to rattle me, X-Man?"

"Can I?"

She shook her head. "Nah. I've worked in some pretty insane kitchens. I got this."

"You got a game plan to make sure the rice doesn't turn pasty?"

"Please." Of course she knew not to cook the rice in with the stew. "That's a rookie mistake."

"Hey," Ryker said. "If you're giving her a tip, you have to give my mom one, too."

"Somehow, I don't think you need to worry about your mom," Lulu said.

"You most definitely do not." Mrs. Olsen worked efficiently, calmly. "I could make this dish in my sleep."

"What're you using for special Cajun spices?" Ryker asked Lulu.

That got her attention. "I thought you said this was Creole?"

"It is," Mrs. Olsen said. "Don't mess with her head, boy. I'm going to win this fair and square."

"Since I don't know the difference between them," Lulu said. "And I've never tasted either, he can't really mess with me. I'm just going with my gut. It's all I can do."

"You confident enough to give me a taste?" Xander asked. "See if you can stand up to your formidable opponent?"

"So little faith in your co-host," Lulu said. "But sure. Hang on a second." After lowering the flame under the skillet, she headed to the pantry, thrilled beyond measure that she'd picked up the jar of peppers she'd bought on a lark. She'd imagined a night with the crew playing around, giving them the pepper challenge.

This is so much better.

Popping it open, she fished one out and then came back to the skillet to give it a stir. She set the pepper on a serving spoon—no, that was just cruel. She cut it in half, then buried it under the vegetables and a slice of sausage. "Okay, here you go. Try this."

He slid it into his mouth and chewed. "It's good. Maybe not as—" His eyes went wide.

"You okay there, champ?"

"What did you put in this?" His voice sounded scratchy—kind of like something had singed his throat.

"It's not as good as my mom's, though, right?" Ryker gave his mom a side hug. "No one cooks like my momma."

"Thank you, baby."

"You've had her rice and beans," Ryker said to Xander.

A sheen of sweat broke out on Xander's face. He was

hunched over, one hand gripping the counter.

"No, wait, you weren't with us on that trip." Ryker was so clueless, he hadn't noticed what was happening with his friend. "You want to know her secret?" He cocked his head at Xander. "Hey, you okay, man? Why're you sweating?"

Color stained Xander's cheeks. "What'd you give me?" He headed over to the pantry and pulled out the jar of Carolina Reapers. "Are you kidding me?" He held it up for the camera.

"If you can't take the heat, you best get out of my kitchen." Lulu grinned.

Dropping the jar on the counter, he ran to the freezer and pulled out a tub of vanilla ice cream. Ryker tossed him a spoon, and Xander scooped out a huge chunk, shoving it in his mouth. He swallowed. "I can't believe you did this to me."

"Is he going to be all right?" the director asked.

"I'm fine." Xander waved it off. "It just caught me off guard." With a slow shake of his head, he gave her an admiring look.

"What did you do to that poor man?" Mrs. Olsen stopped working for a moment to watch the quarterback make a big show of pounding the counter and gasping.

"What'd she do?" Ryker asked.

"Want to find out?" Lulu said

"Damn, woman, no. I'm gonna stay right here with my momma."

"I guess you'll both stop messing with her now," Mrs. Olsen said. "Here, honey. This is my secret ingredient." She handed over a container of smoked cayenne pepper. "I'm not winning 'cause they're distracting you. I'm winning because I've been making this dish going on thirty years."

"You got a football in that big bag of yours?" Lulu asked her.

"No, why?"

"I think the boys should go outside and play catch, while the chefs get down to business."

Mrs. Olsen cracked up. "Oh, I like you, girl."

Lulu smiled, her gaze snagging on Xander, and the warmth and affection radiating off him nearly knocked her off her stride. But she stayed strong, focused on cooking.

Until he mouthed, *I like you, too.*

And then she dropped the wooden spoon and ducked behind the island to pick it up.

There was no playing it cool when that man looked at her like that.

After filming ended, Xander chatted with Ryker and his mom, the crew rolled in to start cleaning up, and Lulu discreetly slipped away.

Her back hurt from standing so long, and she wanted to wash off the heavy make-up and change out of the clothes saturated with the scents of oil and meat.

Before she could turn down the hallway, though, Abigail caught up with her. "When I walked in on you two this morning, I thought, Oh, no, the last thing we need is the leads getting involved. Trust me, it never goes well. But I just watched some of the footage, and the chemistry between you two is magic. He's got this sparkle in his eyes when he looks at you. I wish I hadn't sent out the reel yesterday, because today's footage is spectacular."

"I'm glad to hear it."

"And the hot pepper? It's TV gold. No one saw some-thing like that coming from you. You were the consummate professional, looking for an ingredient in the pantry and serving it to him with absolutely no expression whatsoever. And his reaction? Hilarious. I'm telling you, the ratings are going to go through the roof. We'll still have guests, but I think going forward we'll take the emphasis off the interviews and put it onto the two of you."

"That's good to hear, since tomorrow Xander and I will be competing against each other."

"Yes, I can't wait. We're making this up as we go along, but it's turning out even better than I'd imagined. I've told Xander, and I'll tell you—don't censor yourself at all. We can go back and edit anything out, do a voice-over…just keep riffing with each other." She followed Lulu's gaze to where Xander was standing, arms crossed over his chest, brow furrowed, looking all handsome and broody. Crew members had joined their group, talking with Ryker and Mrs. Olsen. "He's just got that elusive quality, doesn't he?"

"What do you mean?"

"He's mysterious, so you're dying to be the one he tells his secrets to."

True. She'd gotten some of those secrets, and she'd loved it.

"He's supremely confident, so you know he doesn't need you. He radiates this intense alpha masculinity…all those qualities strike something primal in us. We want to be the one he chooses."

Well, so much for feeling like we have some special connection.

Hello, pheromones.

"He also knows how to turn it on for the camera," Lulu said. "Which is the missing ingredient for me. I've never figured out how to fake it."

"Oh, don't shortchange yourself," the producer said.

"You're compelling in your own way. I'll send you some footage, you'll see what I mean. You're fascinating on camera."

"I am?"

"Absolutely. You're intense, passionate…sensual. It's riveting."

Warmth spread through her body. "Well, thank you. That's good to hear."

"And you handled all the interruptions like a champ. I couldn't be happier with the two of you."

They'd had to interrupt filming a dozen times. The food stylist had dashed out to spray the food with cooking oil to make it look fresh. The director called "cut" so often to get the right camera angle, Mrs. Olsen had grown annoyed.

"I'm used to working in busy kitchens," Lulu said. "There's always something that needs attention, so you just learn to multitask and get on with it."

Someone called Abigail's name. She glanced over and lifted a finger. *Hang on.* "All right. You have a good evening, and I'll see you in the morning." She got a few steps before she turned back around. "Oh, and someone's coming to pick up the leftover food for the Women's and Children's Shelter. Will one of you be here?"

Lulu was exhausted. She couldn't even imagine going out. "I'm in for the night."

"Smart girl." Abigail waved before taking off.

Only after she'd walked out the door did Lulu think to ask what time that person would get here. She'd better pack up the food before showering. It struck her, on her way back to the kitchen, that she could make herself a picnic to take to the ledge. *That's a great idea.*

It's so peaceful up there, and it's not too chilly this evening.

While she pulled leftover jambalaya out of the refrigerator, she watched Xander lead Ryker, Mrs. Olsen, and their entourage to the door.

He might not like social situations, but he drew people to him. He could easily meet someone tonight who'd be fun and wild, someone who'd sweep him away.

But that's not a reason for me to hook up with him.

So, she just had to let it go. Let *him* go.

Tearing a sheet of heavy-duty foil, she covered the tray of jambalaya. She didn't know how many lived at the shelter, but she looked around the kitchen to see what else she could give them. She'd made way too much rice, so she'd pack it up. Oh, and she'd bought a bag of yummy oatmeal and chocolate chunk cookies at the store—the kids would love that.

"Is that for the shelter?"

She glanced up to find Xander watching. He stood there like a badass—yet with an intense vulnerability that made her heart pound.

The man makes me stupid.

"You need help?" he asked.

But she wasn't stupid. She was an accomplished chef, so she snapped out of it. "It's no big deal. I've got it. You go have fun."

He studied her like he always did, like he was fishing for clues, angling beneath the surface to catch a glimmer of silver. And she would just die if he could sense how conflicted she was over him.

So, she rallied with a smile. "Where are you taking Mrs. Olsen?"

"I thought she'd get a kick out of Owl Hoot, so we've got a reservation at Wally's." He sealed the lid on the rice, drawing her attention to those big hands that kept her restless and aching at night, as she dreamed of how they'd feel on her body. "You have plans? Going to see your sisters?"

She dropped a bunch of bananas on top of the food in the bag. "Not tonight. Violet's been getting up every two hours, so Coco doesn't want company, and I'm—"

"All peopled out?"

Relaxing, she smiled. "Exactly. I'm just going to throw something together. Eat outside, watch the sunset."

"Yeah? On the patio?"

"Actually, there's a ledge a few miles up the mountain. It's got this amazing view of the valley."

"Is it safe to go alone?"

"Oh, sure. I grew up here, remember? Nothing to worry about."

"Hello?" A deep, gravelly voice filled the quiet bunkhouse.

It was like hurtling back in time, and it was so disorienting she whipped around, her elbow whacking a plastic storage container of rice off the counter. Xander gave her an odd look and picked it up.

Griffin James stood big and imposing in the entryway. "Oh, hey, Lulu. Good to see you." He gave her a chin nod. "I'm here to pick up food for the shelter."

The object of her teenage crush, Griffin was tall, muscular, and inked. Talk about mysterious. He wore it like a cloud of cologne. In high school, he'd walk down the hall and everyone would turn to watch him. He'd seemed older, wiser, and since he'd kept to himself, it had only reinforced the perception that he was beyond their years.

And yet he'd always been the one to put his body

between people fighting and ward off bullies with a menacing look.

She'd loved him with every fiber of her being.

And the whole time he'd been madly in love with Stella.

"Just putting it together now." They hadn't talked since the night of her rehearsal dinner.

But she wasn't a teenager anymore, and her days of being breathless around that man were long gone. "Come on in. I'm thinking what else to add."

Worn jeans and motorcycle boots, hair he didn't bother to tame and scruff that said he hadn't shaved in a couple of days made him look like a man who lived in his own zip code.

Xander moved out of the kitchen and crossed the room. "Alexander Wilder."

They shook hands. "Griffin." He looked between them, like he was trying to figure out if he'd interrupted something. And then he hooked a thumb over his shoulder. "I'll wait in the truck." And then he turned and strode outside.

"Is that *the* Griffin?" Xander asked.

She pulled boxes of unopened cereal out of the pantry. "Sure is."

"He still affects you."

The edge of jealousy in his tone surprised her, and she softened. "Not *that* way. I just didn't expect to see him."

"I wouldn't blame you. I might've gotten a little wood there myself."

She laughed. "Yeah, he's pretty striking."

"Not a big talker, that guy."

"He's always been quiet." There was something different about him, though. He seemed burdened.

"X-Man, let's go," Ryker called from the doorway.

Xander held up a finger. "You want to come with us?"

"Thank you, but I'm actually looking forward to my picnic."

Laura, the stylist, with her gorgeous mane of blonde hair, slim figure, and stylish clothes, dashed back into the house and approached Xander. "Hey, can you follow me home? My brother needs my car tonight." She seemed animated and excited. "I'll just ride with you to the restaurant. Reservation's at seven, so we'll be a little late, but they're going to order a pitcher of margaritas first thing anyway."

The way Laura's hand rested on Xander's forearm, as though she had that kind of familiarity with him, made Lulu's stomach twist. The stylist caught her watching and broke into a big smile. "Do you want to come with us? Reservation's for eight, but it's no problem to add another chair."

"I'm good, but thanks for asking."

"You sure? We haven't hung out yet, and I'd love to get to know you better."

That right there—knowing exactly what to say to people, having that perfect ease in social situations? That's what Lulu aspired to. "Me, too. I've got plans tonight, but let's for sure hang out another time."

"All right then." She beamed up at Xander. "Ready?"

He hesitated a moment too long, and Lulu knew he had to show Ryker's mom a good time—she'd flown out here from New Orleans—so she reassured him with a pat to his arm. "I got this." She added a jar of applesauce to the bag. "You guys go. Have fun."

He lingered another moment. "Okay." And then they took off.

And she had the strangest sensation, like the rope that tied them together grew tighter with each step he took away from her.

With one more look around to see what she could add, she lifted the bags and headed outside. While Xander's group stood around, deciding who would go in which car, he had his head tipped back, taking in the mountain. He caught her looking at him, but he didn't smile, didn't give her a single indication what he was thinking.

Boot soles crunched the dirt, and she saw Griffin approaching. "I put together as much as I could."

He took the bags from her. "Thanks."

"Sure." She walked with him to his truck. "So, how've you been?"

"Good." He carried the bags to the bed of the truck. "Anything breakable?"

"No. It's jambalaya, cereal, rice, some fruit." Should she bring up the elephant in the room? He and Stella had broken up seven years ago. *That's old history. Better leave it alone.*

He stowed the bags in the bed, then turned to face her. When he didn't say anything, her thoughts got jumbled, and she blurted, "Have you been in touch with Stella at all?"

Dammit. She got hot, flustered. *Of all the things to say.*

You'd think I'd learn after twenty-six years on this planet to just let other people fill the silence.

It hadn't even been a long stretch.

"Not at all. Okay, well, I better get going. I've got a few more pickups." Griffin got into the driver's seat.

Way to drive him away. "You still running the motor-cycle shop?"

"Yeah. Still doing repairs, but I've expanded. We're doing custom bikes now."

"That's perfect for you."

His confusion reminded her they'd never had any real conversations, so he'd never told her his dreams. That the only reason she knew about his interest in custom bikes was because she'd obsessed over him.

That the night she'd gone to proclaim her love, he'd been working on his first project. And he'd stopped to have a heated, fiery moment with Stella.

Tension vibrated between them, and she wished she'd never brought up her sister.

But he finally said, "It is." The engine roared to life, and he nodded. "See you tomorrow."

"Okay, bye." She waved like she was watching a parade march by.

Why am I so awkward?

Xander's car followed behind Griffin's, and the area once so lively went quiet.

She stood there for a few moments, watching the plume of dust from their tires as they drove down the road. She felt the chill in the air, heard the crickets. Some of the crew stood around a grill, the smell of woodsmoke in the air. None of them noticed her, so she turned back and went inside.

Times like this she wondered if she'd always be alone.

It was a possibility she had to accept.

And maybe that's okay. She had a career she loved, family she adored, and never enough hours in a day. She had a full life.

Maybe it was enough.

It might have to be.

Chapter Twelve

EARLIER IN THE DAY, MORE MAVERICKS HAD FLOWN in from Maui to meet with Cassian about summer camp. So, after dropping Mrs. Olsen off at the resort hotel, they'd met up with the guys at Wild Billy's.

Now, Xander stood at the bar, nursing a very nice scotch. Word had obviously gotten out that the team was in town, because the place was packed, noise level dialed up to a roar.

Someone bumped into him, sloshing his drink over the rim of his glass. He shifted away but got crammed up against Andre's sweaty back. Fuck, he wanted to get out of here.

He wondered if Lulu had come back from her hike. If he'd stayed in with her, they might be stretched out on the couch, maybe her feet in his lap. He'd like to stroke her smooth calves, slide his hands up her thighs. *Yeah*. Desire heated his bloodstream just like the whiskey.

He'd like to see her expression go all lusty and hot.

She'd be wild and passionate in bed, he just knew it. That's where she'd let go.

He wanted her hair brushing across his chest, as she straddled him. Her hands roaming, while she pressed open-mouthed kisses down his body. And at the thought of her sucking his cock into her hot, wet mouth, electric heat tore through him.

Holy shit. You've got to stop that. Turning toward the bar, he subtly adjusted himself.

Vaguely, he caught bits of the story Daryl was telling about a trip they'd taken—some wild adventure they'd had a few years ago on a yacht. Xander had never gone on those trips, so he tended to zone out when they talked about them. Plus, he'd never been much for alcohol, so drinking stories bored the crap out of him.

His mind wandered back to Lulu. It was a nice night —not as cold as it had been. She might be sitting on the patio, feet propped on the lip of the brick fire pit. Gazing up at the stairs, maybe hanging out with—

Griffin.

He straightened so fast, his stomach slammed into the bar.

He'd seen how flustered she'd gotten around him, watched her wave at him with a frantic look, like she hadn't wanted him to leave.

What if he'd come back? What if she'd *invited* him back?

Because she was quiet, watchful, sometimes it came off as shy. But she wasn't. She was bold and went after what she wanted. What if she'd texted Griffin to come share a bottle of wine with her and catch up?

She'd ask him those thought-provoking questions, get him to open up to her. Because when that happened, a bond formed. A trust. He'd feel close to her.

He'd start paying attention to her in a way he never had before.

And then he'd notice the slide of her silky bangs across her cheek. He'd catch the lazy trace of her fingertips on her arm—a caress he couldn't help but feel on his own skin.

And then he'd want her.

She'd cook for him—that's what she did. She fed people. She figured out what you loved, and she gave it to you. She made you feel special through food.

Fear sliced him open.

She'd wanted Griffin for years. But she hadn't had the confidence back then.

She had it now.

If she wanted Griffin today, she'd get him.

Laura returned from the bathroom and wedged herself between him and Ryker's back. "Okay, so my dad operates the gondola at the resort, and he's going to turn it on for us." She touched his wrist, standing close enough that her breasts pressed into his biceps. "You can bring four guys... or it can be just us?" She gazed up at him with hope shining in her eyes.

Lulu wouldn't want just one night with Griffin. She'd want the whole enchilada. And Griffin would have to be out of his mind to miss the chance to be with her.

What if the connection she'd always imagined with him turned out to be real?

What if Griffin was The One?

He can't be, because I am.

Then what the fuck are you doing here? Xander didn't want to stand around listening to drinking stories, and he didn't want to ride a gondola with anyone other than Lulu.

There was only one place he wanted to be, and he couldn't come up with a single reason why he wasn't there.

Because his life *wasn't* football. If he never got another contract, he'd still be breathing, eating, functioning. *Life* was about relationships.

It's about who you live it with.

It was about Lulu. And even if she didn't want to have sex with him yet, he still chose her.

Over anybody else, even if they were never anything more than friends, he wanted to be with her. "It sounds great, but I'm going to pass."

Laura's smile weakened. "You sure? It's a gorgeous view at night."

"I'm sure."

Because there was only one view that interested him.

Passing the bison preserve, Xander eased up on the accelerator.

Calm the fuck down.

But he couldn't. Because it was so clear.

So what if he wasn't going to stick around Calamity?

What did any of that matter when he had Lulu fucking Cavanaugh in his life? It all seemed so crazy, the way he'd convinced himself to keep his distance from the one person—seriously, the only person—he'd ever had a real connection with.

He turned down the lane to the bunkhouse.

Almost there.

Thank Christ.

He glanced at his phone. No response to the text he'd sent her on his way out of Wild Billy's. Fortunately,

Calamity was a small town, so he'd made it back in under fifteen minutes.

The RVs were lit up, and a group of people sat on logs framing a bonfire. One of the guys strummed a guitar.

The moment he parked, he ran into the bunkhouse. "Lulu?" But he felt the emptiness like a stone cavern, and he knew she wasn't there. Still, he headed to the patio. "Lu?" he called into the night.

Okay, so she was still at that ledge place. He pulled out his phone.

Xander: Where are you?

He waited, about to lose his mind, but she didn't respond.

Hearing laughter, he hurried out the door. He joined the group seated around the fire. "There's some ledge with a good view, not too far away. Anyone know how to get there?"

"I do." One of the interns got up and came over. "Want me to take you?" She set her hand on his arm.

His skin bristled—like it always did when a stranger touched him. How had he never taken it for what it was: proof that he was wired for one woman and one woman only? "No, that's okay. Is it far?"

"It's literally right up the mountain. Come on, I'll take you."

"I just need to know where it is." He wasn't showing up with another woman, not when he wanted Lulu to himself. "Is it easy to get to?"

"Totally. You know that path behind the bunkhouse? It leads to the base of the mountain. Once you get there, turn right and take the trail until you get to a clearing. You can't miss it."

"You looking for Lulu?" A woman came out of an RV

and joined them. "Last I saw, she was talking to that guy, the one from the shelter."

His pulse pounded. "Griffin?"

She shrugged. *I don't know his name.*

"Thanks." Frantic, he pocketed his keys and headed through the house and out the French doors. He checked his phone one more time. Nothing from her.

Xander: call me when you get this

What he really wanted to say was, *Don't hook up with Griffin.*

He's not the right guy for you.

He could imagine Lulu's expression when she said, *I used to have the biggest crush on you.* Her smile was contagious, so of course Griffin would warm up to her. He'd notice the way she tipped her head back when she laughed, all that glossy, dark hair tumbling, and he'd want to feel the silkiness in his fingers.

He jogged along the path. "Fuck." Why had he wasted so much time? Why had he convinced himself he only had a few weeks with her this summer?

He wanted more.

He would *always* need more with her.

Good thing she'd brought a blanket. The air had cooled as twilight settled over the valley. Lulu reached for another chocolate-covered strawberry, enjoying the way the lovely creamy, sweet flavor balanced out the acidity of the fruit.

Clusters of lights were just starting to glitter in the towns of Jackson to the right, Calamity right below, and the village on the left. Which meant it was time to pack up and head back down the mountain. Animals came out at night.

She'd had a lovely picnic. It couldn't have been more beautiful and peaceful, and if she'd managed to stop thinking about Xander—*is he having fun? Who's he hanging out with?*—she might've totally enjoyed herself.

As she sealed up the chicken pesto, she became aware of the distinct sound of someone running on the path. Not a jogger. Nope, this pace was frantic.

Which meant trouble. She threw off the blanket and stood, ready to either help someone or make a run for it.

But then she saw him.

Xander. He burst into the clearing, all wide-eyed and out of breath. "You're still here."

"What's wrong? Is everyone all right?" God, what if something was wrong with the baby?

"Fine." His chest heaved with exertion. "Everyone's fine."

"Then, what're you doing here?"

He gestured to the blanket and the multiple containers of food. "Are you with Griffin?"

Griffin? "No, I'm alone." *Obviously.* She gestured around her.

"I need to talk to you."

"You ran all the way up here to talk to me? God, I thought a mountain lion was chasing you."

"Do you still have feelings for him?"

"For *Griffin*? No, I already I told you. Why are you even asking?"

He lunged for her, hands gripping her upper arms, his gaze skimming over her features, as if she were precious to him. "The thought of you being here with him drove me crazy."

"Why?" she whispered. *What's happening right now?*

"Because I want to be with you." He pressed his mouth to hers, softly, gently. "Only you."

And then he kissed her.

It was soft, sweet, but his body was tight with restraint. She wanted him—God, did she want him—but her instincts were screaming. Because she knew, unless he truly let go, pushed through everything that held him back—she'd never really have him. Not all the way.

And she didn't want the superficial connection he'd had with his exes.

Her gut told her she needed to matter to him so much that he broke.

And maybe that would only happen if she broke with him. *Maybe that's been the problem all along. Me, holding back, waiting to be absolutely certain how a man feels about me.*

Instead of taking a leap of faith and kissing him back.

Clasping her hands around his neck, body pressed up against his, she opened her heart, her soul, and let herself fall into him. And it was…dizzying.

He licked into her mouth, tasting, testing, his hands caressing her bare arms. Everything about him was tentative, careful, and it wasn't nearly enough.

"What part of me do you want?" Breathless, she lowered her forehead to his chest. "Because if you just want my body for a night or two or three, that's just…I mean, if you know me at all, you have to know that won't work for me."

"I don't want another serious relationship. I want to finally start my career in football. I want my shoulder to heal so completely it's like it never happened."

Okay, nothing he wanted had anything to do with her. Crushed, she took a step back.

But he didn't let her go. He reached around to her ass. "But here's what I figured out. None of the things I've been chasing mean anything compared to this." He squeezed.

"My ass?"

He laughed. "No, *us*. Whatever I thought mattered... it all changed when I met you. And now...I *have* to be with you. I didn't want another relationship because neither of the ones I've had was right. This is different. We fit." He grew frustrated. "I realized tonight I could be a franchise player, reach all my goals, and it would be a hollow victory because the quality of my life—the stuff that matters—doesn't come from my career. It comes from talking to you, spending time with you. Nothing feels better than being with you."

She flung herself against him, lifting up on her toes to reach his mouth. His kiss was hot, urgent, and sent her senses spiraling. She thought she might melt from the heat of his desire, and when she whimpered, he bent his knees, lifted her, and carried her to the blanket.

"You want this? Us?" His eyes were wild.

"More than anything."

And then it happened. He broke. Abruptly, he lowered her onto the ground, and his kiss turned desperate, savage, his cock grinding against her stomach. Aching for him, she tilted her hips to notch him right where she needed him most.

Yanking up her T-shirt, he pulled it over her head. Then, he sat back on his heels, taking her in, before pressing a hand over her heart. "You're mine." He brought it to his chest. "You understand?"

She nodded, so out of her mind with want and need she couldn't speak.

"Gotta taste you." He jerked down the cup of her bra and sucked her nipple into his mouth.

She moaned at the wild sensations coursing through her, scraping her fingernails through his hair, and holding him close. Oh, God, she never wanted this moment to end. She was on fire.

Reaching behind her, he unclasped her bra, roughly jerked it off her arms, and let it drop. Filling his hands with her breasts, he said, "Jesus." His voice sounded rough, almost choked up. "Look at you. You're beautiful." He pushed them together, licking first one nipple, and then the other.

Pressing kisses down her stomach, he reached for the waistband of her leggings and tugged them off. She lifted her hips, so he could free her of her clothing.

Just as he lowered between her legs, she said, "Shirt off." He gave her a look so heated, blood roared in her ears. He bunched the material at the back of his neck and yanked it over his head, exposing those broad, strong shoulders.

Then, he pushed her thighs open, his gaze filled with lust. Kissing her inner thigh, he licked between her legs, and that first swipe of his tongue against her clit made her sizzle. She opened wider for him, squirming as he pressed open-mouth kisses that were so lusty, so hungry, she found herself grabbing fistfuls of his hair.

"*Xander.*"

All those delicious sensations streaming through her coalesced, spinning her so fast she flew right out of her body, becoming nothing but lust, desire, and a hunger so intense she grew frantic with it.

The current of energy flooding her made her tremble, as sensations heightened. She could tell it was going to be bigger than any climax she'd ever had. She released his hair to clutch the blanket, just before bursting into a million fiery stars.

For long moments, she coasted across a sky of euphoria.

By the time she came back into her body, he was gazing at her with so much reverence and wonder, she nearly cried.

He kissed her mouth with pure possession. "Gotta have you."

She didn't think she'd ever been happier than this moment. Getting up on her knees, she unbuckled his belt and yanked down his jeans. His erection sprang free, so hard it hit his stomach. Grasping him, she licked up one side and swirled her tongue around the head.

With a hiss, his big hand sifted through her hair. "Not gonna last long." He watched her through half-lidded eyes.

She sucked him into her mouth, the tip of her tongue flicking.

Too soon, he pulled out with a groan. "Lay back down." Just as he lined himself up, he groaned. "I don't have a condom."

"I'm on the pill."

His chin jerked up. "I haven't been with anybody in a long time, and I got tested before the playoffs."

"Oh, this is going to be good."

His lustful expression made it hard to be still. "Everything with you is good." Slowly, he slid inside, watching her expression as he filled her. When he bottomed out, his eyelids fluttered closed. "Jesus. Never felt anything like it."

She grew desperate, restless, and she wiggled her hips to encourage him.

He just smiled. "Hang on. Give me a second. We're never gonna have another first time."

Joy burst in her chest. She kissed this beautiful, perfect man, and he pulled out, slamming back into her. And then he took her with hard, powerful thrusts.

"So fucking hot…" He had his mouth at her ear. "Feels so good…want you, want you so bad."

His body grew hot, his back went damp, and he shifted the angle so his cock powered over her sweet spot. A flash fire tore across her skin, and her neck arched. "*Yes*. God. Oh, my God."

With a punishing grip, he rammed into her again and again, those powerful arms trembling. And then he slammed in hard, hips twisting, as he grunted and held his body tightly to hers. He ground against her, frantic.

When he finished, his shoulders sagged, his breath hot on her neck. "Mine."

Chapter Thirteen

Lulu tried not to watch him. They were being filmed, for God's sake. She needed to pay attention.

But it wasn't easy.

Powerful arms crossed over his muscular chest, Xander stood listening intently to the greenhouse manager. His blonde hair had grown out some since Maui, and she liked it a little windswept. He looked more roguish…more hot surfer.

Last night, after losing their minds at the ledge, they'd gone back to the bunkhouse and done it all over again. She'd explored every inch of that golden skin and the hard planes of his chest, gripped the taut globes of his ass. *Gah.* He was so hot. Passionate, sweet, and just so *sexual.*

Crap.

I'm totally staring.

Stop it.

The whole day, though, he'd been touching her. As they'd talked to vendors, he'd hold her hand behind their backs. When the filming stopped so the producer and photographer could discuss a shot, he'd cup her neck and give her secret kisses.

Best day ever.

They'd started at the farmers market early this morning, where she'd wound up buying so many vegetables, baked goods, and jars of jam that she'd needed a wagon to get it all to the van. She had tons of stuff to donate to the shelter.

Afterwards, the whole crew had a lovely picnic under the shade of a tree at the fairgrounds, and while she'd had to endure sitting at the other end of the table and watching everyone flirt with the handsome, broody quarterback, she'd gotten to know people a little better.

Next stop, they'd visited Delilah Lua's hydroponic farm, which sat at the edge of the Bowie property, right along Highway 191. Inside the three-story glass building, rows of vertical conveyor belts rotated plants that grew in nutrient-filled water.

After a lengthy tour, they'd checked out the store, where Lulu had bought infused vinegars, sausages, jams, and bath and body products all made by local artisans.

Now, they'd just explored the massive greenhouses Delilah had recently built.

"When she first moved here, she was frustrated by the lack of produce." The manager gestured to the rows of peach and pear trees. "Delilah visited one of the area's hydroponic farms and liked it so much she decided to build one of her own. She sells to restaurants and grocers all around the valley, so now we have fresh produce year-round in Jackson Hole."

"This is amazing." Lulu had never seen anything like it. *An indoor orchard—imagine that.* "I've been away seven years, and I can't believe the changes here." Thanks to the billionaires and celebrities that lived in the area, Calamity had always been cutting edge, but this kind of innovation brought the small mountain town to a new level.

And the possibilities for a chef—well, it just changed the whole landscape.

"*Hey.*" Beside her, Xander's arm flew up, batting at something. "What the—" He spun around, both hands slicing the air like he was in a karate tournament. "Shit."

"Are you okay?" Lulu asked. "What's wrong?"

He did this insane dance, hopping on one foot, nearly losing his balance, and she had no idea what was going on until she spotted the bee dive-bombing him.

Oh, wait. There were two—no, three bees.

Laughing, she shook her head. "I guess that answers my question on how you handle pollination."

"Why are they attacking me?" Xander arced around in a balletic move.

The manager looked concerned. "Are you allergic?"

"What? No. Not that I know of." He dropped to a squat. "What the hell?"

Laughing so hard she had tears in her eyes, Lulu swatted at the bees. The moment she remembered the filming, she glanced to the camera operators…yep, all three were trained on him. "All right, come on, let's get out of here." She got a hold of his arm, but he wrenched it free, batting at his ear. "Oh, my God, I can't even say you're overreacting, because they're absolutely in love with you."

"They're harmless," the manager said. "Honestly, they're alfalfa leafcutter bees, and they're not aggressive at all."

"No?" He gave her an exasperated look. "Not at all?" He swooped back and spun. "Jesus, why me?"

Lulu laughed. "Because of your sweet, sweet nectar."

He paused long enough to hold her gaze, eyes lit with joy. "You are so going to get it later."

"Will I, though? Because you're just not all that intimidating right now."

The camera operator had one hand on his knee, bent forward, as he laughed too hard to film.

Xander ducked and cut sideways, agile and graceful.

"Are you wearing cologne?" the manager asked.

"No. Jesus, no."

Lulu grabbed his arm and tugged. "How about I do it with you, so you don't look so weird?" She led the way out of the greenhouse, doing a duck and weave kind of dance, and everyone followed, cracking up.

Once in the sunlight, Xander calmed down. "What the hell was that about?"

Lulu cupped his cheek. "Everybody loves you. You should be used to it by now."

"I heard this buzzing right in my ear. Freaked me out."

"Apparently, even bees like the strong, silent type."

The manager shut the door and approached him. She leaned in for a sniff. "Maybe it's the laundry detergent. What brand do you use?"

"Oh, trust me, it's just *him*," Lulu said. "The pheromones are strong on this one."

He scowled at her, while answering the manager. "I don't know. Whatever's in the bunkhouse."

"It's very fragrant."

"Aw," Lulu said. "They thought you were a pretty flower. They wanted to pollinate with you."

He ran his fingers through his hair and shuddered. Finally noticing the cameras, he pointed a finger at them. "You're not airing that."

"Sure they are," Lulu said.

He cut her a look, and the whole world fell away. No more mountain backdrop, no sage meadow, no parking lot or Highway 191. It was just the two of them, grinning at each other so big and wide she felt like she could topple in and get swallowed whole.

As the laughter settled down, the producer said, "We might have to use some of it. It was good stuff."

"At least you looked good doing it," the camera operator said.

"Hey, maybe you'll get a gig on *Dancing with the Stars*. In fact, that could be your audition reel," Lulu said.

"We done here?" someone asked.

"No, we still have the segment with Delilah," the director said.

As they talked, Xander reached for Lulu and drew her away from the group. "You have any idea how hard it's been not to kiss you today?"

"We've snuck some in."

"That's not the kind I'm talking about." With a quick glance to make sure the others weren't looking, he hauled her up against him and pressed a hot, wet kiss on her mouth. It was…exhilarating, exciting, and just so *beautiful*. To be wanted in a way that matched her own needs…to be so together in this with him…it just hit her so hard. Resting her forehead against his chin, she let out a shaky sigh.

He lowered his mouth to her ear, and right when she thought he was going to say something sexy, he whispered, "They were *bees*."

She laughed. "I know. It was terrifying."

"I was under *attack*."

"Under attack by the great alfalfa bee?"

"It wasn't a single bee. It was a swarm."

"Hey, guys," the director called. "Since we ran out of the greenhouse a little early, Delilah's going to meet us out here." He motioned for the camera operator to start filming. "Here she comes now."

"Everything all right?" Delilah, the stunning, bubbly chef approached with a basket in either hand.

"Hey, Delilah." The manager gestured to the visitors. "This is Lulu Cavanaugh and Alexander Wilder, hosts of *The Gridiron Grillers*."

Every time Lulu heard that title, she died a little inside. She'd presented a dozen other ideas, but none had taken. "So nice to meet you, Delilah."

"Good to see you again," Xander said.

"Hey, X-Man." Delilah set her baskets down. "So, what do you think of my indoor farm?"

"It's amazing," Lulu said. "I remember when Callie Bell's mom moved the farmers market into the old Town Hall for the winter months. That was a really big thing for us here, since our growing season's only four months. But this…" She gestured to the buildings. "I mean, the possibilities are so exciting."

"Did you get to taste anything from the hydroponic farm?" Delilah asked.

"We did, and I bought a ton of stuff to take home."

"Oh, good. A lot of people say the produce doesn't taste the same, that without soil it loses its flavor. But it's not true. It's all about the nutrients you add to the water." She lifted the baskets. "How about a taste test?"

"What've you got there?" Xander asked.

"Oh, I just put together a few things. Ten things, to be exact." She looked from one to the other with a mischievous grin. "Ten *mystery* ingredients." The woman was adorable.

"Why do I get the feeling you're pulling a *Chopped* on us?" Lulu waved a hand between her and Xander.

"Because I am. You guys up for it?"

"Oh, I don't know, Xander's just suffered a huge *trauma*. I'm not sure he's up to the challenge."

Xander snatched a basket out of Delilah's hand. "Are we going to stand here chatting or are we going to cook?"

Back in the bunkhouse, Lulu stood at her end of the island throwing Xander a challenging look. *You ready for me to beat your ass?*

He cupped a hand and gave her a *Bring it* gesture.

The glimmer in her eyes made him frown. He knew she was up so something.

He was right, and she couldn't wait.

"All right you two," Delilah said. "Go ahead and open your baskets."

Ignoring the cameras, the boom mic, and the bright lights, Lulu quickly scanned the contents, her mind going to work.

Delilah stood between them, calling out the ingredients that would be highlighted on the screen for the viewers. "You've got elk sausage, bosc pears, black cherry balsamic vinegar—"

"Whoa." Xander jumped back, arms swinging. He did another of his comical yet controlled dances, and the entire crew cracked up. With a dramatic sigh, he looked right into the camera. "They stuck a bee in my basket." He cut Lulu a look. "Funny."

She laughed. "Clock's ticking. Better get to work."

He shook his head. "I don't know how you pulled it off, but I'm guessing it happened when you 'forgot' your phone."

She'd left him waiting in the van as she'd run back into the greenhouse. The manager had captured a bee in a mason jar for her. "I set my phone down, but I must've gotten distracted by your spontaneous breakdancing routine. You've got some moves."

He smirked. "Right. Of course, this has nothing to do with the fact that I drank some of your special coffee the other morning."

"Did *you* think to get those beans when you were in Maui? No? Oh, that's right. *I'm* the one who made a special trip to Kona to get them."

"One cup."

"Which, if you do the math, means one cup less for me. So, of course, I had to hide them." She shook her head. "It's like living with three sisters all over again."

He snorted. "That was a clever hiding spot you found in the media center."

"Wha—how did you know that?"

"Because I smell them every time I walk in the door. Second drawer, by the way. My olfactory skills are on point." He chuckled. "It's cute how she thinks I can't smell coffee beans."

"Maybe you should use your olfactory skills right now." She tipped her chin toward his end of the island. "How's it going over there? You need to make a call or something? I'm assuming your mommy's standing by?"

Someone on the crew chuckled.

"Knowing my mom, she's definitely watching." He looked into the camera and waved. "Hi, Mom. But, no, I'm good. I got this. You should worry about yourself over there. You probably forgot that Delilah only gave us an hour, and you've spent the first ten minutes of it trying to defend hiding coffee beans. Meanwhile, I've got a nice roux going."

"Roux, huh? Did you read that word off the little cheat sheet written on the palm of your hand? Is that how you got through Stanford?" She picked fresh herbs from the potted plants.

"If my mom were here, she'd probably show you my diploma. She put a yellow highlighter through the part that says *magna cum laude*." He shrugged. "I'm a bit of an overachiever."

"Couldn't quite hit suma, huh?"

"Well, not with the whole Heisman thing junior year."

Lulu couldn't hold back her laughter.

"Given the way you took down Ryker's mom, though," Xander said. "I probably *should* be scared. You're ruthless."

"I'm in it to win it. And, of course, it doesn't hurt that *my* mom hung my Diplôme de Cuisine *and* Diplôme de Patisserie on the wall of her office." She made sure to haul out her very best French accent.

He raised his brows. *Impressive.* But then waved a hand. "Yeah, still not scared. Got anything else?"

"Just skills. Lots and lots of skills." Realizing his techniques to distract her were working, she got busy. "Okay, Man-Who-Brings-the-Bees-to-the-Yard. Let's leave it to Delilah to decide who's the better chef. No need to rely on petty distractions."

"Says the woman who went to the trouble to catch a bee and put it in my basket."

"Worth it. Did you hear yourself squeal?" She looked to the crew. "Hey, can we get a replay of his dance moves at the farm? That'd be way more entertaining than watching him chop an onion." She fake-cringed. "His knife skills need some work."

"You like my moves, huh?" He shrugged his brow.

"Oh, yeah." She smiled, casting a glance at him at the same moment he looked at her. Their gazes connected, and electricity arced between them. She felt the zap in her heart.

But as much as it thrilled her, it scared the crap out of her.

Because she wanted a future with this man more than anything she'd ever wanted. But she couldn't see it.

As soon as either one of them got the call they were waiting for, they'd be gone, back to their real lives.

And she'd have nothing left of him but the photographs spread across social media of his exciting life far away from her.

"Time's up," Delilah said. "Step away from the counter."

Lulu had already finished. She was just swiping the spots of sauce off her white plates.

"Pretty sure your clock's broken," Xander said. "That was the fastest sixty minutes of my life."

"Less time dancing, more time cooking," Lulu said.

"It was a *bee*."

"Okay, you two." Delilah came around the island. "Let's see what you've come up with. We'll start with Lulu." She gestured to the plate. "What have you made for me?"

"I wanted to celebrate the bounty of vegetables and herbs from your farm—"

"Suck-up," Xander muttered.

Crew members chuckled, but Lulu didn't miss a beat. "So, I prepared an Italian stew called ciambotta." With a saucy grin to Xander, she said, "In my spare time, I also whipped up bruschetta, since cooking those gorgeous tomatoes would've been a crime."

Xander peered into his dish and made a comical expression of *Uh oh.*

"And I whipped up a quick little fruit compote with fresh ginger, mint, a splash of brandy, and lemon zest."

"That's it." Xander untied his apron and threw it down. "I concede." He stalked over to them, picked up a bruschetta, and popped the whole thing in his mouth.

"She doesn't get extra points for the amuse-bouche or the dessert, so hang on and let me taste everything." Delilah dipped a spoon into the stew. "Oh, man. That's good." Grabbing a clean one, she tasted the compote. "Are you kidding me with this? I don't even have words for the perfection of your cooking, the marriage of flavors…the *vividness.*"

"Thank you." Still, after all these years, hearing those words, watching that dreamy expression…nothing felt as satisfying as the way people responded to her food.

"Can you guys go to commercial break or something so I can sit here and eat every single bite?" Delilah said. "No one needs to watch me fall into a food coma."

"Or…you could try my dish. Before the greens wilt and the show's over." Xander had the most adorable put-out expression—but the glint in his eyes revealed his sense of humor.

"I suppose." Delilah said it on a sigh.

"You know, this isn't very professional." Xander wagged a finger between the two women. "This chef bonding thing."

Even Lulu laughed. There was something so appealing about him. He knew he was on Lulu's turf, and he was just here to have fun. And it was utterly charming.

"Okay, X-Man, what've you got for me?" Delilah asked.

Using his nickname was intentional, meant to be a constant reminder why the show was named *The Gridiron Grillers*.

"I made a charred okra and corn salad with spicy sausage, and a pear and rosemary vinaigrette."

"What's that now?" Lulu headed over, genuinely intrigued. "Pear and what?"

Xander turned his back to her. "This is between me and Delilah. You had your turn."

Lulu made a *gimme* motion with her hand, and Delilah reached around him to pass the salad over. Lulu took a bite. "Are you kidding me? You literally get paid to play catch with your buddies, and you produce this? Pear and rosemary vinaigrette?" She thrust the plate back to Delilah, giving Xander a glare. "Who are you, really?"

He grinned. "I'm just a ball player, standing in front of a judge, asking her to love his dish."

"You did not just rom-com me," Lulu muttered. "He's literally, like, the perfect man."

He grinned at her, a look so intense, so filled with affection, she felt happiness spill out of her heart and tumble right down to the soles of her feet. Her whole body tingled.

Taking the plate back, Delilah dug in and took a bite. "Mm. Mm, mm, mm. This is fantastic." She looked between them. "You two are unbelievable. One is a traditional chef, who understands the chemistry and measures out each ingredient, and the other's intuitive. He just wings it. And both of these dishes are surprising and layered and absolutely delicious. Honestly, I'd serve both in my restaurant. Which one of you's looking for a job?"

"Actually, we both are," Xander said.

Again, laughter filled the kitchen, but the comment sliced right through her.

Oh, no.

Oh, Xander.

He'd heard from the Mavericks. She just knew it, because while he maintained his smile, she could see fear hidden in his eyes.

They didn't offer him a contract.

He's got to be gutted.

She started for him, but they were on-air, and she couldn't do that. In fact, she needed to get the focus off his comment. "But which one is *obviously* better? I mean, the clear winner?"

"They're both completely different, but equally complex," Delilah said.

"That's not how this show works," Lulu said in a teasing tone.

Delilah laughed. "Hey, this is Calamity, the land of outlaws. We make our own rules."

"But if you had to give one of them an award…?"

Xander cracked up. "Just give it to her. She obviously needs the feedback more than I do." He looked into a camera and mouthed, *Fragile ego*.

"Okay, okay," Delilah said. "Give me a minute. I have to taste them again. And by taste, I mean lick these plates clean."

"You want to taste mine?" Lulu asked Xander.

"Nuh uh." Delilah wrapped an arm around the plate. "I'm the judge. I get all the food."

Lulu shrugged. "I just feel like when I win, he should know why. You know? Just so I won't have to listen to him crying softly into his pillow tonight."

"I'm not going to *cry*," Xander said. "But if I did cry, it wouldn't be *softly*."

"Yeah, true. You're more of a wailer. Remember the Carolina Reaper I gave him the other day? Right after they turned off the cameras, he ran into his room, shut the door, and let out the kind of shriek you only hear in slasher flicks."

"Well, that happens when your brain bleeds out through your eyes." He pretended to be annoyed.

"Amateur."

"Okay." Unable to stop laughing, Delilah waved her hands to shut them up. "Let me take one more bite of each before I announce the winner."

In that moment, Lulu didn't think she could be happier. She'd been so disappointed to lose *The Wild West Woman* cooking show and hadn't been sold on the new format. But now—just based on their chemistry, their repartee—it had become something she could be proud of.

And it's so much more fun than a solo gig.

A different side of her personality had come out thanks to Xander—and the production company liked it.

Happiness spread through her, making her warm and...full.

Hidden by the island, Xander reached for her hand and gave it a squeeze. Her heart filled to bursting.

She wanted to see that look in his eyes—playful, affectionate, with a sizzling amount of lust—forever.

She never wanted this to end.

But he was a free agent now, and she didn't know what

the next step would be for him. All she knew was that football had to come first.

Xander would do whatever it took to find his home in the NFL.

This show would fall to the bottom of his priorities.

And so will I.

Chapter Fourteen

WITH THE PHONE AT HIS EAR, XANDER SAT ON THE edge of the mattress, bare feet planted in the thick blue carpet.

"It's clear they consulted with their physical therapists and orthopedic surgeons," his agent said. "And there just wasn't enough support behind the idea that the training facility could accomplish a 'miracle.'"

"But they didn't talk to my team here in Calamity, which is the point, isn't it?" Xander asked. "This is ground-breaking treatment. That means no one else knows what it can do."

"Believe me, I told them that. I also brought up your performance during the play offs. I told them they were making a huge mistake."

"Doesn't matter. I'm damaged goods. I get it." *I don't want to be a backup anyway.*

But now what?

Who's going to sign a twenty-six-year old quarterback with two shoulder injuries?

Jesus, is there any hope here at all?

"It's bullshit, but I'll tell you this. You're wasted on the Mavericks."

Ah, Christ. Here it comes. He didn't want to hear it. Not another word. It was the same spiel he'd heard from everyone for five years.

"You're a fucking phenom. You proved it in the play-offs, and you're going to be a franchise player. You're better than your dad, your brothers…you're better than Cassian."

"Yeah, okay. I've got to get back to the set." *Liar.* The moment they'd finished filming, Xander had locked himself in his room to return his agent's call.

"You know how I thought this show was the wrong move? Well, I'm damn glad you didn't listen to me. It's exactly the kind of exposure you need. Hey, when are you filming at the training center?"

"Day after tomorrow." But the real question was, *When will it air?* Training camp started next month.

A knock at the door got him off the bed. He hoped like hell it was the one face he wanted to see.

Yes. Those warm hazel eyes looked up at him with warmth and kindness. *She knows.*

She saw the phone and started to leave, but he reached for her and pulled her in. Once she entered, he closed and locked the door.

He'd missed everything his agent had said the last few minutes, but he didn't care. Because it was all noise. Until a coach wanted him to try out with his team, there was nothing to talk about. "Hey, Niall. Let's pick this up later. I've got to go."

"Sure, okay. I'm on this, X-Man. But listen to me. You focus on your shoulder and leave the other stuff to me. I guarantee you'll by playing by July."

After he disconnected, he hurled himself onto the bed.

"Hey."

"You heard from the Mavericks."

Leaning against the headboard, he stretched out. "Yep."

"You want to talk about it?"

"Nope."

She sat on the mattress. "How can I make you feel better?"

"Show me your tits."

She acted all demure. "I feel so objectified." And then she grinned, pulled her shirt off, and sent it sailing.

He'd only been teasing—he hadn't wanted to sink back into the sense of hopelessness—but she'd just rolled with it, and now the sight of those plump breasts in a pink lacy bra set his body humming with interest. He lifted an arm, bent it behind his head, and settled in for the show.

As she crawled toward him, she put an extra bounce in each move. When she reached him, she sat back on her heels and unclasped her bra. Pulling down the straps, she shimmied her shoulders, and the bra dropped off, a pink scrap of lace set against the white duvet.

"You're a tease." He gave his dick a squeeze. "Go on."

Straddling his thighs, she cupped her breasts and pushed them together, creating deep cleavage, and then she jiggled her lush mounds. "You good now?"

He chuckled. Man, she made everything better. "No. All you've done is create a new problem." He glanced at the throbbing bulge in his jeans.

"Oh, yeah. That's a *big* problem." Slowly, she popped the button, then slid the zipper down. Watching his reaction, she pushed under the waistband of his boxer briefs, only just grazing his cock. With her other hand, she shoved up his shirt.

Fuck, he needed more. But he loved the way his body got her all worked up, loved the way she teased him. Everything she did got his pulse pounding.

Leaning over, ass in the air, she braced her hands on either side of his hips as she licked the length of him. "And a hard one, too." She gripped him in her warm hand and jerked him.

The pressure felt so good, he arched off the bed. When she sucked him into her hot mouth, he grunted, drawing up his knees to knock her over. She toppled onto his chest, her hair all tousled, lips parted. "What're you going to do about it?" he asked.

She planted her hands at either side of his head and brushed her nose across his cheek, her breath a warm gush at his ear. "I could fuck you."

Hearing those words come out of that sexy mouth turned him wild. He jackknifed up, gripping her arms and hauling her up to the pillow. As he rolled off the bed and pulled down his pants, she undressed in record time.

Naked, he flopped back onto the mattress. "Get on me."

Once she'd settled on his thighs, she let her hands wander over his chest. Her fingers fanned out, as she caressed him. "You're a very sexy man." She stretched forward, her breasts bouncing and making him unbearably hard. One hand pumping his cock, she kissed him, slow, sexy, and full of dirty promises.

His skin tightened, and he went hot all over. *Game over.* "Come here." He ran his hands down her back, smoothing over the curve of her ass. Grabbing her cheeks, he squeezed, spreading her open for him. "I've never wanted anyone the way I want you."

She sucked in a sharp breath and ground herself all over his cock.

"I'm gonna fuck you so hard." He lined up his cock and nudged into that hot, slick cleft. "You ready for me?"

Eyes glazed, she pushed back onto him, hips restless, and he knew that was the only answer he was going to get. He slid inside, every single one of his nerve endings lighting up.

"Oh." She sat up, shifting until she got him in deep. Her eyelids fluttered closed, and he started moving her, lifting her and slamming her down in rhythm with the punch of his hips.

Consumed by her fresh peach scent, her silky hair gleaming in the late afternoon light, her big, round breasts bouncing, and his cock sheathed in her slick heat—he felt his climax bearing down on him. He was so wound up, so wild, he flipped her over, pushed open her legs with his knees, and thrust deep. She gasped, looking lust-drenched and desperate for more.

"Jesus, Lu. *Fuck*."

Reaching behind her for the headboard, she pressed her palms flat and fucked him right back. Their skin slapped, their bodies grew damp, and a flush spread across her chest, up her neck, and pinkened her cheeks.

His pulse pounded, his spine tingled. "You make me crazy."

With her dark hair spilled across the white pillowcase, she lifted her hips off the mattress and gasped.

She was coming. Already. He shifted, dragging across her clit, and her eyelids popped open. "Xander." She slammed up hard against him, grinding her hips and crying out.

"You're the sexiest woman I've ever seen in my life."

Not a chance could he last, not with this goddess writhing on his cock. He reached for her sensitive bud, and a hit of satisfaction shot through him when her body jerked at his touch.

As he swirled her honey all around the sensitive nub, pleasure saturated her features, and that was it. He couldn't hold back the torrent of lust crashing through him. With the first shot, he threw his head back, his body went rigid, and he gripped her hips tightly to power into her in short, fast bursts. "Fuck. Fuck. *Fuck*." He nearly blacked out from the intensity of his climax. Slowing his thrusts, he gently pulled out and collapsed next to her. He stroked the hair off her face, as this surge of affection swelled, rose, and crashed over him.

She let out a contented sigh, fingertips caressing his forearm. "Did I make you feel better?"

"I just wanted to see your tits." Chuckling, he tucked his face into her neck. "So, I'd say you went above and beyond."

He didn't know what would happen tomorrow or next month or a year from now.

But in that moment…he had everything he needed.

"Cut." The director stepped forward. "We've got to make a quick switcheroo."

Lulu stepped aside, while the food stylist replaced plates of real food with fake. The pale yellow and flaky egg yolks now looked vibrant, thanks to a creation of mango and orange.

Lulu was in awe of how real it looked. "Everything

you do is magic. I would never know that's not an egg yolk."

"Ah, thank you. I love my job." The woman dashed off to make another replacement, returning with sausage patties made out of oatmeal and cocoa powder.

A wall of heat warmed her side, and she reached for Xander's hand. She wanted to lean back against him, feel his arm wrap around her waist. She wondered if her skin glowed with all the desire streaming through her.

"Okay," the stylist said. "All set."

Everyone went back to their places, and the director said, "Let's pick up right where you left off. And…action."

"I stayed at the Inn for a couple of nights," Xander said. "And I can tell you it was some of the best food I've had in a long time."

"Yeah, Chef Jonny's the best." She paused for impact. "Such a shame he can't make it today."

Xander stilled. She'd gone off-script.

She'd taken a risk with this surprise, and she hoped he wouldn't be pissed at her.

"What's going on?" he asked.

"A man with seven kids and a busy restaurant…when isn't something going on? But actually, he's fine. We just have a surprise guest for you."

"A surprise?" He sounded confused. "For me?"

She checked out his wary expression. "Somebody doesn't like surprises."

"When you have two older brothers who get off on torturing you, it has a way of keeping you on your guard."

She caught Abigail's hand circling. *Keep talking*.

"What's the worst thing they ever did?" Lulu asked.

"You want me to pick *one*?" He shook his head. *Not possible*. "I will say, the one that sticks out, was when they

210

finally told me I could join their club. They'd built a fort in our backyard and made a sign that said, *You must be this tall to enter.*"

"Let me guess, it was exactly an inch taller than you."

"You're a quick study."

She raised her fingers. "Three sisters."

"So, anyhow, the day finally came when they said I could join. And the price for entry? Snacks. I thought, *I can do that.* I wanted to impress them, so I bagged up everything I could find in the pantry. Chips, pretzels, granola bars, you name it. I dumped it all in my wagon and raced over there—"

"How old were you?"

"Six. So, I get there, out of breath, pumped to finally be included, only to find the place is empty. They'd moved their fort somewhere else."

"Now, hang on a second." His oldest brother came sauntering out of the hallway.

"Matt?" Xander rounded the island to greet him. They hugged, slapping each other's backs. "What're you doing here?" He spun around to Lulu. "*He's* not our guest, is he? He burns frozen waffles."

She glanced toward the hallway, where Scottie and his mom came out.

"What the—" He jogged toward his mom, lifting her off the floor and hugging her.

If Lulu hadn't already been sure about her feelings for him, it would've happened right then. What was sexier than a man who loved his mom?

"You're the guest?" He set her down.

"Sure am," his mom said.

"Oh, man." He covered his face with a hand. "I don't stand a chance."

"I'm not so sure about that." A petite woman with a blonde bob and earthy style, his mom gazed up at him with love and good humor. "You're a pretty good chef yourself."

As he drew his other brother in for a hug, he kept his focus on his mom. "Tell me we're making Treasures of the Sea?" he asked her. "'Cause that's my only hope."

"You don't know your co-host very well, do you?" His mom smiled at Lulu. "She's the one who chose the dish."

"Awesome." He turned to his brothers. "Can't believe you guys are here."

"Yeah, and a good thing, too," Scottie said. "We can defend our honor."

Their mom rolled her eyes. "You can't defend a story like that. You two were old enough to know better." She wrapped an arm around Xander's waist. "I'm sorry they hurt you, sweet boy."

"And there it is," Scottie said. "Favoritism at its finest."

"I don't have a favorite," their mom said.

"Oh, please," Matt said.

"Well, if you didn't want me to show favoritism, I guess you shouldn't have been so mean to him. Hm?"

Abigail motioned for Lulu to get back to the script. "So, I have a little story. When I was a teenager, I was obsessed with the farm-to-table restaurant concept. I did tons of research and made all these collages, and do you know which one stood out and became my absolute favorite?"

Scottie wrapped an arm around his mom's shoulders. "My momma's?"

"Yep. It was so romantic and lovely…just my ideal. So much so that I begged my parents to take me there. I actually had my Sweet Sixteen at Café Akasha." They'd already talked about it on the phone, so his mom would have to pretend to be surprised.

"*No*. Are you serious? Isn't that something, how life put us together like this?" The woman gave her a hug. "You know, I don't believe in coincidence. I believe we manifest everything in our lives, and I'm just so happy to be part of yours."

"Me, too." When Lulu pulled away, she said, "To this day, your restaurant is up there as one of my all-time favorites."

"I'm touched to hear that."

"So, how did the restaurant get started?" Lulu asked. "What was your original concept?"

"Well, I was a mom of two very loud, energetic boys. My husband played football for the 49ers, and he was gone for long stretches. I was a thousand miles away from my family, and I felt overwhelmed and very much alone. So, I cooked. I started out making my own baby food, then I tried bread…and it just grew as I learned about whole foods and nutrients and all of that good stuff."

"As her first taste tester," Matt said, "I can speak with some authority that it wasn't all good."

His mom laughed. "No, it certainly wasn't. But I fell in love not just with food but with its magical properties. And one day I realized I needed more in my life. I needed something of my own, so I had the idea to open a little café."

"And that little café turned into one of the most successful and beloved restaurants in the world," Lulu said.

"Well, when you do the thing you love…when you find your passion…it all comes together, doesn't it?" Mrs. Wilder looked at her like they were on the same page, that this show was where Lulu belonged.

She wished that were true. But it wasn't. It was nothing more than a stepping stone.

And she wanted so badly to be where she belonged in her career.

"Proud of you, Mom," Xander said.

Lulu got all gooey inside at the way he so freely showed his mom affection.

"Love you, too. All three of my boys."

"All right, you guys ready to cook?" Lulu said.

"You bet we are," Scottie said.

"You've never even cracked an egg." Xander pushed on his brother's shoulder. "What do you know about cooking?"

"I'm not here to make anything." Scottie gave his signature charming grin. "I'm here to help my momma whoop your ass."

"Okay, so, you're going to make your mom's signature dish, Cioppino del Gado." Lulu gestured to the gingham towel covering the rectangular basket. "We're only giving you the ingredients found on Café Akasha's menu. The rest is up to you to create. Go ahead and get to your stations."

His mom and brothers gathered at one end of the island, and Xander stood by himself at the other.

"Hm." Lulu framed the scene with her hands. "What's wrong with this picture? Oh, I know, it's totally out of balance." She moved to stand next to Xander. "Need a hand?"

"I'll take your hands any day of the week."

She grinned. "Let's do this."

"Hang on. If you're helping me, then who's judging?" When his dad came out of the hallway waving, Xander's jaw dropped. "Dad." He took off to greet him.

The older man gave him a bear hug. "Good to see you."

"I can't believe this."

His dad pulled away. "All right. Let me take my place." He settled on a bar stool, aware of everyone staring at him. "Well, don't just stand there. Impress me!"

And then it was on, both groups huddling as they worked out a game plan.

"I'm all yours," Lulu said. "Just tell me what you need me to do."

Xander tore open the netted bag of mussels. "Do you want to wash the tosaka?"

"Sure."

With the camera focused on his mom, he leaned closer. "Was this your idea? Did you arrange this?" He scraped the debris off the mussels with a knife.

"I did." It just seemed so wrong that he hadn't told his family about the Mavericks. She understood why—she'd done the same thing when she'd gotten fired. But she knew they loved him and would rally for him, maybe even have their own insider knowledge or connections to help him. She headed for the sink with the seaweed and called back to him over her shoulder. "Rinse and then set in water for five minutes?"

"Perfect."

"Are you angry?" she asked quietly.

He glanced up at his family. "Not at all. I like having them here."

"Darn." Popping open a jar of brined sea grapes, Scottie tried to dip his big hand in it but couldn't get past the two huge Super Bowl rings.

Here it comes. They didn't know about the Mavericks, so they didn't know it wasn't a good time to tease him.

"Damn. I can't get the sea grapes, Mom."

"What's that?" His mom was busy with the clams, so she didn't see the game.

"Here, let me see." Matt tried jamming his big hand inside, but his ring caught on the rim. "Nope. Can't do it either."

"Do you think it could be because of our giant, diamond-encrusted Super Bowl rings?" Scottie asked.

The crew members laughed, causing his mom to look over. "Boys, seriously? Leave your brother alone and get cracking on the foundation."

Of course, the guys were too busy laughing.

With the seaweed soaking, Lulu brought it to the counter and pressed a hand to Xander's lower back to let him know she was there. In spite of his easy-going grin, he was overheated. And she didn't think it was because of the lights.

Well, then. What was that expression? *Turn around is fair play.* "I've got some pastry dough I can use to make fresh tarts to serve with our dish." She kept her tone matter-of-fact. "Do you want me to get that going? It just needs to be rolled out and set in the molds."

He gave her a confused look. "Sure."

"Are we doing dessert, Mom?" Scottie asked.

"No. We're being judged on cioppino. Dessert won't count."

"If I have to eat cockles," his dad said. "At least let me wash it down with something sweet."

Thank you, Mr. Wilder. Lulu pulled out the dough she'd set in the fridge that morning for tarts. She'd planned on making some for the Women and Children's Shelter. "Here." With a knife, she sliced the large lump of dough in half. "I've got plenty. Just use some of mine."

In the junk drawer, she rummaged around for the container of heat-sensitive ink she'd noticed when she'd first moved into the bunkhouse. Poking her finger into one of the halves, she squeezed drops into it and gently kneaded the holes to smooth over them. Handing it to Scottie, she said, "I'm making a simple French apple tart, but I'll leave it to your mom to figure out what she wants to do."

Xander cut her a look. He knew she was up to something, and the corner of his mouth hitched.

"Cool, thanks." Scottie nudged his mom. "What do you want me to do?"

"We'll keep it simple, too. Why don't you sprinkle some flour on the cutting board, knead it a little, and then roll it out? We'll cut it into strips, cover them in sugar and cinnamon, and bake them."

"Your mom used to make that every holiday for you boys," their dad said. "Remember?"

"I do," Matt said. "She did that with the leftover dough when she'd make pies. Here, give me half. I want to make some."

Lulu brought them another cutting board and a tub of flour. "Here you go." She smiled warmly and went back to work, knowing full well they'd watch to see how she rolled it out. Planting the heel of her palm in the ball, she flattened it, and then worked it with both hands, instead of using a rolling pin.

"Dude, what're you doing? Go wash your hands." Scottie pointed to his brother's dough. "That's disgusting." It had purple streaks in it. "No one's going to eat that."

"What the…? Look, it's not just mine. Yours has it, too." Matt swiped the flour off his cheek, leaving a streak of purple. "Mom, why's it purple?"

Both of them looked to Lulu who worked serenely to press the dough into the tart shells.

"What've you done?" His mom pointed her knife at them. "It's on your faces."

"What?" With his dough-smeared fingers, Scottie swiped a purple streak across his mouth. "Is it gone?" He rubbed even more color over his jaw.

Lulu's shoulders shook with laughter.

Matt laughed. "You look ridiculous."

"You should talk," Scottie said.

And that was it. Lulu and Xander burst out laughing.

His brothers shot her a look.

"Is this you?" Scottie asked. "You did this?"

"What?" Matt asked. "What'd she do?"

"Me?" Lulu said with wide, innocent eyes.

"This is about the rings, isn't it?" his mom asked. "It's about time someone put them in their place."

His dad smiled. "Well played, Lulu. Well, played."

―――

With a surge of gratitude, Xander grabbed Lulu's hand and led her to the bedroom.

"What're you doing? Your family's out there."

But he could hear the thrill in her voice, so he shut the door and lifted her against the wall, kissing her with all the heady desire, gratitude, and affection crashing through him. He loved when her hands went around his neck and her ankles crossed at his lower back, loved the way she kissed him like there was no world outside the door, like the only thing that mattered was this moment, getting closer to him.

She made him feel special, wanted, needed. She made him feel happy and aware and…just so fucking alive.

I'm falling in love with her.

He pulled away, resting his forehead on hers. "Thank you."

"You're welcome. Except, now your family's going to hate me. I made the great Wilder brothers purple on national television."

"My parents thought it was hilarious, and it's about time I retaliated. But that's not what I'm thanking you for." He kissed her again. "I like you, Lulu Cavanaugh."

"Xander?" His mom knocked on the door.

"Everything all right?" his dad called.

She scraped her hand through his hair. "I like you, too."

He set her down. "Everything's great. Hang on a sec." He grinned, tucking those errant bangs behind her ear and cupping her chin. "I meant, thank you for bringing my family out here."

"I thought you might be angry about it, but the thing is, I know you think of your brothers as these gods but they're not. They're your family, your equals. The age gap doesn't matter anymore. Your family's here because they love you. I just…I hope you'll let them support you." She opened the door and stepped into the hallway. "Hey."

He listened to them for a minute—his parents thanking her, his brothers laughing—and while he sure as hell didn't want to tell them, he knew she was right. Matt and Scottie weren't his rivals.

He'd been waiting until he became a franchise quarterback, when he'd be at their level, to have a real relationship with them. But that seemed pretty stupid now.

His mom came into the room, followed by his dad

and then his brothers. He waited for Lulu to come back, but she didn't. And so he was alone in this.

He'd always looked up to his brothers. Big and powerful, they were good guys with lots of friends. They'd followed the rules in life and had been rewarded with good marriages and great careers.

And Xander hadn't. No matter how hard he'd tried, he'd always fallen short.

And he had to wonder if it was because he'd been following the wrong rules. He'd forced himself onto *their* path—and maybe it wasn't the right one for him.

A shock of cold hit the back of his neck. *Am I not meant to play ball?*

Scottie stared at himself in the dresser mirror. "When's this shit gonna come off?"

"I don't know," Xander said. "I don't even know what she used."

"She's hilarious," his mom said.

"Says the woman who doesn't have purple all over her face." Matt rubbed at the ink on his hands.

"Son." His dad clapped a hand on his shoulder. "Really glad to see you."

"Yeah, thanks for coming all the way out here."

"We were thrilled when Lulu called." His dad gave his shoulder a squeeze before letting go. "How's it going? Any word from the Mavericks?"

His breath caught in his throat, the word loser appearing in his mind's eye, but he batted it away. "Yes."

The room went quiet, all eyes on him, the anticipation heavy as humidity.

"No contract."

"Damn," Matt said on a low breath.

"You're a free agent?" his mom asked.

Xander nodded.

"Good," Scottie said. "You don't want to be a backup. It's your time, man. This is it."

But Xander was done with all the cheerleading. "Stop. It doesn't matter how good I used to be. It doesn't matter what anyone expected my career to look like. This is where I wound up. If Cassian gets hurt—and there's always a chance he will, Coach needs someone he can count on. And he's convinced any defender's going straight for my shoulder. I get it."

"He knows about the training center, right?" Matt asked. "The work you're doing?"

Xander nodded. "He knows."

"Look, we'll make some calls." Matt pointed a finger at Scottie, their dad, and himself. "We'll get you some try-outs."

"I don't want courtesy tryouts. Put yourself in my shoes. How are you going to feel showing up to work out with a team when everyone knows you're only there because the coach is doing your dad a favor?"

He could see they absolutely got it and felt vindicated.

Until his dad gave him a hard look. "You don't want to use your connections to get a try-out, then get an internship with the lighting crew. Get a job selling cleats in a sporting goods store. If you're going to be embarrassed on the field because you called in a favor, then go back to school and get another degree. But if you want to play ball, you don't even think about that shit. You keep your focus on playing and training and proving to every coach out there that you're the best damn quarterback this league's ever seen. We all need help sometimes, son. Put your ego aside and play ball."

Chapter Fifteen

KNOWING HIS FAMILY WOULD GET A KICK OUT OF THE costumed actors and staged shoot outs, Xander took them to dinner at the Saloon. A woman in a bustle dress played an old-time piano, and their waiter wore chaps and a holster.

They'd had a great time—lots of laughter and sharing family stories—and just as the evening was winding down, he got up to use the restroom. Scottie followed him. His brother—the loudmouth jokester in the family—was unusually quiet, until they washed their hands in the sink, regarding each other in the ornate mirrors.

"What's up?" Xander asked.

He'd never seen his cocky, confident brother uncomfortable, not a day in his life. Everything Scottie had worked for had come true, thanks to his disciplined work ethic. "I feel like shit."

Great. Pity. Exactly what he hadn't wanted. "Nah, Dad shook me out of it. There's no room for ego if I'm going to get where I want to go. I got this."

"Not about that. About the rings. Shit timing for it. I didn't know… about the Mavericks."

In this moment, he had a chance to steer the relationship around. Instead of looking up to his brother, it was time to be his equal. And the scary-ass part was that it meant he could lose him.

Xander didn't want that—but at the same time, it wasn't much of a relationship if all he did was pretend to be like them. "It's never a good time."

A jolt passed through Scottie's body. He stiffened.

They stood there with wet hands, watching each other in the mirror. Anxious, Xander plowed ahead. "It's not funny, and I don't like it. I don't know how to explain what it's like growing up with older brothers who never wanted anything to do with me, who're both living these perfect lives—and to just always feel like an outsider in my own family." The words spilled out fast, with an edge he hadn't intended. But, man, he was pumped. "And when you show off those rings—I want to throw them at your heads. Because I've been sitting on the bench for four years, and now I don't even have a fucking team." His voice shook with anger.

No, it's not anger. It's fear.

And for the first time he decided to just own it. "My career might be over before it started."

"We're assholes." Scottie looked stricken. "I don't… we're uncomfortable, so we use humor. We don't know what to say. It doesn't make any sense. You outclass us on the field. Everyone knows that. We just got lucky, and you can't catch a break. Jesus, Xander, you should have seen us during the play-offs. We were so damn happy watching you do what you were born to do. It was like letting a horse out of the barn. And then…" He lowered his head. "Fuck. To see you go down like that." He snatched some towels and handed them to Xander, then pulled out a few more for himself. "I'm sorry. I guess we should have had this conversation, instead of making jokes."

By the time they got back to the table, his parents and Matt were just getting up. The bill had been paid.

"Hey, this was my treat," Xander said.

His dad shrugged. "I got it."

They all headed out the door and strolled along the boardwalk. On the street, a crowd gathered to watch the costumed jailor walk a scruffy actor in chaps to jail. A stagecoach clattered by, and a cowboy dropped off his horse and looped the reins on a hitching post.

"I love this town." His mom looped her arm through his.

"Thought you'd get a kick out of it."

"One day, we'll have to rent a place here. Did you see the schedule at the amphitheater? They do Shakespeare plays one night a week throughout the summer."

"Sounds right up your alley."

"I had so much fun today. I'll tell you, I watch a lot of cooking shows, and I've never seen one like this. It's fun… it's different. I think you've got a winner here."

He nodded.

"You like doing it? I know it's not something you ever saw yourself doing."

"I do, actually."

She shook his arm. "My son, man of few words. You were like this as a kid. I'd pick you up from football practice and ask how school went and get one syllable. 'Fine.' You didn't even tell us you'd won the Heisman. We had to find out in a press release."

He shrugged. That was December, junior year. Scottie had just led his team to the play-offs. It was a big deal.

"You were such a sweet, sensitive boy. You know, I always imagined you as a chef."

"A chef?"

"Oh, yes, you came alive in the kitchen. You'd get this crease…" She tapped the space between her eyes. "Right here. You were so creative…the things you came up with…" His mom sighed. "You're a natural."

They turned into the hotel, crossing the gleaming marble lobby. Up ahead was a sweeping staircase with shiny brass banisters and burgundy carpet. Wood paneled walls and a dramatic crystal chandelier made the place look historic and grand.

"You come alive around Lulu, too."

LJust hearing her name sent pleasure through him. He missed her tonight. Her sister and brother-in-law had a meeting for the upcoming Chocolate Festival, so they'd asked Lulu to babysit.

"She's special, isn't she?" his mom asked.

"She is."

Holding onto his arm, his mom stopped him. "No, I mean, really special. It's nothing like how you were with Kayla and Steph."

His senses sharpened.

"You always seemed impatient around them. Like there was something you'd rather be doing."

He could see that. "Well, you never much liked Steph anyway."

"Steph's wonderful, but we thought you got married for the wrong reasons." In a helpless gesture, she lifted an arm and let it drop. "Your career had just crashed and burned."

"Yeah, exactly, and she got me through rehab. She was there for me through the whole thing."

"I know. She kept your spirits up, and I appreciated that very much."

His dad and brothers approached. "We're going to grab a drink."

"We'll be right there," his mom said.

His dad looked between them, clearly wondering what they were talking about so intensely, but he just nodded and strode into the bar. Xander and his mom watched for a moment, as everyone turned to look at the three tall, fit, good-looking athletes.

"Come sit with me." She led him to a red velvet couch right between a wedding gown store and a high-end boutique. "I'm just glad Steph never got pregnant, because that would've changed everything."

"Hard to do when she moved back home after three months."

"Well, you were together for years before you moved to Boston." She patted his knee. "But now that we're talking about it, why on earth did you stay married all that time?"

"You know her family, it's—"

"I do know, but I'm asking why you stayed with *her*."

What could he say that wouldn't make him sound like an asshole?

"Ohh." His mom sounded defeated. "Of course."

"What?"

"How did I not see this? You wanted to be like your brothers, that's why you stayed married." Awareness lit her features. "We all married our college sweethearts."

"Yeah, I guess there's some truth in that." But it was a lot more complicated.

"Well, it's a good thing Steph moved back home. Marriage is hard, and you'd better have a strong foundation if you're going to make it through the hard times. I got pregnant six months after my wedding. So, between your dad being the new kid on the team, and me being pregnant in a new city, away from my family…it wasn't good." She looked down at her hands. "I thought about leaving him, countless times. Just like Steph, I wanted to move back home where I'd be supported by a big family and childhood friends. But I loved your dad too much to leave."

"Steph and I weren't like that."

"No. I think you had a nice friendship, but you never looked at her the way you look at Lulu. And I've only been here one day."

"How do I look at her?"

"Like you're smitten. Like you can't get enough of her."

He shifted uncomfortably. "I like her, but it's not like it can last."

"Why's that?"

Until he'd met Lulu, his mom was the only person he could talk to. His best memories were of the two of them in the kitchen, laughing, talking, working through problems…yeah. He loved his mom. "Because we're going in completely different directions. This show's a launching pad for our careers. I'm moving wherever my next contract sends me, and she'll be a chef de cuisine in a city Michelin covers. That's her endgame."

"Huh." She gave him a sly grin. "So, a chef and a football player can't possibly wind up together?"

"To be fair, you and dad were already married. You had two kids when you started your restaurant. Lulu and I don't know where we'll wind up, and both of our jobs are all-consuming."

"Okay, well, as long as you're looking for reasons for it not to work, then I can only assume you're just having fun for now."

As his mom surely intended, the comment didn't land right. "No, it's more than that."

"Yeah, that's the impression I'm getting. If you want some unsolicited advice—"

"I do. But only from you." He wrapped an arm around her and tugged her in close. "'Cause you're my momma."

"You know, I might not have favorites, but you're my baby, and I will always treasure the time we had together in the kitchen."

"Me, too, Mom."

"Let me just say this, okay? I've seen a lot in my almost sixty years, and one thing I know for sure, love—real love, the kind that rocks your world, that lives deep, deep down — doesn't come along very often."

He let her go. "I never said anything about love." If this seismic shift taking place in his body meant anything —and it did—then he was lying. He cleared his throat. "It's too soon to put a label on what I feel, but it's…"

"Big." She placed her hand over his. "I can see it, sweetheart. Everyone can."

"Yeah, but that's how all relationships start out. You wouldn't get involved if you didn't feel that crazy kind of attraction. Who knows if this is any different?"

She smoothed a hand through his hair. "You're sweating, and you went from talking about Lulu to talking about relationships in general, so I can see this conversation upsets you. I'll just tell you how I knew—and continue to know—that your dad is the only one for me, okay?"

He found himself nodding, because he needed her to articulate the feeling in his heart.

"In thirty-eight years of knowing your father, we've had some terrible times when I've seriously doubted if I could stay with him. But not once did I pack a bag and walk out the door. Because in spite of my anger—and, truthfully, there've been times I even thought I hated him —deep down, I've always felt this…" She turned thoughtful. "I can only describe it as a bond holding us together. It's a feeling, not something I can put into words. But it's that deep-down, rock-solid feeling that insists I stay put. It tells me what your father and I have is real and can't be broken."

"It's way too soon to know if Lu and I have that kind of bond."

"Well, it was something I felt right away. And, honestly, I think when you know, you know. It just sort of clicks. I know your dad felt it, too. Listen, maybe it *is* just fun for now with Lulu. Who knows? All I'm saying is careers aren't obstacles. Your dad and I learned we could get through anything as long as we made each other the priority. Because at the end of the day, he wasn't going to grow old with football, and my last thought when I died wasn't going to be, Gosh, I sure hope they liked my quiche. Our careers end, our bodies give out, but love endures."

She'd done it. She'd expressed his heart. And it scared the shit out of him. "Those are some powerful words, Mom, but it's hard to have a serious conversation when there's a gunslinger coming our way."

· · ·

After saying goodnight to his family, Xander headed to his car. He had one thing on his mind, and that was seeing Lulu.

That bond his mom talked about? He already felt it. Had from the beginning, when he'd felt that undeniable tug as Lulu had walked out the door in Maui.

He hadn't been able to explain it, so he'd dismissed it.

But now…yeah. That's exactly what it felt like.

Missing her, he grabbed his phone and gave her a call. But as soon as she answered, he heard nothing but a baby screaming. "Lu. What's going on?" He couldn't hear her over the shrieking in the background. "I'm on my way."

Even from the street, Xander could hear the cries. He jogged up the walkway, leapt up the porch stairs, and knocked. Peering through the windowpane, he could see Lulu rocking, while a little girl stood on the couch, patting the infant.

They didn't hear him, so he rang the bell. Lulu whipped around, and they both came hurrying over to let him in. The walk to the door seemed to have quieted the baby, and now she shuddered and drew in shaky breaths.

The little girl gazed up at him. "Are you Auntie Lu's boyfriend?"

"Yes, I am." He dropped to a crouch. "I'm Xander. You must be Posie."

"My baby sister's mad. She won't stop crying."

"I see that. Any idea what's got her all fired up?" He stood, reaching for the swaddled baby.

Lulu hesitated, holding her firmly in her arms while bouncing in place.

"I've got four nieces and nephews. One of them had

colic, so this is nothing I haven't seen before. Do you have a baby carrier?"

"Yes." Posie dashed into the dining room, pulled a dangling strap, and caught the swath of fabric in her arms. She brought it to him.

He held it out in front of him to try and figure out how to wear it. Each sling was so different.

"Here." Posie stepped onto a chair and helped him put it on. "You gotta wrap this one around and tie it right here."

"Got it. You're good at this."

She released a sigh. "I know."

What a cutie. "You're a lot like your aunt Lu."

Her eyes went wide. "I am?"

"Oh, yeah. Smart and clever, calm during tough times. You're just like her."

"I want to make cookies as good as hers."

Lulu shook out her arms, now free of eight pounds of baby weight. "Well, then, I guess we'll have to practice more together."

Posie gazed up at her in awe. "Can we make fairy cookies?"

"I've never made them, but if you've got a picture, I'm sure I can figure out how."

He slid the swaddled baby into the sling. "How about this? I'll take Violet on a walk around the block, and you guys get crackin' in the kitchen. That way, when your mom and dad get home, they'll have cookies right out of the oven."

"Can we?" Posie's face lit up with hope and excitement.

"That's a great idea. They'll be home in half an hour, so

we'd better get a move on." Lulu got up on her toes and kissed his cheek, whispering, "Thank you."

Happiness rushed through him. He hadn't had many opportunities to help her, but he'd do just about anything for this woman.

Once outside, he walked toward town, the warm weight of the infant on his chest. Violet's eyes were open, and she blinked, her tongue poking out of her little rosebud mouth.

In all his years with Steph, he'd never thought about children. Seemed weird, now that he thought about it. She came from a big family, so he'd seen her around her nieces and nephews, but he'd never pictured her as a mom to his kids.

He'd never gotten that sense of home with her. Of rightness. Seeing Lulu cradling a baby, though, the six-year-old sister helping out, had hit him hard.

This is too crazy. He'd known Steph six years and hadn't felt anything like this for her, and he'd only known Lulu for six weeks...*come on.*

His breath caught in his throat because it happened again. That tug.

That deep and absolute certainty.

He couldn't see the future. Hell, he didn't know if Lulu felt anything close to this.

But it didn't matter. Because he got it now, what his mom had been saying.

His head had finally caught up to his heart...

...the place where Lulu lived.

"If it doesn't taste good, they'll cheat. That's just a fact." Aisha, the chef at the Antigravity Training Center, opened a storage container. "And every athlete staying here has a diet specific to his or her needs, as set out by a nutritionist." She showed them a hearty cookie. "I leave these out for them all day long. They're basically peanut butter and oats with a tiny amount of butter, sugar, baking soda, and salt. Try it."

"They look so good." Lulu grabbed one and took a bite. "Mm, they're fantastic."

"And healthy. Keep in mind, they're high calorie for people who spend six, seven hours a day training."

Lulu looked right into the camera and grimaced, setting the cookie down.

"Sometimes, when I'm in a particularly good mood," Aisha said. "I'll add chocolate chips or dried cranberries. Those are gone in a flash."

In the massive, state of the art kitchen, two sous chefs were hard at work prepping for dinner, while the line cooks chopped and stirred.

The chef reached for another container. "Since I'm so limited in the kinds of food I can serve, I have to focus on variation. We do a lot of oatmeal here, so I'm always looking for ways to make it taste different. They love it with almond milk, peanut butter, and bananas. But their absolute favorite is when I use a chocolate protein powder and almond butter. They swear it tastes like a peanut butter cup."

"You're making me hungry. I can't imagine why anyone would need to cheat here."

"Thanks. I try." Aisha smiled. "Hey, where did Xander go?"

They'd planned for this moment, so Lulu played it up.

"Good question." She swung around, checking out the kitchen. "Xander?"

"Given this place is basically his second home and playground," Aisha said. "I bet he found his playmates."

"Let's go find out."

Aisha led her and the crew out of the kitchen and across the cafeteria. Well, *cafeteria* conjured images of long tables and the stink of hot dogs in the air. The Bowies had created something truly impressive here. The dining area looked like any high-end restaurant with a variety of seating arrangements.

The chef led them outside to a gorgeous, sunny June day. "Whoa." She looked towards the bright green, neatly mown field. "Can I credit that arm to my super special Sunday oatmeal?"

They watched Xander send a football flying across the lawn—a trip that seemed endless given how far away the receiver stood—and land in the basket of Ryker's hands.

"Holy shit," the cameraman whispered.

Lulu may not follow football, but she'd been around it enough—not just on television but among her dad's friends and the men he'd mentored over many, many years —to recognize a spiral so flawless it gave her chills.

She knew right then he had to get a contract.

She'd forgotten for a few weeks there, wrapped in the bubble of the bunkhouse and the cooking show, but that man had a destiny to follow, and it had nothing to do with Lulu or Calamity.

Alexander Wilder was meant to play football. One day, he would lead a team to the Super Bowl.

She'd always known she wouldn't get to keep him, but she'd had so much fun playing house that she'd blocked it out. She'd have him for the next couple of weeks, but then she had to let him go.

If she was so sure about that, why did it feel like forcing the wrong piece into a puzzle? The sense of resistance inside her was so strong, it almost felt like a mandate to fight for him.

Was that just the silly side of her that longed to find her match?

It can't be Xander. It couldn't. They were both destined for other things.

Continuing toward the field, they found the physical therapist and the facility's in-house doctor standing in the bright sun, both wearing baseball caps. On the grass, Cassian threw the ball to Xander. Just as he caught it, three enormous guys tackled him.

"Oh, my, God." The reaction might've been scripted, but her tone held authenticity because...that was one hard sack. "His shoulder."

The physical therapist kept her eyes on the field. "Just watch."

The guys climbed off him, and Xander popped up, laughing and shoving them. One of the guys made a grab for the ball, but Xander threw a long pass to Cassian.

"I thought he's here to get physical therapy," Lulu said. "Not get *tackled*."

The very fit woman turned serious. "He's already had physical therapy and then a long period of rest. He was cleared to play months ago. Luckily, he never suffered a tear and the clavicle's never been displaced. He's here because we've gotten some promising results with ligament-strengthening exercises."

"We promised to make him better than new." The doctor smiled, as he watched Xander reach the goal posts and do a crazy victory dance. "And I believe we've delivered."

"So, you're saying when he leaves here, it'll be like he never had an injury at all?" Lulu asked.

"That's exactly right." The doctor watched yet another football sail across the field.

When the ball landed in Cassian's hands, the location director said, "Cut. And that's a wrap." She smiled at their guests. "Thanks so much for meeting us out here."

"Our pleasure," the doctor said. "Now, if you'll excuse me, I've got to get back to work."

As the camera crew shut down their equipment and started back toward the parking lot, Lulu lingered. "We're really grateful you took the time to be on the show."

"I wanted to do it," the physical therapist said. "I meant what I said. This new treatment's going to change the world for him."

At that moment, Xander noticed they were done filming and jogged over. The closer he got, the harder it was for her to stand still, so she took off and met him halfway.

She brushed the hair out of his eyes. "You looked good out there." He hadn't cut it all summer, and she loved it.

"I got some good news." Grabbing her arm, he led her behind a tree. "Tortino's out. The Seahawks need a QB."

It took a moment to make sense of the lingo. "Wait, there's an opening for a quarterback?"

"Yes."

"And you're going to try out?" She threw herself into his arms. "Oh, my God, Xander. This is fantastic."

He glanced toward his friends, and she could tell he was uncomfortable.

"They don't know?"

"Gonna keep it on the down-low for now."

"I can't believe this. I'm so happy for you." He still seemed uneasy, and she had a feeling she knew why. How many times had he thought he was getting his big break? "This is the first bit of hope you've had in seven months, so we'll take it."

"Yeah, Lu." He smiled. "We'll take it."

Chapter Sixteen

"So, I have news." Gigi came back into the living room with a bottle of wine.

Lulu sat curled up in one corner of the couch, while Coco slouched at the other end, feet propped on the table and hugging a throw pillow over her belly. "We're listening."

The baby had been asleep for a solid hour and a half, and Posie had crashed right at her bedtime. Things were improving in the Cavanaugh-O'Neill household.

Perched on the edge of the coffee table, Gigi said, "I'm retiring."

"What?" Coco sat up.

But the news didn't come as a shock to Lulu, so she traced a fingertip on the rim of her glass and listened.

Coco crossed her legs. "I know you hated the Lollipops, but you finally got where you wanted to be with your own band. Why retire now, when you're only a year into this new direction?"

"I love my band, and I love the music we're making together. But..." Gigi poured wine for herself and then topped off Lulu's glass. "The thing is, you guys, I want to get off the treadmill. Contractually, I'm obligated to tour, which puts me on the road for three hundred days next year. And it's hard to be creative when you're traveling and surrounded by people all the time and away from your family and fiancé."

"That sounds exhausting." Coco reached for a handful of grapes and popped one into her mouth.

"Everything sounds exhausting to you," Lulu teased.

"True."

"The point is that…I don't want to be on the road for a year. I guess…" Gigi glanced to the baby swing hanging in the doorway. "You know how Mom kept us busy when we were growing up? We never got to hang out, stay in our pjs all day, and watch reality TV?"

"You're giving up your career to stay in your pjs and watch TV?" Coco asked with a smile.

Their oldest sister chuckled. "Some days, yeah, that's exactly what I want to do. But mostly, I want to make a home. I want…a baby. A family."

"You shouldn't feel guilty for wanting something other than a career." A twist of envy had Lulu setting her wine glass down. Gigi had already grabbed the brass ring. She could slow down, take time off, do whatever she needed to be happy. She'd earned it.

I haven't made it yet.

I will, though. This show will get me to the next level.

And once she got her Michelin star, she could pull back on the throttles.

"I couldn't agree more," Coco said.

"That's the thing about life. We get to keep reinventing ourselves." *Look at me.* Never in a million years would she have imagined doing a cooking show. "If you want to retire and be a mom, do it. And then, in a couple of years, if you get itchy and want to go back to performing, you can do that, too."

"I definitely question my sanity in giving up a career I worked so hard for." Gigi gazed into her wine glass. "Because making a come-back won't be easy. I won't be relevant anymore."

"You've toured the world, you have six platinum albums, you've hit the top of the charts...you've done it all." Lulu admired her sister so much. "You can take time off to start a family."

"I hate to break it to you, but having kids is not a break," Coco said. "If you're in pjs all day, it's because you're so exhausted you never made it to the shower. Or you haven't done laundry in two weeks."

Both of them looked at Coco and saw a woman on the edge.

"Oh, honey." Lulu reached for her, and then all three sisters were locked in a hug and Coco was sobbing. They held her while she cried it out.

Finally, Coco pulled away to grab a napkin and blow her nose. "I'm so tired you guys. Posie was such an easy baby. I never could've started my business if she'd been anything like Violet. I love her. You know I do, but she's killing me. This is the longest she's slept since she was born."

"It's time to get some help," Gigi said. "Even if it's just a mother's helper, someone to take Posie out of the house for a couple of hours in the afternoon."

"I know." Coco wiped her eyes and sat back. "But it's all temporary. Eventually, Violet won't need to eat every two hours, and things will get back on track. Beckett's amazing. I pump, so he takes some of the nighttime feeding shifts."

"Now, are you going to tell us why you keep checking your phone?" Gigi asked Lulu.

Caught, she shoved it behind a throw pillow. All night, she'd struggled to keep her mouth shut, since she couldn't say anything when Gigi lived with the quarterback of the Mavericks. "Nothing. It's just…Xander's out of town." She wished she could talk, though. She was a ball of anxiety. "He usually calls me before bed. I like to hear how his day went."

"God, I hope it went well," Gigi said. "We're so excited for him."

"What do you mean?"

"Doesn't he have his try-out with the Seahawks?"

Had she inadvertently said something? *That would be terrible.* "How do you know that?"

"Cassian told me. Why, is it supposed to be a secret?"

"He doesn't want anyone to know." *In case it doesn't work out.*

"Oh, there are no secrets in the NFL. It's a small world."

"If he gets it, what does this mean for the two of you?" Coco asked.

Bingo. "I don't know. I can't even think about that. He's so good, you guys. He needs to play."

"I know." Gigi clapped her hands. "That game during the playoffs? We were in the locker room, waiting for X-ray results and watching the game on TV, and even in all that pain, Cassian goes, 'Good thing I got here first, or he'd have my job.'"

"And then he gets injured all over again. He *needs* this." Since they didn't mind, she pulled her phone out and set it on her knee. She supposed not hearing from him was a good thing—it meant he was still with the team.

"What do *you* need?" Coco asked.

"I need him to play in one of the five U.S. cities that Michelin reviews." Lulu said it with a sad smile. "But that's unlikely."

"I didn't ask about your fantasies." Coco said it softly. "I asked what you need."

Good point.

"Are you in love?" Gigi asked.

"Well, I mean, it'd be ridiculous to say I'm *in love* with him. It hasn't even been two months."

"But?" Gigi prodded her.

"But I've never felt anything like this. He gets me. I know I said that about Trace, but this is different." She grew anxious. "I don't even want to talk about it, because as soon as he signs a contract, he's gone. And as much as I want that for him—and I do—I really, honestly do—it also means I'm going to lose him."

"So, how close are you guys?" Gigi asked. "You've been pretty tight-lipped."

She had, hadn't she? *Habit.* She hadn't grown up confiding in her sisters, so they weren't her go-to girls. *They are now.* "The best thing is that I've been totally myself with him from the start. I didn't think anything would happen between us, so he's only ever seen the real me, and he *likes* me. You guys, we have so much in common, and I'm talking about the important stuff. We're on the same page, so we get what each other's going through."

"That's so great, Lu." Gigi squeezed her hand.

Anxiety got a grip on her. "It is, but I don't get to keep him, so I'm trying to keep my feelings in check."

"Oh, honey, that's just not you," Gigi said. "You're passion. You're fire."

"You realize you still haven't told me what you need," Coco said.

Her sisters waited patiently for her to come up with an answer, but she already knew. She only held back because she'd never confessed it to anyone. It seemed so childish or…idealistic. Like some fantasy she'd gotten from movies and books.

But she wanted their perspective. "I need what you guys have. That one person who makes me feel less alone in the world. My soulmate. The love of my life."

"And is Xander that person?" Coco asked.

A roiling anxiety had her shifting. "How can I answer that? I love being with him. I love talking to him. I love the way he smells, and the way he smiles. I love the way he touches me. You know how in romance books the heroine melts at the hero's touch? I never understood that before. I'd never felt that kind of heat, that need that goes so deep it feels…"

"Out of control?" Gigi said.

"Desperate?" Coco asked.

"Yes, and I love it. I love the way I let go so completely when I'm with him. I love—" Terror sliced through her.

Her jaw snapped shut.

Gigi had a knowing smile, while Coco looked a little worried.

"Well, there you go." Lulu's tone said, *I hope you're happy.* "I love him." She sounded as helpless as she felt. "I do."

"Does he feel the same way?" Coco asked. "Or is he just having fun while he's in Calamity?"

"I know he feels totally comfortable around me. He's

for sure attracted to me." *The way he looks at me, touches me, the things he says…yes, absolutely.* "But I think he's wired to achieve, just like I am. It's easy for us to be together while we're both in a holding pattern, but the minute he signs a contract, he'll go back into beast mode, where he's all about training and playing. He'll go all-out to prove himself."

"That makes sense," Gigi said. "But we're not talking about mutually exclusive things. He can be focused on the team and in love with you."

"It's different with you and Cassian. He's been in love with you half his life. I've only had a couple weeks with Xander."

"Look, every couple has their own story," Gigi said. "You can't compare mine to yours. I'm just saying love is powerful. It trumps everything, so if you're right for each other, you don't write each other off because of careers."

"Letting him go because you're afraid it won't last seems about the saddest thing you could do," Coco said. "Why not come at this from the opposite direction? If you've got something special here, put everything you've got into it. You did that with your career, why wouldn't you do that for him? For love?"

"You know, those are some pretty wise words for a woman who hasn't slept in a month." *And I like them a lot.*

"And what about you?" Gigi asked. "We're talking about him signing a contract, but what's next for you?"

Fear got hold and gave her a good shake. "I don't have a single clue. If Xander quits, the show might not air. And then everything I'd hoped to gain from it goes up in smoke."

"Any chance they'd give you your own show?" Coco asked.

Up until this moment, the timing had been too good to be true. Not that she reveled in *The Farm Woman's* failure, but it had offered her a unique opportunity. Any day now, the announcement would go live that *The Gridiron Grillers* would be debuting in that time slot.

"Realistically, it'll take the Seahawks and his agent time to hammer out an agreement, and then the contract will go to the lawyers, so we'll probably have enough time to get this season in the bag. It's just that, if the network wants more, they're going to want football players. Not just me, the chef." She reached for her wine and took a sip. "So, I really don't know what's going to happen. I have to hope one season is enough to grab the attention of the kind of restaurateur I'm looking for."

"You could move to Seattle with him." Gigi said it quietly, seriously.

"We're not there yet. There's no way he's thinking like that." But the idea sent a thrill through her. "Besides, I have to think about my career. And Michelin doesn't cover Washington."

Both of her sisters gave her pointed looks. *Do you hear yourself?*

Coco reached for a handful of almonds. "Okay, well, if you're telling me that a Michelin star matters more to you than a future with Xander, then just enjoy your time with him while it lasts."

"Ouch."

"What?" Coco asked. "You just said you wouldn't go to Seattle because of a *star*. I mean, cool, you get your star and then what? Then, you'll finally be happy?"

"I'm happy."

Both sisters stared at her for a moment before bursting out in laughter. Lulu had no choice but to join them.

Happy, my ass.

Coco swatted at them. "Shh. You wake up that baby, you're dead to me."

When they quieted down, Gigi asked, "But, for real, if it meant you got to be with Xander, would you take a job in a Seattle restaurant?"

"Or open your own." Coco sounded frustrated. "It doesn't have to be world famous. It might actually make you happy to cook what you want instead of trying to achieve some elusive star."

"It's funny because I went on this whole rant to Xander about this exact situation. How I was so sure Gigi would retire soon because of the nature of her career."

"You did? You knew I was going to do this?" Gigi asked.

Lulu nodded.

"Okay, but it's not the nature of *your* career," Coco said. "You don't have a record label that's demanding you tour, and you don't need a Michelin star to be successful. So, what's really holding you back?"

And right then she knew exactly what it was. "Fear." When the truth struck, she had no choice but to acknowledge it. "You guys, I'm terrified to believe this is real. Nothing has ever felt so right. I mean, he says and does all the things I could ever dream of—the man makes me swoon with how much he likes me, respects me, *wants* me. And I believe him, I do, but look how wrong I was about Trace. I want to trust that this is real, that he's my person, and we're going to figure out how to make it work, but what happens when he's back to playing, and his needs change? When I'm in my happy place cooking, and he's in high profile situations and expects a socially confident woman by his side…"

"Lu." Coco's voice was filled with affection.
And that's just not me.

The moment he pulled up to the bunkhouse, Xander threw open the door and grabbed his duffle bag.

He couldn't wait to see her. From the moment he'd left two days ago, he could've sworn he'd caught whiffs of her peach scent on his clothes and skin.

He felt like a teenage boy with a crush—something he'd never experienced before.

The door was wide open, as the crew brought in two soft boxes and a reflector. He jogged inside, searching for her. He didn't need to look far, because the cameras lights were trained on her, everyone watching, mesmerized.

"This is my absolute favorite dessert, and it's so easy to make." She lifted a wooden spoon. "Look at that. Ribbons of glossy, silky chocolate. And the whole kitchen smells like it. Isn't it sensational? I'm not a fan of milk chocolate, but this rich, dark chocolate makes me weak in the knees."

As if she sensed him, Lulu looked over and broke into a glowing smile.

Had anyone ever been that genuinely happy to see him?

No. Never.

He'd seen himself through his parent's eyes and felt their pride.

He'd seen himself through his ex-wife's eyes and felt her compulsion to keep him happy.

He'd seen himself through the eyes of fans and felt their excitement and predatory interest.

But seeing the warmth and absolute delight in Lulu's

eyes changed him. It made him wake up and live in this one, singular moment. His whole life had been about looking forward, hitting the next marker.

Without even thinking, he made his way to her, watching that smile grow brighter and wider.

"Well, look at that. Clark Kent's in the house." She looked into the camera. "Only instead of a suit he wears jeans and T-shirts in the kitchen, and instead of a cape, he wears cleats and leggings on the field."

He tossed his duffle bag aside. "We don't wear leggings. They're called pants."

"Are they stretchy and form-fitting?" She shrugged. "Leggings."

"They have ties and knee pads. And grass stains." He pointed to her cake. "When's that going to be ready?"

"Well, since we're filming a television show, the finished product is over there."

He practically lunged for it, and she grabbed the back of his shirt. "Slow down there, QB."

"I'm hungry."

"Okay, but first we need to get a nice shot of it. Why don't you grab a string cheese or a fruit cup or something and chill for a minute?"

"You want me to eat string cheese when I can have this?" Grabbing the cake plate, he set it down in front of her.

"Cut." The director motioned to the nearest camera operator. "Let's get an overhead shot of the cake before she slices it."

The food stylist rushed forward to pretty up the plate. She sprinkled confectioner's sugar, set a dollop of fresh whipped cream in the center, and then placed a sprig of mint on top. "Okay, ready."

After they got the still shot, the director said, "And…action."

Lulu sliced a piece and set it on a plate. When she smiled at him—all sexy and soft—it threw him right back to the night before he'd left for Seattle. The lusty look in her eyes, her lips swollen from sucking his cock.

A tingling sensation in his lower back fired up his blood. *Not now, buddy.*

Grabbing a fork, he took a big bite. The rich chocolate flavor hit his taste buds. "Holy…" He stopped himself before swearing on television. "This is insane. How do you *do* this? I've had plenty of good cake in my life. But this… this…" He looked at her, letting her know her talent blew him away.

Abigail made a rolling motion with her hand. *Story time.*

"I'll tell you how. Ever since I was a little girl, I was hyperaware of scents. I used to drive my mom nuts. She'd have all four of us in the bathtub, and she'd be washing our hair assembly-line style, but I'd twist away because I didn't like how the shampoo smelled. She had to take me to the store and let me sniff each bottle until we found a brand I could stand."

Loving the glimpse into her childhood, he took another bite of cake.

"I was super aware of texture, too. I'd throw a fit if my mom tried to get me in tights or wool sweaters. I'm obsessed with the smooth, cool skin of an apple, the slightly gritty taste of jicama. So, honestly, I think I'm a good chef because I'm so aware of it all. Like, you know how people say they can *see* a math equation? Well, I have a sense of what blending cognac and raspberries will taste like. I don't know if I'm wired that way or if spending all my free time cooking formed pathways in my brain."

"You don't have to know. You just have to keep making food this good."

"Oh, please. You grew up in a kitchen. You're the most intuitive chef I know."

"I'm not a chef, but yeah, to be honest, I can sense how things will taste, too."

"You know, for a football player and a chef, we seem to have an awful lot in common."

When she smiled at him like that, like they were the only two people in the room, he just fucking lit up. He wanted to be alone with her, under the covers, skin to skin. He wanted to kiss her and fuck her deep and hard. He wanted to shut out the entire world and just be with *her*.

"And cut." Abigail headed towards them. "That was so great. I love that you walked right onto the set and started interacting. This is going to be a fun little segment." She leaned in. "I've got news." She tipped her head. *Come here.*

As the crew moved in to shut down the set, the producer led them out onto the patio. "It's official. We got *The Farm Woman's* slot." She looked giddy. "Our first show airs *next week*. This is happening."

"I can't believe it." Lulu gazed up at him, and he could read her like a book.

She wanted to know if he was leaving her.

If he'd move to Seattle and forget all about this show…and her.

Not a fucking chance. He hoped she could read that in his eyes, but they'd have to talk about it later.

"So, now, the question is…" Abigail practically shook

with excitement. "Are you ready to sign a contract for season two?"

Lulu didn't answer. She didn't have a job, and she needed this cooking show, so it all rested on him. He wanted to give it to her. Hell, he actually enjoyed doing it with her.

But his life was up in the air. If Seattle passed on him…then he truly had nothing. Between his dad, brothers, and agent, every coach in the league had heard about him.

"I'm interested. Let me discuss it with my agent, and we'll have an answer for you in a couple of days."

"No problem. Totally understand. Keep in mind, we'll work with your schedule, and our filming season is short. Lots of players do other things. Justin Tucker is an opera singer. One of the guys is a farmer, another sells shoes because he wants to own a sporting goods store one day." Abigail grinned. "Yes, I looked into it. So, it's possible. And if we film at this same time next year, I think it might work for everyone."

He was a mess of emotion. It used to be so clear to him—he had one goal, one path: to play ball and lead a team. He wanted it—needed it—but now?

The pull toward Lulu was equally powerful.

And the worst part? Neither was in his control.

Chapter Seventeen

After the press release came out announcing the show, the crew popped bottles of champagne, and Xander and Lulu cooked dinner for everyone.

While some did clean up, others drifted off to play air hockey. Two guys smoked on the patio, and a bunch of people gathered around the karaoke machine.

Xander sat on the arm of the couch watching Lulu perform the B-52s "Love Shack" with wild abandon. She held the microphone as she did a dance that shook her hips and sent her hair swirling.

Earlier, as they'd cooked together, he'd briefly caught her up on his try-out—there wasn't much to say. It went well, the guys seemed okay. But he'd been here before, trying out with teams in the hopes someone would trust he'd rehabbed his shoulder well enough for him to be an asset.

He wasn't going to think about it. He'd hear from his agent when he had news.

Lulu thrust the microphone at him just in time for him to offer his deeper voice as backup. "Love shack baby." Her scent surrounded him, kicking up the want he'd banked for four long days.

"You even sing well, you freak." She smacked him on the shoulder but kept singing.

Not even needing to read the screen, she belted out the lyrics. When she flipped her hair and eyed him with a look of pure sex, he couldn't keep his distance anymore. Wrapping an arm around her waist, he peeled her fingers off the microphone and tossed it onto the couch. The machine rolled right into Prince's "I Would Die 4 U."

He led her in a crazy dance as everyone joined them, singing along. She looked so free, so happy, he had to get closer. He tugged her to his chest. "I missed you."

She threw her arms around his neck. "I missed you, too."

How did she do that, make him feel like a hero just for dancing with her? How did she make the world fall away?

If he had just this for the rest of his life, he'd never want for anything.

Something inside him snapped. It was time to make sure she understood his intentions. Grabbing her hand, he pushed through the group and led her to his bedroom.

"Just to be clear…" He kicked off his trainers and locked the door. "It doesn't matter what happens with Seattle or this show or whatever chef job is next for you, I don't want this to end."

He could see the thrill in her eyes—and the fight to suppress it. "I don't know what that means."

"We've never talked about a future. I think, for both of us, we just wanted to be together–even if it was only for the summer. But I'm telling you I want more. And it's something we need to talk about now, because we've got big shit ahead of us with our jobs, and if we don't lay it out on the table, we might lose each other. I don't want that to happen."

Jobs.

Two months ago, his career was the only thing that mattered. *Now?*

He had his priorities right. "You with me?"

She didn't answer right away, and he appreciated that about her. It meant more that she took time to weigh her feelings.

And yet, if he gave her too much, wouldn't she let her doubts take over? "Talk to me, Lu. Let me know what you're thinking."

"I don't know. We've only just begun—of course I don't want us to end—but long distance doesn't work, not for two people who work as much as we do."

"Cassian and Gigi do it, my parents do it, my brothers and their wives do it. I can't give you answers before we have questions—I have no idea where either of us will wind up. I only know I'll never find someone like you again, that what we have is real, it's special, and I'm not willing to let it slip away."

Her eyes glistened, and she looked torn.

He held her close so she could see the truth in his eyes. "I've never felt anything like this before, and I know it won't come around again because it's you. Only you. *You're* the magic. Will it be hard? Of course. Anything great is worth fighting for. But I'm not going back to a life without you."

The dam broke. She let out a cry, before throwing herself into his arms. "Xander."

"Yeah, baby." His tether to rational thought broke free, sweeping him away. Lifting her, he poured his whole heart into a kiss so deep and hot she could have no doubt about his sincerity.

He carried her to the bed and fell backwards onto the mattress. When she straddled him, he grabbed her ass and hitched her right up onto his cock. Fuck, he was so hard, and she felt so good rocking over him.

Emotion crashed through him. *More*. Pulling up her shirt, he only broke the kiss to yank it over her head, before taking possession of her mouth once again. His fingers fumbled, as he reached behind her and unclasped her bra.

She quickly shucked it off, her hands coming back to cup his face, slide along his jaw, and scrape into his hair. She pulled back, watching him with lust-glazed eyes. "I needed to hear you say that. So badly. But…I'm scared. What if it's only how we feel today? Right now?"

"Does it feel like that to you? Because I've never been more sure of anything in my life." Tipping her over, he tugged off her leggings and tossed them aside. He sat back on his heels, so he could take in the beauty laid out before him. Big, round breasts, the sexy curve of her waist and flare of her hips, and her dark hair fanned out on the white pillowcase...*Jesus*. "You're out of your mind if you think I'm letting you go."

Spreading her legs, he slid a hand under her ass and lifted her to his mouth. Inhaling her feminine scent, he took a swipe along the length of her.

Her fingers fisted in his hair, and her hips arched. "Xander."

He had no words. Driven by need, compelled by hunger, he licked her until she writhed beneath him. Sinking his fingers into her slick heat, he coaxed her into a climax that had her squirming and crying out, as she slammed up against his mouth and pumped her hips.

"Don't stop. Please. Oh, God, Xander, don't stop."

As her muscles slackened, he eased up, watching her features go soft, her eyes dreamy. Letting out a slow breath, she broke into a lazy grin. "I could maybe keep you around."

He sat up, got to his feet, and ripped open the buttons of his jean, yanking them down and kicking them off.

"Commando." She sat up, staring at his erection with a lustful expression. "That's hot."

He gripped his hard, aching cock. "Suck me."

Not taking her sexy gaze off him, she slid her legs off the bed and reached for him. She pressed wet kisses along the shaft, flicked her tongue just beneath the head, and then drew him into her mouth. He hissed in a breath, as need burned through him.

When she swallowed, compressing her throat around him, he groaned. Couldn't take it anymore. "Fuck." He punched his hips, wild, out of control. Hands at the back of her head, he fucked her mouth, his frenzy fueled by her heated expression, her moans, and the way she slipped her hands between her legs. "Touch your tits."

Eyes flaring, she cupped them, pushing them together —*fuck*, making them look huge, the nipples peeking between her fingers. "Oh, Jesus." Lust enflamed him, and his balls pulled in tight. Grabbing his cock, he pulled out of her mouth. "Turn around. Now."

Quickly, she got on her hands and knees, presenting him with her smooth, slender back and that sexy peach of an ass. Gripping her hips, he lined himself up at her glistening, pink opening and plunged home. *Holy fuck*. She felt better than anything. Tight, slick, hot, the friction drove him out of his mind.

He slammed into her, his cock hitting deeper at this angle. Wild with need, he fucked her harder, their skin slapping, their scents mingling. And it wasn't enough. Not nearly enough. No matter how hard, how deep, he couldn't get close enough, couldn't hit that state of connection just out of reach, that elusive fucking oneness.

Frenzied, he lost himself completely in everything Lulu.

With one hand clamped on her hip and the other cupping her breast, he reveled in the heavy weight, the firm flesh jiggling in his palm, and he just couldn't last. The quickening of his pulse, the heightening of sensation, signaled an orgasm so massive, he didn't think his body could withstand it.

And when it hit, it hurtled him out of his body, sent him spiraling through space in a state of perfect bliss. "Fuck." He punctuated each release. "Fuck. *Fuck*." Until he'd spent himself.

"*Xander*."

It was his name that pulled him back to earth, to the bunkhouse, to his bedroom.

She clenched tight around him, throwing her head back and crying out.

Lowering his chest to her back, he wrapped his arms around her, clutching her with all the love in his heart. When his knees could no longer support him, he fell onto the bed beside her, drawing her against his chest. "We're together, Lu. Okay? Tell me you're in this with me."

"I'm with you. All the way."

Now that he had her, he'd never feel alone in this world again.

"I don't want you to give up hope," his agent said.

Right. Xander came out of Calamity Joe's with a breakfast sandwich and a coffee in one hand, his phone in the other. At the end of June, the town was full of tourists, and he didn't want to be around anyone right now. Not after getting this kind of news.

Which was why he'd left the bunkhouse and driven into town. They were in post-production, so much of the crew had been released. Fewer people meant private phone calls garnered more attention.

He headed toward his car. "When do I ever give up hope? It's not in my DNA."

"You got that right. You're a damn Wilder. Look…" Niall sighed into the receiver. "They think you're great. They *know* you are, but they can't—"

A couple of kids skateboarded past him, their wheels clacking on pavement. "Take a chance on someone who's been injured twice. I get it."

"They're going with Jay Devore. Which means his bet paid off."

When the recent college grad didn't get called by the eighth round, he'd decided to pull out of the draft, hoping for an opportunity just like the one with Seattle. It was risky, but it had obviously worked for him.

"He's healthy, hungry…I get it." Xander would have probably made the same choice. "So, that's it. Between my brothers, my dad, you…we've played our hand with all the teams. Everyone knows I'm here, and no one wants me." Fuck, that hurt. He hurried to move past the band playing in the gazebo.

"It doesn't mean it's over, okay? Quarterbacks are

going to get injured, they're not going to perform, and coaches are going to be looking at their short list. You're on it."

"Sure." There was nothing left to talk about.

"Let's go ahead and sign a contract for season two of *The Gridiron Grillers*. Maybe we can even get them to start filming now, while you've both got the time. I'll talk to them. In any event, stay positive, keep training. Your day's going to come."

"We changed the name."

"Sorry?"

"Lulu couldn't stand Gridiron Grillers. She got the name changed in the final hour." Neither of them liked the new name, *Cooking with X-Man and Lu*. But it was better than the original that excluded her entirely.

"Okay, well, whatever they call it, everyone in football's going to be watching it. In fact, let me ask around, see if I can find a coach who cooks. You can invite him on the show. That'll guarantee we draw the audience we're looking for."

"Sure."

Just as Xander opened his car door, a truck slowed. Tyler Cavanaugh pulled up and waved at him. "Oh, hey, man." Both hands full, he gave a chin nod.

"You're living with my daughter, and you bought breakfast at Calamity Joe's?"

He chuckled. "Listen, Niall, I've got to go. Tyler's here."

"Gotcha. I'll get on the phone with East/West. Get started on that contract."

"Sounds good."

"Hey," Niall said. "If anyone knows the coaches, it's him. Ask him if anyone cooks."

"Okay." He might do that. But not today. Today, he'd just be damn disappointed. Pocketing his phone, Xander stepped off the curb. "Sorry, that was my agent. How's it going?"

"Great. What'd you get from Calamity Joe's?"

"Sausage, egg, and cheese sandwich." He held up the bag. "And some breakfast cookies. Got a bunch if you want one."

"Sure."

Xander dug out one of the nut and date-filled bars and handed it over.

"Thanks." Tyler took a bite. "How'd the try-out go with Seattle?"

"Couldn't have gone better." Fear rose, but he focused on the moment, this conversation, the hot sun warming the top of his head. When it subsided, he said, "But they're going with someone else."

"Jay Devore?"

The man really was connected. "Yep."

"I'm happy to make a call—"

"I appreciate it, but I'm pretty sure everyone knows I'm available."

Tyler held up a finger. "One call. Just a friend of mine. I won't say you're looking for a team. I'll talk about the training center, mention that I ran into you there, talked to your physical therapist…I'll keep it casual."

What did he have to lose? "Okay, sure. Thank you."

"I'm sorry it didn't work out." Staring straight ahead, Tyler chewed thoughtfully. "One thing that's always gotten me through the hard times is knowing the only constant in life is change. Today feels like shit, but just like that"—he snapped his fingers—"tomorrow's a whole new world. That's a guarantee. You don't know what your life's going to look like an hour… a month…a year from now."

"I'll try to remember that."

"And here's something else. It might seem like that injury was the worst thing that happened to you, but it's going to turn out to be the best. You'll see. If not for it, you wouldn't have come here and gotten the best care in the world. You wouldn't have gotten this TV show, and you wouldn't have met my daughter."

"You're damn right about that. Lulu's the best thing that ever happened to me."

They'd spent the day shooting ads for the show, but the script had flown out the window when Lulu and Xander had started messing with each other. She had no idea what the editor could pull together with all the footage of them teasing and pranking each other, but she'd never laughed so hard in her life.

Now, they'd just come home from dinner with her family, and Lulu was exhausted. "I can't believe how well that went." The moment she entered her bedroom, she kicked off her ballet flats and curled her toes into the soft, thick carpet.

Xander had gone straight for the kitchen, and she could hear the faucet running and cupboards closing. Changing out of her leggings and blouse, she pulled on sweatpants and an old, super-soft Eiffel Tower T-shirt.

When she came back out into the main room, she found *Just Bake* queued up on the television and a mug on the kitchen counter waiting for the water in the kettle to boil.

Turns out, swooning is real. It's an actual thing.

Because right in that moment, she felt awash in fluttery, romantic feelings.

This man knew her. He listened, he paid attention.

And he took care of her. She was crazy to doubt herself —Trace had never done anything like this.

"You want popcorn or anything?" he called.

When she didn't answer, he came out of the kitchen. "You okay?" He touched her cheek with the back of his hand. "You look flushed."

I love you. But she wouldn't freak him out, so she wrapped her arms around his neck instead and gazed into his warm, hazel eyes. "Thank you."

"For what?" He glanced to the kitchen. "For making tea?" He hunched a shoulder. "You've been going all day. Figured you'd want to wind down."

"For not talking football with my dad all night." She kissed him and then went to pour honey into her mug.

Except when she reached the counter, she found he'd already done it. The exact amount she liked, too.

He headed for the couch and flopped down. "You know that bores me."

"That's not why you changed the subject when my dad brought it up."

When he didn't respond, she sat on his lap and clasped her hands behind his neck. "You did it because of Trace."

"Hey, we all have hot spots. All I need to do is see a Super Bowl ring, and I lose my shit."

"Yeah, but just so you know, I'm not worried about you using me to get to my dad. You don't need him."

"Nope. I just need you."

She braced her hand on his pecs and showed him with her mouth and her tongue just how much she needed *him.*

Her body warmed, heady sensations—*love*—swirled through her.

But just as his big hands made to shift her, stretch her out along him, the kettle whistled. "Let me get that." She got up to pour the water. "You want anything?"

"Nah, I'm good."

After a quick stir, she brought her mug over and set it on the coffee table. He reached for the remote but before starting the episode, he said, "I just want to thank you for the way you've handled the Seattle thing."

She hadn't done a single thing. She wished she could. She'd do anything to get him a contract.

"You're the only one not trying to cheer me up. I don't need to hear how good I am, how any team would be lucky to have me. I know I'm good. I know how well I performed during the play-offs. But, at the end of the day, I'm still not leading a team, and I've run out of possibilities. So, I don't need to hear empty words."

It wasn't that she didn't want to say, *I know it'll happen for you.* Because she did. She completely understood why people rushed to comfort him. No one could believe he was in this situation. She just knew how much it aggravated him to hear it.

Because it's how she felt when someone told her she was a great cook, she should never have been fired. Or that she'll get a new job—a better one—soon.

She could work hard and put herself out there, but there was no guarantee she'd ever catch the goal she chased.

He sat up, reached for her hand. "You know why I'm handling it okay? Because of the one possibility I hadn't considered." He kissed her palm. "Finding you. *Us.*"

Her heart swelled to bursting. *I swear this is too good to be true.*

"My brothers grew up in my dad's world of all football, all the time. But I grew up half in my mom's. And you know how spiritual Café Akasha is?" He grew energized, his eyes shining. "I don't know if I believe in all that woo woo stuff, but there's no denying the reality of my situation. Football has never worked out for me. I'm twenty-six. I finally had my shot during the play-offs and…" His expression said, *I got screwed again.* "But this cooking show fell right into my lap. And the timing? Abigail met us exactly when the network was pulling *The Farm Woman* and needed an immediate replacement. But not something that was waiting in the wings, something sensational. And that was us. Our chemistry. So, I have to believe football's not meant to be. But this is."

Oh, man. That didn't sound right. First, she didn't want to be some consolation prize. But secondly, he didn't actually think he could find the same kind of fulfillment doing a cooking show, did he? "The two things aren't mutually exclusive. We can sign the contract for season two, and you can still train and position yourself for a team to pick you up. It's not over."

"I can't keep investing all my energy into something that hasn't ever panned out. If I hadn't sustained two injuries, sure I'd keep hacking away at it. But look, that's not the point. The point is that I'm happier now than I've ever been. And I've won the Heisman. I've been married. I've been on the roster of the strongest team in the NFL."

She melted a little, realizing she was always too quick to doubt his feelings for her.

"I'm happy, Lu. You make me happy. So, tomorrow morning, I want us to meet with a realtor. I'm going to buy a house." He watched her carefully for a reaction. "I'm moving here."

"What're you saying? Are you talking about…are you asking me to live with you?"

"Yes. Because I never want to live without you again."

"But maybe we shouldn't buy something." *What if I get a dream job? What if he finally gets the call from his agent?* "Maybe we should rent."

"No matter what happens, don't we want a home base here, in Calamity?"

"You're really serious."

"Don't you want it, too?"

Her heart thundered, and she blinked back the sting of tears. It almost hurt to push past her doubts and *believe.* "Yes." She nodded. "Let's buy a house. Let's…God, Xander. Yes."

Using a slotted spoon, Lulu transferred the last of the gnocchi onto a parchment-lined baking sheet. She set it in the fridge to cool, before turning back to add the freshly chopped sage to her golden-brown butter.

Between filming and training, Xander hadn't been able to do more than guest coach a couple of times at Cassian's football camp this summer. Now, though, with the lighter schedule, he could spend more time with the kids.

Tonight, he'd cooked for the coaches, made a whole Mexican feast, so she'd come here, to her favorite place on earth. Chef Jonny's kitchen. She had a craving for her favorite dish.

A key in the lock had Lulu looking up from the skillet.

"That smell." The man himself strode down the hallway and stood before her. "Sage, butter…pasta?"

"Pretty good nose for an old man." She tilted her head so he could kiss her cheek. "You here to get some work done? Or did you forget to turn off the oven?"

"I came to see you. Stopped by the bunkhouse first, but you weren't there. Figured I'd try my luck here." He popped a gnocchi into his mouth. "Mm. Takes me back to the summer between freshman and sophomore year."

"You can't possibly remember the exact date."

"I do. Because it became the restaurant's most requested dish, and I had to tell them my chef moved to Paris."

Ouch. At the time, running had seemed her only choice. She'd convinced herself she'd never belonged anywhere but culinary school, and the fiasco with Trace had only proved it.

In retrospect, she could see she'd gotten lost in classes and then the crazy hours of being a chef, instead of facing her issue with Stella and Trace head-on and maybe growing from it.

Turned out, getting fired was the best thing that could have happened to her. She'd come home. Spent time with her family. Healed. And, for the first time in her life, she had a real relationship with her sisters.

And she had Xander. Warmth bloomed in her chest.

But Chef Jonny didn't need to hear any of that. She sprinkled fresh sage on top for garnish. "Most requested, huh?"

"Yes, and that's the truth."

"Well, it's still my favorite comfort food."

"Does my special girl need comforting?"

Scooping some butternut squash gnocchi into a clean, white bowl, she spooned the butter sauce on top and gently stirred. She lifted it to him.

"I already ate, but I won't say no to a taste. My bride made a lovely meal to celebrate a milestone."

"Ooh, what's the good news?"

"Skylar's pregnant with her second child."

"No way." She dropped the scraper and lunged for him, giving him a hug. "I'm so happy for you." She pulled away. "What a life you've built. You've grown this place into one of the most celebrated restaurants in the world, stayed married for forty years, and raised seven amazing kids. Eight, actually, considering the way you took in Cassian."

Jonny beamed with pride. "Seeing everyone around the table, that's when it hits me, what a good life it's been. Skylar, my baby, she fought falling in love long and hard, so to see her happy with Jinx…and Cassian…he had such a rough go but look at him now. Shows you the power of love, doesn't it?"

Serving herself a bowl, she reached for a fork.

Chef Jonny headed out of the kitchen. "Come. Let's sit down. I have just the wine for this dish."

Following him into the dining room, she set the bowls on a table. At the bar, Chef clinked glasses and popped a cork, before joining her with the white wine.

She tasted it. "This is lovely. What is it?"

"It's a Fiano, an old-vine Chenin Blanc." He reached for his fork. "Now, tell me what's got you cooking comfort food alone tonight."

"Nothing's wrong." *Couldn't be better.* "It's all in my head." She laughed. "I spend way too much time up there."

"Tell me what's on your mind."

"It's all so up in the air, you know?"

"Are we talking about your career?"

"Well, that, for sure. But...today Xander and I went house hunting."

His eyebrows shot up.

"I know. Crazy, right? I want it"—*so much*—"but something feels wrong about it. Like..."

"It's too soon?"

"Honestly, it doesn't feel too soon. I guess I'm just afraid he's using our relationship to cover up a major loss in his life." She supposed it was common knowledge he was a free agent. "He thinks his football career's over."

"Ah. I see."

And I don't want to go all-in, only to have him dump me the second he signs with a team. "We're both in a holding pattern. I'm waiting to get a chef de cuisine job, he's waiting for a contract...so is buying a house a way for him to convince himself he's okay without football, when we both know it's not?"

"How do you feel about living in Calamity? I know your dreams were much bigger."

"I mean, we're talking about a life with Xander. I want it very much. At the same time, I'm totally unsure about my future. If a job comes up in New York City, I have to take it."

"What if a job came up here?

She set down her fork, going very still. "What're you saying?"

"I'm saying, if you stay in town, if you decide to make your home here, then one day *this* could be your kitchen." Chef Jonny leaned across the table and rested his warm palm on top of her hand. "Sixty is coming up much faster than I'd like. At some point, I'll retire. You don't know the business side, but I do. I can teach you everything you need to know, while you're making my customers the kind of food that will make them come back again and again." He sat back in his chair. "I'm saying if you and Xander decide to stay in Calamity, you can rest assured you'll always have a job in my kitchen."

"I can't believe it. *Jonny*." She threw herself into his arms. "That's such an honor."

He tightened his hold before letting her go. "This is where you started, and this is where you belong."

"I've never heard you talk about retiring before."

"I love this world Jacqueline and I have created. And, of course, I've *thought* about retiring but not in any concrete way. But who better to take over than you?" He drank some wine. "If the show doesn't work out, if you don't get another chef de cuisine job, I want you to know you're always welcome here."

Chapter Eighteen

Rain pattered against the windows, and the scents of warm butter and baking bread filled the bunkhouse. Just back from the training center, Xander kicked off his shoes and scraped his fingers through his damp hair.

He heard the women chatting quietly in the kitchen, the clatter of pans, the rush of water in the sink, and a sense of home settled over him.

It wasn't the bunkhouse, and it wasn't Calamity. It was Lulu. He liked the way she lived, loved the peace she brought him.

If he married her, he'd get to feel this every day of his life.

Life's something, isn't it? After his divorce, he'd shoved relationships to the bottom of his list of priorities. He'd been focused exclusively on football. And now he was thinking about spending his life with this woman?

Hell, yeah, I am.

Because he couldn't imagine being with anyone else.

He liked the scent lingering in the bedroom after she

got ready for the day. He got goosebumps watching her cook—she was just so damn sensual. He liked the quiet she brought to his home—and his heart.

He liked everything about her.

On bare feet, he headed into the kitchen, drawn by the sound of their easy conversation.

Lulu had spent the morning at her friend's apiary, and they'd come back here to try out the different flavors of honey.

He watched them for a moment, Lulu rinsing something at the sink, Harley cracking open the oven to peer inside.

"It's ready." The former pro surfer searched a couple cabinets.

"I got it." Lulu grabbed an oven mitt. They'd hung them on hooks for easier access while filming. When she turned back to the sink, she spotted him. "Oh." She snatched the nearest towel to dry her hands. "You're back." With a huge grin, she cupped his face and planted a kiss on his mouth. "Good work out?"

For a moment there, he couldn't speak. Overcome with affection, all he could do was take in this beautiful woman who'd somehow chosen to pour all that passion onto *him*.

He didn't know what the hell she saw that made her look at him like that—like he hung the moon—but he'd never do anything to extinguish that light. "It went great." He gestured toward the flour-strewn cutting board. "What're you making?"

"After our honey tasting party, Harley made baklava."

"Cool. Can't wait to try it."

"Your phone's been blowing up." Lulu tipped her head to the dining room table where he'd left it.

Shit. Thinking of his family, he rushed to get it and saw Niall's name. Abigail had sent the contract off to his attorney, so they might've hit a snag.

Niall: Can you give me a call?

Niall: put the spatula down and call me.

Niall: I've got news on your actual career

Niall: WTF, man. Call me.

Niall: ????

Niall: Look, I got a call from the Wildcats' office. They need your permission to talk to the physical therapist and doctor at the training center.

The Wildcats? Holy shit, could Jones be out? The quarterback had missed a few games last season and no one knew why.

He's supposed to be ready to play this year, so maybe they're looking at me as a backup?

Niall: Check your email. Sent you the form. Sign it. Now.

The idea of being a backup…just made him feel tired.

He glanced into the kitchen and found the women huddled over the baking dish they'd pulled from the oven. He had nothing to lose by letting the team talk to his therapist, so he headed into his bedroom to fire up his laptop.

Seemed crazy, but for the first time, he thought he might prefer to do this show and be with Lulu than be a backup quarterback in the NFL.

Lowering his ball cap to block the afternoon sun, Xander stood by the grill in Cassian's backyard. Someone cannonballed into the pool, splattering him with cold water. A group played volleyball on the lawn, and everyone was laughing and having a good time.

He was about to flip the steaks when he caught a bright spot of yellow. Lulu came out of the house carrying a vegetable platter. She turned back to laugh at something someone said, looking so pretty in a bikini top and a colorful scarf wrapped around her hips.

Holding a bowl of salad, Coco came out behind her, a large blob attached to her chest in a sling. When her husband dangled a swimsuit in front of her, she eyed the pool—a fancy affair with tropical landscaping that made it look like an island resort.

After a moment's hesitation, Coco gave in. She untied the carrier and handed the baby over to her sister, before snatching the one-piece out of Beckett's hand and dashing into the house to change.

That left Lulu alone with a two-month-old baby. She rocked gently, smiling and talking to the little girl.

An image hit him—so vivid, so real, his body went electric, and his heart swelled to a painful fullness. A house filled with kids, a mudroom stuffed with sneakers, a scarred table loaded with dirty plates and lively conversation. Lulu flipping pancakes, him pouring syrup.

He wanted it fiercely.

One hundred percent, no reservations.

Because I love her.

I fucking love that woman.

Only as he started to charge over there and tell her, did he realize he was still holding tongs. The steaks. *Right.* As he flipped them, the juices sizzled, and smoke flared. He still wasn't sure if he believed in all that mystical stuff, but if he did, he could see how every moment of his life had brought him here, to Calamity, to a life away from football.

And he knew, if he'd signed with Seattle, he'd have lost

her. She'd be working in New York City or Paris, and even if they did manage the distance, Lulu would see him on social media with other women, she'd hear rumors of him hooking up on the road.

None of it true, of course.

But it wouldn't matter. He'd seen it all before. Cassian's playboy reputation had almost cost him the love of his life.

Not many relationships went the distance in pro sports.

Mine will. He'd damn well make sure of it.

"Watch this," someone shouted.

Xander turned in time to see Andre leap off the diving board, his big body creating a massive splash. "Hey," Damon barked, holding his tumbler out in front of him, shirt soaked.

Phone vibrating in his pocket, Xander set down the tongs to pull it out. His brothers had been giving him a rash of shit about becoming a homeowner, joking about him buying a minivan and wearing Dad jeans.

Except...this wasn't a familiar number. And no caller ID. Area code 214.

Isn't that Dallas?

The *Wildcats*? No, they'd go through his agent. They wouldn't call him directly.

He could ignore it, but...*what if?* whispered in his mind. He stabbed the accept button. "Hello?"

"Xander?" The deep voice sounded eager.

"Yes." Xander caught the attention of the guys at the table closest to him. He pointed at the grill, and Ryker got up, his chair legs screeching on the concrete.

"This is Coach Ledbetter with the Wildcats."

Shock ripped through him so hard he went dizzy. He

handed Ryker the tongs and headed for the shade at the side of the house.

"You there?" the coach asked.

"Yes. I'm here. Just having a barbecue with some of the guys."

"Great. Listen, do you have a minute?"

He swiped the perspiration off his brow. "Sure do."

"I was about to call your agent, but I'd like to talk to you first. Hope it's okay that Tyler gave me your number."

He'd feel like such an asshole if his blood pressure had spiked, only to learn the guy wanted to be on *Cooking with X-man and Lu*. "Absolutely. What's up?"

"Tyler told me about your show, so if you want to give my wife cooking lessons, that'd be great." A muffled sound was followed by, "I'm kidding. You're a great cook. After I scraped off the burnt parts, the toast was really good." Then, he came back on the line. "Anyhow, I'm not calling about that. Yeah, so, Tyler and I were talking the other day —he knows I've got a situation here. When he told me about the work you're doing at the training center, it helped me make a decision I've been struggling with. I want to thank you for letting me talk to your therapist. I'll bet you're happy with the prognosis."

"You have no idea."

"I'm going to tell you something, we need you. We need a guy who's going to pull us out of this rut. You have any interest in coming to Dallas to work out with my guys?"

"That depends." He needed to be very clear. Because he wasn't fucking up this life he'd just found for more of the same. "Are we talking backup? Or something else."

"I'm looking for a franchise player, Xander. I'm

looking for the man that'll lead this team to the Super Bowl. You think you can do that?"

"I know I can." He sounded as solid and confident as he felt. Not a shred of doubt.

"Yeah, figured you'd say that. How soon you think you can get here?"

"I'm about to demolish a porterhouse steak with my friends. An hour from now, I'll be packed and headed for the airport. Will that work for you?"

Coach chuckled. "Yeah, you're the man, all right. Let me get on the phone with your agent, and we'll have a chat. But I'll let the pilot know he's going to Calamity."

The moment he disconnected, he was on the move. Passing Ryker, he swatted him on the back. "Don't burn 'em."

"I don't burn what goes in my belly."

But Xander was already opening the door and stepping into the air-conditioned kitchen. "Lu?"

She stood at the counter, sunlight pouring in from the window and bathing her skin in a golden glow. "What's up?"

He couldn't lose her over this. He needed her to stick with him.

She tipped the platter toward him. "Caprese. Your favorite." She looked so serene, so beautiful, he almost forgot why he'd sought her out. Her forehead crinkled, and she came right over to him. "You all right?"

He held up his phone. "I just got a call."

She gazed up at him, searching his expression, and he loved that she needed to know how he was feeling. He hadn't known how alone he'd felt most of his life until he'd met her, and the ache had gone away.

"The head coach of the Wildcats just called. He wants me to try out."

"That's great." But she didn't smile. She knew he was conflicted. "You excited?"

"Yes."

"But?"

He scrubbed his jaw. "No buts. It's good." Energy pulsed under his skin. "He thinks I can take them to the Super Bowl."

"You can." She said it so matter-of-factly, he knew she wasn't tossing out empty words.

Uncertainty crawled up his spine like a spider. He paced to the window, gazed out to the bright green lawn at the side of Cassian's house. "What if I can't?" He gave a bitter chuckle. "Wouldn't that be something? The phenom gets his shot…and sucks."

"That would be incredibly embarrassing." She caressed his back. "But even if you did suck, you'd just fight your way back. You didn't suddenly lose every repetition, every drill, every bit of muscle memory from a lifetime of training."

"No."

"But let me ask you this. If someone called me just now and asked me to be the chef de cuisine of one of the best restaurants in the world, and I told you I was terrified and didn't think I wanted to do it, what would you tell me?"

He cut her a look. "I'd say take it."

"Even though I failed in Maui?"

"Yeah, of course. You never asked for help. You didn't tell them you'd never done payroll and hiring. This time, you would. And I know you can do it."

"Me, too, but I'd still be anxious because of how it felt

to be fired. You're scared because you know how it feels to get sacked and hurt your shoulder."

That's exactly right. He let out a breath. "I am." He dreamed about it at night. Woke up sweating.

"If that happens, if you get spooked, then you get a sports therapist to remind you how to block out those fears. To live in the moment, and to live fiercely."

A wave of emotion more powerful than anything he'd ever felt before crashed over him. "I love you."

Her eyes went wide.

"I do." He pulled her against him. "I love you, Lulu."

Happiness bloomed across her features. "I love you, too." She said it on a whisper, voice filled with awe.

"If I do this, we do it together."

"What does that mean, exactly?"

"It means I'm only trying out with the Wildcats if I know we're staying together."

It was like watching an action scene in a movie, as she fought one fear after another, until finally she looked away. "You know I'm not going to give up on us. But I think I know what you're really asking, and I want to take it one step at a time. Go for your try-out and we'll see what happens."

His training at Fin's Antigravity Center had paid off. After a couple hours on the field with the team and another hour with the position coach, Xander'd had his best day in years. One pass after another had fallen right into the pocket.

He felt good. He felt fucking great.

He hadn't even had a chance to shower before Coach had called him into his office. "I liked what I saw, and

Reggie didn't have enough good things to say about you." Carl Ledbetter was a good-looking, fit guy with a full head of dark blonde hair and brown eyes.

"Glad to hear it. It felt good."

Coach sat back in his chair, resting his chin on his steepled hands, eyes gleaming. "I just signed Gunnar Morrison."

"No kidding?" In college, he and Gunnar had been an unstoppable force. For the first time, since landing in Dallas, Xander saw his future. *Here*.

"You think you two still have the magic?"

"If we don't, we'll get it back."

He pushed the chair back and set his elbows on his desk. "Bob Covington hired me three years ago, and I haven't delivered on my promises. These guys just haven't caught a groove together. We've had issues with ego, injuries... But you and Gunnar, you're my dream team. I said it when they hired me, and I'll say it now. If I can get the two of you, we're wearing Superbowl rings next February."

His heart pounded, his blood pumped.

"Does that sound good to you?"

"You know it does."

Someone rapped lightly on the door, before pushing it open. A gorgeous woman sashayed in carrying a fruit salad with a candle in the center. One hand cupped it to keep it lit. "Okay, handsome, I'm bringing the celebration to you." She glanced at Xander. "Don't mind me. I'll only be a minute."

Coach got up, eyes soft, as he greeted the woman who had to be his wife. "I'm sorry. The kid's only in town two nights. He's got to get back to—" Awareness gripped his features and he turned back to Xander. "Ah. Right. I talked to your agent about that show you're working on. Unfortunately, your contract doesn't allow you to do reality television."

"That's not what it is. It's a cooking show. And it films during the off-season."

His wife set the fruit salad down. "Babe, hammer that out once I leave." She gestured for him to blow it out.

He grinned. "I don't need a candle. All my dreams came true the moment I met you. Happy anniversary." He kissed her on the mouth, cupping the back of her head to hold her in place. When they stopped kissing, their foreheads remained pressed together. "I'll be home for dinner, and we'll celebrate then."

"You bet we will." She pulled away and reached a hand to Xander. "Kathy Ledbetter."

"Alexander Wilder. It's nice to meet you."

"All right, I'm going. This..." She lifted the fruit salad before setting it down. "Is less about our anniversary and more about getting good food in him. During negotiations and when training camp's about to start...oh, who am I kidding? Being an NFL coach is 24/7. But it makes him happy, so I can't complain." This time, she kissed Coach's cheek. "See you later."

Carl watched her go, clearly conflicted. "I don't know how I got so lucky." Sighing, his gaze landed on a framed photograph of his family—his wife and three teenage daughters. "All right, you've got a plane to catch. We'll let the lawyers hash out a deal, but I want to see you on the field when training camp starts in two weeks."

On her way to Calamity Joe's, Lulu caught the *Going Out of Business Sale* sign in the window of Duke's Toy Store. She stopped for a moment to take it in.

What in the world?

Every year for their birthdays, her dad used to take each of them here alone on a Saturday morning. They got to choose three gifts. One for themselves, one to share with their sisters, and one for the Women's and Children's Shelter. She had so many memories of that store.

Just as she opened the door of the coffee shop, a message came in on her phone. She stepped inside, out of the glare of the sun, and read it.

Xander: Coming in for a landing.

Excitement flashed through her.

Lulu: can't wait to see you.

Xander: where are you?

Lulu: in town. But I'll head home right now.

Xander: no rush. Not landing for twenty minutes, and then it's a ten minute drive home.

Xander: be naked

Xander: covered in chocolate sauce and whipped cream

Lulu: someone's hungry

Xander: starving, yes. The driver asked if I wanted to grab something to eat on the way to the airport, but I just wanted to come home.

Lulu: at Calamity Joe's. I'll grab you a breakfast sandwich

She took her place in line.

Xander: so we're not sexting?

Lulu: Absolutely not. Mr. Dawson, my eighth-grade math teacher's here. He's ordering right now. *waves at Mr. Dawson*

At that moment, Harley looked up, spotted her in line, and smiled.

Xander: there's a lot of turbulence. This could be our last conversation. Give me something.

Lulu: Dirty or sweet?

Xander: If I'm going to meet my maker, best make it sweet.

Now that he was moving to Dallas, she found it harder to tell him how she felt. Was she still all-in? Yes. But did she one hundred percent believe they'd stay together once he moved?

No. Still, she knew if she wanted it to work out, she'd have to give her whole self. It was just…she felt vulnerable. He'd stepped out of their bubble. He was out there meeting new people, surrounded by eager fans and press and the Wildcats staff…

But if she didn't claim this emotion, this connection to him, she'd be making the first move in distancing them.

Lulu: I love you, Alexander Wilder. Come home to me.

The line moved forward, and she waited. No response.

Not even three dots to show he was writing something.

Well, hell. She'd put herself out there and…maybe he got distracted? Another call? The flight attendant reminding him to buckle up?

She stared at the screen, a fog of fear settling around her.

Seriously, Xander, you've got no response to that?
Nothing?

Finally, three dots floated on the screen, and her pulse quickened.

If he said, *Love you, too*, she'd know his feelings had

cooled. And she understood. He had to go into hardcore football mode. *That's how he's built.*

She'd known this would happen, so she couldn't go getting all devastated.

If he gave her some emojis, it was done. Dead.

Please don't give me emojis.

"Hey, girl. What can I get you?"

But she couldn't for the life of her take her gaze off the screen. Not until his words appeared.

"Lu?" Harley prodded.

"Sorry. Hi. Um, can I get a breakfast sandwich and a chai tea, please? Hot? To go? Both of them."

"Of course." Harley turned to a barista. "Can you take over please?"

"Sure. No problem."

As her friend pulled off her apron and came out from behind the counter, Lulu moved to the pick-up station. She held her breath as those three dots continued to undulate.

Xander: I will always come home to you, because you *are* my home.

Dead.

Lulu Cavanaugh died in Calamity Joe's on July sixteenth from a sudden heart attack brought on by the shocking confession of her boyfriend's undying love and affection.

"Hey, you all right?" Harley came up to her. "What's going on? You looked like you got the worst news just now."

A single tear spilled down her cheek. "I'm an idiot." She didn't wipe it away.

With people crowding around them, waiting for their drinks, Harley grabbed her arm. "Come here." She led them to the other side of the room, to the only free table. They sat across from each other at the tiny two-top. "Talk to me."

"This is just between us."

"Of course."

"Xander's moving."

"Without you?"

She nodded. "He's going to play for Dallas." She leaned closer. "Please don't tell anyone."

Harley just smiled. "I got you."

"And my mind immediately went to, *We're over. It can't possibly work.*" She let out a shaky breath. "I'm afraid he's going to forget all about me."

"And find someone more dazzling?"

Lulu broke out laughing. "I love you. Thank you for getting me."

"Listen, I was there. I had to suffer through the Griffin years."

"Oh, please, I hardly talked about it." She waved a hand dismissively. "I played out the whole thing in my head."

"That's not what I mean. From my perspective, you were this beautiful, smart, creative woman...who watched the gilded boy from afar. As if you weren't in his league."

"Well, I wasn't."

"Wrong. *That's* the part that was all in your head. Lu, you could've dated plenty of guys, but you chose the one who kept to himself, who didn't have a lot of friends. It's almost like he was some blank screen, and you projected all your insecurities onto him."

The simple truth hit like a nuclear blast, incinerating everything she'd ever believed about herself.

"I guess, because you come from this super outgoing family, it made you feel weird because you weren't like them. Like, your parents were always throwing galas and fundraisers for their foundation, when all you wanted to do was stay home and cook. Your mom and sisters would get new dresses and shoes, the stylist would come do their make-up and hair, and there you were with dirt stains on your knees from planting in your garden." When Lulu didn't speak, her friend's brow creased with worry. "I'm sorry. I shouldn't have said all that."

"No, it's just sort of mind-blowing, that whole perspective."

"Well, all I know is that everyone has insecurities, and you can either let yours hold you back, or you can make them your bitch."

"Here you go." The barista brought over her chai and the breakfast sandwich in a wax bag. He also set down a plate of muffins and scones. "Thought you might like a little something with your tea."

Lulu pulled herself together enough to give him a smile. "Thank you."

"Harley?" the barista asked. "Want anything?"

"No, thanks. I'm good. Give me five more minutes?"

"No rush. We got this."

Once he left, Harley said, "These are the honey muffins and scones I was telling you about."

"Oh, yummy." She broke off a piece and took a moment to taste the flavors. "Pecans, ginger…is that lemon zest?"

"Yes, you weirdo. I was making a bunch of things at once, and I started to scrape the lemon peel over the batter and caught myself before I ruined the whole batch. Of course, you would taste the three tiny little specs that fell in."

"That's why they pay me the big bucks." She took another bite. "Actually, no one's paying me anything."

"Look at us. I mean, we had such big dreams, and now we're both back in Calamity."

"I like it here."

"I know. It's just been a hard adjustment for me. It'd help if I knew what I wanted to do next."

Lulu broke off a piece of the scone. "You must have some ideas."

"The obvious choice is for me to be a sports agent, or something like the social media coordinator for the World Surf League."

"But?"

"I don't want to watch other people surf. I want…" Harley tapped her fingertips on the table.

"What do you want?"

Her friend leaned in, like she was about to reveal a deep, dark secret. "I want to bake."

Lulu smiled. "You make it sound like you're confessing your dream in life is to make skin suits. Why is baking bad?"

"I'm an athlete. I'm not a baker."

"Isn't there some saying about how we are what we do? You've got an apiary, you're baking muffins and scones and cookies for your mom's shop…?"

"Yeah, I know." She tipped her head towards the wall. "Duke's retiring."

"I saw that. I can't believe he's going out of business."

"He can't compete with the big box stores, so he's moving. He says he wants to be closer to his kids anyway."

"He can't do that." Lulu said it with a laugh. "That's our childhood he's walking away from."

"I know, right? Remember those stick candies we used to get?"

"Cherry for me."

Harley raised a hand. "Root beer."

"Do you know what's taking its place?"

"Well, funny you should ask." Harley picked up a muffin. "Is it crazy to put a bakery there? In the center of town?"

Well, this is interesting. "The rent's pretty high. You might want to go a few blocks back. Or maybe the Half Moon shopping plaza?"

"Yeah, but I figured since my mom's selling coffee right next door, I could take down this wall and add more seating."

"Oh, I see where you're going with this. I like that. You'd have to sell a whole lot of muffins, though, to cover Main Street rent. What about offering breakfast? Maybe picnics for backpackers and hikers?"

"Yeah, but then it wouldn't be a bakery. It'd be a café."

"True. Well, you don't want to take away your mom's business, so you could let her have the muffins, and you can do croissants and donuts. You know those apple pies you can get at McDonald's? Those hot pockets of yummy deliciousness? You'd have lines out the door for those."

"Oh, God, here she goes. I feel like I need to stand back and just let this happen."

Realizing what she'd just done, she sat back. "I just took your idea and ran right off the ranch, didn't I?"

"You did, and I love it. Go, go, go."

"Okay…" A vision hit her. A store that looked like all those restaurant images she'd saved over the years. Rustic, big tables loaded with cake plates, huge wooden bookshelves stacked with jars of jam and bags of scone mixes. A refrigerated section of take-away dishes.

And a café. *Where I can cook whatever I want.*

Her breath hitched—like she was in an elevator as it whisked straight up to the penthouse.

A feeling of rightness took hold of her.

Harley smiled. "You have more. I can see it on your face. Just go with it. Riff for me, girl."

"Well, I'm just thinking out loud here, but you know what kind of business would be enough to cover rent? What if we did a gourmet store, where we not only sold picnic baskets for hikers, but we had a whole section of prepared foods for people who come back from a day out on the trails and just want to crash in their hotel rooms? Imagine if we had theme baskets. Night Under the Stars, Fourth of July."

Harley clapped. "Did you just say we?"

"No. God, I didn't mean literally me. You'd have to hire a local chef. I was just throwing out ideas."

"What if we catered parties, too?"

Lulu laughed. "Listen to us, turning a simple bakery into an empire. We're a perfect fit, aren't we?"

"I think we are."

Her phone vibrated.

Xander: landed. You naked yet?

Happiness shot through her.

"Is that him?" Harley asked.

"Yeah, I should go."

"If I did this, would you consider doing it with me?" Harley asked.

"For something so outside the realm of what I saw myself doing with my life, I did get awfully excited there for a moment." And, oddly, far more enthusiastic about this idea than taking over the Homesteader Inn. "And I do think it's something I'd like—but it'll have to be later. I have a few more bells to ring in my career. In the meantime, I'd be more than happy to help you get it started. It would be a no-brainer to get investors for something like this."

Harley walked her out. "I love your ideas. I've actually missed you a lot over the years." They hugged. "I don't know where it came from, this idea that you're not good enough, because you're so full of energy and ideas. You were a really good friend to me, Lu. After Ben dumped me? You were there. Girl, you've got to change the conversation in your head. Xander would be crazy to let you go."

She hugged those words close to her heart.

She had a feeling she would need them in the coming days.

Chapter Nineteen

AFTER SETTING THE BREAKFAST SANDWICH IN THE warming oven, Lulu filled a kettle and lit the burner. Just as she grabbed the French press, she heard the tinny sound of Kane Brown blasting outside.

Xander. She dashed out of the kitchen and threw open the door. *He's home.*

Leaning into the car, he pulled out his duffle bag, giving her an outstanding view of that very fine ass. His long sleeve T-shirt hugged his muscular back and worn jeans accentuated strong thighs.

When he turned to face her, his expression brightened with pure joy. She made a run for him, and he took off, meeting her halfway. Dropping the bag, he grabbed her bottom, kissing her like he was starved for her.

He didn't know it, but she needed this.

She needed to be loved this hard, this deep, this thoroughly.

Her whole life she'd longed for it, but she'd never imagined really finding it. She'd thought it was a weakness, her immature need for the kind of companionship that didn't exist.

But it did. He was living proof.

And now—

Oh. Carrying her with him, he dropped low to pick up his bag and strode into the bunkhouse. Kicking the door shut, he headed down the dark, cool hallway.

Burying her face in his neck, she breathed in the scent of clean clothes and fresh soap. "Missed you." She went sailing through the air, landing with a bounce on his mattress. Before she could pull herself together, he was stripping out of his jeans and T-shirt.

"You like that dress?" He had a dangerous glint in his eyes.

"I love it, why?" Anticipation had her shaky, as she drank in his taut belly, the ridged abs, and smooth, tan skin.

"Then, you better take it off." He stood like a warrior, hands on his hips, ready to plunder. "Now."

Scrambling to sit up, Lulu reached for the hem and pulled the dress over her head.

And then he was on top of her, kissing her, one hand cupping her breast, the other gripping her bottom. "You're naked for me." When he plucked her nipple, she sucked in a breath.

Soon as she'd gotten home, she'd stripped off her panties and bra, ready for him. "Figured you'd want easy access."

"That's fucking hot." His mouth pressed a trail of kisses down her neck, along her collarbone, until it closed over her nipple. "Mm." His tongue licked and swirled, his erection hot and heavy on her thigh.

Her legs fell open, and she hitched her hips, eager to

be filled with him, to be swallowed whole by his desire. He made her feel wanted, sexy.

He gave her everything she'd ever craved.

She reached for him, closed her hand around his thick length, but he batted her away. "Touch me, and it's gonna be over."

"I can't wait."

"You're gonna have to wait. Gotta visit all those places I missed while I was away."

"Mm." She swished her bottom, settling deeper into the down duvet. "That sounds good."

He lavished his attention on her other breast, his tongue sucking and flicking, before pressing a trail of kisses down her stomach. When she pushed the top of his head, he chuckled, and then spread her legs wider to lick her inner thigh and the sensitive spot behind her knee.

His relentless, sensual touches drove her into a frenzy, and she reached between them again, giving him a hard squeeze.

"Nuh uh. Not done catching up yet."

"That's sweet and all." She lifted so suddenly he didn't have a chance to brace himself and flipped him over. "But it's been four days, and I'm going to need to speed things up here." She kissed his neck, licking a slow path down his chest and following the happy trail that led to her most favorite place. Her hands glided down his shoulder to his biceps and squeezed. "You are just delicious."

Straddling him, she shifted lower until she sat on his thighs. She licked all the way up his hard length and then back down, doing it again and again, making him slick and wet. She had him panting by the time she sucked him into her mouth. And then, when she flicked her tongue under the sensitive head, his back arched off the mattress and he shouted, "Fuck."

She loved seeing this disciplined man lose control. Loved that she could turn him wild. Her hand pumped in rhythm with her mouth.

Wrapping her hair in his fist, he jerked up, pulling her off him. "Get on me."

Wasting no time, she sat up on her knees, gripped him, and sank down. She took him deep, until he filled her completely. Hands planted on his chest, she rocked slowly, her body on fire from the smoldering look in his eyes.

He groaned, gripping her ass and moving her on him. He was so hard, so thick, and every time she slammed down, he passed right over her pleasure center. Faster and faster, the friction wound her up until every cell hummed and vibrated, the erotic song reaching a frenzied beat.

"Fuck, yeah. Look at you. So fucking hot." He reached for her breasts, held them lightly, so he could feel them jiggle in his palms, just how he liked. And then, as he punched his hips up, he squeezed them, pinching her nipples, sending a jolt of electric heat through her.

Euphoria washed in, saturating her, and then his finger touched her clit, and she sizzled. "*Xander*." It only took a few swirls to shatter her. She writhed on him, her body twisting, her fingers fisting in the blanket.

Perspiration glistened on his handsome face, his features went taut, and his ass lifted off the mattress as he pounded into her, punctuating each hard snap with a "*Fuck*."

With his head tipped back, his jaw hanging open in a silent, desperate scream, he came inside her. After a few slow pumps, he eased out, and she collapsed beside him.

He lifted his arm, and she snuggled against his body. With a hand on his chest, she could feel his rapid breaths.

"I missed you." His tone, desperate, harsh, caught her attention. "I didn't like it."

The intensity in his eyes made her squirm. *What's he saying?*

He sat up. "I don't want to be away from you." Catching her under her arms, he hauled her onto his lap. "If things work out with the contract, will you come with me?"

Move to Dallas? Pushing away, she got up and found one of his dress shirts hanging off the back of a chair. By the time she'd shoved her arms through the sleeves, he was standing behind her.

"Hear me out—"

"What would I do in Dallas?" A riot of emotion fought within her. The naive teenager who'd crushed on a boy she didn't know at all, who'd been ready to marry a guy who only wanted to be a Cavanaugh, wanted to shout, *Yes!* That girl would follow him anywhere.

The woman who'd won Student of the Year out of a pool of chefs from every accredited cooking school in the world, who'd scored the coveted job at Sublime, who'd recovered from her first and only failure by creating a Food Channel cooking show…that woman was confused… lost…scared.

So, he got to live his dream, but she had to give up hers? *Is that what he's asking?* That didn't feel right, but she couldn't think straight. "You know how much that Michelin star means to me. Exactly what your contract with the Wildcats means to you."

"I do know that."

"So, then, what about my career?"

"I know Michelin doesn't cover Dallas yet, but it has chefs who've worked in starred restaurants before. There's this guy, Daniel Costello, he earned a star in Chicago, and now he's got a restaurant in Dallas. And he's just one example. It's a big enough city to draw top chefs. I'm thinking you could be the one to put Texas on the Michelin map."

Fear collapsed into a pile of dust and debris. She walked right into his arms. "I'm a nut."

"No, you're not. I *am* being selfish. I know it's not the path you want, and that's why I did some research to see if it was even feasible for you to consider coming with me. It's not the exact right fit, but you could make it happen in Dallas."

She pressed her cheek to his chest. "I'm sorry for over-reacting."

"It's okay. And I understand if you don't want to come with me. I just don't want to be without you."

She pulled away. "It'll be different once you start playing. You're going to want to prove yourself to the coach and your teammates, you're going to be hellbent on leading them to the playoffs."

"Lulu, I know I've told you that meeting you has changed things for me. That for the first time, I see football as my career, and you're my heart. My home. But I'm asking you to give me a chance to *show* you."

The world tipped sideways, and she reached for the dresser. Her mind raced, and she couldn't get a handle on what she was feeling.

They wouldn't work if she didn't go with him. She knew that. Their jobs were too demanding. But, at the same time, what if she moved, gave up her dreams—only for the relationship to crash and burn?

She was torn, and nothing made sense right now. "Chef Jonny offered me a job."

"Okay." He sounded quick, efficient, like he was in crisis mode, securing the situation. "I didn't see that coming. But...we can make that work. As long as we don't end because I'm playing in Texas."

"No, I'm not taking it. Not right now. He said I'll always have a job with him, and that one day, if I wanted, I could take over for him. The Inn could be my restaurant."

"That's amazing."

"I don't even know why I told you about it. He's not ready to retire, and I'm not..." She lifted her hands. "I don't know what I want." No, she did know what she wanted.

She wanted to move to Dallas to be with him—but she also wanted—*needed*—to get back on track. She couldn't end her career with a failure like Maui.

"You want me to know that you have options, and that's fair. I'm asking you to make a huge sacrifice so I can live my dream. But I'll never ask you to give up yours. If that means you stay in Calamity and work at The Inn, then that's what we'll do. You get a job in LA, New York... we'll figure it out."

"With our schedules, long distance won't work." She gazed up at him needing to see something—she didn't know quite what. But she needed...more.

He grabbed her arm. "It will work, Lu. It'll work because I'll quit football before I give you up. I love you, and I'll do what it takes to keep us together."

Determination. That's what she'd needed. And that's what he'd given her. "I'd never ask you to give up football."

"And I'd never ask you to give up your Michelin star.

So, that's settled. Neither of us has to choose. The season goes from July to January. I'll live wherever you are the rest of the year, and I'll come home every chance I get."

He was serious.

He loved her all the way.

"*Xander.*" She didn't know what to do with this much emotion. She felt ripe with it. "I love you so much."

"I love you, too."

"For me, getting a star means I've achieved a certain level of excellence in my field, but it doesn't mean more than us." She got up on her toes and pulled his mouth down to hers, kissing him, slow, sweet, and full of love. "I'm going to Dallas with you."

"Shit, Lu." Color flooded his cheeks. "Are you sure?"

A sense of absolute rightness infused her. "I am. I'm moving to Dallas." She got up on her toes for a kiss, but he held back.

"There's one problem. They're still negotiating my contract, but they're not going to let me do reality television."

"It's not reality—"

"I know. Believe me, we're fighting that point. But they need me to represent the Wildcats' brand. I'm the quarterback, the face of the team."

She grinned so big she knew she had to look ridiculous. "Did you hear what you just said?"

"Yeah." He blew out a slow breath, blinking away the sheen in his eyes. "I can't believe it."

"I'm so proud of you. You did it."

"I did, but I'll tell you something. There's a difference between the happy you feel when you sign a big contract, and the happy you feel when you're holding the one person in the world who gets you, who makes you feel like home, who's going to carry your babies."

"Babies?"

"Yeah, I want to make babies with you. I want everything with you."

She couldn't believe it. Her dream had come true.

Lulu Cavanaugh had found her match.

Xander stepped off the private jet and headed toward the air strip's office. Camera lights flashed, making it hard to see the PR team waiting to greet him.

Once his eyes adjusted, he took in the huge crowd. Must be a celebrity landing at the same time.

"X-Man," someone called.

"Xander."

Whoa. He hadn't expected the paparazzi to show up on his first day in town. He had a full schedule of interviews and press this week, but he'd figured he could at least check into the hotel and have a night to himself.

"X-Man." A tall, slender woman stepped forward and greeted him with a firm handshake. "I'm Marley. This is Cliff, and this is Rocky. The three of us handle the team's public affairs, charitable foundation, and alumni program."

First, Xander shook hands with the suited man. "Cliff, nice to meet you." And then with the young woman. "Rocky, a pleasure."

"How was your flight?" Marley asked.

"Great." He walked alongside them as they headed toward a massive, gleaming SUV.

"You weren't expecting all the fanfare?" Cliff asked.

"Not at all."

"It's a big deal around here, signing a new quarterback." Rocky flashed him a bright smile. "You're going to love this town—the team spirit is insane."

"Frankly, they're excited to have someone new," Marley said. "Gives them hope for the first time in fifteen years."

Rocky opened the door for him. "You ready for all this?"

"You bet." He knew she meant the spotlight, but he didn't give two fucks about that. He was ready to play ball. He liked the guys, liked the coach, and had never been in better physical condition. As he got into the middle seat, he realized his only anxiety was Lulu. She'd stayed in Calamity to wrap up a few things for the show and would join him the day after tomorrow.

The first episode had aired, and the response was unbelievable. Better than anyone had anticipated. So, he couldn't help wondering what would happen if she got an offer to be the chef de cuisine of a restaurant in a city that Michelin covered. He wanted that for her—as much as she wanted him to play for the Wildcats. But he didn't want to live without her.

The distance would suck, but it wouldn't change anything for him. *She's the only woman for me.*

A hand squeezed his forearm. "You okay?" Rocky gave him a warm grin.

Shit, was she hitting on him? He looked at her more closely. With her buttery blonde hair and clear, hazel eyes, she was beautiful. But he didn't get the sense she was flirting. More that she was the type of woman who jumped headfirst into friendships, made you feel like you'd known each other forever.

Which was great for someone who worked in PR. *She puts people at ease.*

"I told them we didn't need three of us greeting you." She rolled her eyes. "Ridiculous. I'm like, let me pick him up myself. I'll check him into his hotel, get him a steak." Her expression said, *They're so over-the-top.*

In the passenger seat, Marley twisted around to face him. "So, Rocky's going to get you settled in tonight and bring you to the stadium tomorrow. Then, in the afternoon, she'll get you set up with the relocation specialist."

He nodded.

"If you couldn't tell, the press release has already gone out." Cliff sat on his other side. "We've got a Q and A with reporters tomorrow at noon and interviews through the end of the week." He reached into the briefcase nestled between his legs and pulled out a sheet of paper. "I've already emailed you the schedule, but here's a hard copy. Some guys prefer it."

"Thank you."

"And there's dinner tonight with the GM and some others," Cliff said. "But it's in your hotel, so you can just eat and head up to your room early." He smiled. "Unless you want to go out. Dallas has some of the best nightlife I've ever seen. I'm sure Rocky can hook you up."

"No. An early night would be great."

When silence descended in the car and everyone turned to their phones, he realized he'd given his usual terse responses.

Rocky bumped his shoulder. "You're going to be slammed this week, so if you want to hold off on meeting the relocation specialist, I can show you around town. Keep it casual."

"That might be better, since I have no idea what I'm looking for. Where do the other guys live?"

"Oh, they live all over. This city's pretty spread out. The guys with families live in North Dallas, but the single guys live in high rises. So, I guess that's the starting point. Do you have a family?"

"Yes." He'd immediately thought of Lulu, but then he realized she'd meant wife, kids, dog. "No."

"Okay." She smiled at his weird response. "So, are we talking buying a house or renting an apartment?"

He got a hit of anxiety at the idea of permanence. *Why bother buying?* If he got injured again, this gig would be over before it started. But he recognized right away it was a knee-jerk response to his shoulder.

I'm not injured anymore. And he couldn't think like that. Couldn't allow that kind of negativity in even for a moment. *I'm healed, I'm strong.*

I'm ready to play.

"Apartment." Still, why commit until he knew how it would all work out?

"That's probably best. Take a one-year lease and get to know the city, figure out where you want to live. How many bedrooms?"

"A lot. My girlfriend and I both have big families."

"Will they be staying with you when they visit? If so, we can look at renting a home. We have some gorgeous neighborhoods."

"She's going to want to be near good restaurants, so I don't want a suburb. And I'd rather leave the choice up to her anyway. I want her to be happy."

Rocky's expression grew wistful. "I wish she could be here right now."

"Me, too." *Wait, what?* "What do you mean?"

"To see how much you love her, how she's your priority. I'll be honest with you, this is going to be hard for her. I've seen it—hell, I've lived it. I was married to a player. We didn't last eighteen months."

She seemed way too young to have been married.

She touched his arm. "But I have a feeling you're one of the good guys."

"I love her." *Oh, Jesus.* He'd blurted it out like a kid with a secret.

"I see that. Not that you need my advice, but from the perspective of an ex-wife, I can't tell you how important it is to stay in touch with her. Let her know she's on your mind. Every night you're on the road, call her before you go to sleep. I don't know your relationship, but when you're apart and the guys are partying and pictures show up all over social media…she's going to need reassurance."

"Yeah, thanks. I'll do that." *I want to do that. I'd rather be with Lulu than with anyone else.*

The moment the car pulled into the hotel driveway, the paparazzi rushed in, surrounding it.

"How do they know which hotel I'm staying in?"

"Oh, we put everyone up here," Marley said. "Don't worry. Rocky's already checked you in, and she'll bring you down the cargo elevator for dinner."

"And then I'll be back in the morning and take you to your interviews," Rocky said. "Ready?"

The door opened, and Xander stepped out to flashing lights and microphones shoved in his face.

He thought about Rocky's advice—and knew he'd take it seriously.

Feet propped on her carry-on luggage, Lulu couldn't help glancing at the Arrivals and Departures board yet again.

Yep, flight's still on time.

She couldn't believe she was moving to Dallas.

Only two episodes had aired, but it was clear this show was going to be a huge success. Which meant it wouldn't be long before she had enough clout to get in touch with some of the city's top chefs. She'd meet with them in the coming weeks, but she wasn't in any rush. She wanted her next job to be the right one.

First, she needed to familiarize herself with the Dallas culinary scene, get her bearings, and come up with a new definition of success. Mostly, though, she wanted time to settle in with Xander. They'd lived in a bubble this summer, so now they needed to find a new normal with both of them working demanding jobs.

They'd make it—she knew that. With Trace, she'd never had that peace of mind. She'd been on edge all the time—but now she knew it was because their personalities hadn't fit. With Xander, they were so similar she just knew —no matter how big of an adjustment it might be—their love for each other would last a lifetime.

Restless, she got up, grabbed the handle of her luggage, and wandered toward the shops. Maybe she'd get an iced coffee or something.

This life—man, was it crazy. In a million years, she'd never have imagined moving to Dallas. Or falling in love with a football player.

Passing a bookstore, she realized she didn't want coffee. Instead, she'd get some gum, maybe a magazine. As she entered, she wondered what he was doing right then. Well, it was early afternoon. He was obviously on the field, training with his new team.

She got a thrill. He finally had his shot.

And he was going to kick ass and break records.

I will, too. She just didn't see her path as clearly as she once had.

Grabbing a pack of gum and tin of mints, she headed to the magazine rack, scanned the covers...but nothing really interested her. Maybe she'd just read *Cook's Illustrated* online.

Yeah, I'll do that. She got in the check-out line. She thought ahead to landing. Since he was working, his PR rep—Rocky—would pick her up. Apparently, she'd taken Xander around yesterday afternoon, giving him a brief tour of different neighborhoods.

This weekend, the two of them would look around, decide between renting a house or an apartment. In the meantime, they'd stay at the hotel.

A constant stream of travelers came in and out of the store. The line moved forward, and she scanned the newspapers.

Was that...*Oh, my God.*

Xander? On the cover of a gossip magazine? She had to look again.

It absolutely was. Why would he be on a tabloid?

He had his head lowered—like every celebrity ever who tried to shield himself from aggressive paparazzi—as he headed out of a building. A gorgeous blonde woman gazed up at him with a warm, affectionate smile.

She looked like she knew him well.

What fresh hell is this?

"Excuse me." She cut around the line and lifted the magazine out of the rack. A collage of photos covered the front page.

Look who's moving to Dallas!
X-Man moves fast—on and off the field!

She looked more closely at the blonde. And it was like plunging into frigid water. Sound grew muffled. Her skin went ice cold.

Stella.

The blonde is Stella.

This is not happening.

In another photo, they entered a restaurant. Once again, her sister gazed up at him as if they were intimate lovers. Stella *glowed*.

Lulu shook so badly her knees went weak. One hard twist in her stomach had bile shooting up the back of her throat.

I'm going to be sick.

Xander and my sister.

They'd had a romantic evening together. The photographic evidence was irrefutable.

The most damning photo of all took up the bottom half of the page. Xander and Stella stepped out of an elevator, shocked to see paparazzi.

Guess who overslept for his first day of training camp?
Can you blame him?

In her panic, she tried to put the paper back, but its pages fluttered and bent and wouldn't go into the slot. Flustered, she set her gum and mints down on the counter and took off.

Her wheels clattered as she hurried to the bathroom.

You have to calm down.

Holy fuck. Saliva spilled into her mouth. She was going to throw up.

She couldn't see, couldn't think. She was having a panic attack in the middle of the Salt Lake City Airport.

Get your shit together.

Think. She'd talked to him just that morning. He'd complained about how much he missed her.

Hold on. He'd been married for four years, and he'd stayed true to his wife—even after they'd separated. For *years.*

He wouldn't do this to me.

Last night, they'd FaceTimed. He'd been shirtless in bed.

No way would he ask her to move to Dallas with him and then immediately start screwing around.

I know him. He's not like that.

He loves me.

She started to calm down. *He loves me.* She knew it in every fiber of her body.

Then what's he doing with Stella?

Wait a minute. What's she doing in Dallas?

There's only one way to find out.

Ask him.

Right. She blew out a breath. She'd wait till he finished practice, and then she'd call.

Her phone buzzed. *Gigi. Oh, thank God.* She'd talk to her sister about it. "Hey."

But the only response was silence.

Oh, no. Oh, God. Something's wrong. "What?"

"I just sent you a text." Gigi kept her voice steady, her tone modulated. "Keep me on the phone while you look at it. I'm here."

"I already saw it." No matter how cool she wanted to be about this, she knew she sounded panicked.

"Are you freaking out?"

"Yes." Instead of going into the bathroom, she headed back to the gate. "I need you to make sense of this. Explain to me what Xander's doing with Stella. Of all the women in the world, why her?"

"So, that's why I called." Gigi paused. "Mom and Dad have known where she is all along."

"What?" She ducked into an empty gate. "And they never told us? Why?"

"Look, Coco and I feel the same way. Believe me, we're pissed. But you know Dad. He said he couldn't let his daughter run off like that, so he tracked her down and got her a job."

A chill skated down her spine.

"With the Wildcats. She works for Xander's team." Gigi took a breath. "In their publicity department. That's what she's been doing this whole time."

"We've searched for her for years. We all have. How come we've never found her?"

"She got married."

Lulu dropped the handle to press a cool palm to her forehead. "Stella's *married*?"

"Divorced. She was super young. It happened, like, months after she left us. Some whirlwind romance with a football player. Apparently, he was a real playboy, and they divorced after a year. Anyhow, that's why you see her with Xander. She's the PR rep assigned to him."

"I can't believe this is happening."

"Are you okay? I wish I could be there with you. I can't even imagine how you felt seeing those pictures."

"Did you see her expression? Gigi, she's crazy about him." As shock subsided, true fear edged in. "They look so comfortable with each other."

"That's Stella. That's her secret sauce. She makes people feel good, right?"

Fear spread like poison in her bloodstream, creeping into every corner and crevice, taking over her body. And there was no release valve, no way to purge it.

"You trust him, though, right? I see how *she's* looking at him, but he's not looking back at her like that, Lu. You see that, right?"

"It doesn't matter."

I can't do this.

I can't. "She works with him."

"Yep." Gigi gave her the truth, no bullshit.

She appreciated that. "She's going to be around him."

And if I go to Dallas, I'm going to live with this poison every minute of every day.

"Well, not all that much. It's just the first few weeks, this flurry of interviews. But he can ask for someone else."

"I'm not going to be that girlfriend. The one that makes him ask for a less attractive publicist."

"No, I get that."

An announcement cut into her frantic thoughts. Her flight was boarding. She turned, watching people get up.

"But it's Stella." Gigi sounded confident. "She'd never sleep with your boyfriend."

No, but she'd dazzle him. Lulu would never forget the look in Griffin's eyes, pure, raw, carnal lust. She would never forget watching them kiss.

And Trace? The image of his hands gripping Stella's ass was forever imprinted in her mind.

Standing there in terminal C, people rushing around her, wheels clacking, her stomach pitched. "I can't do it."

"Can't do what?"

"I can't do this, Gigi."

"That's your choice, honey. But at least talk to him first, okay?"

She didn't answer. She'd gone numb.

"Lu?"

"I have to go."

Chapter Twenty

STANDING BACK FROM THE CROWD, XANDER SCANNED every face in the baggage claim area. He checked the monitor. Flight 2366. Yep, right carousel. If he texted her, he'd ruin the surprise, so he forced himself to relax and wait.

"X-Man." A middle-aged man came over, fist raised for a bump. "Welcome to Dallas. Your shoulder good?"

"Never better."

"Haven't bought season tickets in a decade, but I'm definitely going to this year. Good luck, man."

"Thanks." Xander tugged his ball cap lower. He was so fucking grateful to be here, leading a team, that he'd never turn away a fan. But he didn't want to talk to anyone. Not until he had Lulu in his arms. Then, he'd relax.

Because it wouldn't be real until she unpacked—her shampoo in his bathroom, the scent of her coffee in the apartment, her shoes kicked off by the front door.

Until she was actually living with him.

Asking her to move to Dallas was a big deal. Huge. Her goals were every bit as important and meaningful as his. He would never take that from her, but he remembered what she'd said about her sister retiring, how chasing a goal had killed her love for cooking, so he'd asked.

And she'd said yes.

A wave of happiness crashed over him. Lifting the ball cap, he scraped a hand through his hair. Jesus, she'd said yes. And any moment now, she'd come through that door to collect her luggage.

Excitement blew through him, and he covered his smile with the real estate listings his relocation specialist had sent him. He had to get back to practice right away, but they'd check them all out this Sunday. Decide where they'd begin their new life together.

When the last bag left the carousel, he knew she hadn't just stopped at the bathroom. Something had gone wrong. Forget the surprise. He pulled out his phone and dialed her.

She answered right away. "Hi."

"Hey. Where are you?"

"I'm not coming."

"What? Is everything all right?" The back of his neck bristled, and a hundred possibilities exploded in his brain.

She changed her mind.

She got in a car accident on the way to the airport.

She doesn't want to give up her dreams.

She's had some time apart, and she realizes she doesn't want to be with me.

Bullshit. She loves me.

That, at least, he knew.

"I guess you haven't been on social media today." Her cool tone broke through the chatter in his mind.

"What? No. I've been in practice. I just came to the airport to pick you up. Why? What happened?"

"It's better if you see for yourself. Open up *SportsNation*. I'll wait."

He paced to the conveyor belt and sat on the edge. All it took was a few taps on his screen for his world to come crashing down around him.

X-Man's starting in Dallas—and he makes himself right at home.
Is this hottie part of X-Man's signing package?

"Hold on." He shot up. "It's not what it looks like. That's Rocky. I told you about her. She works for the PR department. She's been assigned to me. Come on, Lu, you know I'd never cheat on you."

"Xander, that's Stella."

"What?" Relief knocked him back a step. "*No.* Lu, that's Rocky. Rocky Miller." He'd seen pictures of Stella—she had dark hair, like her sisters.

Did Rocky look like Stella? He didn't know. He hadn't paid attention.

"I told you she left Calamity right after high school graduation." She sounded flat, dull. "Well my dad tracked her down and got her a job with his friend, Coach Ledbetter. The same guy he called when you needed a job. She married one of the players, Logan Miller. They call her Rocky because she's a fighter. She came to them with nothing, took night classes, got a college degree. She didn't take shit from her cheating husband, so, yeah…Rocky is Stella."

"I can't believe it. That's crazy." He paced to the plate

glass window. "But nothing happened between us. I'm not —" What could he say? How did he get through to her? "Lu, all I did was talk about you. It was one of the first things she noticed about me. She said, 'She's a lucky woman.' Because I talked about you. Rocky—*Stella*— there's nothing there."

"Xander, you work with her. I can't do it."

"Then, I'll work with someone else. I'll hire my own PR firm. I don't need her." He glanced at the papers he'd crumpled. "I have places for us. There's one in University Park I think you're going to like. It's a townhouse, and right down the block is a really cool gourmet store. It's kind of like the place you were talking about opening with Harley."

"I can't do it, Xander."

"Don't say that." His desperate tone drew the attention of passersby.

"I just can't."

"*Lulu*, for God's sake, would you listen to me?" A couple of people stopped to watch him, and he turned his back on them. "I don't care about Stella. I don't want her. I *love* you."

"I'm sorry."

Xander threw open the back door of the restaurant and stormed down the hall. "Lulu?"

Once he hit the kitchen, a couple of people in white chef jackets turned to him, startled.

"Where's Lulu?" he demanded.

A line cook looked confused. "She doesn't work here."

Fear speared him. He'd seen pictures of her on

Splashagram in this kitchen. He'd assumed she'd taken the job with Chef Jonny. "Where is she?" Had she moved?

Had she gotten a job somewhere else?

She could be anywhere, and he couldn't take any more time off.

One of the guys shrugged. "No idea." He went back to washing the dishes.

With a curt nod, Xander headed back to his rental car. *Plan.* He needed a plan. Tearing out of the Homesteader Inn's parking lot, he picked up his phone and thumbed the screen to see if he had any messages. *None.* "Dammit, Lu. Talk to me."

Rocky—*Stella*—had quit. Why wasn't that enough to bring Lulu back?

He'd never felt an ounce of attraction or interest in her sister. She paled next to the passion burning in Lulu's heart.

Don't you fucking leave me.

He couldn't do it. Now that he knew what life could feel like with her in it, he couldn't go back to that robotic existence.

Foot heavy on the accelerator, he headed down 191 until the turn-off for the Cavanaugh home. He pulled up to the gate and pressed the button. Fingers tapping the steering wheel, he thought he'd lose his mind if someone didn't answer.

He'd bust down the iron blockade.

"Hello, Xander." A female voice, strong, confident.

"Mrs. Cavanaugh. Is Lulu here?"

In the silence that held for several long beats, his pulse pounded, his knee jackhammered.

"Hey." *Tyler.* "Shouldn't you be at training camp?"

That deep voice rattled him. "Yes, I should."

"You getting fined?"

"Yes, sir. Big fines. And they're going to keep adding up until I talk to your daughter."

"She's not here." Tyler sounded frustrated.

"She's not speaking to us, either." Mrs. Cavanaugh's voice carried the heaviness of guilt and regret. "None of the girls are." She paused. "We didn't tell anyone about Stella."

He could hear Tyler's deep rumble as the two spoke privately but couldn't make out the words.

"Anyhow, she's not staying with us," Mrs. Cavanaugh said.

"Is she still in Calamity?" he asked.

"Yes," Tyler said.

"Tell me where."

"We don't know where." Lulu's mom sounded a little lost.

He believed them. "Okay, thank you." *Now what?*

He just didn't know.

"You going back to Dallas?" Tyler asked.

That was the one thing he did know. "Not without Lulu."

In August, the town was packed with tourists. A row of motorcycles parked perpendicular to the curb, while the bikers picnicked on the town green. A couple of families licked ice cream cones outside of Bliss, and tourists stood under the antler arch to take pictures.

Xander found a parking spot a block away and walked to Calamity Joe's. Once inside, he bypassed the line and strode right up to the counter. "Hey, is Harley here?"

The barista glanced up from the espresso machine. He tipped his head toward the wall. "Next door."

"At the toy store?"

The guy shrugged and went back to work.

"Thanks." He wove his way through the crowd and headed back out into the bright sunshine. If her friend didn't have answers, Xander didn't know what he'd do. Cassian and Gigi were back in Boston for training camp. Coco lived a block away, so he'd try there next.

"X-Man." A teenage boy ran over to him, followed by his younger siblings. His parents took up the rear. "What're you doing here? Can I get your autograph?"

No, Jesus. Just let me go. "You bet."

The kid turned to his mom, who reached into her purse, digging around until she found a pen and receipt.

"What do you think?" the dad said. "Does Dallas have what it takes to win the East this year?"

"I'm counting on it." He handed the pen and paper to the boy.

"Thank you. This is so cool."

"You're welcome."

The parents thanked him, and he quickly made his way to the toy store. Crammed with puzzles, books, and stuffed animals, the place barely had any customers. One entire bookshelf held glass jars jammed with striped sticks of candy in all the colors of the rainbow. Two toddlers played with a tall plastic structure with windows and gears and knobs.

He went right up to the counter. "Harley here?"

"She's in back." The clerk glanced up from the register, eyes widening. "X-Man?"

Ignoring him, he made his way to the back of the store. "Harley?"

The curtain parted, and the woman came to a hard stop, taking him in. "What're you doing here?"

"Have you seen Lulu?"

She kept her cool, but he could tell from the way she grew uncomfortable that his woman was back there.

Fuck that shit. He swept past her. "Lulu?"

A great rush of relief crashed over him at the sight of her sitting on top of a stack of boxes in a small office. "Xander?" She hopped off and came over to him. "What're you doing here? Shouldn't you be at practice?"

"We need to talk."

Lulu looked to the man behind the desk. "Xander, this is Duke. He's moving to Arizona. He actually owns the entire building, and he wasn't going to sell it, but—"

The middle-aged man got up and came around the desk. "But these two are halfway to convincing me that I don't want to be a landlord from six hundred miles away." He smiled. "Harley and I will give you two some privacy."

The moment the two of them left the office, he reached for Lulu's hands. "Stella quit. She's gone. Not that I even noticed her. How could I when all I see is you?" He swallowed against the pain in this throat. "I love you. You know that, right?"

"I do."

"I can't believe you broke up with me. I don't understand. You just..." He was wasting time. He had a whole list of things to say and bitching wasn't a winning game plan. "Did you change your mind? You don't want to be with me anymore?"

Her features crumpled. "I want it more than anything." She looked down at her flip flops. "I handled this terribly." Her gaze swung up. "I love you, Xander. With everything in me, I love you."

"Then, what're you doing?" *This doesn't make sense.* "How can you love me and not want to be with me?"

She looked so conflicted. "No, I do *want* to be with you. But I can't just move to Dallas and be a chef at some random restaurant. This whole thing with Stella was my wake-up call. I got so carried away with not wanting to give *you* up that I gave up something else. My dream."

"I would never ask you to do that."

"But you did. When you asked me to move to Dallas, that's exactly what you did. Xander, I've worked hard for so many years. I was *thirteen* when I had a pop-up restaurant. I gave up every vacation and holiday, all so that one day I could achieve something exceptional. You have to understand that I'll forever regret giving up too soon."

"But you don't have a job yet. Can't you move to Dallas and look for one there?"

She watched him with uncertainty. He *knew* she didn't want to end things. Her hesitancy made it clear she was just scared...seeing him with Stella had spooked her. *It'll be all right.* He just had to convince her—

"I do have a job." Her chin lifted. "I took one this morning."

Panic thrashed in his chest. "You took a job?" He drew in a breath to steady his nerves. "Where?"

He'd never seen her look so vulnerable, so scared. "Paris."

"*Paris?*" LA, they could do. New York, Chicago. But France?

"I called Chef Paul. I only wanted him to keep me in mind if he heard of any job openings. I told him the truth, that I'd gotten fired, that I wasn't ready for a chef de cuisine job, and that I wanted another shot at sous chef.

This time, I'll pay more attention to the business side. And…"

"And?"

"He's not happy with my replacement. He's been interviewing others, and the job is mine if I want it." She pressed her hands together—so hard, her skin turned white.

"Okay. Then, I'll come to Paris every chance I can, and I'll live there in the off season." *We can do this*. He just had to adjust his thinking a little.

"No." In spite of the quaver in her voice, her expression turned resolute.

"What do you mean no? You said you love me."

"It won't work." Her gaze cut away. "With our schedules, it's not possible. You know that."

"Then, I'll quit."

"Xander, no." Now, she was practically pleading. "You have to take your shot, and I have to grab that brass ring. Our timing's off, and I think we always knew that. That's probably why it got hot so fast. Because our relationship had a time limit."

Bullshit. Her tortured expression told him she was lying to herself. *Fight for her*. "It got hot so fast because the moment I laid eyes on you I knew I'd found someone special. I knew it in here." He smacked his chest. "And if you think it's going to come around again, you're dead wrong. What we have is unique to us. And let me tell you something—there's never going to be anything better. Are you going to stand there and tell me you don't believe that?"

"Of course I do." She flared hot, intense. But it didn't last. She went right back to being reserved. "And maybe in a few years, we'll find our way back to each other."

"Find our way…" She didn't love him. Not enough to bust through her own fears. Defeat swept down like a cloak and nearly suffocated him. "Okay."

"Okay?" She looked terrified.

"I love you. I'd quit the NFL to be with you." A weight pressed down on his chest, making it hard to speak. "But that's not the root of the problem. The root is you don't love me enough."

"That's not true."

His heart, swollen with sorrow, sat like a heavy stone in his chest. "It's exactly true. You just let me go." He took a step back—just a test—to see if he could do it—and he felt the tug from deep within. "I spent my childhood fighting to be included with my brothers. I spent my career fighting to overcome injuries. I spent my marriage fighting my instincts and trying to make something work that never should have happened to begin with. But you?"

Xander took in her rosy cheeks and shiny hair, the feminine slope of her shoulders, and couldn't believe he'd never touch her again. Never hold her hand or feel the brush of her fingertips on his chest. "It was right from the beginning. Your passion, your intensity, the way you listen and care, the way you look after I kiss you—that bliss? I'm never going to see that on any other woman's face, because I'm never going to fit with anyone the way I do with you." He reached the door. "I have to get back to Dallas but just know that I'm not moving on. I won't be dating or hooking up. So, if you figure out what I already know— that no matter what either of us achieves, it won't mean anything if we're both alone—I'll be waiting."

Chapter Twenty-One

LULU HAD A HOLE THE SIZE OF WYOMING IN THE center of her chest.

Tonight, her parents had called a family meeting to explain why they'd kept Stella's whereabouts from them. Apparently, after they'd tracked her down through a credit card and offered her a job with her dad's friend in Dallas, her sister had insisted on her independence and privacy. It had killed her parents not to tell them, but they'd made a promise.

Still, as important as the conversation was, Lulu had found it hard to concentrate.

Because she was a mess. She couldn't eat. Couldn't sleep. She just couldn't hang around, talking about things that had nothing to do with what preoccupied her, what *consumed* her.

Xander.

My love.

My heart.

So, Lulu had gone the Homesteader Inn to get a

handle on her devastating loss. She hadn't even been here five minutes before Gigi had knocked on the back door.

In the kitchen, the two of them had made pasta and a salad. They'd heated up a crusty baguette and gone to the front of house to dig in.

Once she realized she'd been playing with her food and not eating, she set her fork down. "I can't believe they made you come home for that conversation."

"You know Mom. We weren't speaking to them, and she wasn't having it."

Family was everything to their mom, and when it was fractured, she got to work healing it. "I think about all those times we'd wonder where Stella was, whether she was homeless or living the highlife on a yacht with a sexy Italian, and they didn't say a word. That's just cruel."

"I don't have kids yet, but if one of them ran off, I can see doing whatever it took to keep her in your sights, you know? Keep the line of communication open." She reached across the table to squeeze Lulu's hand. "But I didn't come home for a family meeting."

"Then, why did you?" With Cassian in training, they'd decamped back to Boston. Gigi was finishing up her album in their home studio.

"Honey, you just broke up with Xander. For you to come out and say you've never felt so lost...this is a big deal."

"I'm so glad you're here."

"The thing is...I'm worried you're doing the exact same thing you did after the rehearsal dinner, when you ran away and got so busy with school you never took the time to deal with what happened."

She hadn't considered that. But honestly, she didn't

think her heart would ever heal, so what was the point in waiting around? "I hear you." She fought back tears. God, when would it stop? Hadn't she cried herself out already? For the past week, she'd holed up in Cassian's empty house, waking up each morning with a pounding headache and salt-dried cheeks. "I'm an idiot."

"No question about it."

"Gigi." She actually laughed. "Me giving up my dream is as ridiculous as Xander giving up football."

"Can we get real for a minute? Because you have to know you didn't break up with Xander to work at Sublime. You broke up with him because you're scared he's going to lose interest in you once he's back in the 'real world.'" She hunched a shoulder. "*That* makes you an idiot."

"That's not why I broke up with him." *Well, maybe a little bit why.* "Two driven people with big careers in different cities doesn't work."

Gigi gave her a pointed look.

"It's different with you and Cassian. You have flexibility. I work sixteen-hour days six days a week. And once I have my own restaurant, it'll be seven days a week."

"Are you going to sit here and tell me you'd rather have a fucking Michelin star than the love of your life? Do you even hear yourself?"

"The whole reason Dad didn't want you and Cassian to get together in high school is because he didn't want you giving up your potential so you could be with your boyfriend while he was out realizing his. How is this different? You would never have been with the Lollipops, which means you wouldn't have had the clout to go off and sign a solo deal with a record label."

"So? I would've taken a different path to success. I hated being a Lollipop. Choosing love doesn't mean losing yourself. Look, the point is that you didn't break up with just some guy. You broke up with Xander."

"God, I know that, Gigi."

"Then, why are we sitting here talking about your *career*. Before you saw him with Stella, you were ready to move to Dallas and find a new direction. So, it just seems really strange that we're not talking about the fact that seeing Stella with Xander opened up an old wound."

"I don't need to talk about it. It gutted me, and I worked through it. And now I've moved on."

"Bullshit."

Ouch.

But that hard look in Gigi's eyes had Lulu bracing for impact. Her sister wasn't going to hold any punches.

"You're not connecting two really important things here. You know that pesky little worry you have that your personality isn't big enough for a cooking show? That Xander needs someone more outgoing? It all comes down to the moment you found Stella kissing Griffin."

"I know that." She pushed back her chair like she might get up. "You think I don't know that?" But she didn't go anywhere. Because deep down she wanted to hear what her sister had to say. She needed someone to steer her out of this terrible, blinding fog.

"I don't think you're connecting that insecurity with your drive to have a Michelin star. If your personality isn't good enough, then your cooking better be. You think reaching that goal will make you special. And, to you, special translates to happy and secure, but you're wrong. Because it's nothing more than your comfort zone. You want to know real happiness? Step the hell out of it and go for something that'll dazzle *you*. Who cares if some reviewer loves your food? Who cares if you get a hundred five stars on Yelp? The only thing that matters is how you feel about yourself. And I can guarantee you'll never feel all that great as long as you're a coward."

"I'm not a coward."

"No? Then why are you leaving for Paris tomorrow instead of Dallas? You can make a name for yourself anywhere. Xander's mom did it in Tiburon, and Jonny did it in Calamity."

Lulu couldn't argue with that logic.

"And since we're doing this right now, let me just say one more thing. I think you're holding onto those wounds like they're some kind of armor. Like they're going to shield you from getting hurt again. They won't. They'll just keep you lonely and sad. And at the end of your life, you might have that Michelin star, but you won't have Xander by your side and all the children you two could've had together."

Oh, God. For one precious moment she saw it, felt it, lived it. Xander, their children, their home, their love. Joy roared in, driving out all the sorrow, the worry, the doubt.

Until she remembered…it was too soon for all that. *I'm only twenty-six.* She'd taken one swing for the fences, and she'd failed. She had to swing again.

Something clattered in the kitchen, and Lulu jumped up. "That's probably Chef Jonny. He likes to check in on me." She hurried into the kitchen to greet him. "Hey—"

But it wasn't Chef. It was Griffin. He stood tall and inked, his mood dark. Reaching for a loaf of bread, he said, "Hey, I'm just grabbing a bite to eat."

"Well, here, let me put the rest of this in a take-away container."

"No, that's okay."

"I made plenty. Just give me a second to put it together."

"I don't need anything fancy. I'll make a peanut butter sandwich or something."

"You're a grown man. You can do better than PB and J."

He didn't smile. "It's not for me."

Oh. She wanted to ask him what in the world was going on that had him volunteering at the shelter and sneaking food for someone, but they weren't that close. So, she kept her tone light. "Well, if you want a sandwich, have at it. But if you think your…friend might want homemade pasta and salad, I've got plenty."

"Okay, sure. Thank you."

She opened a cabinet and pulled down a container and plastic lid. As she spooned the pasta into it, she said, "I'm guessing you heard we found Stella."

"No, I haven't heard anything." He went quiet and still. "She okay?"

"Yeah. She's been living in Dallas, working for the Wildcats. She quit, though." She gave a bitter laugh. "After pictures went viral of her with my boyfriend."

God, she missed Xander. So damn much.

When he'd walked out the door, he'd taken a piece of her soul.

"Stella the savior, saving you from another rotten apple?"

"Not this time. This time, I'm told I'm being a coward." Gigi was probably right about that. "I was at the airport, ready to move to Dallas to be with him, and right there in the bookstore, I saw the two of them on the cover of a gossip rag. It just…killed me." She flicked her gaze up to him. "I don't know why I'm telling you this."

"Because I'm one of the guys you caught her with."

"Oh." Her cheeks flamed. "That was…embarrassing. You didn't even know I existed."

"I knew. We went to school together, you worked in my dad's kitchen. Of course I knew. You kept to yourself, like me."

"Well, in any event, I broke up with him because I'm moving, and we all know long distance doesn't work. But my family seems to think I'm afraid to go there again, like I can't bear to compete with Stella's beauty, her personality…her flair."

"They think I was with her for her looks?" He shook his head. "Doesn't work like that. There's no shortage of beautiful women in the world. I was with her because we fit. She gave me purpose." He took the box from her and headed toward the door. "Thanks a lot. I'll see you around."

"Griffin?"

He stopped.

"Have you found anyone else you fit with in all these years?"

"No." He reached for the handle and pulled open the door. "And I'm not going to either."

Exhausted from a long day of work, Lulu kicked off her clogs and headed into the galley kitchen. Traffic and music brought her lively Paris neighborhood into the small apartment. It also brought the heat and humidity of an

August night, but she liked the windows open. It felt less claustrophobic that way.

Pouring herself a glass of wine, she sat on the couch, drawing her legs up. She'd only been back in Chef Paul's kitchen three days, but she loved it. Loved him, loved the menu. It was great.

Everything's great. Restless, she glanced at the coffee table for something to do. *Do I want to finish that book?* Or get back to the show she'd been watching?

If she had to be honest, nothing really interested her.

Except Xander. She couldn't stop wondering what he was doing, how he was feeling about his new team. It had to be hard to earn respect, figure out personalities—

Oh, shut up. She was so tired of stuffing down her emotions. It was just…if she actually faced them, she'd crumple.

But I'm not at work. I'm home, and here I can admit it.

I love him.

She tipped her head back and closed her eyes. *I'm so lost without him.*

Every minute of every day she longed to reach out—to let him know she was thinking about him, missing him, aching for him.

A knock got her up and moving. And it was almost a relief, that sting of adrenaline from having a stranger at her door at midnight. *Because it's an emotion other than grief.* "Who is it?"

"It's Mom."

"Mom?" She unlocked the bolts and threw the door open.

Looking chic in black leggings, an oversize T-shirt, and a peacock blue pashmina shawl thrown around her shoulders, her mom charged into the apartment. Seeing her glamorous mother in this small, one-bedroom apartment only highlighted how shabby and sad it looked.

She gave her mom a hug, breathing in the signature scent created for her specially by a designer. "What're you doing here?"

"We need to talk." Her mom set her leather tote on the floor and unwrapped the shawl.

"You flew all the way from Calamity to *talk* to me? Mom, I spent the whole summer there. We talked all the time." Fear slammed into her. "Is everyone all right? The baby? Dad?"

"Everyone's fine." Her mom gestured around the room. "You shouldn't be here."

"Oh, it's just temporary. I moved so fast I didn't have time to look around. I'll find a better place soon. It's good for now. I love the location."

"I mean in Paris. You shouldn't be here."

"What? Sublime is one of the best restaurants in the world."

Earnest, intense, her mom moved toward her. "Look, you need to understand something. When I got discovered, I was only fourteen. Some fancy lady approached me in the mall and made me promises that I couldn't resist. My parents didn't want me to go, they wanted me to stay in town, marry a local boy, live their safe, small life, but I begged them. And it wasn't just for me. I wanted to put an end to their constant struggle to pay bills."

"Mom, I know all this."

"Listen." She drew in a breath. "I was too young to take on an international modeling career. I never had a chance to figure out who I was, what I wanted in life. So, when Gigi was born with that big talent...and you had this *passion*...I jumped into action. I was absolutely driven to make sure you got to have the kind of fulfilling, authentic life I never had."

She hated to see her mom so distraught. "I don't blame you for anything."

"You damn well should. Because when I met your dad, I made the choice to retire, to have a family. I could've gone into acting or run my own make-up line. I had options, but I didn't want them. I wanted the life I created in Calamity. That was my choice, *my* happiness. The other night, Gigi asked me if I'd ever bothered to ask what *you* wanted. And I had to really think about that, because I couldn't come up with a single time that I did." She reached for Lulu and drew her in for a hug. "I'm sorry, baby."

"For what? You gave me a wonderful life, you gave me opportunities. I wouldn't be here right now living my dream in Paris."

Her mom pulled away. "This is your dream? Living alone in this apartment, away from the man you love?"

It hit like a punch to the chest, pain so jarring it radiated through her bones.

"If I'd ever bothered to ask what you wanted, would you have said, *I want to marry a good man and have babies and cook good food?*"

The pain grew sharper, making it hard to breathe.

"You didn't start out wanting to be the best chef in the world. You started out with a garden, with an interest in seeing what you could do with the vegetables you grew. I couldn't sleep last night, couldn't even close my eyes on the plane, because the truth is…all you ever wanted was a farm-to-table restaurant. You never once said you wanted a Michelin star."

Lulu's pulse fluttered out of control, and she could

barely pull in a breath. "Mom, stop. It's okay. I'm not angry with you."

But she didn't stop. Her mom plowed ahead. "Gigi said something that cut me to the quick. I was talking about you and Stella, saying how I wished she'd come home so the two of you could reconcile, and then maybe you could move on from feeling like you weren't enough, and she said, 'Stella has nothing to do with it.' And you know what? She's absolutely right. Honey, Stella loved you with every fiber of her being. She accepted you just the way you are."

Oh, my God.

Stella.

She didn't know how deeply she'd missed her sister until this very moment. When her mom broke down the barrier.

Her legs were so shaky, she had to sit on the arm of the couch.

"*I'm* the one who made you feel you weren't enough. Every time you achieved something, I pushed you to reach for the next level. I signed you up for a more advanced class, got you an opportunity with an even better chef. And I never once asked if you wanted any of it."

"I know you love me, Mom. I never doubted that you wanted the best for me, for all of us."

"Lulu, what do you want?"

She couldn't push a single word past the hard knot in her throat.

Her mom set her hands on Lulu's shoulders. "Sweetheart, close your eyes and picture your future. Picture yourself happy. Can you see it?"

Yes. God, yes.

Clear as day.

"Now, I'm going to ask you again. What do you want?" The words came out drenched in emotion.

Lulu's body shook with the force of holding back.

"Do you even know?"

Lulu nodded. "I do."

Chapter Twenty-Two

"It just came on the market, and it ticks all your boxes." The relocation specialist punched the ignition button of her Mercedes and got out of the car.

As Xander sat there, trying to find the energy to open the door, the engine ticked. The house sat on a small patch of grass in a nice neighborhood in University Park. Lulu would like it. Some of the best restaurants in the city were a block away.

But without her, he didn't care where he lived. All he needed was a place to crash after a rough day of practice. Still, he should go in, because for some stupid reason he held out hope that she'd come back to him.

See, the thing he wanted to tell her was that he'd had two shoulder injuries. He knew exactly what it felt like—even after he'd been rehabbed and given clearance to play—to experience ghost twinges from the wound site. Every time he got sacked, every time he landed on his shoulder, he got walloped with that same shock of fear that his career had just ended.

So, he knew she was experiencing her own ghost

twinges from the wound Stella had inflicted with Griffin and Trace. And his Lulu, she was fierce. She wouldn't let fear hold her back from the kind of love they had.

She will *come back to me.*

He just knew it.

The relocation specialist rapped on his window. "You coming?"

Getting out of the car, he followed her up the walkway.

"It's got exceptional flow, a gourmet kitchen, and French doors in the kitchen, dining room, and all three bedrooms that lead to a sensational balcony that overlooks the pool." The twenty-something's heels clicked on the stone. "Look at this landscaping. Isn't it to die-for?"

"Sure."

She unlocked the door and pushed it open, making a gesture for him to enter first.

Hit with the scent of vanilla and the barest whiff of peaches, his heart about exploded. *Lulu.*

She's here?

And then he took in the scene. Fairy lights draped the walls, candles flickered on every surface, and the dining room table glittered with silverware, china, and wine goblets. Music played softly in the background, and the woman stood so close he could hear her breathing.

Fuck. How had she gotten the impression he was open to this kind of shit? All he'd ever done was talk about Lulu. He took a step away from her. "This is not cool." He gave her a hard look. "I have a girlfriend."

The woman had balls. She didn't look the least bit hurt. "I thought you said she broke up with you?"

"So? I'm still very much with her. I *love* her, and that's never going to change." He was so fucking done with people thinking they could touch him or hit on him just because he wore a jersey. "I can't believe you'd pull a stunt like this, when you know the only reason I'm looking for a place is for when she comes back to me."

"I did." *That voice.* "I came back."

He whipped around. "Lulu?" A fireball of adrenaline sped through him so fast he went weak. Closing the distance between them, he lifted her into his arms. He went light-headed with relief. "You're here."

"I love you." She kissed him. "I love you so much." The kiss turned desperate, and she scraped her hands through his hair.

"I can't believe you're here." He hauled her hard up against him.

"I missed you. I'm sorry I put us through this."

"Don't ever do it again." He framed her rosy cheeks in his hands. "I couldn't stand being away from you." His hand slid to the back of her neck, as his tongue stroked into her mouth, tangling with hers.

Only then did he remember the woman. "Fuck. I'm sorry—" But she was gone. The door closed. "I thought my relocation specialist was hitting on me."

Grinning, she shook her head. "She helped me set this up."

God, she smelled good. Fresh peaches, and that inimitable scent that felt like home. But they needed to talk. He had to know her plans. "Did you go to Paris? What happened?"

She smoothed her hands down her dress. "I told Chef Paul I didn't want the job and that he should continue interviewing other chefs."

"You what?" His heart was beating too fast, sending blood crashing through his veins. "Don't want it?"

She shook her head. "What's a star going to prove? That I'm special? I prove that every time someone tastes my food. I'm so damn special Xander Wilder *loves* me. I'm special enough that Chef Jonny wants me to carry on his legacy. I'm special just because I'm me."

Happiness spread through him. For the first time since they'd met, he knew with absolute certainty they were going to last. Because she got it. She finally understood. "You are, Lu, you're the most special woman in the world. So, you're moving here? You're living with me?" He needed to be very clear.

"I am. Griffin said something that really got to me. I made some crack about Stella's beauty and, you know, what guy could possibly resist it. And he looks at me like I'm the lamest person he's ever met and goes, 'You think I was with her because she's pretty?' He said, 'No, it's because we fit. She gave my life purpose.' And it made me think about us, and how from the moment we met, we just fit. I mean, you were ready to give up football and be on a cooking show. As if that would've made you happy."

"It would."

"I believe you. Even though you love football, you'd have been happy just to be with me."

"Right, because you give my life purpose. Football is a career. And I like it more than any other thing I could do to earn a living. But the heart and soul of my life is loving you."

When she gazed up at him with awe, he realized he hadn't told her enough about his feelings. And he'd correct that right now. "You know how Chef Jonny would parade you around the restaurant and the customers would rave about your food?"

She nodded.

"And then what would happen? After that?"

"Then, I'd go home and…"

He could see the moment she got where he was going with this.

"And be alone. And feel empty."

"Exactly. It feels good to win a game and read about how well I played, but then I walk off the field, and I'm alone. And with you in my life, I don't have any holes, there's no emptiness. I feel complete. Lulu, I love you, and there's nothing I want more than to spend the rest of my life with you." One thing still troubled him. "But what will you do here?"

"This might sound crazy, but I want to write cookbooks."

"That doesn't sound crazy at all. It's perfect. I can't imagine anything making you happier than spending your days creating new dishes and tinkering with them."

"There's a teeny problem, though."

"What's that?"

"Well, I started a business with Harley. It's the Harley Lu Emporium. We're going to sell gourmet products, take-away food, and baked goods. We're in the process of buying the building from Duke. We'll start out with just the toy store space, but as tenants leave, we'll expand our business." She softened. "When I told Chef Jonny I didn't want the job, he said I was an artist, and that being a business manager would kill my spirit, and I know he's right. Nothing has ever excited me more than this emporium."

"Do you need to live in Calamity to do it?"

"Not full time, no. Eventually, though, when a space opens, I'd like to add a café. It's a long way away, but I think that's the restaurant I want to run."

"So, for now, you're okay making Dallas your home?"

"Xander, my home is you. If you're in Dallas, I'm in Dallas."

The best idea he'd ever had came out of nowhere, and he reached for her hand. "Let's get out of here."

"Um, I sort of signed the lease on this place. It's ours."

"No, I mean, out of Dallas. Let's go on a trip." Knowing she'd never want a big wedding, he'd already researched places to elope.

"We can't. Preseason starts in six days."

"Exactly. Which means this is my only free time until February."

She grinned. "The season ends in December. Already planning on the Super Bowl, your very first season?"

"You know it."

"Cocky. I like that."

"You got your passport handy?"

A slow grin spread across her beautiful features. "I do."

His heart filled with love, he dropped to a knee. "Lulu Cavanaugh, will you make me the happiest man in the world and be my wife?"

She hurled herself at him, toppling him onto his back. Pressing kisses all over his face, she said, "Yes, yes, yes."

"Good. Then, pack a bag. We're getting married."

"*Now?*"

"Right now. I'm not going to wait another day to start my life with you."

Epilogue

LULU HAD A WONDERFUL FAMILY AND A COUPLE OF very good friends. She'd had some of the best bosses she could ask for.

So, her acute sense of aloneness had never really made sense.

Until this moment.

With her bare toes covered in warm sand, she breathed in the scent of the fresh gardenias woven around the arbor and gazed into the eyes of her one true love. Xander was the missing piece of her soul, and she knew that because with him she finally felt complete.

Against the backdrop of waves crashing onto the shore, the reverend performed the service in his gentle, soft voice. As she faced her groom, their hands clasped, Lulu's heart had never been so full.

It was all she could do to stay put and not throw herself into Xander's arms. "I'm just so grateful to have you." Her hand flew up to cover her mouth. "Oh, my God, I'm so sorry. I didn't mean to say that out loud. I'm sorry. Please, go on."

Xander brought her hands to his chest and pressed them over his heart. Color rose to his cheeks. "I probably think that ten times a day, every day. Sometimes, I'm in the middle of a play, and I get this feeling…" He drew in a breath, clearly fighting emotion. "I'm grateful, too."

The reverend chuckled. "Well, we're close to exchanging vows, anyhow." He glanced from one to the other. "Fast forward or keep going?"

"Fast forward," they said at the same time.

"Well, then…" The reverend gestured to her. "You got a good start. Carry on."

Blinking back tears, she knew she had to get this right, make Xander understand how very much she loved him. "The only thing that's ever mattered to me is what's in here." She touched first her heart and then his. "That soul connection. And Xander, that's what we have. When I'm with you, I'm home. I'm my very best and most true self. With you, I've found my match, the love of my life, my *soul mate*, and I will never take that for granted, not for one single second. Alexander Wilder, I promise to love you, respect you, cherish you, and adore you every minute of every day for the rest of our lives. I will be faithful and loyal, and I will listen to you, encourage you, and inspire you. I'll comfort you in the hard times and prank you when you get a little too cocky."

Tipping his head tipped back as he laughed, Xander swiped the tears off his cheeks.

When the reverend asked if she was done, she nodded.

"All right, then, Xander…" The older gentleman tipped his chin to him. "You may say your vows."

"Lu, people come to my mom's restaurant for anniversaries and weddings, anything that celebrates love and romance. As a kid working there, I'd watch those couples staring into each other's eyes...and I never understood their connection. I didn't get it all the way up until Maui, when I saw you standing next to the taco truck. Right away, I saw your strength, your honesty, your goodness, and that was the moment I knew why those people had looked at each other like that. They saw the one person who made them feel safe and loved and wanted and understood. You're my person, Lu. The only one in the world for me."

His sincerity, his emotion, had her *shaking*.

"I want your passion, your energy, your drive...I want your touch, your laughter, your conversation. I knew from the moment I met you that you were my forever. Some way, somehow, I knew I'd make you mine. And for the rest of our lives and into eternity, my heart is yours, and yours alone."

Tears spilled down her cheeks, and she reached for him, burying her face in his white linen shirt. Those strong arms wrapped around her, and she could feel the matching tremble in them.

He loves me so much.

Every bit as much as I love him.

"I can't believe I get to keep you forever." She mumbled it in his shirt, but he obviously heard, since his chest shook with laughter.

"And now that you've pledged your love to one another, I'll ask you to present each other with rings." The reverend's voice pulled them apart. "As a circle has no beginning or end, and so it represents infinity, eternity, and equality, may these rings serve as the visual symbol of the words you've both so beautifully expressed. Xander."

Her almost-husband reached into his pocket and pulled out the ring they'd chosen together. A simple rose gold band with a perfect ruby in the center bracketed by flawless diamonds, it sparkled in the late afternoon sunshine.

"With this ring, I marry you." He slid it on her finger. Before she could pull her hand away, he brought it to his mouth and kissed her palm, mouthing, *I love you.*

The reverend smiled warmly. "Lulu."

She slid the thicker gold band off her thumb. "With this ring, I marry you." As she put it on his finger, a sense of absolute rightness, of peace, flooded her. "I love you so much."

Xander cupped her cheek, leaning in for a kiss, and the reverend teasingly said, "Oh, come on, you guys. I have one job here."

Xander's grin set fireworks off in her soul. "Go ahead."

"I now pronounce you as husband and wife. *Now,* you may kiss your bride."

Her husband lifted her and spun her around. He kissed her—softly at first—but then, as always, it deepened and grew hungry.

Finally, she had the sense of completeness, the passion, the companionship, she'd longed for her whole life.

"Forever," he said against her lips.

"Forever."

Thank you for reading WHOLE LOTTA LOVE! Are you dying for the youngest Cavanaugh sister's story? Check out YOU'RE STILL THE ONE! When she's hired as a wedding planner, Stella comes home to Calamity to find the love of her life is the guardian of a troubled teenager. Stella can't help herself, of course, from trying to fix the boy's problems. But if she wants to win Griffin back, she can't be so impulsive, so over-the-top with her ideas…and yet isn't that what the broody, inked, motorcycle-riding hottie loves about her? Second chance romance, redemption…this book has everything!

Do you subscribe to my newsletter? Get on that right now because I've got an EXCLUSIVE novella for my readers in 2022! You'll get 2 chapters a month of this super sexy, fun romance! #rockstarromance #whenyourcelebritycrushbecomesyourboyfriend #teenidol

Need more Calamity Falls, where the people are wild at heart?

KEEP ON LOVING YOU
WE BELONG TOGETHER
THE VERY THOUGHT OF YOU
JUST THE WAY YOU ARE
IT WAS ALWAYS YOU
CAN'T HELP FALLING IN LOVE
COME AWAY WITH ME
WHOLE LOTTA LOVE
YOU'RE STILL THE ONE
THE DEEPER I FALL
LOVE ME LIKE YOU DO

Have you read the Rock Star Romance series? Come meet the sexy rockers of Blue Fire:

YOU REALLY GOT ME
I WANT YOU TO WANT ME
TAKE ME HOME TONIGHT
MORE THAN A FEELING

Look for LOVE ME LIKE YOU DO in September 2022! Grab a FREE copy of PLANES, TRAINS, AND HEAD OVER HEELS. And come hang out with me on Facebook, Twitter, Instagram, Goodreads, and Pinterest or in my private reader group.

Excerpt of You're Still The One

SNOWFLAKES DUSTING HER CHEEKS, STELLA Cavanaugh stepped off the curb to hail a cab.

She loved New York City during the holidays. Christmas lights lit up the buildings on Fifth Avenue, festive garlands strung across crosswalks, and department store windows competed for the most fantastical displays. It was absolutely magical.

Cars whizzed by, but not a single cab had its available sign lit. And that was the frustrating part. *You can never get a cab here when it rains or snows.* Clutching her leopard print faux fur jacket to keep out the cold air, she took a sip of her quickly cooling mocha latte.

Her phone vibrated, and her boss's name flashed on the screen. *Great.* She loved her job. In fact, she was pretty sure she'd been born to plan weddings, but her boss was unreasonable and demanding, calling at all hours of the day and night.

But as the top event planner in the city, Taji Nash could get away with anything. And who was Stella to complain? She'd gotten the coveted job even though she'd had zero experience in the business. *You bet I'll put up with all her crazy demands.*

Taji: can you come back to the office? I can't find the Davenport file.

Stella: you took it into the bathroom with you. Did you maybe leave it there?

Taji: of course not.

With heavy snow predicted, Stella wanted to get back to her apartment. It had been a long, hellish week—who knew so many socialites wanted winter weddings?—and now she wanted to kick off her heels, heat up some soup...

And not think about the damage she'd done to her sister.

Because no matter how hard she pushed forward and tried to build a life independent of her family, guilt pulsed in rhythm with her heartbeat. There was no escaping it.

She'd blown up her sister's latest relationship.

Again.

Strike three. I'm out.

Lulu would never forgive her this time.

Of course, it had all been a huge misunderstanding. This time, Stella hadn't even touched her sister's boyfriend.

How could I have known the new quarterback was dating Lulu?

She couldn't.

But her words didn't hold up against the images splashed all over the tabloids, making it look like some torrid affair. They'd failed to mention, of course, that Stella was his publicist, that she'd literally just met the guy, and her job had been to check him into his hotel and deliver him to the team dinner.

Whatever. The damage had been done, and Lulu had broken up with him.

And I can't do a damn thing to fix it.

A cab slowed, edging closer to the curb. Did she take it or go back to the office?

She shot off a text.

Stella: do you still need me?

Taji: no, I found it.

Yeah? Was it in the bathroom? But there was no point in antagonizing her boss.

Sliding into the backseat, Stella said, "Jane Street and Greenwich, please."

For seven long years, she'd stayed away from home in the hopes enough time would pass for Lulu to move on and be able to forgive her.

Instead, Stella had reset the clock.

As she settled in for the long ride to her studio apartment in the West Village, she checked her emails. Even though she'd worked with an NFL team for so many years, she'd still had to start at the bottom with this new job. *It's fine.* She didn't mind. This was a new industry, and she needed to learn it. But she'd rise quickly—nobody worked harder or smarter, and nobody came up with better ideas than she did.

She might not have a particular talent like her sisters— she was no singer or chef or chocolatier—but she had big ideas.

Her phone buzzed. *Nooo.*

Can't find your keys, Taji?

You tossed them across the room when the Hilton bride cancelled her wedding, so check the planter by the window.

But it wasn't her boss. It was a Calamity area code. "Hello?"

"Stella?"

She didn't recognize the voice, so she grew anxious. "Yes." Were her parents okay?

"This is Diane Petersen. You might remember my name from some of the projects your mother and I have worked on together over the years."

"Of course I remember you. How are you?"

"I'm doing well but let me tell you why I think you're the one who can make things better for me."

Stella smiled. "Okay."

"About a year ago, Brodie Bowie built a lovely chapel in the mountains and asked me to launch the wedding business for the Owl Hoot Resort and Spa."

"That sounds fun."

"Oh, it is, and the response has been overwhelming, but I only agreed to get it started on one condition: that I'd be training someone to take over for me. Well, let me tell you, I've interviewed countless professionals and hired quite a number of people, but no one's worked out."

"It's a tough business."

"Yes, and when I was talking to your mom the other day, she told me you'd recently moved to New York to work with Taji Nash Events, and I knew right then I'd found my replacement."

"Let me stop you right there. I've only been here a few months."

And I ruined my sister's love life for the third time, so there's no way in hell I'm going home.

And yet…this strange yearning reared up.

To go home.

To be with her family.

And worse…

To be in Griffin's arms again. Oh, God, how she missed him.

Plain and simple, Griffin James was her person. And she had a Griffin-shaped hole in her heart that would never heal.

"Here's the thing. Everyone I've hired has had experience. Know what they don't have? The ability to manage people. That's the key in a business filled with pushy moms, bridezillas, wedding party backstabbers, and in-law temper tantrums. I think you know exactly what I mean."

"I sure do."

"And do you know what I remember about you?"

"Tell me."

"How gracious you were to everyone. You were the perfect hostess at your family's events, popular in school and in town, always had a kind word for everyone. You know how to handle difficult personalities. You're a go-getter, you've worked in PR...Stella, I want you to take over the wedding planning business here in Calamity. I'll teach you everything you need to know to be successful."

Her heart pounded, making her acutely aware of how badly she needed to go home. But after what she'd done, how would that work? Maybe if she hadn't just ruined Lulu's latest relationship, she could do it. But she had. And no one would welcome her.

Griffin certainly wouldn't. He hated her.

Could she stand living in a town where he might be married?

Might have *children*?

"I'm sorry, Diane. I love working with Taji"—*lies*. The woman was a narcissist—"and I'm learning so much here. It's just not the right time. Maybe we can revisit this a year from now."

But what if Griffin hadn't moved on? What if he missed her just as badly?

What if she could heal the rift in her family *and* win back the love of her life?

But that was too much to ask…wasn't it?

"I understand. It's a shame, though. I can't think of anyone better to plan Gigi and Cassian's wedding."

Whoa. "My sister's getting married?"

"Yep."

Hope sprung from her heart so swiftly it hurt. "And you're planning it?"

"Well, I'd like *you* to plan it, but yes, they've hired us. So, what do you say? Feel like creating your sister's dream wedding?"

About the Author

Award-winning author Erika Kelly writes sexy and emotional small town romance. Married to the love of her life and raising four children, she lives in the southwest, drinks a lot of tea, and is always waiting for her cats to get off her keyboard.

https://www.erikakellybooks.com/

facebook.com/erikakellybooks

twitter.com/ErikaKellyBooks

instagram.com/erikakellyauthor

goodreads.com/Erika_Kelly

pinterest.com/erikakellybooks

amazon.com/Erika-Kelly/e/B00L0MLWUY

bookbub.com/authors/erika-kelly

Printed in Great Britain
by Amazon